D1547036

The Trombone

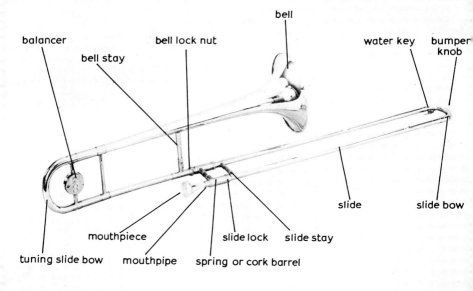

balancer

bell lock nut

bell

water key   bumper knob

bell stay

slide

slide bow

mouthpiece

slide lock   slide stay

tuning slide bow   mouthpipe   spring or cork barrel

Tenor trombone in B♭, medium bore, 8-inch bell: C. G. Conn, Elkhart, Ind.

THE TROMBONE
The Instrument and its Music

ROBIN GREGORY

FABER AND FABER LTD
3 Queen Square, London

First published in 1973
by Faber and Faber Limited
3 Queen Square London WC1
Printed in Great Britain by
Robert MacLehose and Co Ltd
All rights reserved

ISBN 0 571 08816 3

Contents

Illustrations

9

ILLUSTRATIONS

DIAGRAMS

Acknowledgements

The author wishes to thank the following for permission to reproduce illustrations:

The Musée Instrumental du Conservatoire National de Musique, Paris, Plate I; Albert De Visscher, Brussels, publisher of *Les Instruments de Musique dans L'Art et L'Histoire* by R. Bragard and F. J. de Hen, Plate II; The Curator of the Sammlung alter Musikinstrumente, Kunsthistorisches Museum, Vienna, Plate III; The Musikhistoriska Museet, Stockholm, Plate IV; The Curator of the Horniman Museum, London, Plate V; The Musikinstrumenten-Museum, Karl-Marx-Universität, Leipzig, Plate VI; Instrumentenbaumeister Wilhelm Monke, Köln-Ehrenfeld, Plate VII; Reynolds Band Instruments, Lincolnwood, Illinois, Plates VIII, XI and XII; Conn Corporation, U.S.A., Frontispiece and Plate IX; Gebr. Alexander, Mainz, Plates X and XIII; Godfrey Kneller, Esq., Plate XIV; The Vincent Bach Corporation, Elkhart, Indiana, Plate XV.

Thanks are due to the following publishers for permission to reproduce extracts from copyright works:

Boosey & Hawkes, Ltd:
Bartók: Violin Concerto, Ex. 20
Britten: Sinfonia da Requiem, Ex. 34
Prokofiev: Symphony No. 5, Ex. 13
Shostakovich: Symphony No. 9, Exs. 36, 37
Strauss: Salome, Ex. 41
Stravinsky: Octet for wind instruments, Exs. 25, 28
Bote & Bock
Mahler: Symphony No. 7, Ex. 8
J. & W. Chester, Ltd.
Stravinsky: Suite, L'Oiseau de Feu, Ex. 9
Durand et Cie
Ravel: Daphnis et Chloé, Exs. 6, 24
Ravel: L'Enfant et les Sortilèges, Exs. 10, 11, 12, 86

ACKNOWLEDGEMENTS

Ravel: Bolero, Ex. 87

Faber Music, Ltd.

Britten: The Burning Fiery Furnace, Exs. 58, 59, 60, 61

Wilhelm Hansen Musik-Vorlag

Sibelius: Symphony No. 7, Ex. 77

C. F. Kahnt (Agent, Novello & Co., Ltd.)

Mahler: Symphony No. 6, Ex. 72

Alphonse Leduc et Cie

Messiaen: Les Couleurs de la Cité Celeste, Ex. 1

Oxford University Press

Vaughan Williams: Symphony No. 6, Ex. 79

Peters Edition

Strauss: Don Quixote, Ex. 31

Strauss: Till Eulenspiegel, Ex. 83

B. Schotts Söhne, Mainz

Hindemith: Die Harmonie der Welt, Ex. 84

Hindemith: Mathis der Maler, Ex. 69

Stainer & Bell, Ltd.

Holst: The Hymn of Jesus, Ex. 5

Universal Edition (Alfred A. Kalmus, Ltd.)

Bartók: Dance Suite, Ex. 4

Berg: Kammerkonzert, Ex. 40

Berg: Wozzeck, Exs. 2, 19, 32, 44, 53, 54, 55, 56, 57, 74, 82

Berio: Sequenza V, Exs. 88, 89, 90

Janáček: Sinfonietta, Ex. 35

Kodály: Háry János Suite, Ex. 22

Schoenberg: Pelleas und Melisande, Exs. 51, 52

Schoenberg: Variations, Op. 31, Ex. 39

Webern: Six Pieces, Op. 6, Exs. 18, 33, 45

Preface

To me, and no doubt to many others, the trombone has always seemed the most imposing of all orchestral instruments. The sight of a group of gleaming bells raised aloft in their commanding position above the rest of the orchestra invariably engenders an anticipatory feeling of excitement which rarely remains unfulfilled. A moment of drama, it is clear, is about to ensue, whether it be some peremptory pronouncement, an overwhelmingly powerful expression of pomp and grandeur, or the hushed and solemn sounding of some tragic theme. It may seem strange that this versatility is based upon a principle so simple yet so perfect that it has proved almost insusceptible of improvement since its adoption, but herein, perhaps, lies some of the instrument's fascination; that its very simplicity can be put to such numerous and subtle musical ends is one of the many miracles which man and nature, between them, have managed to bring about. In the following pages I hope I have succeeded in conveying how this particular miracle is achieved.

Any account of the trombone as it exists at the present time must inevitably involve some retrospective glances, but no full-dress history of the instrument has been essayed, for several authoritative surveys are already available. However, there has recently been a revival of interest in early music for trombones, leading to the employment of specially constructed instruments appropriate to its performance, and I have therefore included a chapter whose purpose is to give some idea of the problems involved in the recreation of the tonal world of Renaissance and Baroque times, and of the results that have been achieved during their solution.

No real understanding of any wind instrument is possible without some elementary knowledge of its acoustical properties, and a great deal of original if often rather forbiddingly mathematical work has been done on this subject during the past few years. In Chapter 3 I have tried to cover the relevant ground in a reasonably non-technical manner with the aim of making a complex topic intelligible without sacrificing accuracy in the interests of simplification.

The remainder of Part I deals with the various types of trombone in common use at the present time, as well as with some which are less often employed, and this leads naturally to a consideration of the orchestral functions of the instrument. A final chapter reviews some of the recent interesting developments in technique.

Certain omissions will be obvious, and some, at least, of these are intentional. There is no reference, for example, to the thorny subject of the embouchure, for on reflection I have become convinced that in the last resort this is a problem only to be solved by consultation between the player and his teacher. Almost any brass player who has arrived at a satisfactory embouchure will have done so only after having passed through periods of doubt or indecision, during which playing results have given him cause for dissatisfaction in one or more respects, and the problem involved will usually have been diagnosed and finally solved by study with a competent teacher, who can see and hear what is amiss. So far, moreover, as the written word is capable of serving as a substitute for personal tuition it has been authoritatively set down once and for all by Philip Farkas in his book *The Art of Brass Playing*.

Part II consists of a list of music in which the trombone plays a more or less prominent part. By providing dates of publication, when available, and in other ways, I have tried to give some indication whether a particular work is likely to be obtainable, though this has not been possible in every case. Many modern works still in manuscript are included, but it should be noted that these may often be obtained through the composers' organizations of the nations concerned.

Hurstpierpoint ROBIN GREGORY

Note

The following system of notation is used in the text to identify particular notes:

Part I

THE INSTRUMENT

1

General Description

In principle the trombone is one of the simplest of all musical instruments; it is, too, the one most nearly resembling its ancestral type — in itself almost perfect — and therefore the one least affected by the mechanical improvements which have so revolution-ized the technique of other brass instruments during the past 150 years. Basically the technique of the trombone remains what it was when the instrument developed during the fifteenth and sixteenth centuries. With increased technological knowledge minor improve-ments, particularly in the types of alloys used in its construction and in the more scientific calibration of the bore, have been made, but even in its most modern form it is, of all orchestral instruments, the one which players of four or five hundred years ago would most easily recognize in appearance and technique.

The trombone consists essentially of the following parts, shown in the frontispiece: (i) a bell section, which usually incorporates a tuning slide; (ii) the inner hand slides, one arm of which locks on to the bell section, the other ending in a mouthpipe into which fits the mouthpiece; and (iii) the outer hand slides, consisting of two parallel tubes joined at their distal ends by a U-shaped bow or crook, which are so designed as to move easily but without leakage of air over the inner slides.

The major part of the whole tubing is cylindrical, the expansion usually beginning in the bell section. The bore of this cylindrical section varies from about 0·468 inches in the $7-7\frac{1}{2}$ inch belled tenor trombone, to as much as 0·571 inches in the bass trombone with a 10 to $10\frac{1}{2}$ inch bell; thus as a rule the bell diameter is roughly pro-portional to the bore. The expansion which begins in the bell section is continued through the tuning slide, which therefore has a tapered inner bore. Sometimes the wider arm of the tuning slide fits inside the bell tubing and the narrower arm outside the tube

19

leading to the inner slide. The bow of the tuning slide is braced by a stay which often incorporates a weighted balancer. Two more stays strengthen the arms of the bell section still further.

● The bell may be made of any one of a variety of materials. The commonest is brass, but gold brass, nickel-silver, silver and bell-bronze are also used, and recently copper bells made, not from sheet copper, but by electro-deposition on stainless steel forms, have been introduced. This process eliminates the seam found in other types of bell, which is believed by some to affect tone and response.

The bell section is attached to the inner slides either by a tapered portion at the end of the lower slide, which fits tightly into the bell section, or the joint is provided with a lock nut which screws on to a threaded section at the end of the slide. This nut is prevented from slipping off the bell lock receiver by a ring which forms an integral part of the receiver.

The inner slides consist of a pair of parallel tubes braced near the upper end. At this end are fitted the cork barrels, and the outer slides, in the closed position, rest with their ends in these barrels (Fig. 1). The barrels contain rings of cork which act as buffers for the outer slide when this is pushed right home. In many modern trombones the cork rings are replaced by springs, which to some degree are able to take up the pressure of the outer slides, and therefore allow the player some latitude in the positioning of the

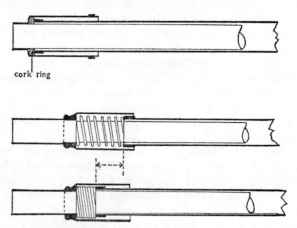

cork ring

Fig. 1. Cork and spring barrels.
Above: cork barrel.
Centre: spring barrel in normal first position.
Below: spring barrel in sharp first position with spring compressed.

slide when it is closed. In this case, intonation of first position notes is almost as capable of adjustment as that of notes in any other position.

● The inner slides are usually chromium- or nickel-plated, or made of a specially hard nickel-silver alloy with chrome finish, as they are subject to considerable wear. At its free end each slide expands slightly into a stocking (Fig. 2) which should be an integral part of the slide. The stocking fits into the outer slide with a clearance of

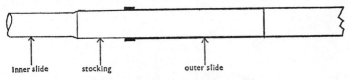

Inner slide   stocking   outer slide

Fig. 2. Stocking at end of inner slide.

only about 0·003 inches, to ensure as airtight a seal as is compatible with free movement of the outer slide. Thus the areas in contact are much reduced, though the stocking slightly increases the inequality of bore between the inner and outer slides. Recent metallurgical advances have made it possible to dispense with the stockings since the inner slides can be made of alloys producing very much smaller frictional forces than in older instruments. Another variation provides fluting along the length of the inner slides, with the aim of promoting a smoother slide action by offering a smaller bearing surface, and also by providing a reservoir for oil in the shallow grooves. The bore of the slides is usually the same in both arms, but occasionally trombones are made with the lower slide of slightly greater diameter than the upper, giving a small expansion in this region. The outer slides, of course, conform, with a tapered crook between their two arms. This so-called duo-bore is intended to give a larger, rounder tone at the expense of brilliance; a typical increase might be from 0·468 inches to 0·485 inches in a medium-bore B♭ instrument.

The upper of the two inner slides ends in a mouthpiece receiver, inside which is inserted a delicate mouthpipe. This includes the venturi (Fig. 3), a small constriction followed by a conical widening, which is a critical point for the response of the trombone. Great care must be taken in cleaning this section of the tubing, for if it is enlarged the tonal quality may well be impaired. It is therefore wiser to use a flexible cleaning brush, with the slides assembled, for this part of the tubing, rather than the cleaning rod and cloth used for the outer slides.

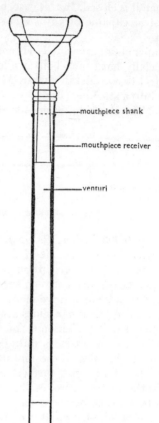

mouthpiece shank

mouthpiece receiver

venturi

Fig. 3. Mouthpiece and mouthpipe.

The outer slide is a U-shaped piece of tubing made of thin brass (0·011 inches or less in thickness), with an inside diameter very slightly more than the outer diameter of the stocking over which it fits. The inside may be plated with nickel-silver providing a bearing surface which moves easily over the chrome of the stockings. If the plating of the stockings is worn, it is unlikely that a smooth slide action will be possible. The crook or bow at the bottom of the outer slides is normally provided with a crook cap and bumper knob as some safeguard against damage to the thin tubing at the point where it is most likely to come into contact with the floor. It is good practice to provide the bumper knob with a rubber tip so that the instrument does not slide away when resting on the knob.

22

The arms of the outer slide are braced at the top by a stay which is held by the thumb and first two fingers of the right hand when the slide is operated. Near the crook, on the under arm of the slide, is a water-key for draining the slide of the condensed moisture which inevitably accumulates there during playing. Sometimes a device is incorporated which enables the water-key to be opened by a lever near the outer slide stay. Occasionally a tuning device, incorporating a screw adjustment with a second stay, is fitted between the arms of the outer slide, but the great majority of instruments utilize tuning in the bell section as previously described. Finally, a slide lock is often provided to prevent the hand slide from accidentally slipping when the instrument is not in use.

One further addition, found on the tenor-bass trombone in B♭ and F, the bass in G and D, and the contrabass in F and B♭ or in F and C, remains to be described. This is the subsidiary coil of tubing, lying in the loop of the bell section and controlled by a rotary valve operated by the left thumb, which enables the instrument to be put into the lower of its two pitches. When the valve is opened, the extra tubing is added to the main tube, thus converting the trombone from tenor to bass, or from bass to contrabass. The exact arrangement of the coil varies from maker to maker (Fig. 4), the chief aim being to avoid sharp bends, which would be acoustically undesirable. Sometimes a second valve is fitted, making it necessary to accommodate an additional length of tubing in the U-bend of the bell section and accentuating the acoustical problems still further. Moreover, some constriction in the tube is more or less inevitable where it enters and leaves the valve if this is not to be excessively cumbersome and slow in action and this, too, has its acoustical effect.

● The valve itself is similar in design to that found in the horn. A mechanical or string action operated from a thumb lever turns a rotor through 90°, converting a linear motion into the necessary rotary motion, thereby diverting the airway through the supplementary tubing. This is illustrated in Figs. 5, 6, 7. If there are two valves the two thumb levers are set side by side so that a small movement of the thumb is sufficient to bring the second valve into operation. Sometimes the two levers are coupled so that depression of the second automatically brings the first into play as well. Maintenance of the valve involves no more than an occasional lubrication of the bearings, examination of the string for wear, and periodical checking of the cork stops for thickness to ensure that the ports in the rotor are in alignment with the knuckles of tubing entering the rotor casing.

23

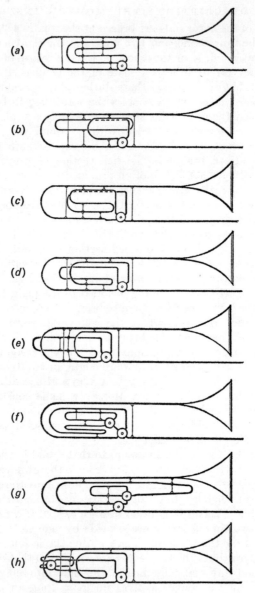

Fig. 4. The F attachment.
(a), (b), (c), (d), varying forms of F attachment.
(e), F attachment with long slide to give flat E.
(f), (g), F attachment with E valve.
(h), F attachment with optional detachable E valve.

24

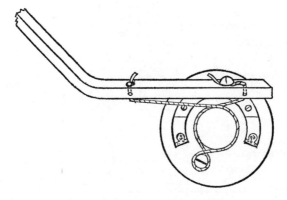

Fig. 5. Rotary valve: string action.

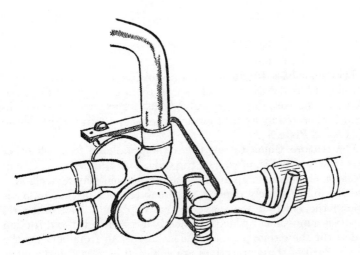

Fig. 6. Rotary valve: mode of action of thumb lever.

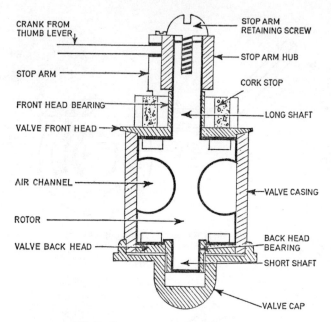

CRANK FROM
THUMB LEVER

STOP ARM
RETAINING SCREW

STOP ARM HUB

STOP ARM

CORK STOP

FRONT HEAD BEARING

LONG SHAFT

VALVE FRONT HEAD

AIR CHANNEL

VALVE CASING

ROTOR

VALVE BACK HEAD

BACK HEAD
BEARING

SHORT SHAFT

VALVE CAP

Fig. 7. Section through rotary valve.

The tenor-bass trombone is occasionally made so that the F attachment is detachable and can be replaced by a simple tenor crook. In this case the rotary valve which forms part of the attachment is operated by a cord to which is joined a thong for the thumb (Fig. 8 and Plate X).

The feature which distinguishes the trombone from all other brass instruments is, of course, the slide. This is a delicate piece of precision engineering, upon whose smooth action playing technique and flexibility largely depend, and maintenance of this action is among the chief of the player's preoccupations. The prime requisite is a movement which is as nearly as possible without friction and at the same time prevents the leakage of air from between the slides. Both of these objectives are achieved in a good instrument by highly sophisticated manufacturing techniques combined with the use of a suitable lubricant, which also serves to prevent corrosion and fill up the pores of the metal. Various lubricating agents are used; some players recommend a brand of skin ointment, others use cold cream, which is occasionally sprayed with water when on the slide. Special slide oil is also available, including

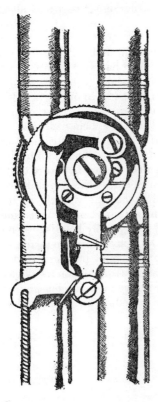

Fig. 8. Rotary valve on detachable F
attachment, operated by cord
and thong.

an emulsion oil for chromium-plated slides, from which ordinary oil tends to run off. Most professional players in this country probably prefer to use cold cream, finding it the best lubricant, the cleanest in use and the longest lasting.

A sluggish slide action may be due to one or more of several causes: (i) the slides, during manufacture, are ground in to ensure a good fit, and sometimes a residue of the powder used remains embedded in the inner surface of the outer slides. Oil from the inner slides gradually allows this to work loose and cause friction between the outer and inner slides. (ii) Small particles of dust and dirt in course of time accumulate in the cork barrels. They may become loosened during cleaning, and are pulled out by the oil on the slide. To begin with, such dirt tends to stick near the tops of the outer slides, causing trouble only in the lower positions, but it

27

slowly spreads down the slides until the higher positions also become affected. (iii) Dents in the outer slides are an obvious source of friction. Often, however, they are so minute as to be almost invisible, and may only affect the slide action when the inner slides have expanded after the instrument has warmed up. (iv) Any action which results in the outer or inner slides being thrown out of parallel in the slightest degree will cause them to drag when in use. This can happen if the outer slides are dropped on the crook, or if the inner slides are held incorrectly while being cleaned. The slides may also become sprung if the lid of the instrument case, where they normally fit when not in use, is opened carelessly by forcing it upwards at one end. The remedy here is to ensure that the slide is not held rigidly by the fasteners across the stay and crook, so that even if the lid is twisted the slides are not twisted with it.

The slides are, in fact, the most delicate part of the instrument. Once they have been damaged by denting or by being thrown out of parallel they are never likely to be quite the same again, even after repair. For this reason the professional player regards his slide as the most important part of his instrument; on its efficiency and ease of movement depend, to a large extent, his ability to perform the rapid and complex parts nowadays demanded of him.

2

Baroque Trombones and Modern Copies

It is not proposed to deal at length here with the history of the trombone, for this has been more than adequately done in Canon F. W. Galpin's famous paper of 1906,[1] to which subsequent writers have added more detail without invalidating its major conclusions. It may, however, be of value to examine some of the structural features of the early trombones, particularly as there has recently been a revival of interest in Renaissance and Baroque music in which wind instruments, and the trombone especially, were used. Efforts have been made to recreate the tonal world of those times in the performance of this music, and examination of such instruments as have survived, and the occasional use of some of them, together with evidence from the music itself and from contemporary accounts of its sound — and even from paintings showing the constitution of the orchestras of the time — leave no doubt that the trombone of the sixteenth and seventeenth centuries possessed a tone quality far removed from that of the present day. Some writers,[2] in fact, go so far as to suggest that the early trombone must be regarded as a different instrument, as distinct from the modern trombone as the viol is from the violin. Every age has its tonal ideal, related to the music of the time; sometimes technology marches ahead of this ideal, less often it lags behind, but in the case of the trombone such changes as have taken place in its construction have been due hardly at all to improved technology and almost entirely to changes in the role it has been required to play in the music of succeeding periods.

Although instruments recognizable as trombones were described and depicted in theoretical works (e.g. Virdung, *Musica getutscht,*

---

[1] *Proceedings of the Musical Association,* 33.

[2] e.g. Egon F. Kenton, *The 'Brass' parts in Giovanni Gabrieli's Instrumental Ensemble Compositions,* Brass Quarterly I, 2, 1957, pp. 73–80.

1511) and represented by artists (e.g. in a painting by Matteo di Giovanna, before 1495) at an even earlier date, the first actual surviving specimens of the instrument come from the second half of the sixteenth century. Six or seven of these trombones are known, all but one by makers from Nuremberg, which was then, and remained for some time, the centre of the art and craft of brass instrument manufacture. The earliest is a tenor trombone, dated 1551, made by Erasmus Schnitzer, and illustrated in Anthony Baines's *European and American Musical Instruments*. Though its tube length would indicate a present-day pitch of about C, there is evidence to show that in its day, pitch standards having since risen, it would have stood in B♭. Comparison of this and other sixteenth century trombones with a modern instrument shows certain obvious differences in structure, and some that are not so obvious without actual examination of the instruments. The features that would particularly affect the tone quality are the following:

(i) *The bore.* Most of these early instruments have a bore of about 1 cm. (0·39 inches) as compared with 0·48 to 0·525 inches or more in a modern tenor, though the 1557 instrument by Jorg Neuschel (0·492 inches) approximates to a modern medium-bore B♭ trombone in this respect. The narrower bore is about equal to that of the 'pea-shooter' favoured until comparatively recently by British players, which had a lighter, thinner but more brilliant tone than is now the ideal aimed at.

(ii) There is a much greater proportional of cylindrical tubing in these old instruments, the expansion beginning only in the last branch and ending in a funnel-shaped bell with practically no flare and a terminal diameter of only 3½ to 4 inches as compared with 7½ to 8 inches in the modern instrument. To the eye, indeed, the bell has very much the appearance of an exponential horn without the sudden terminal expansion which it has since acquired. A bell of this type would tend towards brilliance of tone, the higher partials being present in greater intensity than the lower, which are radiated less efficiently.

(iii) The actual thickness of the walls of the tubing is greater in these older trombones than is the case now. The effect of this would be to make it more difficult, if not impossible, to get these instruments to produce a blaring, brassy tone with a cutting edge in which the metal itself seems to vibrate.

(iv) Perhaps as a consequence the method of staying the instrument appears to have been designed to give the walls of the tubing as much freedom as possible to vibrate unhampered. There are usually three stays, one between the tops of the outer slide, one between the mouthpipe and the middlepipe, and a third between the beginning of the bell expansion and the middlepipe. (On modern trombones there is usually a fourth at the base of the tuning slide in the upper crook, and sometimes a fifth a little lower down.) Though the state of metal technology at the time would have made it possible to attach these stays rigidly, they were often detachable and fixed in position by means of clasps fitting quite loosely over the tubing, with the space between packed with leather or cloth. Tubular stays were sometimes used (as for the slide in the Schnitzer instrument), but the more usual type consisted of a pair of flat pieces of metal hinged on to the clasp and held together by hooks and hasps (Plates I and II). When a flat stay was used on the bell joint the clasp was usually fixed by a pin (Plate IV). In later models the slide stay was sometimes telescopic in order to allow the slide to move easily over the legs of the inner slide, which at this time were not fitted with stockings, so that the bearing surfaces included the whole length of the slide. As already mentioned, the reason for these loose stays may have been the desire not to impair the resonance, and Wilhelm Ehmann[1] attributes the rich partial structure of his copies of Baroque trombones partly to using the minimum number of stays and siting them carefully. Another suggestion,[2] however, attributes no acoustical significance to the structure of the stay, but assigns it the more practical purpose of making it easier to disarticulate the instrument so that in case of damage the offending section could be readily replaced by another. The construction of the trombone by jointing together a number of straight and curved sections using either unsoldered butt or tenon and socket joints covered by ferrules makes this a more than feasible explanation.

(v) *The mouthpiece.* This provides the greatest problem because, being easily detachable, it cannot always certainly be dated as contemporaneous with the instrument with which it is found. So far as can be ascertained[3] it seems that early trombones sometimes, at least, were matched with a tapering mouthpiece of conical shape, more closely resembling the horn mouthpiece of the eighteenth century (though perhaps with a rather more definite throat) than

[1] W. Ehmann, *New Brass Instruments based on old Models*, Brass Quarterly, I, 4, 1958, pp. 219, 223.

[2] E. Halfpenny, *Two Oxford Trumpets*, Galpin Society Journal, XVI, 1963, p. 57.

[3] See, for example, A. Carse, *Musical Wind Instruments*, p. 261-2; R. Donington, *The Instruments of Music*, p. 101; P. Bate, *The Trumpet and Trombone*, p. 71.

that of the trumpet of its time. The general effect of such a mouthpiece would be to produce a mellower tone. Ehmann,[1] however, during his experiments in search of the authentic Baroque trombone *Klangideal,* at one stage used modern trombones with narrow cup mouthpieces designed for jazz instruments, and found that the tone became thinner, softer and 'tighter'; and he later states that exact copies of historical mouthpieces did not prove satisfactory for use with his copies of Baroque trombones, being very narrow and shallow with sharp rims, and giving rise to a spread tone. He concedes that this may have been due to the unfamiliarity of his players with this type of mouthpiece, but nevertheless recommends that they should use modern mouthpieces with as shallow a bowl and as narrow a bore as possible.

There is, then, some conflict of opinion between different authorities with regard to the shape of the cup in mouthpieces used with these early trombones, and the following measurements, taken from two mouthpieces of authenticated dates, together with those of two typical comparable modern mouthpieces, do little to resolve it.

	Length cm.	Rim diameter		Rim width cm.	Cup depth cm.	Shape of cup
		Outer cm.	Inner cm.			
Bass trombone, 1593	9·7	4·0	2·6	0·7	1·8	Hemispherical, sharp throat.
Bass trombone, modern	8·7	3·6	2·7	0·45	2·8	Deep, medium throat.
Contrabass trombone, 1639	–	4·6	3·2	0·7	2·5	Somewhat conical.
Contrabass trombone, modern	9·2	4·3	3·1	0·6	3·1	Deep, medium throat.

It would be unwise to draw any firm conclusions about practice in the sixteenth and seventeenth centuries from these measurements, for there is no means of knowing whether the mouthpieces from which they were taken were typical examples of their time; measurements of modern mouthpieces picked at random from the selection available would give equally inconclusive results. It

[1] Ibid., pp. 217, 218, 223.

would appear, however, that whatever the shape of the cup, hemispherical or more conical, its depth was considerably shallower than is the case today. In general terms a shallow cup gives a brighter tone, but not one of great volume or carrying power, and a deeper cup more volume of a mellower character. No doubt variation between the choices of individual players was as great then as it is today, and it must be remembered, too, that the trombone was used not only to blend with stringed instruments and voices, but also as an outdoor instrument in processions, for *Turmmusik* and so on, when the tonal requirements would be rather different. It is quite possible, therefore, that a player would have used more than one mouthpiece, and have chosen the one appropriate to the occasion.

Whatever the exact acoustical explanation (to which must be added the predilections of the players themselves), there is general agreement that the Baroque trombone was tonally a very different instrument from the modern trombone, and its attributes were probably not very far removed from those ascribed by Ehmann[1] to his modern copies. He claims that 'they speak very easily. No great effort is needed to bring forth the notes. The tone "springs" from the lips . . . It is impossible to blare with these instruments. One cannot produce that distinctive brass tone which is thought of as typical of brass instruments. The tone of these instruments does not have a mechanical effect. It is pristine, straightforward and almost naked. It comes directly from the player, and it is as though a part of nature itself has sounded'.

At this point it should be mentioned that many of the Nuremberg trombones were objects of great beauty, beside which the modern instrument, though still often retaining elegant lines and proportions, has a somewhat severely functional appearance. Though the trombone does not lend itself so readily to decoration as many other musical instruments, the makers seized every opportunity to display their artistry and skill in metalwork. The bell-rim was richly chased, the stays beautifully decorated, even the ferrules were engraved with intricate patterns and the bell-bow guard made an ornament as well as serving a useful function. Many of these features are to be seen in the instruments illustrated in Plates I, II, and III. Two of the most beautiful trombones which survive from the golden age of trombone making were made by members of the Ehe family. The earlier, by Johann Isaac Ehe in 1612, is the oldest known *Quintbass* trombone in existence.[2] It

---

[1] Ibid., p. 223.

[2] Nuremberg, Germanisches Nationalmuseum, No. M I, 168.

shares with the other,[1] made by Johann Leonhard Ehe in 1732, a feature whose significance is the subject of some debate. Each instrument incorporates a loop in the U of the bell section to accommodate the tubing required for the lower pitch, and the loop is fitted with a slide which can be moved forwards or backwards by means of a long rod ending in a handle below the bell stay. Such an arrangement is to be found in other surviving bass trombones (e.g. one by W. W. Haas from the early eighteenth century), and it is also illustrated by Praetorius in his *Syntagma musicum* of 1619. Movement of the slide backwards by the handle lowers the pitch by about a semitone. It can be operated while the instrument is being played so long as the main slide is in the first position, thus giving a downward extension of a semitone, but a more likely explanation of its function concerns the different standards of pitch in use at the time. The *Chorton* of church organs was approximately a semitone below the *Cornett-ton* used by the *Stadtpfeifer*, and if the same instrument was to be capable of playing a role, as it did, both in sacred vocal music and in secular *Turmmusik*, some means of tuning to either pitch would be desirable. This could readily be achieved with such a slide, and doubtless it could also have been used for fine tuning like a modern tuning slide. When the instrument was playing in the higher of the two pitches it could also have been used to extend the downward compass by a semitone. The device could, perhaps, be regarded as a sort of semitone *Stellventil* operated by a handle instead of a valve. In his illustration Praetorius also shows a tenor trombone and by its side a more or less circular crook and a shorter straight shank, conjectured by Carse[2] to be accessory tone and semitone additions to the main tube, presumably for the same purpose as the more elaborate arrangement on the Haas and the two Ehe instruments.

Another feature of interest in the 1732 trombone is the bell, which shows that a more marked flare had already begun to develop by this date, or even earlier (cf. Plate II, a bass trombone by Hanns Hainlein, dated 1668).

An early example of the contrabass trombone, made by Georg Nikolaus Oller in Stockholm, 1639 (Plate IV), presents a very elongated appearance, for the principle of the double slide, although apparently known since the sixteenth century, appears rarely to have been applied before it was resuscitated early in the nineteenth century. (A bass trombone by Jobst Schnitzer,[3] dated 1612, was

[1] Plate III.
[2] Op. cit., p. 254.
[3] Leipzig, Musikinstrumenten-Museum, No. 1908.

at one time believed to be the earliest surviving instrument with such a slide, but it is now known that only the bell section is original, and that the double slide is a nineteenth century addition.) The tubing of the Oller contrabass is about 18 feet long, and since none of this is accommodated as a crook in the bell section the instrument stands nearly seven feet high. With a single slide the positions are so far apart that a very long hinged handle is needed to supply the necessary reach for the lower positions. The slide stays are of the telescopic type. Another point of interest is the involuted bell-bow, apparently serving no more than a decorative function, but more remarkable is the fact that the two arms of the slide are of different bores, an idea which has been revived in this century as the so-called duo-bore or telescopic slide bore (see p. 21).

The alto trombone made by Michael Nagel of Nuremberg in 1663 and pictured in Plate V is less ornate than most of the other trombones so far discussed. Nuremberg was still the pre-eminent centre of brass instrument manufacture at this time, but its products were beginning to assume a more strictly utilitarian appearance. Decoration of the bell garland had not yet disappeared, but this instrument has a plain, somewhat workaday look about it which is in sharp contrast to the magnificence of the trombones by members of the Ehe family and Hainlein shown in Plates I, II and III. It is possible, of course, that these instruments and others like them have had a better chance of preservation partly, at least, because they are objects of beauty, and that they are not necessarily everyday samples of their makers' products. That Nagel was capable of fine decorative workmanship can be seen from a silver trumpet of 1657 in the Kunsthistorisches Museum at Vienna. The instrument under notice, however, has a more plebeian aspect. A feature which gives it a slightly unbalanced look to the eye accustomed to the modern trombone is the unusual length of tubing between the slide and the mouthpiece, and this impression is accentuated by the forward set bell. In modern instruments the bell-rim is usually situated about three-fifths of the way down the overall length — and in the alto often a little less — but in the Nagel alto this fraction is very nearly three-quarters. The bell-stay is of the usual flat type, but the slide stays are tubular, though it is believed that these may be later additions.

The earliest soprano trombones which have been preserved come from the late seventeenth century, though the instrument had possibly been in use before this (see Chapter 8). Plate VI shows a later example made by J. F. Schwabe of Leipzig in 1796, but it may be taken as fairly typical. Like the Nagel alto of over a century before, it has a flat bell-stay and tubular slide-stays. It has a bore of 0·453 inches and a bell-diameter of about 4½ inches, and it is pitched in what was then C. The slide is long enough to provide only six positions, involving the nominal absence of $d'\flat$ from its compass (though a somewhat uncertain version of this note can be obtained at the fullest extension of the slide using a loose embouchure).[1] Its absence is in any case not a matter of great moment since the instrument would normally have been used in its middle and upper registers. It was as the result of an examination and trial of this particular example of its type that Kunitz[2] was led to assert that the soprano was a much-maligned instrument, worthy of a better fate than has befallen it through the centuries.

At the sixth Heinrich Schütz Festival at Herford in 1953 Wilhelm Ehmann tried the experiment of using museum instruments similar to those described above in the performance of music of Schütz's time, with the aim of gaining as accurate a conception as possible of the tone quality appropriate to this music. In spite of some difficulties, such as the fact that the instruments were not well in tune with each other, the results were sufficiently encouraging to lead him to suggest that it might be possible to construct modern versions of these Baroque trombones and trumpets. After testing many of the instruments in the Germanisches Museum at Nuremberg and the Rück collection at Erlangen he selected an alto trombone by Hieronymus Starck of Nuremberg (1670), the tenor by Erasmus Schnitzer already mentioned, and the 1612 *Quintbass* by Johann Isaac Ehe. Modern versions of these were made, not as exact copies, but with the aim of reproducing their unique tonal quality while incorporating more recent technical improvements — even to the extent of including a valve mechanism and F attachment on the B♭ tenor trombone, and an E♭ valve on the F bass. Examples of these modern narrow-bore Baroque trombones are shown in Plate VII. Their attributes, as described by Ehmann, have already been quoted, and make them capable of combining unobtrusively but effectively with voices, woodwind, or strings, or with mixed groups, as, for example, violin, recorder, cello and tenor or bass trombone, or viola, alto trombone, gamba and tenor or bass trombone. These trombones can also be used to play a cantus firmus, or even as continuo instruments, as well as joining with Baroque trumpets or cornetts to form a brass choir.

[1] Dr. H. Heyde, in a personal communication to the writer.
[2] Kunitz, *Die Instrumentation: Teil 8, Posaune*, p. 801. He erroneously states, however, that only four positions are available on this instrument.

3

Acoustics

All brass instruments are of the type known as lip-reed instruments and sounds in all of them are produced by basically the same method. A generator — the lips vibrating across the opening of a mouthpiece inserted into the end of a length of tubing — is coupled with a resonator — the column of air enclosed by the tubing — and sets that resonator in vibration. The pitch of the note so emitted depends on several factors, the most important of which are the length and calibration of the tubing and the mode of vibration of the air column. Somewhat exceptionally, as in the case of the trombone, the column may vibrate at its conventional (but not its true) fundamental frequency, that of the so-called pedal note; more usually the air column vibrates in two, three or more parts, giving notes whose frequencies are generally taken to be integral multiples of the conventional fundamental frequency. These notes, known as harmonics or partials, form a series whose intervals become progressively smaller — the so-called harmonic series shown below for a tube length (about 270 centimetres or nine feet) giving the B♭ series, as in the tenor trombone.

Harmonic series of the trombone in B♭

For a given length of tubing only one series can be obtained; the longer the tube the lower the pitch and the greater, subject to certain limitations of bore, the number of partials capable of being sounded. The wider the tube in proportion to its length the more easily the pedal note speaks, but the more difficult it is to sound the higher partials.

37

The series given above shows the simple theoretical and practical result of causing the air to vibrate in a wholly cylindrical tube open at both ends, or in a wholly conical tube closed at the narrow end. It is, therefore, a gross over-simplification of the state of affairs so far as the trombone is concerned; this instrument is by no means wholly cylindrical, since it expands for about the last two-fifths of its closed length to form a flaring bell many times the diameter of the cylindrical portion. Moreover, the lips of the player form a more or less closed end, and such a closed cylindrical pipe would resonate to give no more than the odd-numbered partials. To state the acoustical properties of the trombone in terms of those of either an open cylindrical pipe or of a closed conical one is therefore a comparatively fruitless proceeding, for it can give no more than a very rough approximation to the truth. The properties of a tube which is neither wholly cylindrical nor wholly conical, and in which the expanding portion is not even a true geometrical cone, must therefore be determined by experiment, or by the solution of wave equations, or by a combination of both. In the case of the trombone the matter is complicated still further by the facts (i) that the proportion of tapered to cylindrical tubing is not constant; the cylindrical part constitutes about 50 per cent when the slide is in the first position, but increases to nearly 70 per cent when it is fully extended, and (ii) that there is also a taper in the mouthpipe, accounting for nearly a tenth of the closed length. Calculation of the frequency relations between the partials of such a tube therefore becomes extremely complicated. In general it may be said that the addition of an expanding portion to a closed cylindrical tube enables a series of partials to be obtained whose frequencies are in more or less integral relation with each other, and that since early times in the history of the trombone makers have arrived empirically at a bore profile which produces this result for a large number of consecutive partials. These vibrational modes are such that they have frequencies which are approximately integral multiples of a certain frequency, that of the pedal note, an octave below the second partial, though the pedal note itself is not in one of the prime vibrational modes of the tube. To put it another way, the frequency in the nth mode is $\frac{1}{2}n$ times that of the second mode, or very nearly so, and the relationship of the second mode frequency to that of the pedal note may be approximately deduced as follows: if f_1, f_2, f_3 . . . are the frequencies of the resonant modes, then for a conical tube, $f_2 = 2f_1$, $f_3 = 3f_1$ . . . and for a cylindrical tube closed at one end $f_2 = 3f_1$, $f_3 = 5f_1$, etc. For a cylindro-conical tube f_2 lies between $2f_1$ and $3f_1$; that is, the true fundamental mode is considerably more than an octave below the second mode. Actually, as Bouasse[1] shows, for the trombone the interval is more nearly a twelfth than an octave. He goes on to say that a definite answer to the question 'What are the true partials of a trombone?' is impossible; the bore profiles of different instruments are not the same, the slide shifts in the various positions vary with the player, and even with the state of his lips, and so on. Hence, he says, whatever the series proper to the tube, the player produces the note he requires by the correct use of his lips. Though the resonant mode frequencies may well not lie exactly at points corresponding to the notes shown in the series above, the generator (the lips) is too massive to be completely dominated by the resonant air column; it will, however, prefer to vibrate at frequencies near to the normal mode frequencies of the tube. In Benade's[2] phrase, the lips are amenable to suggestions from the resonating column so that it is easier for the player to cause them to vibrate at one of the favourite frequencies of the tube. If the lip tension is reasonably correct, the instrument pulls in at the proper pitch; if the instrument itself is of faulty design and the resonant mode is not of the correct frequency the player pulls it into pitch by modifying his lip tension. He is more easily able to do this owing to the existence of what Bouasse terms 'privileged' notes. These are sub-harmonics (of integral sub-multiple frequencies) of the probably slightly inharmonic frequencies natural to the tube, and a cluster of these privileged notes will lie around each of the natural vibratory modes of the tube. This may perhaps be made clearer by reference to the following table, which shows the relevant privileged frequencies deriving from the second to tenth normal-mode frequencies of a hypothetical tube of such a shape that it gives a series which is not exactly in tempered intonation.

From this table it may be seen that the second mode frequency is approximately reproduced as a privileged note of half the frequency of the fourth, one third that of the sixth, and so on. It can also be seen that the lack of a vibratory mode at the pedal note is compensated for by the presence of several privileged notes clustered around a frequency of 58 Hz, an octave below the second mode frequency. In practice the partials natural to the tube will almost certainly not all be exactly in equal temperament — that is, they will be 'slightly bent'. Nevertheless, the presence of a

[1] H. Bouasse: *Instruments à Vent*, p. 309.
[2] A. H. Benade: *Horns, Strings and Harmony*, p. 168.

Normal-mode frequency	f_2	f_3	f_4	f_5	f_6	f_7	f_8	f_9	f_{10}
Tempered frequency Hz	116	175	233	294	350	415	466	523	587
Actual frequency Hz	118	177	233	296	354	407	463	520	580
f/2	59		117		177		232		290
f/3		59			118			173	
f/4			58				116		
f/5				59					116

Table 1.

number of privileged notes close to each partial will help the player to obtain the intonation he desires.

The privileged notes will also account for the existence of the notes $E\flat$ to B' which fill in the trombone player's traditional gap between the first pedal note and seventh position E. These notes, quite recently 'discovered' by some American players, and now being used and taught by them, are members of a similar set of regeneration frequencies to those shown in Table 1, in this case being one half of the third mode frequency and one quarter of the sixth. $E\flat$, for example (frequency approximately 78 Hz), is assisted by a privileged note derived from the third partial $e\flat$ of a fundamental $A'\flat$ and by a second derived from the sixth partial $e'\flat$, and is therefore playable in the third position — though in practice it seems to speak more readily in a long third position. However, this particular set of notes is not so strongly supported as are the pedal notes, and this may explain why they are more difficult to produce (though well worth the effort if an F attachment is not available), and also why they have not been exploited before.

The aim of the designer of a trombone might well be to approach, as nearly as possible, the ideal of causing the resonant frequencies to fall in the scale of equal temperament, by choosing the appropriate lengths of cylindrical and expanding tubing and the exact profile of the latter. In pursuing this aim he will find himself limited to some extent by mechanical considerations — the length of cylindrical tubing, for example, must be sufficient to allow for a slide giving seven positions. It has been widely assumed that the notes of the series produced by cup-mouthpiece instruments are in just intonation. Simple theory treats the trombone as a cylindrical tube open at both ends, and under these conditions the assumption would be correct. In actual fact, as has been shown, these conditions are far from being satisfied; the trombone is a cylindro-conical tube with a more or less closed end (see Fig. 9). Hence it is not likely that calculations based on assumptions which are not actually fulfilled in practice will be anything but very approximately true. It has in fact been claimed[1] that suitable calibration of the bore could ensure that a brass instrument would follow very closely either a just or tempered series, and figures showing the intonational errors of five trumpets of different makes, and presumably of different bore calibrations, seem to bear out this

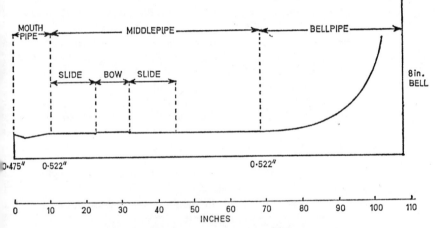

Fig. 9. Profile of typical tenor trombone.
Vertical scale 25 times horizontal scale.

contention, for they show apparently random variations from tempered intonation, sometimes on the sharp side, and sometimes on the flat. There is no coherent pattern in the variations, which are attributed solely to differences in the calibrations of the bores and mouthpieces. Doubtless figures for trombones of different calibrations would show similar irregular deviations from the theoretical values as calculated for an open cylindrical tube, and the bores could be redesigned to put the partials in tune with either just or tempered scales as required, though, as will be seen later, with some effect also on tone quality. It must be remembered, too, that even if the tube is designed to give resonant frequencies at the optimum positions, the influence of the player has to be taken into

[1] Earle L. Kent: *The Inside Story of Brass Instruments*, p. 4.

account. By training or inclination he may play certain notes sharp or flat, or he may lack the skill and accurate control necessary to set his lips vibrating at the correct frequency. If the rate of these vibrations is not near enough to that of one of the resonant modes or of a privileged note, on reflection at the bell the wave may not return in phase with the next, and the result will be a weak and stuffy tone. Even if the lip vibrations are of the correct frequency the vibrations of the air column do not immediately reach their full amplitude; a very short period intervenes during which waves not proper to the tube are damped out and the wave of resonant frequency is built up, eventually, if the coupling between the generator and resonator is tight enough, affecting the vibrating source so that it, too, vibrates more strongly. This short period, leading to the establishment of a steady state in which the instrument actively encourages the vibration of the lips, is known as the starting transient, and the wave form during this period is extremely complex. Similarly when notes are played in succession there is a short interval of time during which the vibration of the air column changes from one condition to another in a manner which is determined by the method of articulation used by the player, and by the way in which the change is made, for example by slide or valve, giving rise to further characteristic transient behaviour. Transient effects, indeed, play a large part in enabling a listener to distinguish between instruments whose tone quality in the steady state may be very similar.

Though in the trombone, as in other brass instruments, the coupling between generator and resonator is tight and the resonator attempts to impose its frequency on the generator, the domination, as already mentioned, is not complete. As a result it is possible for the player, especially by using a slack embouchure, and with the help of privileged notes, to sound notes not in one of the resonant modes of the tube. Notes below E in the seventh position can be obtained by 'lipping', pulling down the frequency of the natural partial, perhaps with some loss of quality and with some degree of uncertainty unless the player is highly skilled. These so-called 'falset' notes have long been known and correspond to the factitious notes quite commonly used by hand horn players. Other partials can be lipped down in the same way, particularly in the lower register, and some players may sub-consciously do this and use a smaller extension of the slide. It is also possible, but less easy, to play sharp, if the lip reed does not submit completely to the regenerative effect of the vibration of the air column. In other words, there is some tolerance around each partial, and particularly below it, so that the player is by no means completely at the mercy of his instrument so far as intonation is concerned, even when he has committed himself to a particular extension of the slide. A by no means inconsiderable part of his skill, in fact, lies in his ability to adjust his intonation in this way to suit the needs of the moment.

The trombone serves the function of coupling the generator to the outside air, at the same time amplifying its vibrations. The air column it encloses resonates efficiently only at certain pitches, depending partly, as already shown, upon its length and shape. The resonant pitches depend also on the speed of sound; if this changes, as it does with a rise or fall of temperature, their frequencies are raised or lowered, since the time taken for the sound to travel is increased or decreased with the same effect as if the column had been lengthened or shortened. Hence the instrument plays sharper when warm. Moreover, in a wholly cylindrical tube the speed of sound is the same for all frequencies, but in a tube including a tapered portion, such as that of a trombone, sounds of low frequency travel faster than those of high, so that the instrument behaves as if it were shorter for low frequency notes than for high.

A third element in the coupled system about which comparatively little is known is that formed by the air cavities of the player's head and chest. It seems very probable that these play some part in the determination of the tone quality obtained, for it is likely that the cavities themselves resonate, as is suggested by stethoscopic observations. Bate[1] believes that this resonance at certain frequencies may 'sometimes assist and sometimes interfere with the lips in their capacity as the vibrating part of the generator'.

We may consider the trombone, then, as an instrument of such dimensions that it is capable of producing a series of partials approximating to the harmonic series already given, but it would be unwise to assume that any particular instrument would actually produce this series either in exactly just or equal temperament. It is the skill of the player himself and his ability to control, by lips and choice of slide shift, the imperfections of intonation almost certainly built into the instrument, that ultimately count.

Tone Quality

It has long been known that no musical instrument produces a pure tone — that is, one vibrating at a single frequency only —

[1] P. Bate: *The Trumpet and Trombone*, p. 14.

though the ear perceives a tone as a note of definite pitch. Such tones are invariably compound, consisting of a number of partials superimposed upon the fundamental note which is that actually perceived. These partials bear to the fundamental the relationship shown on p. 37, and are those of the harmonic series. Their presence in trombone tone is due to the ability of its air column to vibrate simultaneously in a number of different ways, and the number and intensity of the partials present is the decisive factor in determining the quality of tone which the instrument produces.

Analysis of the sounds produced by the trombone makes possible the identification of the partials present and the determination of their relative intensities. The results can be displayed most usefully as tonal spectra, in which the partials are represented by ordinates of appropriate height along a horizontal axis showing their frequencies. Some typical tonal spectra for the trombone are shown in Fig. 10.

Jeans[1] characterises the first few partials as follows: the second gives clearness and brilliance, the third more brilliance, together with a thickening of the tone and the addition of a hollow, nasal quality. The fourth adds yet more brilliance, the fifth a rich, horn-like quality, and the sixth more of the nasal quality. All these partials are part of the common chord of the fundamental, and are concordant. The odd-numbered discordant partials from the seventh upwards add dissonance to the fundamental tone and thus introduce a degree of roughness or edge into the tone — what is recognized as the 'metallic' or 'brassy' character of the instrument. Some of the partials may not be exactly harmonic — that is, not of frequencies which are exact integral multiples of the fundamental frequency — and if the discrepancy is significant these discordant partials, the extent of whose inharmonicity varies from one instrument to another, give further character to the timbre.

The spectrum for the pedal B♭ shows a wide spread of partials, several of them in as great intensity as the fundamental, corresponding to the rich, sharp-edged, metallic sound of the trombone in this register, quite different from the more rounded, 'spread' tone of the tuba at the same pitch. The spectrum for high c'', on the other hand, shows only three partials in any significant strength, and the tone here is smoother and more horn-like in quality. In three of the spectra the effect of the mute is shown in filtering out some of the partials to give a quite different tone quality; this will be discussed more fully later.

We must visualize the lips of the player, the internal profile of

[1] J. Jeans, *Science and Music*, p. 86.

his mouthpiece, and the shape and scale of the tubing combining to create a certain partial structure *inside* the tube, only for this structure to be modified by the flare of the bell, possibly the material of which the tubing is made, and certainly the presence of a mute, when used, to produce the type of spectra shown in Fig. 10. These modifying factors may emphasize, on the one hand, or attenuate or even completely filter out, on the other, some of the partials originally present.

The player's lips, stretched across the opening of the mouthpiece, form the primary generator, acting as a type of pressure-operated double reed which vibrates in such a way as to emit puffs of air at a definite frequency. This frequency is determined by the tension of the lips, their effective length, and the pressure of the air trying to force its way between them. The tension of the lips, of course, is regulated by the player, and

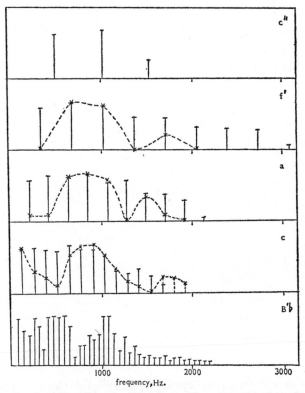

Fig. 10. Tonal spectra of the trombone. Dotted lines show the effect of muting.

obviously accurate control of this tension plays an important part not only in determining the pitch of the note but also its tone quality. The length of the vibrating portion of the lips is fixed by the cup diameter of the mouthpiece; generally speaking the lower the pitch of the instrument the greater the cup diameter used. The air pressure, also controlled by the player, is greater at high pitches than at low, and varies as well with the dynamics required, as shown in Fig. 11.

The pressure of the air behind the lips forces them more widely open, and air rushes out. When the velocity is at a maximum, the pressure in front of them is reduced, and this, in conjunction with their natural elasticity, causes them to come closer together, when the cycle is repeated. The shape of each puff of air depends upon the degree of abruptness with which the shape of the opening

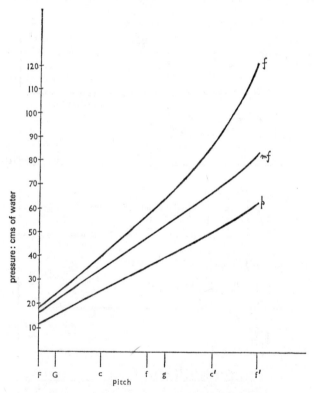

Fig. 11. Air pressures developed in playing the trombone at various pitches, in *p*, *mf*, and *f*. (After Bouasse.)

46

changes, and the fraction of each cycle for which the lips are fully open; these variables are affected partly by the physical characteristics of the player's lips, and partly by his search for a particular tone quality, but in any case will produce a vibration rich in partials, exciting the various vibrational modes of the tube. These, as already described, in their turn will have a regenerative effect on the lips if they are vibrating to produce partials of frequencies equal to or near those natural to the tube, once any other frequencies have been damped out during the short transient period.

• Between lips and tube, however, the mouthpiece intervenes to make its own mark on the partial structure, besides acting as an airtight coupling between them. The trombone mouthpiece, of which typical sections are shown in Fig. 12, consists of a more or less deep cup tapering to a throat which in turn leads to a slightly expanding backbore. This should merge imperceptibly into the mouthpipe of the instrument, which itself contracts slightly to form the venturi, a region whose exact acoustical significance seems somewhat obscure, but which plays some part in matching the backbore to the mouthpipe. The dimensions of cup diameter and volume, the size of the throat, the calibration of the backbore and the fit of the mouthpiece in the mouthpipe are all critical to the manner in which the instrument responds to the player. For each instrument there is an optimum cup volume, and an optimum distance for which the mouthpiece should project into the mouthpipe. Departure from the optimum conditions affects tone quality, intonation, and the 'feel' of the instrument; it is said that a deviation of as little as 0·05 inches can make an appreciable difference.[1] So far as cup dimensions are concerned, a small diameter and volume with a narrow throat give increased resonance at high frequencies, but less good at low; thus high notes will speak more easily and with brighter tone colour, but the likelihood is that they will be sharper than with the optimum cup volume. Conversely, an increase in these dimensions will reverse the effects. The shape of the inner edge of the rim — whether sharp or rounded — has its influence on the ease with which a sharp *staccato* or a good *legato* can be obtained. Yet another factor which must be considered in the choice of a mouthpiece is the amount of lip the individual player is accustomed to get into the mouthpiece.

It can be seen, then, that there is no such thing as an ideal mouthpiece. The requirements are so conflicting that the shape and dimensions which are satisfactory for one element of playing will almost certainly be inimical to others. The usual answer is to

[1] Earle L. Kent: op. cit., p. 7.

compromise and select a 'middle-of-the-road' mouthpiece which does most things adequately but none superlatively. No doubt the best solution would be to have one's mouthpiece tailor-made to match both one's instrument and one's own physical idiosyncrasies, and this can be done, but will prove somewhat expensive. An American maker's catalogue lists forty-two types, varying in cup diameter, depth of cup, size of throat, rim width and shape, and from such a variety it is usually possible for a player to find a model which suits him and his instrument. Another possibility is to experiment with a mouthpiece provided with an adjustable cup, which can be deepened for the low register, and mouthpieces with detachable rims are also available (Fig. 12).

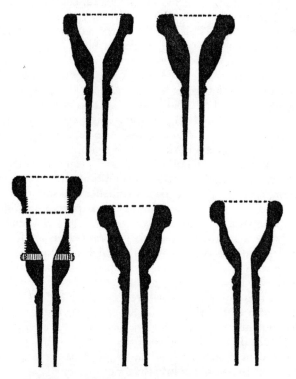

Fig. 12. Mouthpiece profiles.
    Top left: medium cup, medium wide rim.
    Top right: very shallow cup, wide cushion rim.
    Lower left: with adjustable cup and detachable rim.
    Lower centre: medium deep cup, medium wide rim.
    Lower right: bass trombone, deep cup, medium wide rim.

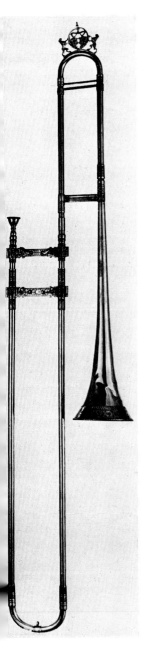

I Tenor trombone: Georg Ehe, Nuremberg, 1619.
(*Musée Instrumental du Conservatoire
National de Musique, Paris, No. 660.*)
above, detail of bell bow guard

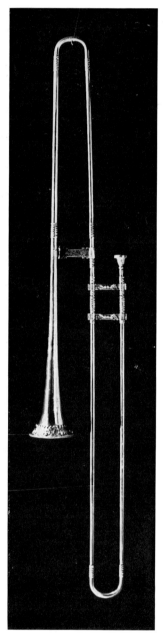 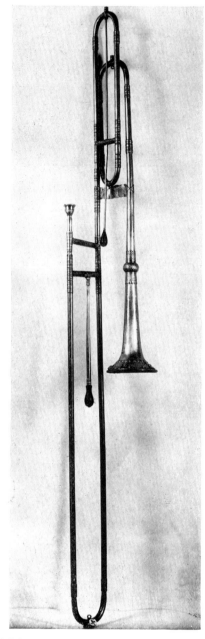

II (*left*) Bass trombone: Hanns Hainlein, Nuremberg, 1668.
(*Musée Instrumental, Brussels, No. 1265.*)

III (*right*) Quintbass trombone: Joh. Leonh. Ehe, Nuremberg, 1732.
(*Gesellschaft der Musikfreunde, Kunsthistorisches Museum, Vienna, No. 202.*)

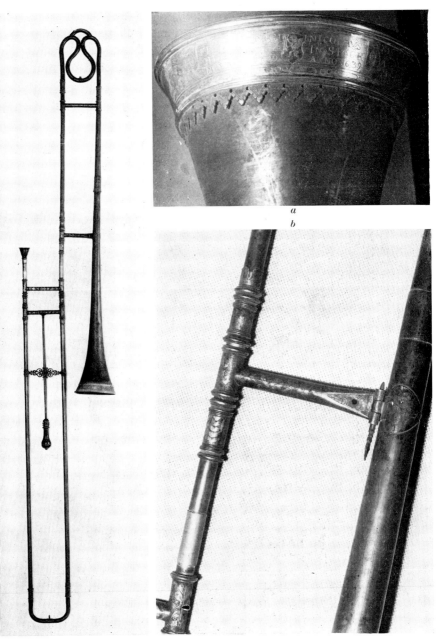

a

b

IV Contrabass trombone: Georg Nikolaus Oller, Stockholm, 1639. (*Musikhistoriska Museet, Stockholm, No. 242.*)
(*a*) Detail of bell garland, (*b*) detail of bell stay, showing pin attachment

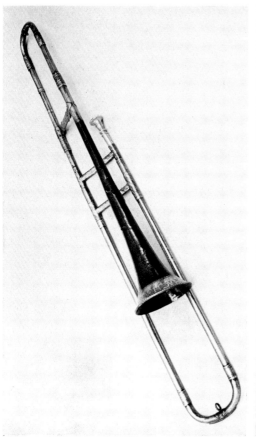

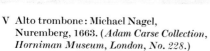

V Alto trombone: Michael Nagel,
Nuremberg, 1663. (*Adam Carse Collection*,
Horniman Museum, London, No. 228.)

VI Soprano trombone: J. F. Schwab
Leipzig, 1796. (*Musikinstrumente*
Museum, Leipzig, No. 1879.)

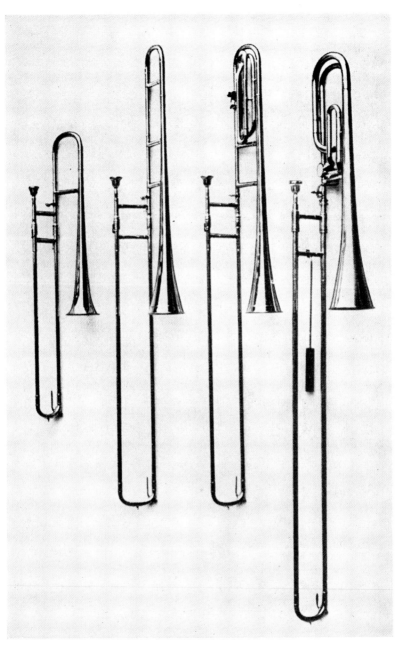

VII Modern Baroque trombones. (*W. Monke, Cologne.*) *left to right*, alto in F,
tenor in B♭, tenor in B♭ with F valve, bass in F with E♭ valve

VIII (*left*) Tenor trombone in B♭, large bore, 8½-inch bell. (*Reynolds, Lincolnwood, Ill.*)

IX (*right*) Tenor-bass trombone in B♭ and F, medium bore, 8-inch bell. (*C. G. Conn, Elkhart, Ind.*)

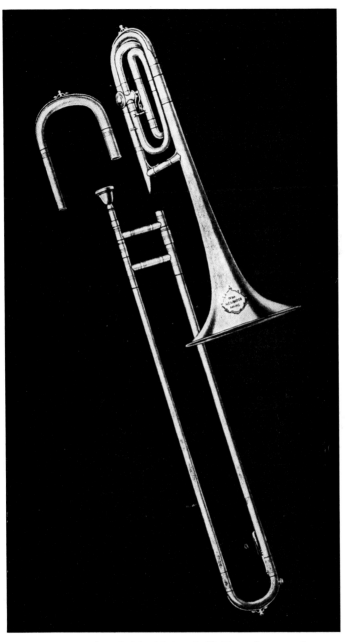

X Tenor trombone in B♭ with detachable F attachment, valve operated by cord and thong. (*Gebr. Alexander, Mainz.*)

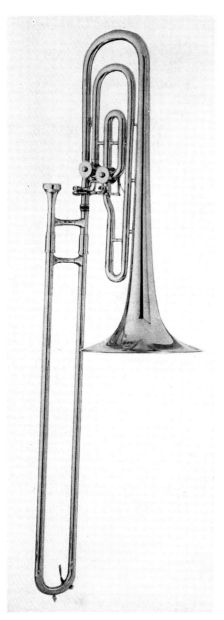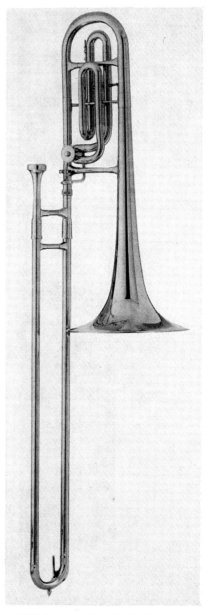

XI Bass trombone in B♭ and F, E slide with adjustable stop gauge, tuning separate from F tuning slide, wide bore, 10-inch bell. (*Reynolds, Lincolnwood, Ill.*)

XII Bass trombone in B♭, F and E, separate tuning slides for each section, wide bore, 10-inch bell. (*Reynolds, Lincolnwood, Ill.*)

XIII Bass-contrabass trombone in F,
C and D (Cimbasso model).
(*Gebr. Alexander, Mainz.*)

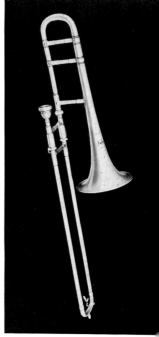

XIV (*above*) Contrabass trombone in C, with double slide. (*Boosey, London.*)

XV (*right*) Alto trombone in E♭, medium bore, 6½-inch bell. (*Vincent Bach, Elkhart, Ind.*)

From the preceding brief account it can be seen that the mouth-piece has a more important acoustical function than merely to provide a comfortable coupling between the lips and the instrument. The throat at the base of the cup provides a more or less sharp edge against which the intermittent stream of air issuing from the player's lips, already possessing its own partial structure, impinges, breaking up into a series of vortices and giving rise to an edge tone of definite frequency depending on the velocity of the stream and the distance of the lips from the edge. If the frequency of the edge tone is equal to one of the resonant frequencies of the tube, oscillations are built up. Once again the vibration of the air in the tube has a strong influence — an acoustical feed-back, as it were — on the period of the vortex formation. The shape of the edge, that is, the throat of the mouthpiece (which is not under the control of the player), and the velocity of the air stream and the distance of his lips from the throat (which are), can have a considerable influence on the partial content of the note, and hence on its tone colour.

We now have a sound whose tonal spectrum has been produced by the combined action of the vibrating lips, the edge tone of the mouthpiece, and the resonance characteristics of the tube. It is unlikely, however, that the tube, which is behaving as a broad-band amplifier — compare the sound produced by buzzing the mouthpiece alone with that heard when the instrument is attached — will possess a flat response over the whole of the frequency range concerned. It is more probable that there will be certain regions in which amplification peaks will occur As a simple example, for a low note such amplification might occur at around the frequency of the fourth partial. If now the note an octave higher is played, the same amplification affects the third partial, and the partial content is altered. A group of such prominent frequencies is known as a formant region, and is attributed by some acousticians partly, at any rate, to the natural frequencies of the metal walls enclosing the vibrating air column. These are constant factors, and all partials within this particular region of pitch are therefore strengthened, irrespective of the pitch of the note actually sounding. The tubing itself, in fact, contributes something to the quality of sound, resonating in sympathy with the vibrating air column at its own natural frequencies. Each type of instrument has its own characteristic formant regions, which play an important part in determining the tone quality of the instrument. The formant of the trombone, though not as strongly marked as those of some other instruments, owing to the large number of partials due to other causes, is shown by Jeans[1] to lie in the region of 900 to 1200 Hz, but this is almost certainly too high. If a recording of a trombone is played at twice the correct speed it sounds very much like a trumpet because the formant is moved up an octave to the pitch of the trumpet's formant. Conversely, if a trumpet recording is played at half speed, the sound is practically indistinguishable from that of a trombone.

If the region of the formant is determined partly, at any rate, by the natural frequencies of the metal of which the instrument is made, it might be expected to vary to some extent if a different metal is substituted for the normal brass, since the speed of sound is different in different metals and the resonant frequencies depend upon this quantity. Trombones have been made entirely of copper, and at the present time can be had in brass, nickel-silver, and in silver-plated brass. Generally, however, it is the bell to which most attention is paid; this is sometimes made of gold brass, with a higher copper content than ordinary yellow brass, or it is plated with nickel, silver or copper. Special bronze alloys are also used. The bell of gold brass is said to give a rounder, more sonorous and compact German-type tone of less brilliance but greater carrying power. Opinion, however, is divided on this point, and the choice of material seems to be more a matter of personal preference than of any objective evidence.

One further factor of considerable significance with regard to tone quality remains to be mentioned. It has already been seen that one of the functions of the bell is to help to fix the magnitudes and locations of resonant peaks, but it also acts as a radiator of the sounds it has helped to create. Technically the bell includes the whole of the tapered portion of the tubing, though the expansion is so gradual when it begins that it becomes obvious to the eye only in the last two feet or so. It is usually stated that the expansion is exponential in form, so that the area of cross-section doubles itself at constant intervals along the axis of the tube. Culver,[2] however, states that this is not so, and that each designer has his own flare coefficient, arriving at its value largely from experimental rather than theoretical considerations. The apparent discrepancy probably arises from the lack of exact definition of the term 'bell'. If the whole of the tapered portion is included, the expansion is usually exponential, or approximately so, for the greater part of its length, though the terminal portion — the last few inches — expands more rapidly still. As mentioned in Chapter 2,

[1] J. Jeans, op. cit., p. 149.
[2] C. A. Culver: *Musical Acoustics*, p. 215.

trombones of the sixteenth and seventeenth centuries lacked this final expansion and had a more funnel-like bell, and their tone appears to have been softer and less metallic than that of modern trombones. Modern reconstructions also lead to the same conclusion. Whatever the exact shape of the bell, it is clear that its acoustical properties are extremely important since nearly all the sound is radiated from it. The larger the effective aperture of the bell compared with the wavelength of the sound it is emitting the better it radiates. The effective aperture size, on the other hand, depends upon the rate of flare; if this is too rapid, low frequency sounds will not be efficiently radiated. Hence the bell is frequency-sensitive and may discriminate against certain partials, as shown for a hypothetical case in Fig. 13. In effect it plays two contradictory roles; it augments the intensity of sound emitted, but if it is too large it reduces the intensity of the upper partials and hence diminishes the brilliance of the sound, but on the other hand if it is too small it does not radiate low frequency sounds efficiently. For a good bass, therefore, the flare must not be too rapid, so that the low frequencies are not discriminated against, and for brilliance the aperture must not be too large, so that the higher partials are not discriminated against.

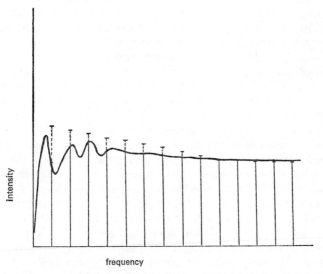

Fig. 13. Effect of the bell on the partial structure of the trombone. The curved line shows the frequency response of the bell, and the dotted lines how it attenuates some of the lower partials originally present in the tone.

A further property of the bell is that it confers some degree of directivity on the sound it emits. In general when the wavelength is small in comparison with the bell-mouth diameter — that is, for partials of high frequency — the bell beams these partials out along the axis of the instrument, but for lower frequency partials the directivity is much less pronounced. As a result the tone quality heard from directly in front of the instrument is much brighter than when it is heard from one side.

The final factor influencing the tone colour is the mute. This may take a wide variety of shapes, some of which are shown in Fig. 14. The material is also very varied; aluminium, brass, copper, wood, fibre, cardboard, rubber, glass and polystyrene are some of the substances which have been used. Most commonly employed in orchestral work are the straight mutes — truncated cones — of metal or a composition material, sometimes plaster or stone-lined, giving the player some range of tonal effects. Jazz players are able to be more adventurous in their choice of mutes and achieve correspondingly wider variety of tone colours. This, rather than a reduction in the volume of sound, is the main function of mutes.

In an exhaustive study of the acoustical effects of the mute Kurka[1] shows that, in fact, its influence is four-fold. There is an attenuation of volume, which is most marked in the lower register, and least in the medium. Most mutes also cause an alteration in pitch, usually in the direction of sharpness, again especially in the low register, though its magnitude may not be great enough to be significantly troublesome. An increased degree of directivity is to be observed, which is more pronounced in the medium and high registers, as if the the mute were focusing the sound in the same way as a lens does light. Finally, and most important, there is the effect of the mute on tone colour. This is most easily seen from Fig. 10, in which the dotted lines show the shape of the envelope caused by muting. From this it is plain that while some partials are reduced in intensity, others — and these frequently the odd-numbered, dissonant ones — are amplified so as to become more conspicuous than in unmuted tone. Moreover, in each case formant peaks are obvious at about the same frequencies, around 800 Hz, with a less well-marked one at about twice this frequency. These results were obtained with a stone-lined mute; other types have their own characteristic formant peaks corresponding to the differences in tone colour observed with different mutes. Kurka recommends that more scientific study should be made of the effects of different mute volumes, shapes and materials on the tone

[1] M. J. Kurka: *A Study of the Acoustical Effects of Mutes on Wind Instruments.*

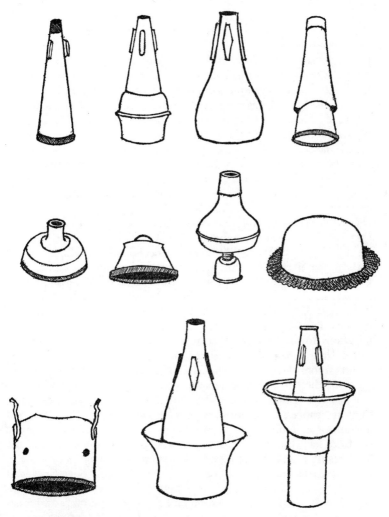

Fig.14. Mutes.
>   *Top, left to right*: Straight mute (composition or fibre); straight mute (aluminium); straight mute (polystyrene); mega mute (clear tone or solo tone).
>   *Middle, left to right*: plunger mute (rubber); plunger mute (metal); wah-wah mute (aluminium); Derby mute (stone-lined).
>   *Bottom, left to right*: bucket mute (vel-ve-tone); cup mute (polystyrene); cup mute (copper, chromium-plated).

colour, and that composers should be more specific in their demands when using muted effects. The bare term *con sordino* can result in a wide variety of tone colours according to the type of mute used by particular players, and Bartók is somewhat exceptional in asking, for example, for cardboard mutes to be used. Kurka also points out that lack of uniform standards in construction leads to considerable variations in acoustical behaviour even among mutes of the same type, and even, in extreme cases, among mutes by the same manufacturer. As a result, the player has to become accustomed to the acoustical idiosyncrasies of the mute, or mutes, he has chosen to use, particularly with regard to pitch. It must be remembered, too, that the response of the instrument is altered when it is muted. A higher air pressure is usually required to produce the same degree of dynamics, and sometimes some adjustment of the embouchure as well.

Consideration of the acoustical facts detailed above will show that the designer of a trombone is faced by more than one dilemma. By his choice of the calibration of the bore and bell, he has to satisfy the partially conflicting requirements of intonation and tone colour. If he alters the shape to provide better intonation of the partials, he will find that he has also altered the tone quality; if he fixes on a shape to give a particularly desirable tone quality, he may find he has also built in some undesirable errors of intonation. Intonation depends mostly but not entirely on the bore calibration of the first three-quarters of the tube length, tonal quality more on the dimensions of the last quarter. In fixing the shape of the bell the designer must have regard to the selection of partials it is going to transmit, and the effectiveness with which they are radiated. He must cope with the problem that the proportion of cylindrical tubing will vary from about 50 per cent of the total length to almost 70 per cent, and he must ensure that the final result is manageable and well-balanced for the player. Until quite recently improvements in design have largely been the result of experience allied to good workmanship and more or less empirical methods. Further research and the advent of more and more sophisticated techniques could well show that some of the defects hitherto regarded as inherent in the instrument may in fact be avoidable.

4

The Tenor Trombone

The technique of the trombone differs from that of all other brass instruments, which are provided with means of lengthening the tube by valves. The trombone effects this lengthening by the mechanically simpler process of moving a U-shaped slide over a pair of parallel inner slides. The length of these slides, determined by the reach of the average human arm, is such that a series of seven positions, corresponding to the seven different valve combinations available on a three-valved horn or trumpet, can be obtained, providing fundamentals covering an interval of a diminished fifth. A further and important point of difference from the valved instruments is, of course, that the intonation in any position except the first (and, if spring barrels are fitted, to some extent in this position too) is entirely within the control of the player, since he has the opportunity for infinitely fine adjustment of the tube length denied to the player of a valved instrument.

At this point it should be emphasized that, though the appropriate slide extensions can be calculated theoretically, in practice they vary from player to player, from instrument to instrument, and even from day to day. This is partly illustrated by the following figures,[1] showing the theoretical extensions required, and some found by actual measurement.

According to theory, therefore, these players would be sharp, for example, in the seventh position, one of them by as much as three-fifths of a semitone, and similar departures can be seen from the theoretical values in the other positions. Hence most players will rightly say that there are no such things as well-defined positions on the trombone which apply in all circumstances and with all instruments; the positions are no more than rough guides, to which the player will make fine adjustment according to the

[1] Partly from H. Bouasse: op. cit., p. 369.

Position	Slide extensions (inches)			
	Theoretical	Player A	Player B	Player C
1	–	–	–	–
2	3·4	2·7	3·0	3·1
3	7·1	6·5	6·9	6·6
4	10·9	8·8	10·5	11·3
5	15·0	13·8	14·6	15·6
6	19·2	17·9	18·5	19·5
7	23·8	21·0	22·1	22·6

state of his embouchure, the context of the note to be sounded, the individual instrument he is using, and the partial being produced. The figures above show that on the whole all three players probably preferred to lip down to the correct pitch and to use a rather smaller extension of the slide. This is possible because there is a certain tolerance around each partial (see p. 42), especially below it and in the lower register. The process becomes more or less unconscious, involving the player's sense of intonation and his pre-knowledge of the exact sound he wishes to produce. Further problems of intonation, moreover, are introduced by the fact that the partials are not all exactly in tune with the tempered scale. It has already been shown that in a cylindro-conical tube such as that of the trombone the higher mode frequencies are not likely to be exact multiples of the pedal note frequency, as in a purely cylindrical or a purely conical tube. These 'slightly bent' frequencies, as Benade[1] terms them, will therefore not necessarily correspond exactly to those of the partials of either the natural or the tempered series. Different instruments will possess different discrepancies of intonation even, Kleinhammer[2] says, in identical models from the same manufacturer. Though Kent[3] has pointed out that it is theoretically possible to design an instrument so that the resonant frequencies lie where they should on the equally tempered scale, this does not seem to have been achieved in practice. It is therefore impossible to state, except in very general terms, the intonational faults likely to be encountered; to some extent each instrument is a law unto itself. Fifth partials are usually slightly flat, and d' may be better as a sixth partial in the fourth position rather than as a fifth partial in first, though it can be sharpened to some extent on an instrument with spring barrels.

[1] A. H. Benade: op. cit., p. 177.
[2] E. Kleinhammer: *The Art of Trombone Playing*, p. 88.
[3] Earle L. Kent: op. cit., p. 4.

Seventh partials are almost invariably badly flat, and for this reason are not normally used on valved instruments. They may occasionally serve a useful purpose on the trombone, though they will need correcting by shortening the normal positions (see Ex. 5), and $a'\flat$, in the first position, is better tuned as an eighth partial in the third position. Ninth and tenth partials are better avoided in the lower positions, but b' and c'' (tenth partials) can sometimes be usefully employed in fourth and third positions. Eleventh partials are very sharp and more or less impracticable except in special circumstances; $e''\flat$ (in a flat first position) and d'' (in a flat second) are possible, but can normally be obtained in other positions.

The main point is that the chromatic scale of the trombone is not a mechanically fixed succession of semitone intervals as, for example, on the pianoforte, but requires each note to be selected from one of seven natural series, each of which can be varied in pitch by the player. It is upon him, and not upon the instrument, that the heaviest responsibility rests for accurate intonation. This is true, of course, of all wind instrument players, but the trombonist is more on a par with the player of a stringed instrument in that the increased latitude in matters of intonation which each of them is allowed brings, with all its advantages, an increased responsibility and the need for a very acute ear.

Kunitz[1] denies that the player of the trombone can train himself to play in tempered intonation; he claims that equal temperament is a calculated and therefore an unnatural compromise, and that a continuous conscious correction within the framework of an orchestral performance is an impossibility. To achieve this the player would have to make an appropriate adjustment to his slide position except when playing the octaves of the fundamentals, since the other partials are unlikely to be in exactly tempered intonation. It has in fact been found[2] that players of instruments in which variation in pitch is possible do not keep to any scientifically calculated standard of pitch — leading notes, for example, are usually played sharp — and there is a continuous harmonic adjustment to the sounds of other instruments. The trombonist, like the string player, depends upon his ear and his musical sensitivity for his intonation, and assesses the exact positioning of his slide accordingly.

For these reasons, all values of tube lengths and slide extensions given should be taken not as exact measurements, but as no more

[1] H. Kunitz, op. cit., pp. 598–9.
[2] A. Wood: *The Physics of Music*, p. 194.

than guides serving to illustrate principles rather than to state fixed quantities.

Each of the seven positions of the trombone provides a series of partials (up to the tenth, twelfth or higher, according to the skill of the player), based upon the fundamental for the tube length of that position. Since the amount by which the tube must be lengthened for each fall of a semitone is about 5·95 per cent of its length, the distance between adjacent slide positions is not constant, but increases as the pitch falls. Thus on a B♭ trombone the distance between the first and second positions is about 3½ inches, and between the sixth and seventh rather over 4½ inches. Table 2 shows the series available in each position. Since the higher partials are more closely spaced than the lower, alternative posi-

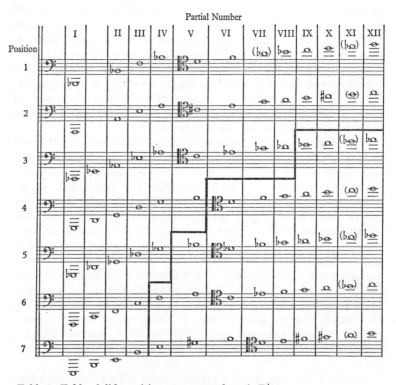

Table 2. Table of slide positions, tenor trombone in B♭.
Slide positions to the right of, and below the thick line would not normally be used for the notes shown, which are available in shorter positions.

tions are available for every note from *e* upwards, but generally speaking, except when it is necessary in order to avoid large and awkward changes of position, the lower positions are not used when there is a choice. It can be seen from the Table that from *g* upwards the player need go no lower than the fourth position, and from *c'* on every note can be obtained in the third or shorter positions. Since emission of the sound is usually easier on a shorter tube, using a lower partial, these short positions would normally be used for notes from *f'* upwards unless considerations of unwieldy slide shifts, or possibly of tone colour, dictate otherwise. Sounds produced as lower numbered partials of fundamentals based on a shorter tube length are somewhat brighter in colour than the higher numbered partials from a longer tube, and partials beyond the eighth are rarely used in the lower positions.

In spite of the statements in many text-books on orchestration to the effect that pedal notes are only possible in the first three or four positions, in modern technique all seven are considered to be within the compass of the instrument.[1] The reason for these statements may well be that on the narrow-bore trombone commonly in use until quite recently (at least in this country and in France), the last few pedal notes were extremely difficult to sound, and when produced, of poor quality. On the medium or wide-bore trombones now almost universally used they speak much more readily.

The pedal notes have acquired an undeserved notoriety and are still, perhaps, not accorded their true value. Forsyth[2] describes them as 'unsatisfactory, rather coarse, and wanting in substance', and if this was ever true it is certainly not now. He goes on to make some derogatory remarks concerning the famous passage in the *Hostias* of the *Messe des Morts* by Berlioz, where eight trombones play pedal notes as the bass of chords completed only by three flutes three octaves above, condemning it unheard by adding that 'it probably sounds very nasty'. It has been suggested that the intention is for the flutes to pick up the partials contained in the trombone tone; it has also been pointed out that at the time of its composition there was no other brass instrument in French orchestras which could produce these bass notes. Whether they were written for practical or dramatic reasons, the effect is certainly unusual, but also rather impressive.

In *Les Couleurs de la Cité Celeste* Messiaen has a basically similar

---

[1] The American trombonist Paul Tanner includes pedal C within his range (see *The Instrumentalist*, Oct. 1968).

[2] C. Forsyth: *Orchestration*, p. 135.

passage (Ex. 1) to which he appends the note 'Les sons graves et sons pédales des trombones, trombone basse et cor doivent être terribles'. Three clarinets, high above, provide a barely audible colouring to these fearsome trombone notes.

(Ex. 1. Messiaen: *Les Couleurs de la Cité Celeste.*)

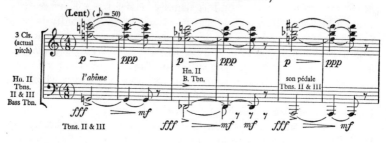

The exact date at which the existence of pedal notes was discovered is not known. Kastner, in the *Supplement* to his *Traité général de l'Instrumentation* (1844), mentions that they had been brought to his notice by a trombonist of the Paris Opera named Schiltz, but they had already been used by Hérold (*Zampa*, 1831), and by Berlioz (in the passage mentioned above, 1837), although the latter had some difficulty at his first rehearsal in persuading his trombonists that the notes were possible.[1] It appears, then, that they did not become part of the recognized technique of the trombone at least until the early nineteenth century. Since that time they have been comparatively sparingly used by composers, and then almost invariably as long sustained notes, not usually lower than $A'\flat$ or G'. In the absence of a contrabass trombone these are not otherwise available in trombone tone, and the tuba, so often used instead, is no real substitute, for the pedal notes have a dark, precise, metallic sound which is completely their own. With the increasing use of wider-bored tenor and tenor-bass instruments they are much more easily produced than previously, and more adventurous use could well be made of them, including those in the lower positions. A short time is needed for the preparation of the embouchure when the notes are to be employed, and again for its adjustment subsequent to playing them, but too much is often made of the supposed difficulties of production.

Pedal notes are also available on the bass trombone. The following passage is unusual in its prolonged use of pedal notes, here

[1] 'These notes are in the instrument and the players must get them out.'

doubled by tuba, contra-bassoon and double-basses and employed more for their weight of tone than their colour.

(Ex. 2. Berg: *Wozzeck*, Act II.)

In fact, this passage is playable only on a tenor-bass or bass-contrabass trombone; the first seven bars use the pedal notes in first, second, third and fourth positions with the F valve, while the next two pairs are pedals (fourth and fifth positions, second and third) on the B♭ side.

Thus the complete compass of the modern tenor trombone extends from E′, the lowest pedal note, to B′♭, the first position pedal; it is then usually stated that there is a gap up to seventh position E, and that thereafter it proceeds chromatically to f″, the twelfth partial in the first position. One method of partly filling the gap is to utilize the so-called 'falset' notes E♭, D and C♯, obtained in the seventh position using a very slack embouchure and taking advantage of the inherent flexibility of intonation available to the player, especially in the low register and below the partial — the same effect as with the factitious notes on the horn. A better method of bridging the gap is, however, available. It is possible to obtain the first four notes, and even the B, by starting in a long third position and proceeding down to a very flat seventh position at the fullest extension of the slide. The acoustical origin of these notes is suggested on p. 40, and it seems that they are connected with the privileged notes which, as Benade[1] says, make it 'possible in principle to have any number of unused vibratory modes, above, below, or mixed in with those forming harmonic series'. Whatever their acoustical provenance, they form a well-defined set, in quality resembling the pedal notes with which they

[1] A. H. Benade: op. cit., p. 195.

61

link up, but, like them, requiring a short time in which to prepare the embouchure.

One curiosity is worth mentioning in this connection. Both in *Das Lied von der Erde* and in his Ninth Symphony Mahler writes a sustained *C*, in the former for first and second trombones, and in the latter for all three, and in each case specifically marks it *Pedalton*. This note is available as a pedal neither on the tenor nor the tenor-bass instrument, though it can, of course, be played as a second partial on the F trombone. It is unlikely that this marking could be a slip of the pen, for Mahler's experience as an orchestral conductor, and still more, the meticulous and detailed markings in his scores, make it clear that his knowledge of the capabilities of orchestral instruments was very wide. These facts lead to the interesting speculation that he might possibly have been aware of the existence of these privileged notes, for the *C* can, in fact be played as such in the sixth position on the B♭ trombone. If these notes were known to the German trombonists of the time (1908–9), they do not appear to have been used elsewhere nor, so far as can be ascertained, are they shown in the teaching manuals of the period. On the other hand it may be that Mahler expected these notes to be played on a tenor-bass instrument with a pedal note type of tone quality.

From *E* upwards the compass proceeds chromatically to *f″*, twelfth partial in first position, but may be extended still higher by players with a strong embouchure. A good tenor player will certainly expect to be able to produce a pleasant tone quality, without strain, up to *e″*♭ (Table 3).

With such a wide range certain technical limitations present themselves, especially on the tenor trombone without an F attachment. Chief among these is the difficulty experienced in playing rapid passages in which large slide movements are required. However smooth and easy the motion of the slide, an appreciable time is needed to shift it the two feet or so between first and seventh positions. Rapid changes between any of the first five positions are everyday fare for the trombonist, and present no particular problem, but a quick passage involving constant interchange between first or second and sixth or seventh positions is almost impossible to play with accuracy and precision. In many cases thoughtful use of alternative positions enables the player to avoid this difficulty, but if the passage involves the sixth and seventh position notes *F*, *E*, *c* and *B* no alternatives are available. The following extract includes progressions where, on a tenor trombone, shifts of this sort are unavoidable.

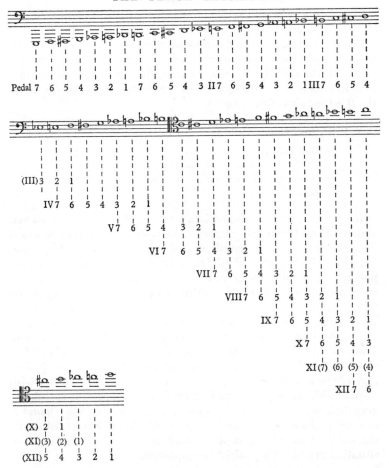

Table 3. Chromatic scale of the tenor trombone in B♭. Roman numerals indicate partial numbers; Arabic numerals positions.

(Ex. 3. Verdi: *Othello*, Act II.)

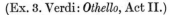

63

Similarly a passage like Ex. 4 is extremely difficult to bring off successfully, and at best would sound (and look) very clumsy in the absence of an F valve. In this case the instrument is muted, but in similar situations without the mute some care might be needed to match the slightly different tone qualities arising from the fact that the A♯ is the second partial of the shortest tube length, while the B is the third of the longest.

(Ex. 4. Bartók: *Dance Suite.*)

In general, when a choice is available, the position is chosen which utilizes the lowest-numbered partial — that is, the one which involves the shortest length of tubing. Quite apart from any question of economy of slide movement these low-numbered partials speak more freely and with a clearer tone than the higher from a greater tube length, which have a slight tendency to be 'stuffy' in tone. Nevertheless, there are many occasions on which the auxiliary positions prove valuable in helping to avoid large slide movements, though they need to be used with discretion. Tone quality must be considered, and intonation, too, requires careful attention; no hard and fast rules can be laid down since so much depends upon the player and his individual instrument, with whose foibles he will be familiar. The seventh partial is invariably very flat, but it can sometimes prove valuable in giving f'♯ and g' in short positions which can be sharpened. The following list shows the most commonly used alternative positions, and the types of situation in which they might be employed.

Normal Position	2	1	2	1	2	1	1	5	4
Partial Number	III	III	IV	IV	V	V	VI	VIII	VIII
Alternative Position	7	6	6	5	5	4	4	3	2
Partial Number	IV	IV	V	V	VI	VI	VII	VII	VII

Normal	2	1	5	2	6	3	4	5	1	3	1	3
Alternative	7	6	5	7	6	3	4	5	6	3	4	3

In Ex. 5 the slide positions are those marked by the composer himself, and since he played the trombone he was perhaps in a better position than most composers to know best how to achieve the result he wanted.

(Ex. 5. Holst: *The Hymn of Jesus.*)

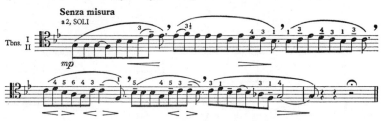

A note appended to the score points out that 'by using the positions marked, the trombone players will avoid the unpleasant smearing of one note into another'. The position $3\frac{1}{2}$ is intended to indicate that the seventh partial *f* in the fourth position is very flat and will need to be sharpened by shortening the slide position.

Examples 6 and 7 show how, when successive notes of a passage are all partials of a particular fundamental, use is made of this fact to remain in the same position. This will obviously make possible the easy execution of arpeggios based on the series of any of the seven fundamentals.

(Ex. 6. Ravel: *Daphnis et Chloé, Danse guerrière.*)

In general, and particularly in quick passages, the shorter the slide shifts that need to be made the better. Thus in the following phrases, if the *d'* is taken in the fourth position instead of the first a saving of some seven inches is made in the first bar, and about fourteen in the second.

(Ex. 7. Verdi: *Othello*, Act I.)

(Ex. 8. Mahler: *Symphony No. 7.*)

From his instruction to give the trombones time, Mahler appears to have had some qualms about their ability to perform these arpeggi in tempo, but a competent player should have no difficulty with them if he uses the alternative position as suggested.

Quite apart from reasons of economical slide movement, the alternative positions can often be used to help promote a good legato. As explained later, a true legato is possible only between two partials of the same series. Hence any interval that can be played without changing position can be slurred, and an astute choice of position may make a slurred interval possible where the normal position will not. An extreme case of this facet of trombone technique is to be seen in Ex. 24 (p. 79).

The Glissando

Though the ability to play a true glissando, in which all the intervening microtones between two notes are heard as the slide shift is made, is a property possessed by the trombone alone among wind instruments, the player's preoccupation is normally to avoid producing such an effect. It might be said, indeed, that a large part of his slide technique is employed in eliminating the minute glissandi which all too readily appear in a change from one position to another if tongue and slide are not perfectly co-ordinated. This is particularly the case in slurred phrases, which easily become blurred or smeared in the absence of a sound technique.

The use of the glissando in serious compositions is comparatively recent; it was probably first used in other types of music by the Negro bands of the southern states of America, the precursors of the modern jazz bands, in the 1880s, and it is known that Arthur Pryor, one of Sousa's trombonists, exploited the effect just before the turn of the century. At any rate, Widor, in his *Technique of the Modern Orchestra* (1904), expressed surprise at hearing it when passing a dance-hall, and thought that it was highly unlikely ever to be used in a symphony; and Schoenberg, when he did write glissandi[1] in his *Pelleas und Melisande* (1902–3), felt it necessary to add an explanatory footnote: 'The glissando on the trombone is executed as follows: the note E is established by the lips as the lowest partial of the sixth draw' — that is, in the seventh position — 'and then the slide is shifted through all the positions in such a way that the chromatic intervals, as well as the quarter-tone, eighth-tone and smaller intervals in between, are clearly heard, as in the glissando of string instruments'. Since then the glissando has become a commonplace of trombone writing, and though undeniably effective in its place, has probably been overdone. It is, however, part of the essential technique of the trombone player. Table 4 gives the glissandi which are possible on the tenor trombone.

The last six diatonic glissandi, though difficult, are just possible. Since they depend upon the close proximity of the upper partials in the region where they are no more than a tone apart, they exist only in the high register. For an upward glissando they involve lipping up the series of partials as the slide moves *out* (not *in*, as in a normal upward glissando), until such a position is reached that the glissando can be completed by the lips without further movement of the slide. The last two of these are lip glissandi extending up to the sixteenth partial, and theoretically could be reproduced in all positions up to the first, giving a diatonic glissando from $b'♭$ to $b''♭$. It is doubtful if any player would think it worthwhile attempting these (except possibly as embouchure practice), since they are highly unlikely ever to be called for in performance.

Composers do not always have a clear understanding of what is and what is not possible when writing glissandi. Except for the last

---

[1] 'It is typical of Schoenberg that at the time he wrote this passage he did not really know whether it was technically possible according to the standards of the time or not, but invented his own technique for its performance.' D. Newlin: *Bruckner, Mahler, Schoenberg*, p. 224.

Table 4. Glissandi.

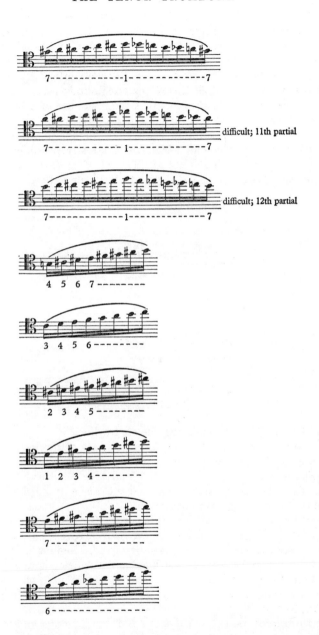

difficult; 11th partial

difficult; 12th partial

six of Table 4, a glissando cannot be made over a larger interval than an augmented fourth, involving the total extent of the slide movement, and it must not involve a change of partial number during its course. Within these limits it can ascend, or descend, or both, and need not, of course, cover the whole interval. Reference to Table 4 will make it clear that the possibilities, especially in the lower register, are strictly limited, though the use of a tenor-bass trombone helps to widen the scope a little.

The examples which follow show the different notations used, and include some glissandi which are not really possible without some faking, either involving an interval of more than an augmented fourth or a change of partial during their course.

(Ex. 9. Stravinsky: Suite, *L'Oiseau de Feu*.)

Here Stravinsky writes out the glissando in full, also giving full indication of the slide positions.

(Ex. 10. Ravel: *L'Enfant et les Sortilèges*.)

In Ex. 10 the glissandi are shown by lines joining the notes which are to be reached at appropriate beats of the bar, and the starting position of each glissando is noted. Ravel scrupulously avoids indicating a glissando to the final *b♮* in the third trombone part, since the first position is reached at the *b♭* and the player must then move to *b♮* in fourth position.

Another example from the same work (in which glissandi are frequently used) shows the same problem in reverse, though here Ravel does not suggest how it is to be solved. The first *b♮* in Ex. 11 must be taken in fourth position, and a quick change to first position *b♭* is necessary before the glissando can be properly begun; the same difficulty occurs several times during the course of the glissando.

A third quotation (Ex. 12) shows a descending glissando for the first trombone in conjunction with an ascending one for the second.

(Ex. 11. Ravel: *L'Enfant et les Sortilèges*.)

(Ex. 12. Ravel: *L'Enfant et les Sortilèges*.)

The obstacles in the way of a glissando extending over a greater range than the slide positions will allow are overcome by Prokofiev by using two trombones which overlap.

(Ex. 13. Prokofiev: *Symphony No. 5*.)

Next are given a few examples of cases in which the composer has written glissandi which are not strictly possible without the use of a valve, and not always even then. It is unlikely that Debussy was acquainted with the tenor-bass trombone, for in his time French custom was to write for three tenors. Yet the simple-looking glissandi in Ex. 14 are not possible for the tenor instrument. Starting on e♭ (third position) one runs out of slide at b♮, and the same applies to the drop from c♭ to g. If spring barrels are fitted, it might be possible to push the slide in to its fullest extent and lip up in the hope of slightly extending an ascending glissando; in this case the only expedient is to push the slide past the seventh position as far as one dares or can manage, and lip down.

(Ex. 14. Debussy: *Images*, No. 2. *Ibéria*.)

The glissandi in another extract from the same work extend over much too large a range to be played exactly as written.

(Ex. 15. Debussy: *Images*, No. 2. *Ibéria*.)

To show more clearly the problems involved, the glissandi have been written out in full below. If the first player starts in seventh position d', his slide will take him only as far as $g'\sharp$; a glissando ending on first position d'' must start on seventh position $g'\natural$. A change from first to seventh position during the course of a glissando is unthinkable. A possible solution is to start at d' in seventh position, lip up the intervening partials (e', $f'\sharp$, $g'\sharp$) and then begin the glissando in the normal way. The other two players are faced with similar problems. The second can begin at seventh position b, lip up to $f'\sharp$, and glissando on up to second position b', while the third must begin at fourth position g (the only possibility), somehow make his way through a thicket of partials to seventh position d', and return with relief to second position g' in a true glissando.

(Ex. 15a.)

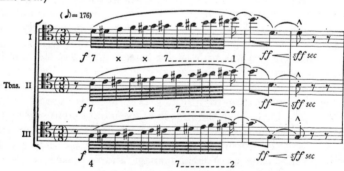

The next example also poses a problem — a downward glissando over a range of an octave to a note which does not exist on the tenor trombone except as, in this context, a somewhat dubious privileged note. Even the tenor-bass instrument will find some difficulty in coping adequately with this big interval. Whichever instrument it is played on, somewhere there will have to be a bridge using a lip glissando to cover the gap, and on the tenor the bottom *D* will only be reached with a very long arm and a very loose lip.

(Ex. 16. Respighi: *Saltarella*.)

Three final examples:

(Ex. 17. Mahler: *Symphony No. 3*.)

(Ex. 18. Webern: *Six Pieces*, Op. 6.)

(Ex. 19. Berg: *Wozzeck*.)

In these passages, no matter what instrument is used, little more than an approximation can be made to the enormous glissandi they involve. Each can begin and end on the right notes; what happens in between depends upon the individual player and the instrument used.

It can be seen that more is sometimes expected from a trombonist than he or his instrument is able to give. When this happens, it is usually owing to an incomplete understanding of the technical capabilities of the instrument on the part of the composer, and

73

though the player, by the exercise of considerable ingenuity, will usually manage to devise some means of coping reasonably adequately with these technical impossibilities, he may understandably become somewhat bitter when a conductor tries to teach him his job.[1]

Occasionally a lip glissando, similar to that employed on the horn, is used. This involves a rapid arpeggio up or down (or both) the partial series of one particular position. An example from Bartók is given; in it he marks the position in which each glissando is to be played.

(Ex. 20. Bartók: *Violin Concerto.*)

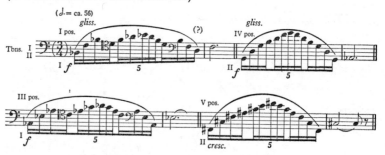

Grace Notes

The playing technique for grace notes is very similar to that for the glissando. For a single grace note no problem arises, provided that the composer has taken the trouble to ensure that the progression lies in two neighbouring slide positions — that is, that the interval is a semitone. Up to *a* a whole-tone grace note is not possible; beyond that it may be obtained either by a slide shift of one position together with a change of partial, or by a lip slur between two adjacent partials in the same position.

When more than one grace note is indicated, more often than not these are written in whole-tone intervals. If the tempo is fast, it is generally not possible to play them as written since there is not time to make the necessary slide changes nor to articulate each note. Many of the grace notes which occur in nineteenth-century Italian opera parts were written with the valve-trombone in view, and on this instrument they are as feasible as on any other valved instrument. The following example shows the type of part, which cannot be played exactly as written on any slide trombone. The

---

[1] See E. Kleinhammer: Op. cit., p. 59.

best that can be done is to play a short glissando before each
crotchet; in the first two bars, for example, from *e* in the seventh
position up to *f♯* in the fifth, and from *g♯* to *b* in the third and
fourth bars. In the last two bars a glissando for the whole interval
more or less reproduces the written notes, though it involves a
rapid shift from second to seventh position after each crotchet.
These alterations, of course, pass unnoticed and do not alter the
general agitato effect.

(Ex. 21. Verdi: *Othello*, Act I.)

If the grace notes are in a slower tempo, they can sometimes be
played as written, utilizing double or triple tonguing in conjunction with quick slide shifts. In Ex. 22 all three trombones could
triple tongue from sixth position through fourth and second to
first, where all three trills can be played, but a simpler and more
effective expedient would be a lip-glissando, with the first trombone in fourth position, the second in sixth, and the third in sixth,
the latter moving up to fifth for the trill.

(Ex. 22. Kodály: *Háry János* Suite.)

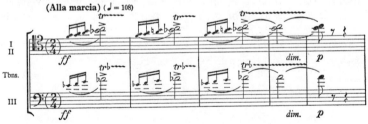

Ex. 23, however, written presumably with the valve-trombone
in mind, needs some judicious editing if it is to be played on a
tenor slide instrument, though it is possible on a tenor-bass. The
first group of grace notes, if played as written, would involve the
slide shifts, 2, 7, 5, 4 and would possibly be feasible if first position
B♭ were substituted for *B♮*; but it would be simpler to omit the *A*

and play a simple glissando from seventh position to fourth. The second is playable in the positions 6, 4, 2, 1 but again a glissando would give much the same effect. The third requires the extremely awkward change 4, 2, 7, 6 and it is not easy to see what can be done to ease the situation and yet keep reasonably close to the composer's intentions; the fourth is a trifle less awkward, but even utilizing the auxiliary positions the player is left with a choice between the combinations 4, 2, 4, 3; 4, 6, 4, 3; or 4, 6, 7, 6, none of which is immediately attractive. Most trombonists would manage to make shift to produce the general effect required in cases like these, without adhering meticulously to the exact notation.

(Ex. 23. Mascagni: *Cavalleria Rusticana*.)

Trills

The trill is not very commonly employed on the trombone, except perhaps for bizarre effects such as those in Ex. 22, for two main reasons. The first is that it has a somewhat cumbersome and inelegant feel about it (though its practice provides excellent embouchure training), and the other, more cogent, that the number of trills available is severely limited. A true trill is made by rapid variations in lip tension, and can only be effected between neighbouring partials of the same series. Consequently it is limited to the interval of a whole tone, and cannot start on any note lower than d. Table 5 gives a list of such trills, the last four of which require

Positions	7	6	5	4	3	2	1
			7	6	5	4	3
					7	6	5

Positions	2	1	2	1	3	2
	4	3	5	4	5	4
	7	6	7	6		

Table 5. Lip Trills.

76

such a high and well-controlled lip tension that they are unlikely to be mastered by any but the finest players. The first seven of these trills begin on the seventh partial, if played in the positions shown in the top line, and this is likely to be flat; and the intonation of some of the others which employ the eleventh partial may not be quite accurate.

A few examples of the use of the trill may be mentioned. Stravinsky uses those on *f'* and *a'* in *L'Oiseau de Feu* and again in *Le Sacre du Printemps*, and Ravel, in *L'Enfant et les Sortilèges* (a veritable compendium of trombone devices), one on *f'♯*. Kodály, in his *Háry János* Suite, writes the higher ones on *a'♭*, *b'* and *c''* (see Ex. 22). The trill on *B♭* of Ex. 7 cannot be played on the tenor trombone, but is possible as a valve trill with an F attachment, using the *B♭* (second partial on the B♭ trombone) and the *c* (third partial) on the F, both in first position.

Semitone trills are possible only by using the slide, alternating it as quickly as possible between two adjacent positions, and these preferably not lower than fourth or fifth. In the nature of things such a trill cannot be as clear-cut as a lip trill, and perhaps fortunately, the need or opportunity for using it is rare.

Chords

The possibility of sounding chords on brass instruments has been known at least since the early nineteenth century, and probably longer. The phenomenon was profitably exploited by the horn virtuoso Eugene Vivier (1817–1900), and in his *Memoirs* Berlioz mentions that during 1842 the Stuttgart trombonist Schrade, in the course of a performance of a solo fantasia, caused considerable astonishment among his audience by sounding the four notes of the dominant seventh in the key of B♭ — E♭, A, C, F — simultaneously. Berlioz felt that composers could well study and profit by this acoustical oddity, but until recently (see Chapter 11) little has been done to follow up his suggestion.

The acoustical explanation generally accepted is that by playing one of the notes of the chord and humming another, resultant first order sum and difference tones are produced to complete the chord, the interval between the two generating notes determining the chord that results. As a rule the difference tone is readily observed, but the summation tone is rather more difficult to hear. The chord which Berlioz noted could have been produced by playing the low *F* and humming the *a*. The frequency of *F* is approximately 88 Hz and of *a* 220 Hz; their difference gives a note of frequency 132 Hz

(*c*) and their sum one of frequency 308 Hz — a somewhat flat
e′♭.

Some of the theoretically possible chords, based on *c* as the lower
of the two generators, are shown in Table 6.

Table 6. Chords.

The two generators are on the left in each case, and the resultant tones on the right. The notes in brackets are not exactly in
tune.

Other acoustically possible chords can be devised; whether they
are realizable in practice depends upon a number of imponderable
factors, chief among which is the range and quality of the voice
which is to provide the second generating tone. Moreover, with
musical instruments theory is by no means always a certain guide;
what is possible on paper is not always feasible in practice, and
conversely the apparently impossible is not infrequently achieved.
The trombonist who wishes to pursue the matter further would be
best advised to experiment for himself; even then his findings
might well not be confirmed by other players using different
instruments and with different qualities of vocal timbre.

Articulation

The trombone is often compared with the stringed instruments in
its ability to achieve accuracy of intonation, but there is a fundamental difference. Whereas the passage from one note to another
on a stringed instrument can be made by a change of finger
position without touching on the intervening notes, the process of
shortening or lengthening a tube cannot be made stepwise except
by means of a valve. If a slide is used instead the change is inevitably continuous. In this physical fact lies the difference between the technique of the trombone and that of all other wind
instruments. It is the price it has to pay for its infinite variability
of intonation, and one of the consequences is that tonguing on this
instrument assumes an all-important role, for in the great majority
of cases a change of position involves a new articulation. It might,
then, be imagined that a flowing legato style is foreign to the nature
of the trombone, but this is far from being the case. It is true that

78

a technically pure legato can be obtained only between different partials of the same fundamental — that is, without movement of the slide, and an extreme and unusual case of such a passage is to be seen in Ex. 20; another which ranges more widely than normal is given in Ex. 24.

(Ex. 24. Ravel: *Daphnis et Chloé.*)

There will be many cases, of course, in which two or more notes of a phrase can be played in the same position, and these can always be slurred together if required; but there will be many more cases in which a legato is marked when the notes of the phrase cannot be played without change of position. Even then, however, it may be possible to produce so close an approximation to a true slur as to be indistinguishable from the real thing. This is achieved when the second note is obtainable as a higher partial from a lower fundamental if the interval is upwards, or as a lower partial from a higher fundamental if downwards. In other words, if the slide moves in the opposite direction from the note progression, outwards for a rising phrase, or inwards for a falling one, the first note will 'break over' into the second as the slide moves, with no more separation between the notes than there is between two valved notes on other brass instruments. On the other hand, if the partial remains unchanged while the slide moves, a glissando is unavoidable unless the second note is tongued. In this type of slurring, known as legato tonguing, the co-ordination between slide and tongue must be extremely precise, with a very gentle stroke of the tongue so that its use can be hardly, if at all, detected. Thus true slurs are obtainable in the following circumstances:

(i) when they are different partials in the same position;

(ii) when the second note jumps up one or more partials as the slide moves out;

(iii) when it jumps down one or more partials as the slide moves in.

A fourth possibility, more difficult to bring off successfully, is to produce a slur when the slide movement and the interval are both in the same direction, up or down, provided there is a change of partial. In all other cases, the second and subsequent notes of a phrase must be lightly tongued. A two-octave B♭ scale will show the possibilities.

Position	1	6	4	3	1	4	2	1	3	4	3	1	2	2	1
Partial Number	II	III	III	III	III	IV	IV	IV	V	VI	VI	VI	VII	VIII	VIII
	★		★	★	★		★	★			★	★			★

An asterisk denotes that the note must be tongued.

It can be seen that of fourteen intervals in the scale only six can be slurred together without tonguing. In a legato phrase of any length, therefore, the player is faced with the necessity of making a considerable number of decisions whether to slur, when possible, or to tongue. In these situations it is probably easier, given a good slide technique and accurate tonguing, to articulate each note; with a competent player the result is indistinguishable from a true legato.

The following, in a slow tempo, gives scope for the imaginative use of alternative positions to promote a smooth legato, and it is informative to examine Ex. 5 from this point of view.

(Ex. 25. Stravinsky: *Octet for wind instruments*.)

In any type of legato playing it is of prime importance, of course, that the lips should continue to vibrate between one note and the next, or a gap appears and the legato effect is lost. This requirement presupposes a quick slide movement if a change of position is needed, and an exact synchronization of slide with tongue if a new articulation is made, in order to avoid an unwanted glissando.

Ex. 26 is a passage requiring fine legato playing from all three trombones, most, if not all of which, will have to be done by use of the tongue.

Staccato tonguing is a commonplace in trombone writing. It may be in single notes (Ex. 27), or in a scale passage (Exs. 3, 28), or in repeated notes (Exs. 29, 30).

80

(Ex. 26. Schumann: *Symphony No. 3*, 4th movement.)

(Ex. 27. Tchaikovsky: *Symphony No. 4*, 3rd movement.)

(Ex. 28. Stravinsky, *Octet for wind instruments*.)

(Exs. 29, 30. Rimsky-Korsakov: *Scheherazade*, Op. 35.)

The latter two cases involve tonguing at the rate of nearly 12 strokes per second and over eight per second respectively. These speeds are hardly possible using normal tonguing techniques, and recourse is had to double or triple tonguing, in which, instead of the usual T-T-T articulation, either T-K-T-K (for double tonguing) or T-T-K (usually, but not invariably, for triple tonguing), is employed. Most authorities[1] insist that a competent player should be able to single-tongue up to a rate of about 9 strokes per second, and that his multiple-tonguing techniques should extend well below this figure, so that there is a good margin of overlap.

A species of articulation less commonly employed is that first used by Richard Strauss as a special effect to represent the bleating of sheep in his tone-poem *Don Quixote* (1899). This is known as flutter-tonguing, and Strauss notated it as in Ex. 31, with a note explaining that parts written in this way were to be performed *mit Zungenschlag*.

(Ex. 31. Strauss: *Don Quixote*.)

It appears that his intention was that the tongue should be fluttered between the lips, intermittently interrupting the air stream and giving a distortion to the tone. This procedure is hardly practicable, for it would interfere with the vibration of the lips, and it is doubtful whether there are any players who actually adopt it. Even though condemned by Strauss as incorrect, the normal method is to roll an R against the front part of the roof of the mouth. To some players the technique comes easily; for others it is well-nigh impossible.

Later composers have also used this effect, and some examples are given below.

---

[1] e.g. P. Farkas, *The Art of Brass Playing*, p. 50; E. Kleinhammer, op. cit., p. 67.

(Ex. 32. Berg: *Wozzeck*, Act III.)

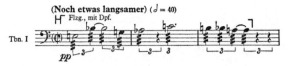

(Ex. 33. Webern: *Six Pieces*, Op. 6.)

(Ex. 34. Britten: *Sinfonia da Requiem*, Op. 20.)

In the Webern example the trombones are unaccompanied except for a held $G'\natural$ on the tuba, three detached chords on the harp, quaver strokes on the brass drum, and syncopated swishes with the *Rute*. The fourth trombone part is somewhat low for flutter-tonguing, though Strauss, in *Die Frau ohne Schatten*, writes a tremolo on $B'\flat$, and Berg, elsewhere in *Wozzeck*, one on A', though he qualifies his instruction by adding 'if possible'.

5

The Bass and Tenor-bass Trombones

Since the very early days of the trombone the bass of the group has been the *Quart-* or *Quint-Posaune*, pitched in F or E♭ a fourth or fifth below the tenor. This instrument was described by Praetorius (*Syntagma Musicum*, 1619), Mersenne (*Harmonie Universelle*, 1636) and Speer (*Grundrichtiger Unterricht der Musikalischen Kunst*, 1687), and Mersenne also mentions that in France a crook was sometimes used which could be inserted into the tenor instrument to convert it into a bass. These instruments, undergoing only the minor changes — different types of stays, a wider expansion in the bell, and so on — common to all trombones towards the end of the eighteenth century, remained the standard bass trombones (together with a slightly smaller instrument in G which became particularly popular in this country) until comparatively recently. Their ranges (excluding the pedal notes) were as follows:

Trombone in F, from   to .

Trombone in E♭, from   to

Trombone in G, from   to

In order to obtain seven positions on these instruments, a slide extension of some 30 inches or more was needed owing to their greater length of tubing. This is more than can be comfortably accommodated by the human arm, and the instruments were therefore provided with a swivel handle attached to the slide stay

84

to give the extra reach. In seventh position the F trombone could obtain the low B' and thus bridge the gap between seventh position E of the tenor trombone and its first pedal note $B'\flat$. The trombone in G lacked the C' and B' which are sometimes called for in works from Mozart's time onwards, but this minor defect was tolerated on account of its magnificent tone quality — 'the finest of all bass trombones'.[1]

With the invention of the valve in the early nineteenth century and the gradual replacement of natural horns and trumpets by fully chromatic instruments their parts in orchestral music became increasingly complex, and trombone parts followed suit. Though the bass trombone had always been able to cope with chromatic parts the greater agility now required created certain problems for this long and somewhat unwieldy instrument. These often involved large and rapid movements of the slide and tended to emphasize the comparative slowness with which these long instruments speak. Some means of easing these difficulties was sought, and in 1839 the Leipzig maker C. F. Sattler, after much experimentation, suggested the addition to the B♭ trombone of a length of supplementary tubing serving to convert it into a trombone in F. This in itself was not a new idea — see the reference to Mersenne above — and the novelty lay in the method employed to bring this extra tubing into play. Sattler placed it in the U-bend of the bell section, and provided a valve, operated by the left thumb, by means of which it could be instantaneously included in the airway. This instrument was first described in an article by G. W. Fink in *Allgemeine musikalische Zeitung*, 41 (1839), which records that the well-known trombone virtuoso Karl Queisser had tested and approved it. Its chief advantage was that the bass trombone slide technique now became no more difficult than that of the tenor, for the slide was still of B♭ dimensions and the handle could be dispensed with. The distances between the extreme positions were no greater than on the tenor trombone, and the flexibility of the instrument and its ability to cope with rapidly moving parts were correspondingly increased.

Sometimes the supplementary tubing was controlled, not by a valve, but by a quick-change pre-set switch (*Stellventil*) similar to that often fitted to the trumpet to switch it from B♮ to A or from C to B♭; or a removable attachment was supplied with a normal B♭ instrument, to be fitted, when required, in place of the tuning slide. Such instruments are still made, but with a valve incorporated in the attachment which is operated by an arrangement —

---

[1] A. C. Baines: Trombone, *Grove*.

usually a cord and leather thong for the left thumb (Plate X, and Fig. 8) — which is part of the attachment. Such an instrument is basically a medium-bore tenor trombone, convertible to F if desired, but weighing less than the duplex instrument with permanent attachment except when used as a trombone in F.

A wide-bore duplex instrument of this type, with a built-in F attachment, gradually ousted the older F and E♭ bass instruments in Germany during the latter half of the last century, and its use is becoming increasingly widespread elsewhere. The attachment has its own tuning slide, enabling it to be tuned independently, and the valve can be used while the instrument is being played in exactly the same way as on any other valved instrument. In effect it serves the identical function of the valve on a double horn, providing a means of instantaneously changing crooks.

The transference of the extra tubing of the bass trombone from the slide to the loop in the bell section, however, brings its own problems. When the valve is in use it adds an extra three feet of tubing to the B♭ instrument, and the distances between adjacent slide positions are therefore greater than on that instrument. The slide is accordingly long enough to accommodate only six positions when the valve is open, and the player must adjust his slide positions according to the actual length of tubing in use at the moment. Though the six positions with the F valve are nominally as shown in Table 7 they are sometimes known by their nearest equivalents on the standard B♭ tube — first, flat (or long) second, flat third, sharp fifth, flat sixth and flat seventh.

Table 7 also shows that first and second positions on the F side duplicate sixth and seventh on the B♭ side. These extended positions are used mainly in the lower register of the B♭ trombone, and are the only means of obtaining the notes c, B, F and E. The F attachment largely eliminates the need to use these positions, since they can usually be replaced by first and second positions with the valve, leading to a much increased flexibility and doing away with most of the big slide shifts which are unavoidable on the single tenor. Thus the following passage, almost unplayable on the latter instrument, becomes quite simple when the F attachment is used.

(Ex. 35. Janáček: *Sinfonietta*.)

86

Table 7. Table of positions for tenor-bass trombones.

    (i) Tenor-bass trombone in B♭/F.
    (ii) Bass trombone in B♭/F /E or in B♭/F/E♭.
    (iii) Bass trombone in G or in G/D/C.
    (iv) Bass trombone in F.
    (v) Bass trombone in E♭.
    (a) Not available on instruments (i) or (ii).
    (b) Not available on instrument (ii).

Further examples of this increased flexibility will be given later.

The second problem concerns the lack of a seventh position on the F side, which means that the low B' which was obtainable on the single F bass is no longer available. Moreover, low C is almost certain to be too sharp, for the following reason. The B♭ tube is acoustically about 115 inches long; the F attachment adds some 39 inches and full extension of the slide a further 48 inches, giving a total length of 202 inches, whereas low C requires a length of about $205\frac{1}{2}$ inches. It is usually possible to pull out the tuning slide of the attachment to provide the extra length, but first position F will now be very flat, for the tube is $157\frac{1}{2}$ inches long instead of the 154 inches needed. With spring barrels it may be possible to take up a little, but not all, of the excess length, and the advantage of using first position on the F side instead of sixth on the B♭ is therefore lost.

Sometimes the tuning slide of the attachment is designed to be capable of being pulled out to give E in the first position. This may just make it possible to obtain B' at full slide extension, and a well-tuned C is then available in fifth position. In practice this is less convenient than would appear at first sight, since there is rarely, if ever, time to adjust the tuning slide when these notes are required, and if the adjustment is made first position F and its attendant series are out of the question as they will be intolerably flat. Since the only point of pulling the slide to E is to provide the B' and C, it would be better, if possible, to pull it still further to a flat E position, and thus allow the B' to be played in a comfortable sixth position (very close to seventh position on the B♭ side), with fifth position C slightly shorter than normal sixth. This would avoid the strain imposed upon the inner slides at full extension, when they bear the whole weight of the outer slides on their extreme ends. A new set of positions will, however, still be required for other notes when the valve is used with the tuning slide extended in this way.

Though expedients like these can be employed to give the C and B' in tune, the problems they involve make them not altogether satisfactory solutions. The player is faced with the unpleasant necessity of playing the whole passage containing these recalcitrant notes in an unfamiliar set of positions, or of attempting to adjust his F slide to the correct length behind his head as he plays. A switch-valve could be used, or a pre-set adjustable slide gauge provided (see Plate XI), but a better solution is to provide another valve automatically putting the instrument into E or E♭ by the addition of a second length of supplementary tubing (Plate XII).

With this valve the player has the two notes available in nominal fifth and sixth positions, if the valve is tuned for a flat E, or in fourth and fifth, if in E♭. He does not need to become accustomed to a third set of positions as with the adjusted F slide since he can use the valve, if he wishes, solely for these two notes; nor need he attempt the impossible feat of tuning the slide while playing; there is no loss of first position *c* and *F*, and no undue strain on the slide as he can tune his second valve slide to give the *B'* in a comfortable position. The single valid objection that the two-valve bass trombone might encounter is that the second valve and its associated tubing increase, by perhaps the better part of a pound, the weight of an already weighty instrument. To meet this objection there has been devised an accessory detachable E attachment which can be quickly fitted to a normal B♭ / F tenor-bass. This can be tuned independently of the permanent F attachment, and would be used only for passages which include low *B'* or *C*. In using this attachment a slight disturbance of the normal balance of the instrument must be tolerated.

This inevitably somewhat involved explanation may perhaps be made clearer by reference to Fig. 15.

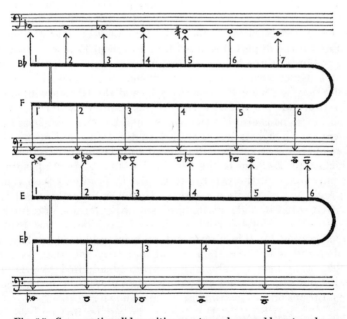

Fig. 15. Comparative slide positions on tenor-bass and bass trombones.

In brief, the tenor-bass and bass trombones exist in the following variations:

(i) The medium-bore single valve trombone in B♭ and F.

(ii) The same instrument with a valve slide capable of being pulled out to E; some models have an adjustable stop-gauge on the slide, and sometimes the slide is long enough to be pulled out to a flat E, or even to E♭, in which case the *Quartventil* becomes a *Quintventil*. Alternatively the F valve can be converted to one in E♭ by a quick-switch valve. These instruments are also built in wide-bore.

(iii) The wide-bore two-valve instrument in B♭, the first valve taking it into F, and in conjunction with the second into E or into E♭. The levers operating the valves are often coupled so that when the second is depressed it automatically takes the first with it. American makers usually describe these instruments as being in B♭/F with slide or valve to E or flat E; German-made trombones of this type are in B♭/F with slide or valve to E♭.

The medium-bore tenor-bass is normally used as a tenor trombone with an extended downward range and the advantage of taking sixth and seventh positions on the B♭ side as first and second on the F. If built in wide-bore it takes the place of the bass in F, but again with an increased range and flexibility. In Germany and Austria second and third players have for many years used the duplex instrument, and even in France, which for long preferred three tenors, a medium-bore B♭/F or B♭/E instrument is being used as a bass trombone. In America the second player may use a medium-bore B♭/F, and the third a wide-bore, with a second E or flat E valve. In this country the tenor-bass is widely used, as is also the two-valve bass, but the older bass in G lingers on, though it has moved with the times and acquired a valve-operated attachment putting it into D. Since it retains its swivel handle its range is thus extended down to *A′* (sixth position). partially filling in the gap between seventh position C♯ on the G side and the first position pedal *G′*. Moreover the attachment can be fitted with a C slide, giving a downward extension of a further tone to *G′* as second partial in the sixth position. A few British players swear by this instrument and are reluctant to bow to fashion and adopt the B♭/F trombone; they say that its tone quality as a bass trombone is constantly admired by visiting conductors who have not previously encountered the instrument. The positions on this instrument are also shown in Table 7.

The uses to which the F valve can be put by first and second players are best seen from an examination of the chromatic scale from *f* downwards. The positions from *f* to *d♭* are nominally the same, whether the valve is used or not, but it must be remembered that fifth position on the F trombone, for example, is a flat sixth position from the point of view of the B♭ trombone. *c* and *B* are often, but not invariably, taken in first and second positions on the F side, and the next four notes, from *B♭* to *G*, in first to fourth positions without the valve, though here again there may be occasions when it is more convenient to use the valve (third to sixth positions). Below this the F side would almost invariably be employed. A few examples will make this clear.

(Ex. 36. Shostakovich: *Symphony No. 9.*)

(Ex. 37. Shostakovich: *Symphony No. 9.*)

(Ex. 38. Berlioz: Overture, *King Lear.*)

91

The first and second trombone parts of some modern composers — for example Strauss and Schoenberg — make the tacit assumption that players will be using tenor-bass instruments, taking them down to E♭, D or C without compunction. A short extract from Schoenberg (Ex. 39) and one from Berg (Ex. 40) give some indication of the technical facility which they expect from their players — a facility only to be achieved by the use of this instrument, which also provides the extended downward range required.

(Ex. 39: Schoenberg: *Variations for Orchestra*, Op. 31.)

(Ex. 40. Berg: *Kammerkonzert.*)

For bass trombone parts an F valve is, of course, essential, and a second E or E♭ valve solves many problems in the lower register, including the provision of a good B♮.

Besides easing such technical difficulties the valve also makes available a second set of glissandi, though these will cover a range of a fourth only, owing to the absence of a seventh position. Whole-tone lip trills are possible with the valve from $b'♭$ upwards, though they may prove more recalcitrant to produce from the greater length of tubing. Yet another possibility is the valve-trill, but this, however, is more restricted in its application than might at first sight be supposed. The valve is operated by the left thumb, but since the left hand is helping to support the instrument the thumb has insufficient freedom to execute a rapid series of movements unless support is available elsewhere. This fact effectively restricts valve-trills to those obtainable in the first position, and possibly in third, when the right hand can support the bell. The following semitone trills are thus made available:

·o = valve open, c = valve closed

But such gains are really minor bonuses arising fortuitously from the presence of the valve, whose real *raisons d'etre* are the increased range it provides and the improved technical facility it makes possible.

6

The Contrabass Trombone

An *Octav Posaun* or trombone doppio in B♭ (an octave below the tenor) was known to Praetorius (1619) in at least two versions; one was a magnified form of the tenor (see Plate IV), while the other incorporated some of the extra length as a crook forming part of the bell bow. Its enormous length, approaching 20 feet, made the necessary slide extensions very large, and it must have been extremely clumsy in action. One solution to the problem was to provide a double slide, with four limbs, in order to halve the shifts between positions, and Galpin[1] mentions that the famous maker Jorg Neuschel of Nuremberg received an enquiry about an instrument with such a slide as early as the 1540s. Even if this improvement was in fact used, the contrabass did not survive the Baroque period, and was revived only in the early nineteenth century, owing its resuscitation to 'the general tendency towards the ponderous and the superhuman'[2] at this time. The idea of the double slide was revived by Gottfried Weber in 1816, and adopted by the maker C. A. Moritz of Berlin when he constructed a B♭ contrabass to Wagner's instructions for the first performances of *The Ring*. Other composers followed Wagner's example in writing for a contrabass, often as the natural bass of the trombone group in place of the tuba, whose wide conical bore gives it a smooth bland tone which destroys the homogeneity of the group. Verdi, in his later operas, Puccini, Strauss, d'Indy, Schoenberg, Berg and Webern have all written for a quartet of trombones in which the lowest of the group is often required to descend beyond the range of the bass and tenor-bass instruments. These parts were normally played upon the double-slided B♭ trombone, or sometimes in this

[1] F. W. Galpin: Op. cit.
[2] K. Geiringer: *Musical Instruments*, p. 232.

94

country upon the Boosey contrabass in C, examples of which are still in occasional use.[1] (See Plate XIV.)

The increasing agility of these parts, however, made a less cumbersome instrument imperative, and in 1921 Ernst Dehmel of Berlin suggested the application of Sattler's *Quartventil* principle to the bass trombone in F, to provide a bass-contrabass instrument with its extra length transferred from the slide to an attachment in the bell section, thus doing away with the double slide. His instrument, as constructed by A. Sprinz of Berlin, includes two independent thumb-operated valves, capable of being used separately or together. The arrangement thus differs somewhat from that of the tenor-bass in that each valve adds a length of supplementary tubing to the main tube; the E or E♭ valve in a tenor-bass merely prolongs the tubing which is brought into play by the first valve and cannot be used separately. In Dehmel's instrument the first, a whole tone valve, puts it into E♭, and the second into B♭; together they give a nominal A♭ — nominal for reasons to be explained later. A somewhat similar instrument, used by the Dresden *Staatskapelle*, is also pitched in F, with a switch valve to E♭ (in later models replaced by a second thumb valve) and a thumb valve to C. Together these give a nominal B♭, and in addition the C attachment can be fitted with a whole-tone slide which, with both valves open, puts the instrument into A♭. A still later model enables all three additional lengths of tubing to be controlled by a complicated thumb mechanism.

On both these instruments there are six positions, down to *C*, when the valves are closed. With the E♭ valve open, six positions take the pitch down to *B′♭*. In Dehmel's design the B♭ valve allows of five positions, down to *G′♭*, and with both valves open, four, giving *F′* as the lowest note. In the Dresden instrument fifth position with the C valve open gives *A′♭* (*G′* is just possible at the fullest extension of the hand slide if the tuning slide of the C attachment is pulled out as far as possible); with both valves *G′♭* is the lowest note, and if an A♭ slide or valve is provided there are four positions, once again giving *F′* as the lowest pitch.

The imperfections of these instruments, improvements though they are on the double-slided contrabass, are bound up with the peculiar mathematics of valve combinations, whereby a drop of a whole tone (for example, from F to E♭) added to one of seven semitones (F to B♭) does not give a total of nine semitones (F to

[1] A. C. Baines (Trombone, *Grove*), states that nine positions are available on this instrument, giving the low *E′* required in *The Ring*, but on the instrument illustrated there are only six, with *G′* as the lowest note.

A♭), but rather less. The problem is similar to that encountered in the valve systems of the trumpet and horn, but here it is aggravated by the greater length of tubing involved. To put an F trombone into E♭ about 19 inches of tube must be added; to put the same F instrument into B♭ about 77 inches. Together this gives a total of approximately 96 inches, which is insufficient to give a drop to A♭, requiring about 105 inches. Alterations to the slides of both attachments, which can be tuned, are possible to provide some or all of the deficient length, but first position notes when either valve is used separately will then be flat, though compensation can be made in the other positions by using shorter slide shifts.

A still more recent development, the *Cimbasso* model devised by H. Kunitz, solves the mathematical problem rather more neatly. This instrument was described in *Das Musikinstrument* (*XII Jahrgang, Ausgabe 7*, 1963) and first made by the *VEB Blechblas- und Signal-Instrumenten Fabrik*, Markneukirchen. It is now manufactured by Alexander, and has been used for some time, especially in the operas of Verdi and Puccini, by the orchestra of the *Komische Oper* in Berlin and the Royal Liverpool Philharmonic Orchestra in England (Plate XIII). It utilizes a bass trombone in F, to which are added two valves which again can be used independently or together. The first, operated by the middle finger of the left hand, puts the instrument into D; the second, an ordinary thumb valve, into C. Together the valves give the equivalent of a contrabass in B♭. The difference between this instrument and those previously described lies in the fact that the addition of tube lengths corresponding to a drop of three semitones (to D), and of five (to C) is very nearly equal to that required for a drop of seven (to B♭). If each attachment is of the correct theoretical length their combined addition will in fact give a slightly flat B♭; if each is made a little shorter the B♭ can be obtained in tune and small adjustments made in the slide positions to compensate for the sharpness that will ensue when the valves are used separately. The slide gives seven positions down to *B* on the F trombone, six with the first valve down to *A'*, and six with the second taking the pitch down to *G'*. With both valves open five positions, with a lower limit of *F'♯*, are possible. In addition, at least six pedal notes on the F side are available; the last three of these are duplicated in the first three positions with the D valve, and the lowest, *C'*, can be taken in first position with the second valve. Its compass is therefore a completely chromatic one from *C'* upwards as far as the player's embouchure will allow, though its chief use is obviously in the lower part of its range. Moreover, all the notes in this extensive compass except $F'\sharp$ and G' can be taken in third or shorter positions, and all above $E\flat$ in first or second, though for most notes there are several alternative positions owing to the fact that the instrument is really four trombones in one. The slide positions for all these instruments are shown in Table 8.

These recent forms of the contrabass trombone combine the chief advantage of the valve-trombone — the flexibility in rapid passages so necessary, for example, in the parts written by Verdi and Puccini for that instrument — with one of the most important assets of the conventional trombone — that of being able to correct the intonation with the slide. The technical demands on the player are, of course, increased, for to his slide technique he must, in some degree, add that of the player of a valved instrument, and he must employ them simultaneously.

The older contrabass trombone in $B\flat$ has never been a popular or widely-used instrument, except perhaps in Germany. During his travels in 1843 Berlioz examined one of these trombones in Berlin, and remarked that 'we have none in Paris, the performers there declining the practice of an instrument which tires their chests. Apparently the Prussian lungs are more robust than ours.'[1] On the other hand one of the comparatively few contrabass players in this country, Godfrey Kneller, asserts that he plays on his Boosey contrabass in C (the instrument mentioned on p. 95 and shown with its owner in Plate XIV) with the same ease and flexibility as on the tenor, and that the physical demands it is said to make on the player are greatly exaggerated.[2] It was certainly an instrument for the specialist, but it was not called for often enough to make specialization worth while except, perhaps, in the orchestras of opera houses. The newer instruments, which are the rather more complex bass-contrabass counterparts of the tenor-bass trombone, must reduce the physical strain on the player so far as the use of the slide is concerned, and also to some extent in requiring less sustained lung-power, owing to the frequent possibility of using the shorter F or $E\flat$ tubes in place of the much longer $B\flat$ one. On the original contrabass notes in the middle and upper part of the range were of necessity played on a tube length varying from about 231 inches (first position) to about 308 inches (seventh position). On the modern instrument a much shorter tube length can be employed, and the physical effort required to set and maintain the

[1] H. Berlioz, *Memoirs*, p. 308.

[2] In the early years of this century the Salvation Army made and used some contrabass trombones. Mr. Kneller possesses one of these sharp-pitch instruments and speaks highly of its design.

Table 8. Table of slide positions for contrabass trombones.
  (i) Contrabass in B♭, double slide.
  (ii) Contrabass in C, double slide.
      On some of the above instruments the slides are long enough to
      provide nine positions.
  (iii) Contrabass in F/E♭/B♭/A♭, Dehmel system.
  (iv) Contrabass in F/E♭/C/B♭/A♭, 'Dresden' model.
  (v) Contrabass in F/D/C/B♭, Cimbasso model, Kunitz system.
  (a) Not available on instruments (iii) or (iv).
  (b) Not available on instruments (iv) or (v).
  (c) Not available on instruments (iii), (iv) or (v).

98

air column in vibration is less. Moreover, most of the notes in this part of the range can be taken in the first three or four positions with a single slide whose operation is no more tiring than on a tenor-bass instrument. The result is seen in much greater flexibility in rapid passage work. Examination of the fourth trombone part in the excerpt from *Wozzeck* (Ex. 44) will show that the player of a duplex instrument need rarely venture beyond the third position, whereas with the B♭ contrabass he would spend much of his time in fifth and sixth positions with occasional forays up to first.

A further advantage lies in the increased range available. Even if the B♭ contrabass player successfully sounded the twelfth partial, this would take him no higher than *f′*, while the same partial on the F side of a duplex trombone is *c″*. At the other end of the compass the pedal notes are hardly possible on the old contrabass, but the first few, at least, can be obtained on the C or D trombone, or with a combination of valves. Since pedal notes on the F side of the tenor-bass are now a recognized part of modern technique, a good player on this instrument can produce a chromatic scale from B′♭ down to G″♭ on the B♭ trombone, continue with the pedals of the F side to fifth position D′♭, thence, if he has a second valve, to B″ or even to B″♭, which is theoretically not there at all. Moreover all except possibly the last are good notes. It might therefore be felt that the wide-bore B♭/F with a second valve is sufficiently versatile to make a contrabass unnecessary, since apart from a few notes right at the bottom it covers very nearly the same range; and parts written for the contrabass are often played on this instrument. The lowest octave of its range, however, consists entirely of pedal notes, which usually need time for preparation of the embouchure, whereas the modern contrabass can take notes down to G′ or G′♭ as second partials, making it easier to cope with moving parts at these depths.

In the same way as the tenor-bass goes a long way towards eliminating the need to use the lower positions for such notes as *F* and *E*, so the contrabass provides the facility for obtaining the quite commonly occurring notes *C* and *B* in the shorter positions. On the F side of the tenor-bass the first of these can only be had in sixth position, while the *B′* is absent altogether unless an E or E♭ slide or valve is fitted.

A further advantage conferred by the valved contrabass is the ability to perform certain grace notes otherwise awkward or impossible. The acciaccatura from *A′♯* to *B′*, for example, which occurs in Strauss's *Elektra*, can be played quite easily if a C or D valve is available, since the notes are playable in adjacent positions; on the old contrabass it would involve a shift from first position to seventh unless the instrument possessed a slide length giving it eight or nine positions.

With a whole-tone E♭ valve a number of trills become possible, though as with the tenor-bass they are restricted to those in the first and third positions. The valves also make available some extra glissandi, though of course these cover a smaller range — a fourth or less owing to the smaller number of positions in the lower pitches.

Rapid chromatic parts, too, are more easily executed with the aid of the valves, as in the following extract:

(Ex. 41. Strauss: *Salome.*)

This could be played in the following positions, as one of a number of possibilities:
(C valve) 6 5 4 3 — (E♭ valve) 5 4 2 1 — 5 4 3 — (C valve) 6 5 3 2 — 4 3 2 — 5 4 2 1, without involving a large number of big shifts.

Considering the advantages offered by these duplex bass trombones it may seem surprising that they have not made more ground. The long-standing and partly unfounded prejudice against the old contrabass here loses what validity it ever had. It is not claimed that in the lowest register of the newer instruments any less effort is required; if very low notes are needed, the price must be paid in extra tube length, whether this is provided from the slide or by a valve. It is clear, however, that the extent of slide movements must be greatly reduced, and also that anywhere but in the lowest register notes can be produced as lower partials of shorter tube lengths than on the B♭ contrabass, with correspondingly less physical effort. It may well be that the complexities of technique introduced by the provision of so many alternative positions to some degree defeats its own ends, and in any case many players tend to be suspicious of too much complicated mechanism.

Another objection — which could equally well be levelled at the tenor-bass instrument — is that the use of a valve has a deleterious effect on tone quality. However good its design, and that of its ancillary tubing, it is usually found that to begin with the valved notes tend to be 'stuffy' in quality, but the ever-increasing use of the tenor-bass shows that with practice the tone quality can be perfectly well matched to that of notes played without the valve. The problem is almost identical with that encountered by the players of other brass instruments 150 years ago when the valve was first introduced. There was then much prejudice against the new invention on the grounds of the inferior quality of the valved notes, but this eventually subsided as the design of the valve was improved and the players became accustomed to the need consciously to match valved and unvalved notes; and this can be done equally well on the trombone. It has been suggested that players are sometimes suspicious of over-complicated mechanisms; the trombone has existed for so long as a slide instrument pure and simple that they jealously and rightly guard the slide principle as fundamental to the trombone. Hence the almost complete rejection, at least for orchestral purposes, of the true valve-trombone (without slide); in spite of its great agility it is felt to have an inferior tone, and of course, acquires the intonational problems inherent in valve combinations while losing the ability to solve them with the slide. The instrument is, in fact, no longer really a trombone, though it may be built to look like one.

But the function of the valve on a tenor-bass or bass-contrabass is not quite the same. These instruments are still fundamentally slide instruments, with all their advantages (and disadvantages); the valve is no more than a quick method of changing from a trombone pitched in one key to another pitched in a different key. It corresponds in its function to the thumb-valve of a double horn which switches the instrument from F to B♭. Basically, of course, any valve must be regarded as fulfilling the same sort of function, but with a valved instrument like the trumpet the tube length is continually being changed by the valves; in the trombone the fundamental method of altering the length is the slide, and the valve is to be regarded merely as a temporary addition to the slide, giving the player a greater notional reach than his physical attributes will actually allow. In other words, it has the effect of increasing the length of his right arm. He still retains the essential ability of the trombonist to adjust his intonation with the slide; he need no longer be (if ever this were the case) of outstanding physical capacity, and he has a more flexible instrument into the bargain.

Despite these facts, the contrabass unfortunately still retains its undeserved reputation as an instrument only for the superman, too unmanageable to be of much use in the orchestra, and not worth the time and trouble required to master it. A vicious circle is thus created; if there are few proficient players, composers will not write for the instrument, and there is even less incentive for players to specialize on it. This is a great pity, for the contrabass is the natural bass to the trombone group in a way in which the tuba, normally used in this role, is not. The tuba is the only wide-bored member of the orchestral brass which has a conical profile, and its tone colour, as a result, is broader and more mellow than that of the trombone, and entirely lacking the sharper metallic character of that instrument. The use of the tuba often thickens the texture, especially when it plays in the low register, where the contrabass trombone would give the passage a much more sharply defined character, without any loss of solidity. Most composers acquiesce in the use of the tuba in a role for which it is not really suited, owing to the unlikelihood of a true trombone bass being available, but some, mainly German and Austrian, have refused to accept this situation and have written for a full trombone group of four, even though they may also have included the tuba to serve a somewhat different function. Wagner was probably the first to employ a full trombone choir in this way, with the lowest part allotted to a contrabass.

(Ex. 42. Wagner: *Die Walküre*.)

In his operas Strauss frequently wrote for a quartet of trombones, and from internal evidence it is fairly clear that he often expected the fourth member of the quartet to use a contrabass instrument. In the following extract, for example, the fourth trombone part could possibly be played on a tenor-bass, but it would involve some quick adjustments of embouchure to enable the $G'\flat$ and $B'\flat\flat$ to be played as pedal notes on the $B\flat$ side, the former in fifth position. With a duplex bass trombone these notes are easily available as second partials.

102

(Ex. 43. Strauss: *Die Liebe der Danae.*)

Many other passages from Strauss's operas could be cited in which the use of the duplex bass would simplify matters for the fourth player. Though some of these operas were written before the instrument existed, the bottom parts often lie uncomfortably low for a tenor-bass, and presumably Strauss envisaged the use of the double-slided B♭ contrabass, which would probably have been available in the larger German opera houses at that time.

Other composers to use a similar trombone quartet include Schoenberg (*Gurrelieder*, 1913) and Berg (*Wozzeck*, 1925; Ex. 44).

Although Berg merely specifies one alto, two tenor and a bass in this work, the lowest part in many places explores the extreme depths and it is doubtful whether any player would feel very happy in it without some means of putting his bass into a lower pitch. It is significant that in more than one place Berg felt it necessary to add a note — 'where possible, 4th trombone; if not possible, bass tuba' — as if he expected that the contrabass so clearly indicated by the look of the part might not always be available.

In the fifth of his Six Pieces, Op. 6, Webern extravagantly employs a group of six trombones for the few bars quoted below — elsewhere in the work he uses only four. The lowest part is playable with a two-valve tenor-bass, though the last muted pedal *A'*, dying away to nothing, might be somewhat difficult to manage. It would be unrealistic, however, to expect to find that comparatively rare bird, the contrabass trombonist, engaged in order to help out with a single note.

One cannot help feeling that not enough use is made by composers of this magnificent instrument, with its dark colour and massive tone. Some of the reasons for its neglect have already been mentioned — exaggerated accounts in many of the standard works on orchestration of the demands it makes upon the player, which are certainly not true of the modern instrument; incomplete comprehension, perhaps, of its potentialities; unwillingness to write for an instrument which is unlikely to be available, and knowledge of the fact that even when a part is provided more often than not it

104

(Ex. 45. Webern Six Pieces, Op. 6.)

will be played by a tuba, or, transposed an octave up where
necessary, by a tenor-bass trombone. Like the soprano trombone,
but perhaps for less sufficient reason, the contrabass has never
managed to gain a firm foothold in the orchestra; it is to be hoped
that the development of the newer instruments described above
may eventually enable it to do so.

7

The Alto Trombone

The alto trombone, pitched in E♭ or F (and more rarely, in E, D or D♭) was one of the group of four mentioned in the sixteenth and seventeenth century treatizes of Virdung, Praetorius and Mersenne. At this time its function was either to act as the topmost voice of the quartet, or as the alto voice when the melody was played by the cornett. In either of these two roles it was used as one of a group supporting or blending with voices, though the group was sometimes given an independent part or was used, with other instruments, in a purely instrumental ensemble to play the Sinfonia to a motet (e.g. Giovanni Gabrieli's *In ecclesiis*), or sometimes a complete composition (e.g. his *Sonata pian e forte*). In addition the usual *Stadtpfeifer* ensemble which played daily from the tower of the *Rathaus* in German towns was a combination of one or two cornetti together with alto, tenor and bass trombones, and it was for just such a group that Pezel composed his *Hora decima* and the *Fünffstimmigte blasende Musik* in the late seventeenth century. A little later Bach was using the same group somewhat conservatively in his Church Cantatas, rarely allowing it to do more than double the voice parts, but at about the same time in Vienna Fux, Caldara and other court composers were treating the alto trombone much more adventurously as an obbligato instrument in their masses and motets. An extract from a work by Fux will show what technique he expected from his alto trombone player.

The outstanding feature of this passage lies not in its tessitura, which is placed firmly in the middle register of the instrument, but in the diatonic agility required from the only brass instrument which was at that time capable of it.

The normal range of the alto trombone reached at least as far as the tenth partial so that the following from Gluck's *Alceste* is not set unusually high.

(Ex. 46. Fux: Antiphon, *Alma redemptoris Mater*.)

(Ex. 47. Gluck: *Alceste*.)

At the end of the eighteenth century the alto trombone, to-gether with the tenor and bass, was still being used in the old style in Church music to support the voices, and also sometimes in the opera orchestra, especially in solemn or tragic scenes, but it was not until the early nineteenth century that trombones became a well-established part of the symphony orchestra. In this role the career of the alto trombone was short-lived, for shortly afterwards the valve was invented, and composers began to treat the valve-trumpet as the treble instrument of the brass group. At about the same time a change in the ideal of trombone tone colour occurred, from the former smooth mellow vocal sound to a brassier type with a sharper edge — the sound described by Berlioz as 'menacing and formidable' — and one which was perhaps better matched to that of the trumpet now so frequently associated with the trombone. In these circumstances Berlioz found the tone of the alto trombone so shrill that he considered its high notes to be of little use, and advocated the French custom of employing three tenors, with a bass trombone only if the music were in four parts and the tenors were capable of holding their own against it. For these and other reasons the alto trombone began to drop out of use, though it lingered on later in Germany than in France and Italy. The following examples, from the first half of the century, show the type of part, in range and style, typically given to the alto trombone during its brief stay in the symphony orchestra.

(Ex. 48. Liszt: *Hungarian Rhapsody No. 2 in* E♭.)

(Ex. 49. Mendelssohn: Overture, *Ruy Blas*.)

See also Ex. 26 (p. 81) from Schumann's Symphony No. 3.

A curiously late example of the use of the alto trombone — curiously because the French were among the first to dispense with the instrument — occurs in Ambroise Thomas's opera *Hamlet* (1868).

Thomas appears to have had a particular affection for this instrument, for he gave it another important solo in the Overture to *Le Comte de Carmagnola*.

The alto trombone then practically disappeared from the orchestral scene, though Bruckner specified the instrument in his symphonies for parts which are comfortably within the range of the tenor and are nowadays usually played on that instrument without, perhaps, quite fulfilling the composer's intentions with regard to

(Ex. 50. Thomas: *Hamlet*, Act 1.)

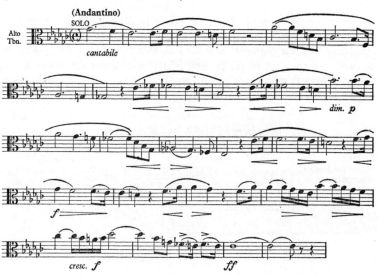

tone colour. The tenor trombone in its high register almost inevitably sounds somewhat forced, so that the tone carries a feeling of tension which may not be required. With the alto trombone in its upper (but not highest) register the sound emerges more freely and naturally with a clear, bright tone, even in pianissimo. Economic circumstances rarely make it possible for a player to specialize on the alto trombone for, as with the contrabass, his services are not often enough called for;[1] and even when they are, the tenor instrument can usually make shift to fill the gap more or less adequately.

In the early twentieth century, the era of mammoth orchestras, some German and Austrian composers felt the need for a high trombone voice and began once again to write for the alto trombone. At one point early in his Seventh Symphony Mahler tentatively suggests that the instrument might be used for a pianissimo which is not, in fact, particularly high for the tenor, but this is an indication that it was once again in use at this time (1905). Schoenberg, too, was writing for the alto in *Gurrelieder* (composed 1900–1 orchestrated 1910–11) and *Pelleas und Melisande* (1902–3). In the latter work he uses it somewhat unadventurously, as if

[1] In his *Conversations* Stravinsky laments the lack of good alto trombone players (e.g. for his *Threni* and for Berg's *Altenberg Lieder*).

uncertain of its capabilities; it is rarely taken above its middle register, and is almost always safely doubled by one or more horns, or trumpets, or one of the tenor-bass trombones specified in the score. Aside from considerations of tone colour (and the frequent doublings do not make it easy for this to tell) it is not clear why it is used, for its part could be played without great difficulty by a tenor. Two examples are given; the first is typical, and the other shows one of its rare excursions into the upper register.

(Exs. 51 & 52. Schoenberg: *Pelleas und Melisande*.)

Berg also uses the alto in *Wozzeck*, partly because he often takes the first trombone beyond what was at the time considered to be the upper limit of the tenor trombone's compass, and partly because of its unique tonal colour, not to be satisfactorily replaced by trumpet tone; and he writes for it with a better appreciation than Schoenberg of its potentialities. At one point he does not hesitate to write for violins and trombone in unison (Ex. 53),

(Ex. 53. Berg: *Wozzeck*, Act III.)

and though he does not use the highest register of all there are many exposed solo passages of which the following are typical.

(Exs. 54–56. Berg: *Wozzeck*, Act II; Berg: *Wozzeck*, Act II; Berg: *Wozzeck*, Act III.)

The last of these extracts poses a small problem, for the lowest note available on the E♭ alto in seventh position is *A*, and the *G* in this passage is quite unsupported.

Large leaps, needing secure embouchure control, are sometimes used, but these are usually doubled by another instrument.

(Ex. 57. Berg: *Wozzeck*, Act I.)

It will be observed that in most of these cases the trombone is muted. Berg has a predilection for this particular tone colour (see

111

also Ex. 44), which well suits the sombre and tragic picture he wishes to paint in this work, and only infrequently, and then with all the greater impact, does he use the unmuted instrument to provide a more massive weight of tone.

The most recent work to make extensive use of the alto is Britten's Parable *The Burning Fiery Furnace*, and here it might almost be said to dominate the score. The small chamber orchestra of flute, horn, alto trombone, viola, double bass, harp, chamber organ and a variety of percussion instruments closely resembles in its constitution the 'cornet, flute, harp, sackbut, psaltery and dulcimer' listed in the Book of Daniel, where the story of the Parable is to be found. Soon after the start of the work the trombone, with a peremptory summons, calls attention to the Herald's opening address, and again, later, adds its menacing commentary when he pronounces Nebuchadnezzar's order that all should worship the Golden Image (Ex. 58.)

(Ex. 58. Britten: *The Burning Fiery Furnace*.)

During the procession of the instrumentalists through the church the trombone has a long and important solo culminating, at the raising of the Image, in a hectic downward glissando through the partials in the first position, six times repeated.

112

(Ex. 59. Britten: *The Burning Fiery Furnace.*)

Further quotations showing how Britten exploits the technical possibilities of the instrument and the demands he makes upon the player in doing so are given below.

(Exs. 60, 61. Britten: *The Burning Fiery Furnace.*)

Ex. 61 shows an unusual use of pedal notes on the alto trombone. These are usually stated to be practically valueless, since they are too thin and weak in tone. This criticism, of course, was applied to the old narrow-bore instrument, but Britten, who particularly requested the use of such an instrument in this work so as to obtain the maximum contrast with horn tone, had no qualms about using the pedals and they prove effective enough in performance. The notes speak more readily on the modern wider-bored alto, though still without quite the weight of tone of the corresponding notes on the tenor.

Many of the parts from which quotations have been given could doubtless nowadays be performed by a first-class tenor player, though in general they would lie rather high. The effect, however, would not be the same, for at the same pitch the alto is using lower partials of a shorter tube, producing a lighter, brighter and less forced tone.

Table 9 shows the chromatic scale of the E♭ alto trombone. For the F alto instrument the scale must be transposed a whole tone upwards. Technical possibilities are, within its own range, the same as on the tenor. Glissandi covering the span of an augmented

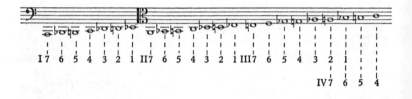

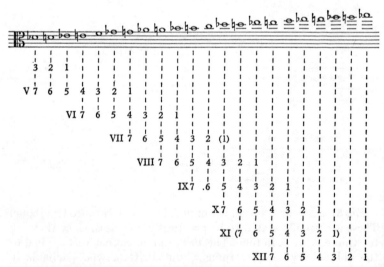

Table 9. Chromatic scale of alto trombone in E♭.
    Roman numerals indicate partial numbers; Arabic numerals positions.

114

fourth are possible for each partial from the second to the tenth or twelfth as shown below for the E♭ instrument:

Whole tone lip trills begin with the seventh partial in the seventh position as the lower note, giving the following:

8

The Soprano Trombone

The soprano trombone has always been the poor relation of the family. Almost from the beginning circumstances have so conspired against it as to allow it to maintain only a precarious existence at best. Composers have sporadically written parts for the instrument without always being certain that it would be available, but it has never really maintained, or even achieved, its apparently rightful position as the treble of the trombone group.

It would seem natural that, once the principle of the slide mechanism had been established, the instrument should be constructed in such sizes as to provide a complete choir of four voices; but if this was done it is curious that no soprano trombones apparently survive which were contemporaneous with the earliest alto, tenor and bass trombones to be found in various collections, which date from the mid-sixteenth century. Praetorius lists a *Diskant-Posaun* but makes it plain that he refers to the alto and that he regarded this as the topmost voice of the trombone choir. Mattheson (*Das neu-eröffnete Orchester*, 1713) specified a small and a large alto, and it is possible that the former may have been the instrument later known as the soprano. At any rate, there seems to have been some confusion of nomenclature, so that comments have been made in which Praetorius's criticisms of the instrument he knew as the *Alt* or *Diskant Posaun*, pitched an octave above the *Quart-* or *Quint-Posaun*, appear to have been transferred to the true *Diskant* of the group — the soprano trombone in B♭, an octave above the tenor. Terry,[1] for example, quotes Praetorius as remarking of the *Diskant* that 'though agreeable for playing a melody, it was too insignificant in tone for concerted music', and

[1] C. S. Terry, *Bach's Orchestra*, pp. 39–40.

then gives this as the reason for Bach's infrequent use of the soprano trombone. Kunitz[1] dates the soprano trombone from the beginning of the sixteenth century, and lays much of the blame for the disrepute into which it quickly fell at the door of Praetorius; he quotes the derogatory 'an Klang und Applikatur nicht genüge' and says that, coming from so authoritative and influential a source this criticism has been unthinkingly accepted ever since by writers, composers and players. Geiringer[2] suggests, by implication, that the soprano had been used in the late sixteenth century, but most other authorities put its appearance in the late seventeenth, the period from which the earliest extant specimens actually survive. In any case, before the end of the sixteenth century the cornett had become the leading treble wind instrument, and it retained this position for the next hundred years. Whether the soprano trombone was in competition with the cornett during this time or not, it is clear that it never became really popular, except possibly in a few isolated cases,[3] and after the invention of the valve it was almost completely forgotten without ever becoming quite extinct. It was still being made in small numbers here and abroad during the nineteenth century, and in the early years of the twentieth a modern wider-bored form was illustrated in the catalogues of some German makers, probably for use in the *Posaunenchöre*. Still more recently the soprano trombone has been used in German performances of Gluck's *Orpheus and Euridice*. In the one case a narrow-bore instrument, played by a trumpeter, was used, but it did not blend well with the remaining wider-bored trombones. In the other a modern instrument, matching the others in bore, was played by the first trombonist, and this proved more satisfactory.[4]

American manufacturers (e.g. Conn) also made a few soprano trombones, probably for use in jazz bands, but as always throughout its history, it never came into common use.

The soprano trombone is usually pitched in high B♭, an octave above the tenor. As with other trombones, the bore of the modern instrument is rather wider than that of the earlier, though the value of 12·6 mm. (0·496 ins.) given by Kunitz[5] for a typical

---

[1] H. Kunitz, op. cit., p. 794.

[2] K. Geiringer, op. cit., p. 186.

[3] An interesting reference to the extensive use of the soprano trombone by the Moravian wind ensembles of the mid-eighteenth century is to be found in the article by Harry H. Hall: *Early Sounds of Moravian Brass Music in America*, in *Brass Quarterly*, VII, 3, 1964.

[4] H. Kunitz, ibid., pp. 800–1.

[5] H. Kunitz, op. cit., p. 802.

example would seem to be on the high side, being about equal to that of a small-bored tenor. The bell diameter is about five inches, and the total tube length in the closed position is less than five feet. Usually this allows a slide length for only six positions, involving the lack of the note *b* between sixth position *c'* (third partial) and first position *b*♭ (second partial). Sometimes the slide itself is extensible by a further two inches or so, putting the instrument into A, but since the inner slides are of fixed length there are still only six positions and *b*♭ is now missing. The extension cannot be made while the instrument is actually being played, so that in effect this is a B♭ trombone with a moderately quick change to A. The mouthpiece normally used has a somewhat shallow cup without a sharp-edged throat. If the inside diameter is too small, the higher partials will be more easily sounded but the tone becomes too shrill and less typically trombone-like. The slide shifts are, of course, very short to a player accustomed to the tenor trombone, and for this reason, and the difference in bore and mouthpiece, the soprano is not an instrument to which he can change at a moment's notice.

The chromatic scale of the soprano trombone is shown in Table 10. The pedal notes, though possible on a modern wider-bore instrument, are not used; at the other end of the compass notes above the eighth partial can be obtained, especially if a narrower mouthpiece is used, but the few composers who have written for the soprano trombone appear not to have taken it beyond this limit. Bach used the soprano only on three occasions, and never took it above *a"*, but even if, as has been suggested, he used the cornett in its place merely because this was a *Stadtpfeifer* instrument and was therefore more readily available to him, the parts are still playable by a soprano trombone. Terry,[1] on the other hand, believes that the cornett replaced the discant trombone because of its more brilliant and effective tone. In either case the instrument was never used in any more ambitious way than to double the soprano voice part. Gluck treated the soprano trombone in very much the same manner in *Orpheus and Euridice*, as also Mozart in his C minor Mass, one of the last works in which it was used, so that it never managed to break free from the older and conservative style of writing and was almost entirely confined to church and opera-house. By the end of the eighteenth century it was practically obsolete, well before the trombone group entered the symphony orchestra. Only on rare occasions, such as the Gluck revival mentioned above, is it resuscitated; more often economic con-

[1] C. S. Terry, op. cit., p. 38.

siderations dictate the use of the trumpet as a not altogether
satisfactory substitute.

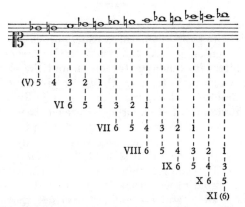

Table 10. Chromatic scale of soprano trombone in B♭.
Roman numerals indicate partial numbers; Arabic numerals positions.

9

The Valve Trombone

To the purist the expression 'valve trombone' is a contradiction in terms. The essential feature of the trombone is the slide, the means by which it alters its fundamental length and the element in its construction which more than anything else gives the instrument its unique character, and in particular its very individual mode of progression from one note to another. However, the application of the valve principle to the trombone soon after the invention of the valve in the early nineteenth century was probably not quite so misguided as might appear at first sight. The opening of a supplementary airway by the operation of a piston or a rotary valve is plainly a more rapid process than lengthening the tubing by the movement of a slide, and no doubt it was felt that this was a necessary step in enabling trombone players to match the greater facility in rapid execution afforded to trumpets and horns by the provision of valves — a facility which was soon to be exploited by composers. It quickly became clear, however, that the addition of valves to brass instruments was not an unmixed blessing, for it brought certain unforeseen problems in its train. The inclusion of tubing which necessarily contained bends of fairly small radius was found to have the acoustical effect of altering the tone quality of the valved notes, and in general not for the better — particularly in the early days when the valves and their associated tubing were still in an imperfect and somewhat crude state. This criticism, of course, was not confined to the trombone, but though in the case of the trumpet and horn the controversy has long since died down, the tone quality of the valve trombone is still held, even with later improvements in the design of the valves, to be inferior to — or at best, somewhat different from — that of the slide instrument. A second problem was connected with the mathematics of valve combinations which, as explained in Chapter VI, inevitably lead to defects in intonation. These defects, of course, were also to be found in horns and trumpets, where to some degree they could be corrected by a variety of expedients — adjustment of the embouchure, compromise on the length of the valve slides, and so on — but they were more pronounced on the longer instruments and presented the trombonist with a problem which he had not hitherto been required to face. It had been his twofold boast that he already possessed an inherently chromatic instrument whose intonation was completely under his control, provided he had acquired the necessary skills. Now he had to choose whether to switch to an instrument with an entirely different technique, whose imperfections were obvious, in the hope of gaining some advantage in flexibility; or to remain faithful to the instrument which had served his predecessors so well during the previous three centuries or more. Though some may have flirted with the valve trombone for a time as a novelty, by 1855 most German orchestral trombonists had gone back to the slide instrument.[1] In Italy the valve trombone gained a surer foothold, and was used especially in opera orchestras for the technically demanding parts which Verdi and other composers wrote for it.[2] To some extent it was also adopted in other southern European countries, but elsewhere it never really caught on, at least for orchestral work. It was, however, more widely used in military bands; in 1867 Czerveny of Königgrätz, for example, was manufacturing *Armee-Posaunen* in four sizes — alto in E♭ or F, tenor in C or B♭, bass in F or E♭, and contrabass in B♭. The valve trombone has obvious advantages when used in marching bands, though in England these have rarely been considered sufficient to offset its disadvantages. Until recently the repertoire of wind bands, both brass and military or concert, has consisted largely of transcriptions of orchestral music, and this may have led in some places to the employment of valve trombones to play parts originally written for bass stringed instruments. In a slightly different field, the valved instrument is sometimes used by the jazz trombonist, presumably on account of its agility, though his often prodigious slide technique would, it might be thought, prove capable of satisfying all the demands he might wish to make upon it. Moreover, by using the valve trombone he loses the ability to make a glissando.[3]

[1] H. W. von Gontershausen: *Neu eröffnetes Magazin musikalischer Tonwerkzeuge*, Frankfurt, 1855.

[2] See D. F. Tovey: *Essays in Musical Analysis*, Vol. 5, O.U.P., 1937, p. 197, for an interesting discussion of Verdi's use of the valve trombone.

[3] But see P. Bate: *The Trumpet and Trombone*, p. 248, for a note on the 'half-valve' technique.

There is still a steady demand for the valve trombone, as is evidenced by the fact that most manufacturers list at least one model in their catalogues, usually in narrow or medium bore, and often with an optional interchangeable slide section. Some of the advantages claimed for it are enumerated here. (i) It has a greater facility in the execution of rapid passages, though this superiority has become steadily less marked over a period of time during which slide technique has gradually improved and the tenor-bass instrument has come into more common use. (ii) It is easier to handle in marching and cavalry bands, and has the virtue of requiring less space in crowded orchestra pits. (iii) It is a useful adjunct for the versatile brass player accustomed to valves who wishes to double on another instrument without having to learn an entirely new technique. (iv) It provides a natural training for a learner who may wish later to change to trumpet, baritone or tuba, or conversely, for one who may wish to switch from one of these instruments. It is, too, a suitable instrument for the young trombonist whose arm is not yet long enough for him to reach the lower positions on the slide trombone. Finally, it is a more robust instrument than the latter, whose fragile slide can so easily be damaged.

The valve trombone is usually made with three parallel arms so as to resemble the slide trombone in appearance. There is no real reason why this should be done, except that sub-consciously one expects any sort of trombone to be of the familiar conformation dictated, in fact, by the need for a slide. The bass trumpet in C or B♭, often played by trombonists, is for all practical purposes a valve trombone, though built in trumpet shape, and a variety of other forms has from time to time been employed, ranging from a tuba-like shape to the circular helicon style, but these are rarely to be found nowadays.

The length of tubing in the valve trombone is equal to that of the equivalent slide instrument with the slide closed, and the valve system is conveniently situated for operation by the right hand. The valves, piston or rotary, are almost always of the descending type, lowering the pitch by a whole tone, a semitone, and a minor third respectively. Separately or in combination they give six different fundamentals corresponding to those of positions 2–7 on the slide trombone. Two main forms are made; the so-called short model, whose front bow projects only a few inches in front of the bell mouth, and the long, which is about the same overall length as the slide instrument. By far the commonest pitch is the tenor B♭, but quite recently German manufacturers have listed the following rotary valve trombones in their catalogues: soprano in C, alto in

E♭ or F, tenor in C (as well as one in B♭), a 3- or 4-valve bass in F, a 4-valve bass in C, and even a 6-valve contrabass in F, with three valves operated by each hand.

Another 6-valve instrument, of a rather different type, was designed in about 1910 by the Brussels firm of Lebrun in an attempt to deal with the faulty intonation of the ordinary valve trombone, and a seven-piston version of this instrument was introduced into the Queen's Hall orchestra by Sir Henry Wood without any lasting success, though Bate[1] states that a similar instrument is still in use at the Brussels Opera. It employs Sax's principle of the independent ascending valve; with all the pistons up the instrument is equivalent to a slide trombone in its seventh position. Depression of the sixth valve cuts out enough tubing to give sixth position, of the fifth valve fifth position, and so on. The valves are never used in combination, so that each can be correctly tuned for its own particular position. The extra valve on the seven-valve version is a descending one, putting the whole instrument into F as on the ordinary tenor-bass, but the valve loops are now no longer of the correct length, being tuned for a B♭ trombone, and the results of using any other valve in combination with it would seem to be highly dubious, having the same effect as using the B♭ slide positions on the tenor-bass trombone with the thumb valve depressed.

[1] Op. cit., p. 221.

10

The Trombone in the Orchestra

The history of the trombone in the orchestra is a strange and somewhat chequered one. For an instrument which sprang, fully armed, as it were, from the head of Euterpe it is surprising what difficulty it experienced in gaining and establishing a firm foothold in the orchestra once that had become a fully organized body. The earliest surviving parts which were specifically written for trombones date from the end of the sixteenth century, and they were then, and for long afterwards, used mainly for the accompaniment of vocal Church music and, more rarely, in opera. Their chief function in either sphere was to form a group, often with cornetti, which doubled the choral parts, a function to which the vocal style of playing then employed well suited them. During the seventeenth century trombone writing changed but little, and it is curious that on the whole composers made little use of an instrument with greater potential than several in more common use. Even though slide technique had not as yet been fully perfected — Speer[1] in 1687 regarded the trombone as a diatonic instrument though he recognized that it was capable of producing semitones in positions lying between the four he described — by virtue of the slide principle the trombone was in a much better position than the trumpet to deal, in its own range, with melodic material. Nevertheless, during the latter part of the seventeenth century and for most of the eighteenth the trombone eked out a somewhat precarious existence as an orchestral instrument. It was still used in Church music, and for a time, in Vienna in the early eighteenth century, even reached the status of solo obbligato instrument in the religious music of the Court composers (see Ex. 46), but this was no more than an isolated and local phenomenon. The increasing popularity of the horn, another instrument which, in its early days

[1] D. Speer: *Grund-richter Unterricht der Musikalischen Kunst.*

124

at least, could not compare with the trombone as a diatonic and melodic instrument, may also have contributed to its decline. The players were still there; the *Stadtmusiker* in Germany continued to provide a source from which they could be drawn, but their services were called upon mainly for the more popular kinds of music-making, or for ceremonial and civic occasions. Always rated lower in public and princely esteem than the exclusive trumpet, the trombone seems at this time to have acquired a plebeian and almost old-fashioned image, so that it passed through a period of comparative stagnation during which its technique progressed slowly, if at all.

The revival of the trombone as an orchestral instrument began in the last quarter of the eighteenth century. Gluck was one of the first to recognize its expressive possibilities and to use it in a more adventurous way when the dramatic situation demanded. He wrote for a group of three, or in *Orpheus*, four, including a soprano, and at times used them in unison, a method of employment which had rarely been attempted up to this time. His example was followed, a little later, by Mozart, who confined the trombones to his operas and masses, and even then reserved them for solemn or tragic moments. One number in *Idomeneo* is accompanied only by horns and trombones, but the classic example of the dramatic use of trombones comes from the final scene of *Don Giovanni*.

Mozart commonly used the trombones harmonically as a group; a well-known exception occurs in the *Tuba mirum* of his Requiem, in which he uses a single trombone as an obbligato instrument in the style of the Viennese Court composers of the early part of the century. Forsyth[1] pours unjustified scorn on Mozart's writing in this movement (Ex. 63), but the part is not unidiomatic and it must be assumed that his experience of the sound of this obbligato was associated with the brassy bravura style of playing prevalent at the time he was writing, a style far removed from the smooth vocal quality that Mozart imagined and that would nowadays be available.

An earlier work in which the trombone was used as a *concertante* instrument has recently come to light. This is a symphony of 1763 by Michael Haydn, in the third movement of which the trombone is given a part of virtuoso quality, complete with trills at practically all phrase cadences.[2] But at this time the employment of the trombone in the concert orchestra, especially as a solo instrument,

---

[1] C. Forsyth: op. cit., p. 149.
[2] For a description of this work see the article by T. Donley Thomas: *Michael Haydn's 'Trombone' Symphony*, in *Brass Quarterly*, VI, 1, 1962.

(Ex. 62. Mozart: *Don Giovanni*, Act II.)

and later:

126

(Ex. 63. Mozart: *Requiem*; *Tuba mirum*.)

was a rarity, and the credit for its introduction into the symphony is usually given to Beethoven, who used a group of three for the first time in his symphonies in the finale of the Fifth. (Trombones had been used earlier in some of the 'battle' symphonies popular at the time; their earliest symphonic appearance was in Franz Beck's Symphony in E♭, c. 1760.) Thrilling though their entry is, Beethoven's use of the trombones, here and elsewhere, showed little advance on the older style of writing. He used them harmonically, often with the rest of the brass and occasionally, when the valveless trumpets and horns were unable to match their versatility, independently, with the alto trombone being given the melody. From this time on, trombones were regarded as an accepted part of the symphony orchestra, though they were by no means always employed. Mendelssohn, for example, looked upon the trombone as too solemn and noble an instrument to be used except on very special occasions.

Gradually composers began to reveal unsuspected or, at any rate, unexploited facets of the trombone's character. Though to begin with they still used it as a group instrument, and therefore harmonically, its melodic possibilities, previously only tentatively explored, were given more scope. The blossoming of the Romantic movement, with its emphasis on the emotional content of the music and its expression by expanded and more highly coloured orchestral means, inevitably had its effect on trombone writing at this time. It was quickly realised that in the *tutti* trombones could give powerful expression to a wide range of emotional situations varying from the jubilant to the sinister. Whether as the cause or the effect of this realisation the ideal of trombone tone underwent a marked change in the direction of greater brilliance. Berlioz's well-known characterization of the trombone in his *Traité de l'Instrumentation* (even though couched in highly coloured terms) is an accurate enough assessment of the mid-nineteenth century view of the instrument, and this view, generally speaking, determined the orchestral uses to which the trombone was put during the succeeding sixty or seventy years.

Berlioz begins by characterizing the trombone as, above all, an epic instrument. 'It possesses,' he says, 'in an eminent degree, both nobleness and grandeur,' properties which composers have recognized from its earliest days; two brief examples are given from a multitude which could have been chosen.

(Ex. 64. Brahms: *Symphony No. 4.*)

(Ex. 65. Bruckner: *Symphony No. 8.*) See also Exs. 26, 42.

Berlioz continues, 'It has all the deep and powerful accents of high musical poetry, from the religious accent, calm and imposing',

(Ex. 66. Brahms: *Symphony No. 1*.)

'to the wild clamours of the orgy'; here let Berlioz provide his own example, in which, as he describes it, 'the brass seem to vomit curses and answer prayer with blasphemy'.

(Ex. 67. Berlioz: *Harold in Italy*.)

The trombone can 'chant like a choir of priests',

(Ex. 68. Rimsky-Korsakov: Overture, *Russian Easter Festival*.)

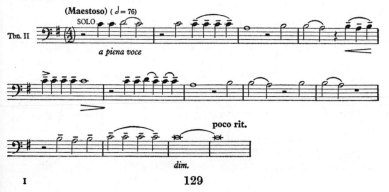

(Ex. 69. Hindemith: *Mathis der Maler*.)

'threaten'

(Ex. 70. Rimsky-Korsakov: *Scheherazade*.)

'lament'

(Ex. 71. Mahler: *Symphony No. 5*.)

'ring a funeral knell'

(Ex. 72. Mahler: *Symphony No. 6.*)

'raise a hymn of glory'

(Ex. 73. Beethoven: *Symphony No. 9.*)

'break forth into frantic cries'

(Ex. 74. Berg: *Wozzeck*, Act II.)

'or sound its dread flourish to awaken the dead or doom the living'.

(Ex. 75. Verdi: *Requiem.*)

Berlioz goes on to differentiate between the tonal qualities of trombones played at various dynamic levels. 'In a fortissimo', he says, the tone is 'menacing and formidable', and he cites the D minor scale (Ex. 76) upon which Gluck founded the chorus of furies in the second act of *Iphigenie auf Tauris*.

(Ex. 76. Gluck: *Iphigenie auf Tauris*, Act II.)

'In simple forte', on the other hand, 'trombones have an expression of heroic pomp, of majesty, of loftiness . . . they no longer menace, they proclaim'.

(Ex. 77. Sibelius: *Symphony No. 7*.)

'In mezzo forte in the medium register, in unison or in harmony with a slow movement, trombones assume a religious character.'

(Ex. 78. Mozart: *Die Zauberflöte*, Act II.)

'The pianissimo of trombones applied to harmonies belonging to the minor mode is gloomy, lugubrious.'

(Ex. 79. Vaughan Williams: *Symphony No. 6.*)

In soberer and less dramatic terms than those of Berlioz the chief functions of the trombone in the orchestra might be categorized as follows:

(*a*) To provide a broad harmonic background in the *tutti*. Here the trombones are often used in conjunction with the rest of the heavy brass (a misleading term insofar as it implies that the sole function of the group is to supply a massive and penetrating weight of tone, whereas it is equally effective in soft chordal passages). Frequently both melody and the accompanying harmony

135

are assigned to the massed brass; Wagner's and Bruckner's scores, for example, provide innumerable instances of this rich and opulent colour. Trombones alone, close spaced and in the upper register, give an effect of blazing brilliance:

(Ex. 80. Dvořák: *Carneval Overture.*)

more widely spaced and placed lower one of solemnity and majesty (Ex. 66).

(*b*) To delineate a melody, the trombones being used either in unison (Ex. 69) or in octaves (Ex. 81).

(Ex. 81. Berlioz: Overture, *Le Carnaval Romain.*)

This is fairly common practice; less usual is the employment of trombones in a contrapuntal manner, as in Exs. 72 and 82.

From the end of the nineteenth century onwards the trombone has more frequently been used to reinforce active string parts; in Ex. 83, for instance, three trombones double bassoons and cellos in a staccato chromatic passage of some complexity.

It is also used in a similar role in slower sostenuto passages; in Ex. 84 the three trombones are doubled at the octave by two clarinets and a bass clarinet.

(*c*) Trombones are often used to provide a rhythmic foundation (Exs. 29, 30), and, in an almost percussive role, to supply accentuations by means of sharp, detached, sforzato chords. These uses are functions of the ability of the trombone, in common with other brass instruments, to utilize a wide variety of articulations and types of attack.

(*d*) The use of a single trombone as a solo instrument in the

(Ex. 82. Berg: *Wozzeck*, Act II.)

(Ex. 83. Strauss: *Till Eulenspiegels lustige Streiche.*)

(Ex. 84. Hindemith: *Die Harmonie der Welt.*)

orchestra is less common and has not, perhaps, been sufficiently exploited. There has been a tendency to assume that such solos are likely to sound over-sentimental, and this is a real danger to be avoided both by composer and player. Sibelius (Ex. 77) succeeds magnificently in doing so; Mahler's 'more intimate and personal type of melody'[1] lies closer to the border-line, but the listener should not be misled by the fact that at its first appearance Mahler marks the solo *Sentimental*, which does not imply any sort of self-indulgence.

(Ex. 85. Mahler: *Symphony No. 3.*)

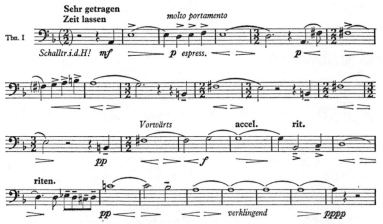

Almost at the opposite extreme are Ravel's excursion into the jazz style of the twenties (Ex. 86), and the solo where the trombone takes its turn with the melody in his *Bolero*.

Both are set in the high register, where the trombone loses its solemnity and acquires a more frenetic character.

From the examples given, it may be seen how the conception of the orchestral function of the trombone has been expanded over the past 150 years. For long its chief role had been a harmonic one, with only occasional forays into the melodic field. Three- and four-part trombone writing is still common, but the technical demands upon the player have continually increased. Moreover, the instrument has been required to play a progressively more independent role, and since the beginning of this century its parts have become highly chromatic and rhythmically much more complex. Duplication of lower string or woodwind lines is frequent and the trom-

[1] W. Piston: *Orchestration*, p. 278.

(Ex. 86. Ravel: *L'Enfant et les Sortilèges*.)

(Ex. 87. Ravel: *Bolero*.)

bonist takes these tasks in his stride. With the development of the
atonal and serial styles of composition the trombone finally
abandoned what vestiges remained of its old-fashioned image as a
solely 'vocal' instrument, and its angular parts with their awkward
intervals presented yet another challenge to the player. Gunther
Schuller,[1] indeed, gives Schoenberg the credit for 'opening up new
horizons for underdog instruments such as the trombone', and
Berg was not slow in following Schoenberg's example, as reference
to the extracts from *Wozzeck* will show. A modern trombone part
bears but little resemblance to the slow-moving, square-cut style

[1] *Horn Technique*, p. 85.

of writing of earlier times, and is often recognizable as such only by its position in the score.

What of the future? An attempt is made in the following chapter to describe some of the extensions of technique which the modern trombonist may soon have to master as a matter of course. Their use in orchestral work is as yet only tentative, but a composition by Roger Smalley, *Pulses 5 × 4*, provides a pointer to the demands which may be made on the orchestral trombonist of the future. Scored for five groups, each of three brass instruments and drums (two of these groups use three trombones each, the others horns and trumpets), the work consists of 30 Moments, some of whose material is fully composed, and some of which, within certain guide-lines, is improvised. As the composer[1] comments, 'the necessities of instantaneous invention can produce developments and extensions of instrumental technique hitherto undiscovered even by the players themselves'. They are required to use many of the techniques described in Chapter 11; for example, to produce microtonal beats with other players, and with themselves (by humming), to use vibratos of controlled but varying widths, to superimpose rhythms on continuous held pitches by different types of articulations or by rhythmic movements of a plunger mute, and so on. In one Moment, for instance, one group of trombones pulsates with its mutes and the other with its slides. 'There are', in the words of a highly favourable review by Stanley Sadie,[2] 'hushed growls, muted moans, gentle burbles, hefty sustained blasts'. In such works technical virtuosity will be taken for granted, but a further essential will be an active and sustained imagination to be exercised by the player in improvising in conjunction with others; and this new element may well be part, at any rate, of the picture of the future, for trombonists as for other instrumentalists.

[1] He describes the work in an article in *The Musical Times*, 1516, June, 1969, pp. 597–599.

[2] *The Musical Times*, 1518, August, 1969, p. 853.

11

Recent Developments in Technique

The structure of the trombone has changed relatively little during the past 500 years. Apart from the addition of the valve during the nineteenth century, a development which has eased certain technical problems but which has not radically altered the technique of the trombone, such improvements as have been introduced have been of a comparatively minor character. The provision of a tuning slide, or of a water-key, the addition of stockings to the inner slides, the use of new alloys and more sophisticated methods of manufacture — all these have made life easier for the player without in any way suggesting that they could lead to extensions of technique. It might well have been thought that with an instrument of such antiquity there could be little, if anything, new to learn about its technical possibilities. The technique of the violin, for example, developed over a period of about three hundred years, but eventually became stabilized about the middle of the nineteenth century, since when there has been no significant further advance. The trombone virtuosi of the early part of last century, in much the same way as Paganini did for the violin, made the apparently impossible possible; by their execution of rapid passage work they showed that slide technique could be developed still further, and their facility in trills indicated that there was still something to be learnt about lip technique. Moreover, they set new standards by their clarity and precision and by their beauty of tone. Since then, until comparatively recently, it seemed that a state of stability had been reached and that no further advances were possible.

This has now proved not to be the case. A combination of circumstances, not always easy to trace, but less connected with the structure of the instrument than with the attitudes of mind of some of those who play it, has led to several striking extensions of its technique. Some of them, no doubt, cause shudders to run down the spines of more conservatively-minded trombonists because, they would affirm, they use the instrument in a manner that is foreign to its nature. From their point of view this is a valid objection; if the trombone is regarded in its traditional light as a dignified, majestic instrument whose chief glory is its beautiful *sostenuto*, then to subject it to such apparent indignities is bound to be looked upon as a debasement of its character. It is a mistake, however, to believe that the trombone is limited to a few stereotypes of expression; new techniques have given it a wider range of expression, and modern composers are beginning to exploit these techniques with serious intent. Their works should therefore be approached with an open mind, for though the idiom may be recondite and some of the technical devices used far removed from the ordinary trombonist's experience, yet they represent an interesting line of development in their attempts to increase the expressive possibilities of the trombone. Whether one finds them successful or not, they provide a stimulus to fresh thought about the instrument.

Many of these extensions of technique have been developed primarily by jazz musicians during the past fifty years or so, and have only gradually been taken over by players in other fields. No attempt will be made here to trace the development of the jazz trombonist's technique, but mention of a few salient points will make it clear that his influence can be discerned in many of the modern works for trombone. A combination of factors ensured that the jazz instrumentalist was given much greater scope for experimentation than the symphonic player. Many jazz musicians had little or no formal schooling on their instruments — some indeed were unable even to read music — and this fact must inevitably have led them, during the process of teaching themselves, to experiment in an attempt to discover the potentialities of their chosen instruments. Moreover, the element of improvisation inherent in jazz must also have resulted in an intensive search for means of increasing the expressive possibilities of the instruments in use. Thus the trombonists, not being subject to the more or less strict disciplines imposed on the symphonic player, evolved for themselves a variety of styles far removed from the orthodox. Generally speaking, it might be said that the jazz trombonist plays in a less cultivated, less restrained manner, in which he is much more able to assert his individuality. To what is often a virtuoso technique, both of slide and of lip, he adds one or more of a number of stylistic features based upon a very large compass, a variety of articulations, the use of a formidable arsenal of mutes, distortions of tone, various degrees of vibrato, slide and lip glissandi and so on, which he describes in a unique and colourful jargon. 'Gutbucket', for example, implies a spontaneous, natural, earthy — even crude — style of playing, raw and vulgar by symphonic orchestral standards; 'the growl', often produced in conjunction with a plunger mute, is a distortion of tone quality giving a rough, rasping effect imitative of jungle sounds. Some players have had an abrupt, explosive style; others, wishing to express themselves through their instruments even more explicitly, with the aid of the wah-wah mute evolved the 'talking solo' in which the trombone speaks an almost human language. Microtones, in the form of 'blue notes', have been freely used, and the 'terminal vibrato', the 'rip' and the 'smear' are commonly used methods of beginning or ending sustained notes, involving the employment of the lip glissando.

For some of these effects there is no recognized musical notation, and when the solos in jazz were almost always improvised there was no need for one. But when composers in other fields began to use some of these devices, as well as some of their own invention, as they have recently done, a more precise indication of their intentions became necessary. The first of several pieces for solo trombone which have been written during the past few years was Berio's *Sequenza V*, and it may be taken as their prototype. Although it utilizes many of the now normal trombone techniques such as double and triple tonguing, flutter-tonguing, and slide glissandi, there are several more esoteric features for which the composer has had to devise special notations. The whole work is played with a plunger mute, and a separate line of the score is included to indicate the degree of closure of the mute. At some points it is to be rattled inside the bell according to a given rhythmic pattern. A special type of harmonic glissando is notated, in which the same note is to be obtained as various partials of different fundamentals, for which the positions are given. At one place a continuous slide movement is indicated by a visual pattern above which articulations are shown so that sounds are produced irrespective of the exact position of the slide. At other places audible sounds of inhalation through the instrument are to be made, and there is a special sign for a 'breathy sound'. The player is often required to vocalize at various pitches, sometimes while simultaneously playing his instrument in the orthodox manner, sometimes with his lips away from the mouthpiece; occasionally he imitates human speech with his trombone, using the mute as an aid to the production of vowel sounds. Simultaneous slide and vocal glissandi, in the same or in opposite directions, add further complications. Finally, an extremely wide compass ranges from pedal *A* to *f″* at the top of the treble clef. Three short extracts are given in Exs. 88–90 to show the type of notation used.

(Exs. 88–90. Berio, *Sequenza V*.)

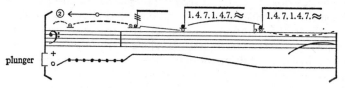

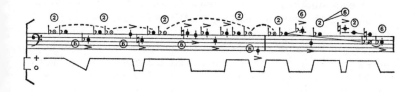

With some of the double sonorities, when the difference in pitch is only microtonal, a sort of beat is set up; this is the 'growl' invented by the jazz trombonists, and it can be felt by the player as a vibration in the cavities of the mouth and throat. It is sometimes suggested that the effect is actually produced by growling at the back of the throat while playing, but whether the growl produces the oscillation, or the oscillation the growl, is really immaterial. At other points, where the divergence between the pitches is wider, more or less well-defined chords are heard, the difference tone being the more prominent.

It should be emphasized that this particular piece, dedicated to the memory of Grock the clown, is comic in intention, and that the player, in addition to a virtuoso technique and complete command of several new technical devices, must possess some histrionic ability, for he is required to make visual gestures designed to remind the listener of the famous clown.

The same is true of Alsina's *Consequenza*. Vinko Globokar, an unrivalled exponent of this new genre, describes the piece in these words[1]: 'The soloist acts a sort of play with himself, having at his disposal beyond visual gestures, different sound sources, as for example blowing, reproducing the "white noise" of electronic music, various noises produced by the plunger or the foot, as well as the sharply contrasting use of the distorted sound of certain vowels. When the "normal" sound of the trombone suddenly appears, Alsina fastens on it and develops from it an extremely aggressive instrumental virtuosity, verging on the impossible, having as aim the total exhaustion of the soloist'.

Globokar's own *Discours II* for five trombones (or for one player in a multiple recording) is a further attempt to extend the expressive possibilities of the trombone. He starts from the thesis that human speech and the playing of the trombone have much in common — not only a similarity in tone colour between some vocal sounds and those obtainable from the instrument, but also in the means by which they are produced. By using these resemblances and his ability to imitate, with the help of various mutes, most of the vowel sounds and many of the consonantal, he aims at creating a sort of language in which the trombones can hold conversation with each other. Beginning, like primaeval man, with rude and faltering attempts at speech, they gradually achieve an articulateness which culminates in almost conspiratorial fashion with strange whisperings and susurrations. Here again further steps are being taken down a road first tentatively entered by jazz trombonists. Whether or not it proves to be a cul-de-sac remains to be seen.

To summarize, recent technical developments in trombone playing include the following:

(i) The range has been extended at both ends of its compass. It is now taken up to g'' by some players as a matter of regular practice — not so much because it is frequently used at this height, but because such practice makes for greater security in those parts of the upper register which may be more commonly required. It is possible to go even higher with a strong embouchure and the sixteenth partial $b''\flat$ is not out of the question. At the other extreme all seven pedal notes are considered to be feasible, taking the instrument down to E' if it is a tenor, and a fourth lower if it has an F attachment. Moreover it is possible to fill in the gap between seventh position E and the first pedal note even if there is no F

---

[1] Sleeve-note of the D.G.G. record 137005, on which he plays this and other pieces, including that by Berio and his own *Discours II*.

valve by making use of the privileged notes, so that the range of the tenor trombone may now be taken to extend from E', the lowest pedal note, chromatically to g'' or above, some four octaves or more.

(ii) Slide technique, perhaps owing to the example of jazz trombonists, has become even more flexible, so that a trombone part sometimes nowadays has almost the look of a cello or bassoon part. Associated with this increased agility must be a corresponding facility in articulation.

(iii) A much greater range of timbres is now available to the trombonist, again largely owing to the enterprise of jazz players in evolving and bringing into use a wide variety of mutes. So far composers of symphonic music have not taken full advantage of these different tone colours and rarely specify any particular type of mute.

(iv) Vibrato is an element of style which has always been a technical possibility on the trombone, but one which would have been out of place in most cases in the older *sostenuto* type of part. With the advent of the jazz trombonist as a soloist it has, however, become an important element in his individual style; so much so, indeed, that it has been maintained that 'a jazz musician may be assessed more simply by his vibrato than by any other particular in his style'.[1] It can be produced by the lips or throat, but more effectively on the trombone with the slide. Whether, or how far, it should be used in orchestral music is a debatable point, but there is certainly scope for its employment in solo pieces. So far, however, many of these pieces have tended towards an abrupt, explosive style which excludes the possibility of using vibrato as an expressive element.

(v) Perhaps the most radical of recent technical innovations has been the use of what have been called 'multiple sonorities', and of extraneous sources of sound. Although there has been a freer and more adventurous exploitation of some of the traditional techniques, the use of the voice in conjunction with the instrument is, apart from a few tentative essays in chord production, a completely new departure. It takes a variety of forms, including humming, whispering, breathing audibly in and out through the instrument, tonguing without actually sounding a note and, with the aid of mutes, the imitation of speech. By no stretch of the imagination can some of the sounds thus produced be called beautiful, but plainly they are not intended to be so.

In sum these innovations allow the trombone to display a new

[1] H. Panassié and M. Gautier: *Dictionary of Jazz*, p. 263.

side to its character, which is at the farthest possible remove from the comparatively unobtrusive and amenable nature it possessed in Renaissance and Baroque times; perhaps in accord with the ethos of the age it has developed a commanding, even aggressive side to its personality, eloquent and capable of expressing a wide range of emotions, but in a language which does not pretend to elegance. Lovers of the trombone must decide for themselves whether this is a development of which they can whole-heartedly approve. The important point is that it is evidence of fresh thinking about the instrument. There are, of course, limits to the technical capacity of any instrument, but it is only as the result of the demands of composers who are interested in the trombone and knowledgeable about it, and of players who wish to feel more stretched than they are by the greater part of the trombone repertoire, that these limits will be reached. The trombone is probably the most versatile of all brass instruments; present developments enable it to exhibit some facets of this versatility, but still others may possibly be revealed in the future which, whilst equally demanding technically, will enable it to express new ideas in a way as yet unimagined.

Part II
THE MUSIC

Introduction

The trombone is not normally regarded as a solo instrument. There have, however, been two short periods in its history when it has emerged from the comparative obscurity of its group to take the limelight. The first of these was in the early eighteenth century, when various minor composers, particularly in Vienna, took to using it as an obbligato instrument in their religious music. The employment of the 'thin-toned, austere, alto trombone' in this role was in sharp contrast to its brief and more profane moment of glory in the first half of the nineteenth century. This was the time of the virtuoso in almost all fields of instrumental music, and the trombone was not without its exponents to show off its paces in showy pot-pourri, variations and display concertos of negligible musical worth.[1] Spurred on by the increasing interest in the wider-bored instrument and the invention of the *Quart-Ventil*, these virtuosi enjoyed a fame on a par with that accorded to pianists such as Thalberg, but by about mid-century the trombone had once again disappeared from the scene as a solo instrument.

There are signs, however, that a third renaissance, partly inspired, perhaps, by the virtuosity of such jazz players as J. J. Johnson, Kai Winding, and Jack Teagarden, has begun, this time with the trombone in the role of an unaccompanied instrument, and as a member of chamber music groups. The chief characteristics of the earlier virtuosi were their smooth cantabile playing and their agility in rapid passages, trills and so on, which were not normally regarded as idiomatic to the trombone. One of them was said to have embellished the introduction to Mendelssohn's *Lobgesang* as follows:

[1] See M. Rasmussen: *Two Early Nineteenth Century Trombone Virtuosi*, Brass Quarterly, V, 1, 1961.

The modern virtuoso approaches his instrument from a different standpoint. He takes the technical facility for granted, and adds to it a wider compass and the whole range of new effects described in Chapter 11, whose declared aim is to extend the expressive possibilities of the trombone. These extensions of technique, fascinating, amusing, or infuriating as they may be to the individual trombonist, appear to have a somewhat limited application, and unless they are sparingly used they will soon become as cliché-ridden a part of the trombonist's vocabulary as the now outworn glissando. Until recently the chief claim of the trombone to a place in the sun has been its ability to draw a melodic line of almost vocal quality, as Baroque composers well understood; ingenious experimentation has shown that there are other sides to its character, but it would be a pity if concentration on these were allowed to obliterate its more traditional role.

It must be admitted that trombone and pianoforte do not make a well-matched pair. Though there is a comparatively extensive repertoire for this combination, it is mostly of an ephemeral nature, and likely to be of more interest to trombonists than to the listener at large. Many of these solos are contest pieces designed to test technique rather than sound any great depths. On the other hand, there would seem to be no valid reason why, with the example of jazz music to follow, the trombone should not be successfully employed as a solo instrument in a concerto. Nevertheless, it has nothing in its literature to compare with the Mozart horn concertos or even the Haydn trumpet concerto. No major composer has attempted a concertante work for trombone; the nineteenth-century virtuoso pieces are of little interest musically though they throw some intriguing sidelights on the history of the golden age of the virtuoso. None of the more modern works has achieved a permanent place in the repertoire, and it now seems unlikely that the trombonist will ever possess a first-class full-dress concerto to match those available to the players of most other wind instruments.

The trombone is by nature a gregarious instrument, probably at its best in company with others of its own kind, or with near relatives. As a consequence there is a considerable body of music, old and new, original and transcribed, for trombone ensembles. Of these the four-part group has the most extensive repertoire, and rightly, for there is no more glorious sound than that of a trombone quartet when it plays in the vocal style of the sixteenth century sackbuts. As mentioned in Chapter 2, a recent development has aimed at encouraging the use of copies of Baroque trumpets and trombones by the *Posaunenchor* movement in Germany, for the accompaniment of choral music of the period, and for the performance of the intradas, canzonas, sonatas and tower music of such composers as Pezel, Schein and Reiche, with something approaching the authentic tone quality — lighter, softer and mellower than that of modern trombones. These instruments are now available from several makers, including Helmut Finke of Herford, Gebr. Alexander of Mainz, and Wilhelm Monke of Cologne. To hear Tiburtio Massaino's Canzona for sixteen trombones played on these instruments in one of the great Italian cathedrals would be an overwhelming experience.

The brass ensemble, though not a modern phenomenon, is a medium which has attained great popularity, especially in the U.S.A., during the past twenty years or so. In instrumentation it ranges from three or four instruments to large brass choirs, with or without associated percussion. The smaller combinations of up to five players can be regarded as chamber music groups, the brass equivalents of the string quartet or quintet but with the difference that the composition of the group is less standardized. The brass trio is usually of horn, trumpet and trombone, or of two trumpets and trombone; the quartet of two trumpets and two trombones, or one of the trumpets may be replaced by a horn. The quintet has more or less settled down to an instrumentation of horn, two trumpets, trombone and tuba (there are several American, and a few British, permanent groups of this composition), though there are plenty of works for other combinations. Most of these quintets are fairly short, rarely lasting more than ten minutes in all; in such small groups as these the instruments must play more or less continuously and there is no possibility of any great variation in timbre or texture. A high proportion of them require players of professional or near-professional standard.

With the sextet the borderland of chamber music is reached. The traditional composition of this group in the U.S.A. was horn, two trumpets (or cornets), trombone, baritone and tuba; in Germany three trumpets and three trombones are favoured, on the model of the old tower music and for a rather different repertoire. A combination of two horns, two trumpets and two trombones is flexible and gives opportunities for a variety of textures and colours, and contrast between a group of sharp-toned instruments and one of mellower timbre is provided by two trumpets and a trombone as against two horns and a baritone or tuba.

Larger groups than these must be considered to fall into the category of the brass choir, a particularly American conception in which the brass section has been lifted more or less wholesale from the symphony orchestra, sometimes with the addition of a baritone and of percussion instruments, and provided with a wide range of serious and often impressive works.[1] Composers from other countries have written for the same medium, but by far the greatest bulk of the music comes from the U.S.A. The comparatively few British works are mainly by composers who have resided in the U.S.A., and they have few chances of performance in this country, where the accepted brass ensemble is the brass band, with a different instrumentation and a repertoire consisting either of transcriptions or of specially written pieces of a lighter nature. These are not listed here. In the U.S.A., on the other hand, the Music Departments of almost every University and even high schools have their own brass groups capable of tackling much of the ever-growing body of music for these ensembles.[2] The French repertoire is not large and consists mainly of fanfare-like pieces, and the Germans, with their brass ensembles concentrated largely in the *Posaunenchor* movement, rely mostly on the Baroque inheritance, with a sprinkling of modern works and contemporary chorale settings.

There exists an extensive and rapidly increasing mass of music which has been arranged or transcribed for brass instruments, much of it taken from the Renaissance and Baroque periods. Most of these works were not specifically written for brass — some indeed were originally vocal pieces — but the evidence shows that the sharp line of distinction now made between vocal and instrumental music was at that time much more blurred, and the instrumentation much less precisely specified. This is often shown by the titles the works were given as, for example, Anthony Holborne's *Pavans, galliards, almains and other short Aeirs both grave, and light, in five parts, for Viols, Violins, or other Musicall Winde instruments* (London, 1599), or the frequently occurring phrase *buoni da cantare et sonari con ogni sorte di stromenti* — to be sung and played on every sort of instrument. The purist need not therefore turn up his nose at these modern transcriptions, though he will be justified in casting a careful and critical eye on the standard of editing, which is by no means always as high as it should be; and the player need feel no secret guilt about performing

[1] Several of these are critically examined in a series of articles by Mary Rasmussen in *Brass Quarterly*, II, 2, 3, 4. She foresees some interesting developments in this area, particularly in the region lying somewhere between jazz and 'serious' music.

[2] A 1964 survey estimated that there were some three million brass players in the U.S.A. at that time.

them, providing that he realises that a considerable responsibility rests upon him — accustomed as he probably is to playing only nineteenth- and twentieth-century music — to study the style of this music and to aim at the type of sonority apt to the period. Enterprising brass players in search of still further material of this sort will find many helpful suggestions in the article *Finding Unusual Brass Music*, by Jan LaRue and Gene Wolf, published in *Brass Quarterly*, VI, 3, 1963.

There is a large body of choral music with accompaniment for brass ensemble — sometimes a group of trombones alone is used, but more frequently these are associated with other brass instruments. Even from the prejudiced point of view of one who never fails to find the sound of a group of well-played brass instruments exciting and inspiriting, it must be admitted that much of this repertoire is of little musical value, belonging, as Mary Rasmussen puts it, 'largely to the realm of social history, contributing its bit to the reconstruction of the *Klangideal* of the past rather than to the concert programs of the present'. Nineteenth-century German composers were only too ready to celebrate the occasion, national, religious or merely local, with a new work for chorus and brass. Even so, a careful sifting — which would indeed be a work of supererogation — might well dredge up the occasional pearl-containing oyster.

On first thoughts it is, perhaps, surprising to find the trombone figuring in any list of chamber music apart from that for small brass ensembles, since it might be expected to dominate the proceedings too completely, both physically and aurally. Its image is still that of Berlioz's 'epic instrument', liable to 'break forth into frantic cries, or sound its dread flourish to awaken the dead or to doom the living'. It is too often forgotten that in its earlier history it was constantly used on an equal footing with viols, recorders, and the human voice, and that the pendulum has swung back in this direction; the tonal ideal now sought for is not the sharp-edged brilliance of last century, but a smoother, more vocal quality. Composers have once again used it in this role, in which the trombone is able to combine on equal terms with strings and woodwind without any fear that it will find itself out of place. As a result the chamber music list makes strange reading; sixteenth- and seventeenth-century composers rub shoulders with those of the twentieth, and there is little or nothing from the intervening period. The reader who is interested in this modern trend should refer to Robert Gray's article, *The Trombone in Contemporary Chamber Music*, published in *Brass Quarterly*, I, 1, 1957.

Section 6.9 goes beyond the bounds of true chamber music, including works for larger ensembles, some for wind instruments alone.

It must be emphasized that the list which follows makes no claim to be exhaustive, and in any case, like all such lists, it is inevitably out of date before it is published. It is hoped, however, that its scope is wide enough to meet the needs of most trombonists. Many sources have been tapped during its compilation, but especial mention must be made of the extensive bibliographies published in *Brass Quarterly*, to whose editor, Miss Mary Rasmussen, I am greatly indebted for permitting me to make use of them.

No attempt has been made at a critical evaluation of the works included, for two good reasons. With such a large body of music involved, it is not possible for any one person to have had the opportunity of examining or hearing more than a small proportion of it; at the risk — or even in the certainty — of including a considerable amount of third-rate music it was felt that any attempt to make a selection would be bound to involve arbitrary decisions which could well have excluded some worthwhile works. Secondly, it is a common experience that even third-rate music can often be fun to play, though of little or no interest to a listener; and there are many works whose pedagogical value more than compensates for any lack of musical interest. The list may therefore have something of the appearance of a rag-bag, but there is almost certain to be something in it for most tastes and purposes. The reader who requires a more critically selective list is referred to Miss Rasmussen's excellent *Teacher's Guide to the Literature of Brass Instruments*.

Sources

In addition to publishers' catalogues, the following sources have been consulted or are referred to in this list of works. Where an abbreviation has been used, this precedes the title of the source in the following list.

	Altmann, W. *Kammermusik-Katalog*. 5th ed., Leipzig, Hofmeister, 1942; 6th ed., 1945.
AMC	*MS list of works for brass instruments*. New York, American Music Centre, Inc.
AmZ	*Allgemeine musikalische Zeitung*. Leipzig, Breitkopf & Härtel, 1798–1848; Rieter-Biedermann, 1866–82.
ASCAP	*ASCAP Symphonic Catalogue*. New York, ASCAP, 1959.
B	*Baker's Biographical Dictionary of Musicians*. 4th ed., New York, G. Schirmer, 1940; 5th ed., 1958.
	Catalogue of Chamber Music in the BBC Library. London, BBC, 1965.
Blom	Blom, E., *Everyman's Dictionary of Music*. London, Dent, 1946; 2nd ed., 1958.
BMI	*Pamphlets on American Composers*. New York, Broadcast Music, Inc.
BMIC	*Chamber Music by Living British Composers*. London, British Music Information Centre, 1969.
BQ	Rasmussen, M. ed. *Brass Quarterly*. Durham, New Hampshire, 1957–65; *Brass and Woodwind Quarterly*. Durham, New Hampshire, 1967–
	British Catalogue of Music. London, British National Bibliography, 1957–
	Catalogue des Éditions Centre Belge de Documentation Musicale. Brussels, CeBeDeM, 1965.
CFE	*Catalog of Composers Facsimile Edition*. New York, American Composers Alliance, 1957; Supplement, 1958.

157

CG *Catalogue of Members' Compositions, Vol. I,* and *Composer:* Journal of the Composers' Guild of Great Britain. London, Composers' Guild of Great Britain, 1958–

Chapman, R. *Flute Technique.* London, Oxford University Press, 2nd ed., 1951.

Chase Chase, G. *America's Music.* New York, McGraw-Hill Book Co., 2nd ed., 1966.

CMC *Catalogue of Canadian Chamber Music.* Toronto, Canadian Music Centre, 1967.

CM Lib. Fairfax, B. comp. *MS list of works for wind instruments.* Deposited with the Central Music Library, Westminster, London.

Cobbett, W. W. comp. & ed. *Cobbett's Cyclopedic Survey of Chamber Music.* London, Oxford University Press, 1929; 2nd ed., 1963.

Cowell Cowell, H. & Cowell, S. *Charles Ives and his Music,* New York, Oxford University Press, 1955.

MS list of works for wind instruments. Prague, Czechoslovak Music Information Centre.

Cz *Music News from Prague.* Prague, Czechoslovak Music Information Centre, 1968–

D Dale, Delbert A. *Trumpet Technique.* London, Oxford University Press, 1965.

Day Day, S. comp. *Classical Record Catalogue.* London, The Gramophone.

Catalogue Général des Disques microsillon. Paris, Diapason.

Catalogue of Instrumental Music. Amsterdam, Donemus, 1961.

Catalogue of Vocal Music. Amsterdam, Donemus, 1961.

Catalogue of Orchestral Music. Amsterdam, Donemus, 1964.

Catalogue of Instrumental Chamber Music. Amsterdam, Donemus, 1965.

E Eitner, R. *Biographisch-Bibliographisches Quellen-Lexicon.* Leipzig, Breitkopf & Härtel, 1900; Graz, Akademische Drucks und Verlagsanstalt, 1960.

Engel Engel, H. *The Solo Concerto.* Cologne, Arno-Volk Verlag, 1964.

Ewen Ewen, D. *American Composers Today.* New York, H. W. Wilson Co., 1949.

Farish, M. K. *String Music in Print.* New York, R. M. Bowker, 1965. *Supplement.* New York, R. M. Bowker, 1968.

F   Fétis, F. J. *Biographie Universelle des Musiciens.* Paris, Didot, 1867–70; *Supplément et Complément.* Paris, Didot, 1878–80.

Fleisher   *Catalogue of the E. A. Fleisher Library.* Philadelphia, privately printed, 1933–45.

          Fontes artis musicae. Listes Internationales selectives. Kassel, Bärenreiter, 1962–

FST   *Catalogue: Svensk Instrumental-Musik.* Stockholm, Föreningen Svenska Tönsattare, 1964.

G   *Grove's Dictionary of Music & Musicians.* London, Macmillan, 4th ed., 1928; Supplementary Vol., 1945; 5th ed., 1954.

Ga   Gardavský, C. ed. *Contemporary Czechoslovak Composers.* Prague, Panton, 1965.

          Goldman, R. F. *The Wind Band, its Literature & Technique.* Boston, Allyn & Bacon, Inc., 1961.

Gor   Gorgerat, G. *Encyclopédie de la Musique pour Instruments à vent.* Lausanne, Éditions Rencontre, 2nd ed., 1955.

          Hartmann, H. ed. *Bielefelder Katalog der Schallplatten klassischer Musik.* Bielefeld, Bielefelder Verlagsanstalt.

Gram   *The Gramophone.* Harrow, General Gramophone Publications, Ltd., 1922–

H   Helm, S. M. *Catalog of Chamber Music for wind instruments.* Ann Arbor, Mich., National Association of College Wind & Percussion Instrument Instructors, 1952.

Ho   Howard, J. T. *Our Contemporary Composers.* New York, Thomas J. Crowell Co., 1941, 1948.

Ho2   Howard, J. T. *Our American Music.* New York, Thomas J. Crowell Co., 1965.

          Husted, B. F. *The Brass Ensemble: its History & Music.* Rochester, University of Rochester Press, 1961.

I   *The Instrumentalist.* Evanston, Ill., The Instrumentalist Co.

IL   *The Interlochen List of Instrumental Ensembles.* 4th ed., Interlochen, Mich., National Music Camp, 1963.

          Katalog der Abteilung Noten. Darmstadt, Internationales Musikinstitut, 1966.

          Jacobs, A. *A New Dictionary of Music.* Harmondsworth, Penguin, 1958, 1967; London, Cassell, 1962.

          Jensen, J. R. *A Bibliography of Chamber Music for*

French Horn. Fullerton, Calif., F. E. Olds & Son, 1964.

K   King, R. *Brass Players' Guide to the Literature.* North Easton, Mass., R. King Music Co., n.d. and *Selected Brass Music.* North Easton, Mass., R. King Music Co., 1967, 1968.

Kroll, O. *The Clarinet.* (rev., and with a repertory, by D. Riehm.) London, Batsford, 1968.

La   Dufourcq, N. ed. *Larousse de la Musique.* Paris, Librairie Larousse, 1957.

L. & B.   Lang, P. H. & Broder, N. ed. *Contemporary Music in Europe.* London, Dent, 1966.

Langwill, L. G. *The Bassoon & Contra-Bassoon.* London, Benn, 1965.

Machilis, J. *Introduction to Contemporary Music.* New York, W. W. Norton, 1961.

MBE   *MS List of works for brass ensembles.* New York, Modern Brass Ensemble.

MGG   Blume, F. ed. *Die Musik in Geschichte und Gegenwart.* Kassel, Bärenreiter, 1949–1968.

MT   *The Musical Times.* London, Novello, 1844–

MS List of works for wind instruments. Oslo, Norsk Komponistforening, 1965.

Notes. Washington, Music Library Association, Inc., 1943–

Opperman, K. *The Repertory of the Clarinet.* New York, Ricordi, 1960.

P   Pazdirek, F. *Universal-Handbuch der Musikliteratur.* Vienna, [1904–10?].

R   Reis, C. R. *Composers in America.* New York, Macmillan, 1947.

Rasmussen, M. *A Teacher's Guide to the Literature of Brass Instruments.* Durham, New Hampshire, Appleyard Publications, 1964.

Rendall, F. G. *The Clarinet.* London, Williams & Norgate, 1954.

Richter, J. F. *Kammermusik-Katalog (1944–58).* Leipzig, Hofmeister, 1960.

Ri   Richards, D. *The Music of Finland.* London, H. Evelyn, 1968.

Rie   Riemann, H. *Musiklexicon.* 12th ed., Mainz, Schott. 1959–61.

RT   *The Radio Times.* London, BBC.

Catalogue: *Samfundet til Udgivelse af Dansk Musik*, Copenhagen, Samfundet, 1956; *Supplement*, 1964.

S   H. Seeger, ed. *Musiklexicon*. Leipzig, Deutscher Verlag für Musik, 1966.

Schwann   *Schwann Long-playing Record Catalog*. Boston, Mass., W. Schwann, Inc.

Schweiz   *MS List of works for wind instruments*. Zürich, Schweizerisches Musik-Archiv, 1966.

Slon   Slonimsky, N. *Music of Latin America*. London, Harrap, 1946.

     Sonorum Speculum: Mirror of Dutch Musical Life. Amsterdam, Donemus, 1959–

T   Thompson, O. *International Cyclopedia of Music and Musicians*. London, Dent, 4th ed., 1956; 5th ed., 1964.

     Thurston, F. *Clarinet Technique*. London, Oxford University Press, 1956; 2nd ed., 1964.

V   Valentin, E. *Handbuch der Chormusik*. Regensburg, G. Bosse, n.d. [1953–58].

VDK   *Komponisten und Musikwissenschaftler der Deutschen Demokratischen Republik*. Berlin, Verlag Neue Musik, 1959; 2nd ed., n.d. [1966].

Ve   Vester, F. *Flute Repertoire Catalogue*. London, Musica Rara, 1967.

     Clough, F. F. & Cuming, G. J. *World Encyclopedia of Recorded Music*. London, Sidgwick & Jackson, 1952; *Supplements I–III*, 1952–57.

WWM   *Who's Who in Music*. 4th ed., London, Burke's Peerage, 1962; 5th ed., 1969.

ZfM   *Zeitschrift für Musik*. Offenbach a.M., Steingräber, 1920–

Abbreviations

A	Alto (or contralto)	bcl	Bass clarinet
acc	Accordeon	bn	Bassoon
ad lib	ad libitum	br	Brass instruments
althn	Althorn	ca	Cor anglais
arr	Arranged by	cel	Celesta
B	Bass voice	cch	Children's chorus
b.	born	ch	Chorus
Bar	Baritone voice	cl	Clarinet
bar	Baritone (instrument)	comp	Compiled by
		cong	Congregation
bc	Basso continuo	cont	Continuo

ct	Cornet	orch	Orchestra
cto	Cornetto	org	Organ
cym	Cymbal	perc	Percussion
d.	died	pf	Pianoforte
db	Double bass	quart	Quartet
dbn	Double bassoon	quint	Quintet
ed	Edited by	picc	Piccolo
elec	Electric	rec	Recorder
euph	Euphonium	rev	Revised
fch	Female chorus	S	Soprano
flghn	Flügelhorn	sax	Saxophone
fp	First performance	saxhn	Saxhorn
glock	Glockenspiel	stg quart	String quartet (2 violins, viola, violoncello)
gt	Guitar		
h	Hand		
harm	Harmonium	stgs	String orchestra
hn	Horn	T	Tenor
hp	Harp	ten hn	Tenor horn
hpcd	Harpsichord	timp	Timpani
l h	Left hand	trb	Trombone
mand	Mandoline	trp	Trumpet
mar	Marimba	v	Voice
mch	Male chorus	vcl	Violoncello
MS	Manuscript	vib	Vibraphone
MzS	Mezzo-soprano	vla	Viola
n.d.	No date	vla d'am	Viola d'amore
n.p.	No place	vln	Violin
ob	Oboe	wind quint	Wind quintet (flute, oboe, clarinet, horn, bassoon)
ob d'am	Oboe d'amore		
ondes M	Ondes Martenot		
Op	Opus	ww	Woodwind
oph	Ophicleide	xyl	xylophone
opt	Optional		

Notes

(*a*) When the instrumentation of a work is denoted by figures, these are in the order:

Flute, oboe, clarinet, bassoon — horn, trumpet, trombone, tuba — violin, viola, violoncello, double bass.

Other instruments are denoted by their names or abbreviations.

(*b*) When the key of a work is given, a capital letter indicates a major key, and a small letter a minor key.

(*c*) A † before the title of a work indicates that a commercial long-playing recording of the work has been traced.

(*d*) An * after the abbreviation for a source indicates that the source refers to the location of the manuscript or an early edition.

Contents

1. Trombone and pianoforte

Absil, J. 1893–	Suite	(K)
Alexander, J.	Sonata	GMPC, 1967
Alschausky, S.	Waltz Aria	Sikorski
	Arietta	Benjamin
	Waltz-Aria No. 2	Benjamin
Ambrosius, H. 1897–	Sonata	Hofmeister, 1958
Ameller, A. 1912–	Kryptos: Étude	Hinrichsen, 1958
Andersen, A. 1845–1926	Andante religioso	Benjamin
Andersen, E. 1914–	Sonatina	Hansen, 1968
Arensky, A. 1861–1906	Concert Waltz in B♭	RS, 1952
Arrieu, C. 1903–	Mouvements	Amphion, 1966
Bachelet, A. G. 1864–1944	Morceau de Concours	Leduc; IMC, n.d.
Baervoets, R. 1930–	Impromptu	Maurer, 1958
Baeyens, H.	Introduction & Cantabile	Brogneaux
Bagge, J. G.	Barcarolle	Benjamin
Bakaleinikoff, V. 1885–1953	Meditation	(K)
Barat, J. E.	Pièce en Mi♭	E. & S., 1923; Leduc
	Andante & Allegro (1935)	Leduc; IMC, n.d.
	Morceau de Concours (bass trb)	Leduc
	Introduction & Serenade (bass trb)	Leduc
	Introduction & Danse (bass trb)	Leduc
	Reminiscences de Navarre (bass trb)	Leduc
Barillet, R.	L'Enterrement de Saint-Jean	Leduc, 1960
	Hans de Schnokeloch (bass trb)	Leduc, 1961
Barraine, E. 1910–	Andante & Allegro	Salabert, 1958
	Chiens de paille (bass trb)	Jobert, 1966
Bartá, L. 1928–	Concertino (1964)	SHV, 1966
	Sonatina (1956)	(Ga)
Bartovský, J. 1884–1964	Concertino	(Ga)
Bassett, L. 1923–	Sonata	King, 1967
Baudo, S.	†Petite Suite	(K)
Beach, B.	Suite	AMP, 1957
Beaucamp, A. 1921–	Cortège (bass trb)	Leduc, 1953
Becher, H. 1863–1941	Capriccio	(K)

Belcke, F. A. 1795–1874	Fantasie	Benjamin
Bennett, D.	Trombographic	
Benson, W. 1924–	Aubade	Piedmont, 1959
Berthold, T.	Fantasie	Benjamin
Bigot, E. 1888–	Variations	Leduc, 1949
	Impromptu	Leduc, 1947
	Carillon et Bourdon (bass trb)	Leduc
Bitsch, M. 1921–	Impromptu (bass trb)	Leduc, 1957
Blazevitch, V. 1881–1942	Concert Sketch No. 5 (Ed. Satz)	Leeds, 1946
Boda, J. 1922–	Sonatina	King
Boeck, A. de 1865–1937	Fantasie	Gervan, 1954
Boizard, G.	Diptyque: Aux Statues de Bomarzo (bass trb)	EMT, 1967
Bolotin, S. W.	Scherzo	RS, 1956
Bonneau, P. 1918–	Capriccio	Leduc, 1946
Boutry, R. 1932–	Choral varié	Leduc, 1956
	Trombonera	Leduc, 1956
	Capriccio	Leduc, 1957
	Tubaroque (bass trb)	Leduc, 1955
	Tubacchanale (bass trb)	Leduc
Bozza, E. 1905–	Ballade	Leduc, 1944
	Hommage à Bach	Leduc, 1957
	Ciaccona	Leduc, 1967
	Allegro et Finale (bass trb)	Leduc, 1953
	New Orleans (bass trb)	Leduc, 1962
	Thème varié (bass trb)	Leduc, 1957
	Prelude & Allegro (bass trb)	Leduc, 1953
Brant, H. 1913–	Funeral Music for the Mass Dead (2 trb)	CFE
Bréard, R.	Pièce de Concours	Lemoine
Brown, C. 1898–	Méditation	Leduc, 1955
	Recitatif, Lied & Final (bass trb)	Leduc, 1961
Büchtger, F. 1903–	Vier kleine Stücke	Bosse, 1964
Büsser, H. 1872–	Piece in E♭, Op. 33	Leduc
	Cantabile & Scherzando, Op 51	Leduc
	Concert Piece in E♭, Op 55	IMC
	Variations in D♭, Op 53	(K)
	Étude de Concert, Op 79	E. & S., 1927; Leduc
	Phoebus Variations, Op 87	Leduc
Büttner, M. 1891–	Improvisationen, Op 6	Hofmeister
	Improvisationen Nos. 1 & 2	Benjamin
	Improvisationen Nos. 3 & 4	Benjamin
Cabus, P. 1923–	Fugue en Toccata	Maurer, 1958
Capdeville, P. 1906–	Sonate concertante	Leduc, 1966
Cardew, C. 1936–	Three Pieces	
Casinière, Y. de la 1897–	Thème varié	Leduc, 1958

166

Castelucci, M.	Intermezzo capriccioso	
Castérède, J.	Sonatina (bass trb)	Leduc, 1958
	Fantaisie concertante (bass trb)	Leduc, 1960
Catelinet, P. 1910–	Old Macdonald had a Farm	Hinrichsen, 1953
Charpentier, J. 1933–	Prélude & Allegro (bass trb)	Leduc, 1959
Childs, B. 1926–	Music	CFE
Cimera, J.	Improvisation	Remick, 1949
	Recitative & Caprice	Remick, 1949
	Valse d'Amour	(K)
	Caprice charmante	Kjos, 1956
	Spring Caprice	Kjos, 1956
Clergue, J.	Impromptu	Lemoine
Clérisse, R.	Prière	Leduc, 1959
	Thème de Concours	Leduc
	Pièce lyrique (bass trb)	Leduc, 1957
	Voce nobile (bass trb)	Leduc
	Idylle (bass trb)	Leduc
	Romance (bass trb)	Leduc
Cook, E.	Bolivar	(K)
Cools, E. 1877–1936	Allegro de Concert	(K)
Cowell, H. 1897–1965	Hymn & Fuguing Tune No. 13 (1960)	AMP, 1960
Crocé-Spinelli, B.	Solo de Concours	Leduc
Croley, R.	Divertissement (bass trb)	(K)
Daneels, F.	Petite Pièce	Maurer, 1961
David, F. 1810–73	Concertino in E♭, Op 4	
	(Ed. F. Grube)	Benjamin 1956
	(Ed W. Gibson)	IMC, 1961
	(Ed R. Müller)	Zimmermann, 1961
		Hofmeister, 1958
Davison, J.	Sonata	Templeton, 1966
Debaar, M.	Légende et Caprice	Brogneaux
Defaÿ, J. M. 1932–	Danse sacrée et Danse profane	Leduc, 1954
Defossez, R. 1905–	Concerto	Metropolis
Delcroix, L. 1880–1938	Légende, Op 64	Leduc
Demersseman, J. 1833–66	Introduction & Polonaise, Op 30	Benjamin
	Cavatine, Op 47	Benjamin
Depelsenaire, J. M.	Légende nervienne	(K)
Deprez, J.	Pièce de Concours	Maurer, 1960
Désenclos, A. 1912–	Plain-Chant et Allegretto	Leduc, 1965
	Suite brève dans le goût classique	Leduc, 1965
Desportes, Y. 1907–	Fantaisie in B♭	Leduc
Desprez, F.	Fantaisie concertante	Maurer, 1962
Devos, G.	Deux Mouvements contrastés (bass trb)	Leduc, 1960
Dewanger, A.	Humoresque, Op 89	Leduc, 1954
Dhossche, R.	Invocation	(K)
Diethe	Variationen	Benjamin
Dondeyne, D.	Cantabile et Caprice	Leduc, 1958

Douliez, V.	Andante, Op 53	Maurer
	Introduction & Andante, Op 54	Maurer
Dubois, P. M. 1930–	Cortège	Leduc, 1959
	Deux Marches	Leduc, 1960
	Suite	Leduc, 1965
	Cornemuse (bass trb)	Leduc, 1961
	Piccolo Suite (bass trb)	Leduc, 1965
Dubois, T. 1837–1924	Solo de Concert	Leduc; IMC, n.d.
Duclos, R. 1929–	Doubles sur un Choral	Leduc
	Sa Majesté la Trombone	Leduc, 1948
Dutilleux, H. 1916–	Choral, Cadence & Fugato	Leduc, 1950
Dvořáček, J. 1928–	Inventions (1961)	CHF
Ebner, C.	Romance, Op 44	
Eisfeld, T. 1816–82	Rezitativ und Cantabile	Benjamin
Fayeulle	Bravaccio (bass trb)	Leduc, 1958
Fischer, M.	Intermezzo	Westend
Fleischmann, O.	Concertino, Op 35	Benjamin
Fleming, R. 1921–	A Musician in the Family (1952)	CMC
Frackenpohl, A. 1924–	Pastorale	Rochester, 1957
Franck, M. 1892–	Fanfare, Andante et Allegro	Salabert, 1958
Francl, J. 1906–	Meditation, Elegy & Dance	SHV, 1965
Friedemann, A.	Concert-Variations, Op 8	Oertel
Fuhlisch, G.	Posaunen-Erfolge	Sikorski
Gabaye, P. 1930–	Complainte	Leduc, 1957
	Tubabillage (bass trb)	Leduc, 1959
Gabler, E.	Metamorphosen (Freie Variationen über zwei eigene Themen)	Benjamin, 1954; Sikorski
	Ballade	Benjamin
	Elegie	Benjamin
	Capriccios Nos. 2 & 3	Benjamin
Gagnebin, H. 1886–	Sarabande	Leduc, 1953
Galelli, G.	Canto del solitario	Drago, 1956
Galliard, J. E. ca. 1687–1749	Six Sonatas in a, G, F, e, d, C (Ed K. Brown) 2 vols	Hinrichsen, 1960 IMC, 1963 Schott, 1946; M. & M., 1946
Gallois-Montbrun, R. 1918–	Aria	Leduc, 1952
Gardner, J. 1917–	Romance	Schott, 1952
Gaubert, P. 1879–1941	Morceau symphonique	Leduc, n.d.; IMC
	Cantabile et Scherzetto	(K)
Gedalge, A. 1856–1926	Solo de Concours	Gaudet; IMC
Geib, F.	Serenade, Op 10	Mills
	Nocturne, Op 7	Mills
	Cavatina	
	Dialogue, Op 11	
	Caprice, Op 4	

Geissler, F. 1921–	Sonatine	Hofmeister, n.d.
George	Sonata	(K)
Giffels, A.	Sonata (Ed T. Beversdorf)	Southern, 1964
Goepfart, K. 1859–1942	Konzertstück	Benjamin
Golubev, E. 1910–	Sonata, Op 36/2	RS, 1956
Gregson, E. 1945–	Divertimento	Chappell, 1968
Grković, B.	Sonatina	UKBH, 1958
Grube, F.	Waltzer Rondo	Benjamin, 1955
	Concertino	Benjamin, 1958
	Ballade und Polonaise	Benjamin
	Posaune bei guter Laune	Benjamin
Guenther, A.	Concertino	Benjamin
Guide, R. de 1909–62	Suite, Op 32/3: Les Caractères du Trombone (1956)	Leduc, 1958
Guilmant, F. A. 1837–1911	†Morceau symphonique, Op 88	Schott; IMC, n.d.
Hansen, T. 1917–	Introduktion und Scherzo, Op 22	Benjamin
Hartley, W. S. 1927–	Arioso	Interlochen, n.d.
	Sonata concertante (1956–8)	Interlochen, n.d.
Henry, O.	Divertimenti di tre toni (1958)	Boston, Composer, 1960
	Passacaglia & Fugue (bass trb)	King, 1963
Hervé, A. de	Introduction & Finale	Bosworth
Hess, E. 1912–	Capriccio, Op 57	Helbling
Higuet, N.	Larghetto e Allegretto	Maurer, 1961
Hildingsen, A.	Arioso	Benjamin
	Romance	Benjamin
Hindemith, P. 1895–1963	†Sonata (1941)	Schott, 1942
Hlobil, E. 1901–	Intermezzo	Artia
	Canto emozionte, op 43	(Cz)
Höser, O.	Romanze	Benjamin
Hoof, J. van 1880–1959	Divertimento (1935)	Metropolis, 1952
Horowitz, J. 1926–	Adam-Blues	Novello, 1969
Hoskins, W. B.	Recitative & Aria	CFE
Houdy, P.	Largo & Toccata	(K)
Hugon, G. 1904–	Introduction & Allegro	EMT, 1961
Hutchison, W.	Sonatina	C. Fischer, 1966
Imbrie, A. 1921–	Three Sketches	Shawnee
Jacobi, F. 1891–1952	Meditation	Southern
Jaruszewski, E.	Konzertstück	Benjamin
Jehmlich, R.	Concertino, Op 3	Benjamin
Jenkins, C. 1889–	Legend in d	Bo. & H., 1922
Jörgensen, A. 1881–1947	Suite	Hansen
	Am Abend	Benjamin
	Légende	Benjamin

Jones, R. W.	Sonatina (1958)	Interlochen, n.d.
Jong, M. de 1891–	Konzertstück, Op 50	Brogneaux, 1950
Jongen, J. 1873–1953	Aria & Polonaise, Op 128	Gervan, 1944
Kaï, N.	Légende (bass trb)	Leduc, 1962
Kaiser, E. b. 1850	Adagio	Benjamin
Karg-Elert, S. 1877–1933	Sinfonia Kanzone (1926)	MS(MGG)
Karjalainen, A. 1907–	Polonaise, Op 1	(Ri)
	Small Solos, Op 35	(Ri)
Kelly, R. 1916–	Sonata	CFE
Klaus, N.	Sonata	King
Knight, M. 1933–	Introduction & Allegro	Tritone, 1962
Kopelent, M. 1932–	Four Pieces	SHV, 1963
Kreisler, A. von	Sonatina	(K)
Krejčí, M. 1891–1965	Sonatina (1948)	SHV, 1961
Krol, B. 1920–	Capriccio da camera, Op 35	(K)
Kuehn, (S?)	Adagio	C. Schmidt
Kühne, J. C.	Concertino	Benjamin
Kummer, G.	Variationen	Benjamin
Kurpínski, K. 1785–1857	Cavatina	PWM
Kuusisto, I. T. 1933–	Coelestis Aulae Nuntius (with org)	(Ri)
Kvapil, J. 1892–1958	Suite	(Ga)
Lafosse, A.	Trois Pièces de Style	Leduc, 1956
Lamy, F. 1881–	Choral varié	Leduc, 1949
Leclercq, E.	Concertino	Leduc
Leduc, J. 1932–	Arioso & Danse	Leduc
Lehner, F.X. 1904–	Sonatine	Bosse, 1964
Leibowitz, R. 1913–	Four Bagatelles, Op 61	(RT, Sept. 9, 1967)
Lepetit, P. 1893–	Pièce de Concert	Leduc, 1955
Lodeon, A.	Campagnarde (bass trb)	Leduc
Löwe, C.	Die Uhr	Benjamin
London, P. 1904–	Trombone Serenade	Hansen
Lonque, A. 1908–	Novelette	Maurer, 1960
	Scherzo-Capriccioso, Op 68	Maurer, 1961
Looser, R. 1920–	Variationen-Fantasie über ein eigenes Choralthema (1958)	Henn, 1958
Lotzenhiser, G.	Interlude	Belwin, 1965
Loucheur, R. 1899–	Hialmar (1947)	Durand
Luening, O. 1900–	Sonata (1953)	Highgate [ca 1967]
Maes, J. 1905–	Morceau de Concert	(K)
McCarty, P.	Sonata (bass trb)	Ensemble, 1963
McCoy, E.	March	
McKay, G. F. 1899–	Sonata	Remick, 1951
Maniet, R.	Pièce in C	Brogneaux, 1954
	Marziale	Maurer, 1957
	Poco Allegro	Brogneaux
	Introduction & Scherzando	Maurer, 1956

Manns, F. 1844–1922	Romanze	Benjamin
Manzo, S.	Concertino	Zanibon, 1967
Marc-Carles	Introduction & Toccata	Leduc, 1961
Margoni, A.	Après une Lecture de Goldoni (bass trb)	Leduc
Marteau, M.	Morceau vivant	(K)
Martelli, H. 1895–	Sonata, Op 87 (bass trb)	Phillipo
	Suite, Op 83	Phillipo
	Sonata, Op 100	Eschig, 1966
	Dialogue (bass trb)	Eschig, 1966
Marter, G.	Thema und Variationen	Benjamin
Martin, F. 1890–	†Ballade (1940)	UE, 1941
Massis, A. 1893–	Impromptu	Leduc, 1949
Masso, G.	Suite for Louise	Kendor, 1966
Matěj, J. I. 1922–	Informatorium (38 pieces)	Panton, 1966
Maurat, E.	Petites Inventions, Op 21/3	Eschig, 1966
Mazellier, J. 1879–1959	Solo de Concours	Leduc; IMC
Mellers, W. 1914–	Galliard	Schott, 1952
Mercadante, S. 1795–1870	Salve Maria	C. Schmidt
Meulemans, A. 1884–1966	Rhapsodie	Gervan
	Concertino (1953)	CeBeDeM, 1959
Minet, F.	Air varié	Metropolis
Missa, E. 1861–1910	Morceau de Concours (1904)	Leduc
Mitscha, A.	Sonata	PWM, 1953
	Romans	PWM, 1965
Monaco, R. A.	Sonata	Colombo, 1969
Morel, F. 1926–	Pièce in f	UMP
Morrissey, J. J.	Song for Trombone	Marks, 1960
Mühlfeld, R. 1856–1907	Romanze (1879)	Benjamin
Muehlfeld, W.	Konzertstück, Op 7	Benjamin
Müller, B. E. 1825–95	Gebet (with org)	Zimmermann
Müller, J. I.	Praeludium, Chorale, Variations & Fugue (1839) (bass trb) (Ed A. Ostrander)	Musicus, 1959
	Concertino	(K)
Müller, W.	Trombologie	Steinbacher, 1948
Muller, J. P.	Concerto-minute, Op 4	Maurer, 1960
Neibig, A.	Konzertstück	Benjamin
Nelhybel, V. 1919–	Suite	GMPC, 1968
Nestico, S.	Reflective Mood	Kendor, 1964
Niverd, L. 1879–	Légende	(K)
Nux, P. V. de la	Solo de Concours	Leduc
Orlinsky, H. B.	Konzertstück	Bosse, 1967
Ostrander, A.	Concert Piece in fugal style (bass trb)	Musicus, 1960

	Sonata in g (pf ad lib)	Musicus, 1960
	On the Fairgrounds	Musicus, 1956
Ostransky, L.	Concertino	Rubank, 1966
Parlow, A.	Fantasie über ein Tiroler Volkslied,	Benjamin
1822–88	Op 103	
	Romanze, Op 175	Benjamin
Parrott, I. 1916–	Sonatina (1958)	MS (Composer, Univ. College of Wales, Aberystwyth)
Pascal, C. 1921–	Improvisation en forme de Canon	Durand, 1959
	Pastorale héroïque	Durand, 1952
	Sonata en 6 minutes 30 (bass trb)	Leduc
Paudert, E.	Berühmte Aria	Benjamin
	Fantasie marziale	Benjamin; Sikorski
Petit, P. 1922–	Grave (bass trb)	Leduc, 1953
	Fantaisie (bass trb)	Leduc, 1953
	Wagenia (bass trb)	Leduc, 1957
	Thème varié (bass trb)	Leduc, 1965
Pfeiffer, G.	Solo	E. & S., 1899;
1835–1908		Leduc
Planel, R.	Air et final (bass trb)	(K)
Podešva, J. 1927–	Concertino (1949)	(Ga)
Poot, M. 1901–	Impromptu	Eschig
	Étude de Concert	Leduc, 1958
Popp, W. 1828–1903	Gesangszene, Op 278	Benjamin
Porret, J.	Six Equisses	Baron
	Concertino No. 7	Billaudot
	Concertino No. 8	Billaudot
Presser, W. 1916–	Sonatine	Tritone, 1962
	Rondo	Tenuto, 1967
Ragwitz, E.	Sonatine	DVM, 1968
Rakov, N. P. 1908–	Aria	RS, 1955
Raph, A.	Russian Sailor's Dance	(K)
Raphling, S. 1910–	Lyric Prelude	(K)
Rasse, K.	Concertino	E. & S.; Leduc
1873–1955		
Read, G. 1913–	De Profundis (with org)	King
Reiche, E.	Concert Piece No. 2 in A	Benjamin
Reutter, H. 1900–	Ostinato	Leduc, 1957
Rex, W.	Concertino	Benjamin
Rivard, W. H.	Sonata	
Rivière, J. P.	Burlesque	Leduc, 1958
Ropartz, J. G.	Pièce en e♭	E. & S., 1908;
1864–1955		Leduc, 1953; IMC
	Andante & Allegro	Leduc
Rousseau, S. A.	Pièce concertante	Heugel, 1898
1853–1904		
Roy, K. G. 1924–	Sonata, Op 13	King [1963]
Rueff, J. 1922–	Rhapsodie	Leduc, 1962
	Concertstück (bass trb)	Leduc, 1960

Sabathil, F.	Divertissement, Op 54	Benjamin
	Mein Lied, Op 80	Benjamin
	Sehnsucht: Lied ohne Worte	Benjamin
Sachse, E.	Concertino (Ed A. Hansen)	Rahter [ca 1953]
		Sikorski; IMC,
		1957
Saeys, E.	Ballade, Op 216	Maurer, 1960
Saikkola, L. 1906–	Grave (with org)	(Ri)
Saint-Saëns, C.	Cavatine, Op 114 (1915)	Durand, 1915;
1835-1921		RS, 1958
Salzedo, C.	Pièce concertante, Op 27	Leduc, 1958;
1885–1961		IMC, n.d.
Sanders, R. L. 1906–	Sonata in E♭	Gamble, 1948
Schampaert, J.	Fantasie dramatique	Metropolis
Scharschmidt, K. G.	Rezitativ und Variationen	Benjamin
Schibler, A. 1920–	Blues	Henn
Schiffmann, E.	Intermezzo, Op 53 (with org)	Rahter; Benjamin
		1954
	Concert Piece, Op 67	Sikorski, 1944;
		Benjamin, 1957
Schoemaker, M.	Concertstuk	Gervan
1890–1964		
Schroeder, W. 1895–	Andante cantabile	Nordiska; Hansen
Schroen, B.	Fantasy Sonata	Jurgenson, 1900
Semler-Collery, J.	Fantasie lyrique	Eschig, 1960
	Dix Etudes lyriques	Eschig
	Saxhornia (bass trb)	Leduc, 1959
	Barcarolle & Chanson bachique	Leduc, 1953
	(bass trb)	
Serocki, K. 1922–	Sonatina	PWM, 1955
Shepherd, W.	Nocturne & Rondolette	Southern, 1962
Sheriff, N. 1935–	Piece for Ray	IMI, 1966
Simons, G.	Atlantic Zephyrs	C. Fischer
Smita, V.	Concert Aria (Rev. M. Hedja)	SNKLHU, 1958
1822–1908		
Spillman, R.	Two Songs (bass trb)	Musicus, 1963
Šrámek, V. 1923–	Suite	SHV, 1966
Stekke, L.	Variations, Op 24	Gervan
Stevens, H. 1908–	Sonatina	Peer, 1968
Stojowski, S.	Fantasia	Leduc, n.d.;
1869–1946		PWM, 1953
Strauwen, J.	Capriccio	Brogneaux
Takács, J. 1902–	Sonata, Op 59	Sidemton, 1957;
		Mills, 1954
Tamba, A.	Fantaisie	Leduc, 1965
Tcherepnin, A. N.	Andante	Belaieff; Bo. & H.,
1899–		1955
Telemann, G. P.	Sonata in a (Ed K. Brown)	IMC, 1966
1681–1767		
	Sonata in f (Ed A. Ostrander)	IMC
Thilman, J. P.	Concertino giocoso	Hofmeister, 1954
1906–		
	Concerti espressivi (with timp)	Peters, 1966

173

Tisné, A.	Elégie & Burlesque, Op 32	Leduc, 1965
Tkachenko, P.	Elegy	RS, 1963
Tomasi, H. 1901–	Danse sacrée (bass trb)	Leduc, 1960
Tournemire, C. A. 1870–1939	Légende	Leduc, 1920
Tournier, F.	Arème	Ed Rideau Rouge
Townsend, D. 1921–	Chamber Concerto No. 2	Mercury, 1965
Trevarthen, R.	Sonata (1959)	Louisville
Tuthill, B. C. 1888–	Fantasy Piece, Op 10/2	(K)
Uber, D.	Panorama	Adler, 1962
	Sonata	(K)
	Mississippi Legend	Adler, 1960
	Autumn Sketches, Op 56	Ensemble, 1966
Vachey, H.	Two Interludes	Leduc, 1966
Vandermaesbrugge, M.	Prélude et Danse	Maurer, 1960
Vasiliev, S.	Konzertstück	RS, 1954; Hofmeister, n.d.
Verees, E.C. 1892–	Konzertstück	Gervan, 1954
Vidal, P. A. 1863–1931	Solo de Concert No. 2	Girod, 1897; Leduc, 1921
Watson, W.	Sonatina	Shawnee, 1962
Whear, P. W.	Sonata	Ludwig, 1963
White, D. H. 1921–	Sonata	Southern, 1967
Wigy, F.	Légende	Maurer, 1962
Wilder, A. 1907–	†Sonata	(Schwann)
Wilenski, I.	Two Arias	RS
Wynne, D. 1900–	Sonata	MS? (WWM)
Zagwijn, H. 1878–1954	Equisse (1947)	Donemus, 1947

2. Trombone with Orchestra

2.1 *Trombone with Orchestra*

Albrechtsberger, J. G. 1736–1809	†Concerto in B♭ (1769) (Ed G. Darvas) (Alto trb, stgs)	EMB, 1968
Alschausky, S.	Concerto No. 1 in B♭	Rahter
	Concerto No. 2 in B♭	Benjamin
Andersen, A. 1845–1926	Concerto	Benjamin
Beckerath, A. von 1901–	Concerto (1948)	(fp, Munich, 1948)
Belcke, F. A. 1795–1874	Concertino, Op 40 (1832) (Ed A. Hansen)	Benjamin, 1953
Berghmans, J.	La Femme à Barbe (No. 4 from La Chenille)	Leduc, 1958
	Concertino	Leduc, 1954
Berlioz, H. 1803–69	Oraison funèbre, from Symphonie funèbre et triomphale (with band)	Br. & H.
Bigot, E. 1888–	Impromptu	Leduc, 1927

174

Blazhevitch, V. 1881–1942	Concerto No. 2 in D♭ (Ed A. Lafosse)	IMC
	Concerto No. 5 (Ed A. Ostrander)	IMC
	Concerto No. 10 (Ed A. Sedrakiana) (Ed A. Ostrander)	RS, 1963 IMC, 1965
Bloch, E. 1880–1959	Symphony (1956)	Broude, 1956
Böhm, C.	Still wie die Nacht	Benjamin
Bonneau, P. 1918–	Fantasie concertante	Leduc, 1950
Borden, D.	Concerto	MS
Boutry, R. 1932–	Concerto	Leduc, 1963
Bozza, E. 1905–	Ballade, Op 62	Leduc, 1944
Bresgen, C. 1913–	Concerto in g	(MGG)
Bruns, V. 1904–	Concerto	
Bucci, M. 1924–	Concerto for singing instrument	(K)
Büttner, M. 1891–	Concerto	Benjamin; Sikorski; Schauer
Cimera, J.	Concerto	Remick, 1950
Clapp, P. G. 1888–1954	Dramatic Poem (1912; rev. 1940)	(Blom, T)
Coker, W. 1928–	Concerto (with band)	Presser, 1961
Creston, P. 1906–	Fantasy, Op 42 (1948)	G. Schirmer, 1951
David, F. 1810–73	Concertino in E♭, Op 4 (Ed F. Grube) (Ed Mueller) (Ed W. Gibson) (Ed R. Müller)	Benjamin, n.d. C. Fischer IMC, 1961 Zimmermann, 1961
	Concertino, Op 5	Hofmeister, 1958
Delden, L. van 1919–	Piccolo Musica concertato, Op 79 (3 trb, stgs, timp)	Donemus, 1963
Dubensky, A. 1890–	Concerto (1953)	(Ho)
Freed, I. 1900–60	Rhapsody (1951)	(Ho)
Gillis, D. 1912–	Dialogue (with band)	Mills, 1958
Gräfe, F.	Grand Concerto	Rahter, 1953; Sikorski; IMC; CB, n.d.
Grøndahl, L. 1886–1960	Concerto (1924)	Samfundet, 1954
Grube, F.	Concerto	Benjamin
Guilmant, A. 1837–1911	†Morceau symphonique, Op 88	Schott; IMC
Halahan, G. F. C.	Concertino (stgs)	(WWM)
Hartley, W. S. 1927–	Concerto (3 trb, band)	Ensemble, 1967
Henneberg, A. 1901–	Concerto	(L)
Herf, F.	Concert Piece	Leuckart
Hofmann, C.	Concerto	Benjamin

175

Holmboe, V. 1909–	Concerto, Op 52	
Hovhaness, A. 1911–	Concerto No. 3, Op 94; Diran (stgs)	King, 1962
	30th Ode of Solomon, Op 76; Overture (stgs)	Peters, 1967
Howarth, E. 1935–	Concerto	(WWM)
Jacob, G. 1895–	Concerto	Williams, 1956
Jörgensen, A. 1881–1947	Suite, Op 22	Hansen
	Concerto	Benjamin
Karjalainen, A. 1907–	Concerto, Op 16	(Ri)
	Scherzo, Op 12	(Ri)
Karkoff, M. I. 1927–	Concerto, Op 35	FST
Kincl, A. 1898–	Concerto	(Ga)
Köjer, K. H.	Profile: Heitere Suite (3 trb)	Hannover, 1961
Kubín, R. 1909–	Concerto (1936)	MS (Ga, MGG)
Kühne, J. C.	Concerto in Form einer Gesangsszene (1886)	(Engel)
Larsson, L. E. 1908–	Concerto, Op 45/5	Gehrmans, 1957
Lebedev, A.	Concerto (bass trb) (Ed A. Ostrander)	Musicus, 1960
Leopold, B. 1888–1956	Greetings to the Fatherland (1956)	(Ga)
Lucký, S. 1919–	Divertimento, Op 12 (1946) (6 trb, stgs, perc)	CHF
McCarty, P.	Sonata (bass trb) (stgs)	Ensemble, 1963
Maes, J. 1905–	Konzertstück	MS?
Martin, F. 1890–	†Ballade (1940)	UE, 1941
Maštalíř, J. 1900–	Fantasy (1952)	(Ga, WWM)
Matej, J. I. 1922–	†Concerto No. 1 (1952)	SNKLHU, 1959
	Concerto No. 2 (Sonata)	Panton, 1966
Meyer, (L. von?)	Concertino	(Engel)
	Potpourri	(AmZ, 17, 1815)
Milhaud, D. 1892–	†Concertino d'Hiver (1953) (stgs)	AMP, 1957
Mitchell, L. C. 1923–	Concerto grosso (1961) (3 trb)	MS (BQ, VI, 1)
Mokrousoff, B. 1909–	Concerto (1935)	MS? (G)
Müller, C. G.	Concertino (Ed A. Hansen)	Benjamin, 1953
Nesterov, A.	Concerto, Op 11 (Ed W. Gibson)	IMC, 1958
Nicholson, R. W. 1907–	Overture (stgs)	(WWM)
Novosad, L. 1922–	Fantasy	(Ga)
Nowakowski, J. 1800–65	Concertino (Ed W. Gibson)	PWM, 1967; IMC, 1958; Benjamin
Parris, R. 1924–	†Concerto	
Parrott, I. 1916–	Concerto (with band)	Musica Rara, 1968
Platonov, N.	Concerto	RS, 1962
Premru, R. E. 1934–	Concerto (1955)	Premru Music

Pressen, W. 1916–	Rondo	(K)
Reiche, E.	Concerto No. 2 in A	Zimmermann; Leeds; IMC
Reschofsky, A.	Concert Fantasy	Leuckart
Rimsky-Korsakov, N. 1844–1908	Concerto (with band) (Ed W. Gibson)	RS IMC, 1958
Rothmüller, M. 1908–	Divertimento (stgs, timp)	Bo. & H., 1955
Schäfer, F. 1905–	Concerto	(Ga)
Schibler, A. 1920–	Concerto, Op 55: Signal, Beschwörung und Tanz	A. & S., 1958
Schuller, G. 1925–	Fantasia concertante (1947) (3 trb)	MS (BMI, Ho)
Serly, T. 1900–	Concerto (1952)	Southern
Serocki, K. 1922–	Concerto (1953)	PWM, 1955
Shilkret, N. 1895–	Concerto	MS
Smolanoff, M.	Concerto, Op 21	(K)
Späth [Spaeth, A.?]	Concerto (2 trb)	MS? (AmZ, 35, 1833)
Spillman, R.	Concerto (bass trb)	Musicus, 1962
Spisak, M. 1914–65	Concertino	Leduc, 1951
Stark, R. 1847–1922	Ballade, Op 20	(T)
	Historiette, Op 30	(T)
Tanner, P.	Aria (with band)	Holly-Pix, 1967
	Concerto (2 trb, with band)	Holly-Pix, 1965
Tiede	Fantasie	MS (AmZ, 46, 1844; Engel)
Thilman, J. P. 1906–	Concertino giocoso, Op 47	Hofmeister, 1954
Tomasi, H. 1901–	Concerto	Leduc, 1956
Tuthill, B. C. 1888–	Concerto, Op 54	King, 1969
Vacek, K. V. 1908–	Bagatelle (stgs)	(Ga)
Vaćkář, D. C. 1906–	Charakteristikon	CHF
Vasiliev, S.	Concerto (Ed Enke)	RS
Verees, E. C. 1892–	Concerto	Gervan
Vidal, P. 1863–1931	2e Solo de Concert	Leduc, 1921
Villette, P.	Fantaisie concertante	Leduc, 1962
Xenakis, I. 1922–	†Pithoprakta (2 trb, stgs, perc)	Bo. & H.
Wagenseil, G. C. 1715–77	†Concerto (Ed K. Janetzky)	SM [1963]
Weber, A. 1930–	Concerto	Leduc, 1968
Weber, M. 1854–1906	Dramatische Szene in italienischer Weise	(Engel)
Zador, E. 1894–	Concerto (1967)	MCA, 1967

2.2 *Trombone and one or more other instruments, with orchestra*

Andriessen, J. 1925–	†Movimenti hn, trp, trb, stgs, timp	Donemus, 1965
Asriel, A. 1922–	Vier Inventionen (1963) trp, trb	VNM, 1966

M

Berghmans, J.	Concerto grosso hn, trp, trb, stgs	Leduc, 1957
Castérède, J.	Concertino trp, trb, stgs, pf, perc	Leduc, 1959
Defaÿ, J. M. 1932–	Concerto trp, trb	Leduc, 1954
Depelsenaire, J. M.	Concerto grosso 2 trp, trb	Choudens
Dijk, J. van 1918–	Concerto trb, vln, vcl	Donemus, 1961
Donatoni, F. 1927–	Concertino 2 hn, 2 trp, 2 trb, stgs, timp solo	Schott, 1953
Etler, A. 1913–	†Concerto (1967) br quint, stgs, perc	Continuo, 1968
Fabian, W.	Concerto grosso cl, sax, trb, stgs, pf	IPA, 1959
Fortner, W. 1907–	Phantasie über die Tonfolge b-a-c-h- (1950) fl, ob, bcl, hn, trp, trb, vln, vla, vcl, 2 pf	Schott
Haydn, M. 1737–1806	Divertimento in D (Ed L. Kalmár) cl, bn, trb	Musica rinata 7, 1965
Henze, H. W. 1926–	In Memoriam: The white Rose fl, ca, bcl, hn, bn, trp, trb, stgs	Schott
Hindemith, P. 1895–1963	†Concert Music, Op 50 (1930) 4 hn, 4 trp, 3 trb, tuba, stgs	Schott, 1931
Husa, K. 1921–	Concerto br quint, stgs	(WWM)
Kauffmann, L. J. 1901–44	Festliche Musik (1943) 2 trp, 3 trb, stgs	MS (MGG)
Kirchner, L. 1919–	Toccata (1955) ob, cl, hn, bn, trp, trb, stgs, perc	AMP
Klebe, G. 1925–	Divertissement joyeux, Op 5 cl, hn, bn, trp, trb, stgs, perc	B. & B., 1949
	Espressione liriche (1956) hn, trp, trb	Schott
Koetsier, J. 1911–	Concerto trp, trb	Donemus, 1966
	Music 3 trp, 3 trb, 2 stg orch, timp	(Re)
Kox, H. 1930–	Sinfonia concertante hn, trp, trb	Donemus, 1956
Kreutz, A. 1906–	Dixieland Concerto cl, trp, trb	MS (ASCAP)
Kreutzer, C. 1780–1849	Concertante bn, 3 trb	MS?
Kunert, K. 1911–	Concerto (1966) hn, trp, trb	MS (VDK)
Looser, R. 1920–	Konzertante Musik (1951) trb, hp, stgs, timp	MS (B)
Mabellini, T. 1817–97	Gran Fantasia fl, hn, trp, trb	MS? (MGG)

Martin, F. 1890–	†Concerto (1949)	UE, 1950
	wind quint, trp, trb, stgs, timp, perc	
Matthus, S. 1934–	Kleines Orchesterkonzert (1963)	DVM
	2 fl, 3 trb, hp, pf, stgs, perc	
Meyer, E. H. 1905–	Concerto grosso (1966)	Peters
	2 trp, trb, stgs, timp	
Mihalovici, M. 1898–	Variations	EV
	2 trp, 2 trb, stgs	
Monnikendam, M. 1896–	Concerto	Henmar
	trp, trb, org	
Morrissey, J. J.	Concerto grosso	Chappell
	2 trp, trb	
Raasted, N. O. 1888–	Sinfonia da chiesa, Op 76	Samfundet, 1947
	2 trp, 2 trb, org, stgs, timp	
Raphling, S. 1910–	Concerto (1953)	(Ho)
	ob, trb, stgs	
Roger, K. G. 1895–1966	Concerto grosso, Op 71 (1951)	Moeck
	fl, ob, cl, trb, stgs, timp, perc	
Schelb, J. 1894–	Concerto	SM
	trp, trb	
Schibler, A. 1920–	Concerto, Op 59 (1959)	A. & S., 1959
	hn, trp, trb, hp, pf, 2 stg orch, perc	
Schmidt, O. 1928–	Pièce concertante, Op 19	Hansen, 1967
	trp, trb, hp, pf, stgs, cel, perc	
Starer, R. 1924–	Concerto a tre	MCA, 1965
	cl, trp, trb, stgs	
Tchemberji, N. 1903–	Suite concertante	RS, 1935
	hn, trp, trb	
Tolar, J. K. 17th Cent.	†Sonata in C	MAB, Vol. 40, 1959
	bn, 4 trp, 4 trb, stgs, cont (Ed J. Pohanka)	
Weinzweig, J. 1913–	Divertimento No. 5 (1961)	CMC
	trp, trb, band, perc	
Werdin, E. 1911–	Festliche Musik	Schott
	3 trp, trb, stgs	
Wuorinen, C. 1938–	Concertone (1960)	CFE
Yudin, M. 1893–	Concerto	(T)
	3 fl, 3 trb, stgs	

3. Trombones alone

3.1 *One Trombone*

Alsina, C. 1941–	†Consequenza, Op 17 (1966)	B. & B., 1969
Arnold, M. 1921–	Fantasy, Op 101	Faber, 1969
Austin, L. 1930–	Changes: Open Style (1965) (trb, tape)	(Chase; MT, Dec. 1966)
Bassett, L. 1923–	Suite	Louisville, 1967; Colombo, 1969

Bavicchi, J. 1922–	Preludes, Op 21	Ensemble, 1967
Berio, L. 1925–	†Sequenza V	UE, 1968
Bernstein, L. 1918–	Elegy for Mippy II	G. Schirmer, 1950
Boutry, R. 1932–	Concertino	Leduc, 1958
Cage, J. 1912–	Solo for sliding trombone	(K)
Childs, B. 1926–	Sonata (1961)	Tritone, 1962
Croley, R.	Variazioni piccoli, Op 44/1 (bass trb)	Louisville, 1965; Colombo, 1969
Druckman, J. 1928–	†Animus I (trb, tape)	MCA, 1967
Globokar, V. 1934–	Discours (trb, tape)	(MT, Feb., 1968)
Hovhaness, A. 1911–	Mysterious Horse before the Gate (trb, 5 perc)	Peters, 1964
Kupovič, L. 1936–	Das Fleisch des Kreutzes (1962) (trb, 6 timp, 3 tam-tams, church bells)	UE
Ostrander, A.	Sonata in g (bass trb, pf ad lib)	Musicus, 1960
Presser, W. 1916–	Partita	Colombo, 1969
Reinhardt, B. 1929–	Music	IMP, 1965
Reuter, F. 1896–1963	Suite, Op 23	Zimmermann, n.d.
Sear, W. E.	Sonata	Avant, 1966
Shulman, D.	Three Gymnastics	Weintraub, 1951
Stockhausen, K. H. 1928–	†Solo (trb, tape)	UE
Stout, A. 1932–	Proclamation	Louisville, 1967; Colombo, 1969
Swift, R.	Composition	CFE
Wilenski, I.	Variations on a Moldauisches Theme	RS, 1955

3.2 *Two Trombones*

Blazevitch, V. 1881–1942	Concert Duets	RS; IMC; Omega; Leeds, 1947
Blume, O.	Twelve Duets (Ed W. Gibson)	IMC, 1959
Breve, R.	XVth Century Song	
Catelinet, P. 1910–	Suite in miniature	Hinrichsen, 1966
Cornette, V. 1795–1868	Six Concert Duets	CB, n.d.
Couillard, H.	Quatre Études en forme de Duos	Southern
	Douze Duos concertantes	Southern; Leduc
Henning, C. 1784–1867	24 Easy Duets (Ed A. Ostrander)	IMC, 1960
Henry, O.	Rondo pequeno	Composer, 1960
Kahila, K.	Andante & Allegro	Musicus
Nuten, P.	Duo capriccioso	Metropolis [1953]
Raphling, S. 1910–	Sonatina (1955)	(K)
Russo, W. 1928–	Duets, Op 35	Brown, 1961
Stoker, R. 1938–	Four Dialogues	Hinrichsen, 1952
	Three Inventions (1966)	Leeds

THE MUSIC

Tanner, P.	Duets, Vol. I	Holly-Pix, 1966
Telemann, G. P.	Six Sonatas	M. & M., 1959
1681–1767		
Uber, D.	20th Century Duets: 2 vols	Adler, 1960
	Ten Concert Duets	Musicus

3.3 *Three Trombones*

André-Thiriet, A. L.	Suite, Op 204 (Ed R. Dhellemmes)	Lemoine, 1966
1906–		
Bamberg, K.	Trio	Merseburger
Bartsch, C.	Choral, Danse nonchalante et Fanfare	Maurer, 1965
Bozza, E. 1905–	Andantino (1963) (Ed R. Dhellemmes)	Lemoine, 1966
Bruckner, A.	Equali	Ensemble, 1965
1824–96	(Ed Q. Maganini)	C. Fischer
Cariven, M.	Andantino cantabile (1961) (Ed R. Dhellemmes)	Lemoine, 1966
Chase, A.	Eight Trios	Cor, 1963
	Three Waltzes	
Cornette, V.	Three Trios (Ed Osborn)	Ensemble
1795–1868		
Desprez, F.	Triptyque	Maurer, 1965
Franco, J. 1908–	Three Inventions	CFE
Haan, S. de 1921–	March, Waltz & Quasi Adagio	Hinrichsen, 1959
Hennebelle, J.	Petite Fanfare (1961) (Ed R. Dhellemmes)	Lemoine, 1966
Jacobson, I. D.	Three Thoughts	Mills, 1962
Kindermann, J. E.	†Symphonia in E aus Deliciae Studiosorum, 1643	DTB, XXI– XXIV, 1924
1616–65		
Knab, A.	Sechzehn Choräle: 2 vols	Br. & H.
1881–1951		
Lannoy, R.	Prélude (1961); Fanfare (1960); Fuguette (1960)	Lemoine, 1966
Lo Presti, R. 1933–	Trio	C. Fischer
Moulaert, R.	Suite (1939)	CeBeDeM, 1959
1875–1962		
Müller, R.	Ausgewählte Trios	Zimmermann
Porret, J.	Fragonard	(K)
Premru, R. E. 1934–	Two Pieces (1952)	Ensemble, 1965
Schiffmann, E.	Phantasy, Op 66 (timp ad lib)	Hofmeister, 1941
Schilling, H. L.	Partita: Singet, preiset Gott mit Freuden	Möseler, 1964
1927–		
Soret, M.	Studio 6 (1961) (Ed R. Dhellemmes)	Lemoine, 1966
Stieber, H. 1886–	Turmmusik Nr. 2	Hofmeister, 1953
Tanner, P.	Imitation	Holly-Pix, 1966
	Larghetto	Holly-Pix, 1966
Tournier, F.	Pièce en forme d'Ouverture à la française (1960)	Lemoine, 1966
	Sicilienne (1961)	Lemoine, 1966

Uber, D.	Carnival	Adler, 1960
	Modern Trios (Manhattan Vignettes)	Musicus
Znosko-Borowsky, A. 1889–	Scherzo, Op 13 (Ed W. Gibson)	RS, 1955 IMC, 1960

3.4 *Four Trombones*

Ameller, A. 1912–	Chorale Cathédrale Scherzo, Op 92	Hinrichsen, 1960
Atherton, P. 1910–	Suite	(RT, May 1, 1969)
Bark, J. 1934– & Rabe, F. 1935–	Bolos (1962)	Hansen, 1964
Bassett, L. 1923–	Quartet	Morris, 1954; King, 1960
Beethoven, L. van 1770–1827	Three Equali (1812) (Ed R. King)	Br. & H., n.d.; King, 1961; Ann Arbor, 1949; Ensemble, n.d.
Blacher, B. 1903–	Study	
Blaževitch, V. 1881–1942	Valse de Concert (Ed F. Cofield)	King Rubank, 1957
Borris, S. 1906–	Largo & Presto	
Boutry, R. 1932–	Cinq Pièces à quatre	Leduc, 1961
Bozza, E. 1905–	Trois Pièces (bass trb or tuba ad lib)	Leduc, 1964
Busch, C. 1862–1943	Meditation	C. Fischer
Butts, C. M.	Suite	Shawnee, 1966
Catelinet, P. 1910–	Two Divertissements: Romance & Tambourin	Hinrichsen, 1953
	Three Pieces	(K)
Chapman, R. 1916–	Suite of three Cities	Peters, 1960
Charpentier, J. 1933–	Quatuor de forme liturgique	Leduc, 1960
Clapp, P. G. 1888–1954	Concert Suite No. 1 (1938)	Bo. & H., 1955
	Concert Suite No. 2	Bo. & H.
Cohen, J.	Rondo	Interlochen, 1961
Colby, C. L.	Allegro con brio	Gamble
Defaÿ, J. M. 1932–	Quatre Pièces	Leduc, 1954
Dillon, S. 1944–	Suite (1966) (with 6 timp)	BMIC
Domroese, W.	Intermezzo	
Dondeyne, D.	†Suite	EMT, 1960
Dubois, P. M. 1930–	Quatuor	Leduc, 1962
Ebbage, D. A. 1942–	Sonata	(WWM)
Eisbrenner, W. 1908–	Scherzo	

Elton, A. 1935–	Quartet, Op 26 (1963)	BMIC
	Quintet, 'J.F.K.', Op 28 (1963) (with perc)	BMIC
Essex, K. 1915–55	Fanfare & Fugue	
Frackenpohl, A. 1924–	Quartet (1948; rev. 1967)	Ensemble
Fuss, H.	25 ernste und religiose Stücke	Zimmermann
Glasser, S. 1926–	3 Dances, Op 6 (1961)	BMIC
Globokar, V. 1934–	Étude pour Discours (4 trb in multiple recording)	(RT, Sept. 9, 1967)
Gow, D. 1924–	Suite, Op 57 (1961)	Musica Rara, 1967
Haubiel, C. 1894–	Processional	CP
	Recessional	CP
	Moderni	Belwin
	Romantico	Belwin
Hawthorne-Baker, A. 1909–	Partita (with timp)	BMIC
Hemel, O. van 1892–	Donquichotterie (1962)	Donemus, 1962
Hlouschek, T. 1923–	Divertimento (1960)	MS (VDK)
Hornoff, A.	Suite	Hiob, 1953
Jacobs, G. 1895–	Suite	Bo. & H.
Johnson, C. W.	Cragged Pass	Rubank, 1961
Jones, D. 1912–	Sonata (1957)	BMIC
Koepke, P.	Élégie heroique	Rubank, 1957
	Scherzo caprice	Rubank
Langley, J. W. 1927–	Suite (1959)	Hinrichsen, 1961
Lantier, P. 1910–	Quatuor	MS?
Laudenslager, H.	Three Preludes & Fugues	Cor, 1963
Leontiev, A.	Protyazhnaya	
Maas, A.	Two Quartets in B♭	Ackermann & Lesser; 1920; Oertel; CB
McCarty, P.	Recitative & Fugue	King, 1960
McKay, F. H.	Festival Prelude	Barnhouse
	Pageant March	Bo. & H., 1962
	Intermezzo	Remick
Maes, J. 1905–	Fragment	Maurer, 1964
Maniet, R.	Divertimento	Maurer, n.d. [1959?]
Marc-Carles	Lamento et Marche	Leduc, 1963
Massis, A. 1893–	†Suite	EMT, 1964
Meulemans, A. 1884–1966	Suite (1942)	CeBeDeM, 1958
Müller, J. P.	Choral & Variations	Maurer, 1959
Müller, R.	Ausgewählte Quartette, 3 vols	Zimmerman
Nelhybel, V. 1919–	Six Pieces	GMPC, 1966
	Three Organa	Colombo, 1965
Olander, E.	First Suite (Ed H. Ferguson)	G. Schirmer, 1951, 1962

Ostransky, L.	Prelude & Galliard	Rubank, 1961
	Donnybrook	Rubank, 1961
	Two Episodes	Rubank, 1961
Otten, L. 1924–	Suite (1951, rev. 1966)	Donemus, 1957, 1967
Peeters, F. 1903–	Suite, Op 82 (1955)	Peters, 1959
Premru, R. E. 1934–	In Memoriam (1956)	Ensemble, 1967
Raph, A.	Burlesque	Cor, n.d.
Raphling, S. 1910–	Quartet	Adler
Ristić, M. 1908–	Suite (1938)	MS? (MGG)
Rueff, J. 1922–	Deux Pièces brèves	Leduc, 1956
Sanders, L. 1906–	Scherzo & Dirge	AMP, 1948
Semler-Collery, J.	Petite Suite	
	Deux Pièces	
Serocki, K. 1922–	Suite (Ed A. Tauros)	PWM, 1954, 1967
Steel, C. 1939–	Four brief Diversions	
Stretton, A. J.	Four Quartets	
Tanner, P.	A Study in Texture	Holly-Pix, 1965
	Just Bach	Holly-Pix, 1965
Telemann, G. P. 1681–1767	Concerto (Arr. A. Lumsden)	Musica Rara
Tomasi, H. 1901–	Être ou ne pas être (bass trb solo, 3 trb)	Leduc, 1963
Uber, D.	Three Miniatures, Op 29	Ensemble, 1967
Waelput, H. 1845–85	Andante cantabile	MS (MGG)
Walker, R.	Preambule	Pro Art
Woyrsch, F. von 1860–1944	Mors triumphans, Op 58 (1915)	Oertel
Wright, D. 1895–1967	The Age of Chivalry	Weinberger, 1961

3.5 *Five Trombones*

Globokar, V. 1934–	†Discours II (multiple recording, or 5 players)	Peters

3.6 *Six Trombones*

Phillips, B. 1907–	Piece	King, 1953
Tanner, P.	El Cangrejo (with 4 perc)	Holly-Pix, 1965

3.7 *More than Six Trombones*

Adler, S. 1925–	Five Vignettes (12 trb)	OUP, 1969
Ott, J.	Suite (8 trb)	C. Benny
Villa-Lobos, H. 1887–1959	Preludio from Bachianas brasilieras No. 1 (arr. G. Smith) (8 trb)	AMP, 1968

184

4. Brass Ensembles, including trombone(s)
(horn, trumpet, trombone, tuba, other instruments)

4.1 *Two Instruments*

Alexander, J.	Trio of Duets	0110	Southern, 1968
Baines, F. 1917–	Three short Pieces	0110	Williams, 1959
Borden, D.	Fifteen Dialogues	0110	Ensemble, 1962
Butterfield, D.	Seven Duets	0011	DB, 1960
Catelinet, P. 1910–	Suite in miniature	0110	Hinrichsen, 1952
Defossez, R. 1905–	Quatres petites Pièces	0110	CeBeDeM, 1957
Glinka, M. I. 1804–57	Four short Fugues	0110	King, 1963
Goldman, R. F. 1910–	Duo	0110	Mercury, 1950
Henry, O.	Three serial Duets	0110	Boston, Composer, 1960
Irons, E. D.	Pedro y Amigo	0110	
Kahila, K.	Twelve Duets	1010	
	Andante & Allegro	1010	(K)
Kupferman, M. 1926–	Available Forms	0110	GMPC, 1966
Lester	Three Duets	0110	WIM
Raph, A.	Three display Duets	0110	Musicus, 1956
Raphling, S. 1910–	Prelude & Toccata	0110	(K)
Schwadron, A. A.	Duo in odd Meters	0110	(K)
Schwartz, E. 1936–	Essays (1966)	0110	Tetra, 1968
Uber, D.	Programme Duets	0110	Musicus
	Double Portraits	0011	Brodt, 1967

4.2 *Three Instruments*

Ardévol, J. 1911–	Tercera Sonata a tres	0210	IIM, 1945
Armbruster, R.	Scarlattina	1110	(Schweiz)
Bassett, L. 1923–	Trio	1110	King, 1968
Beckwith, J. 1927–	Five Pieces	1110	CMC
Bentzon, N. V. 1919–	Trio, Op 82	1110	Hansen, 1964
Bialosky, M.	Two Movements	1110	King, 1954
Blacher, B. 1903–	Divertimento, Op 31 (1948)	0110-pf	B. & B., 1958
Borris, S. 1906–	Suite	0210	Möseler [1961?]
Breydert, F. M.	Trio	0210	AMP, 1968

185

Brun, H. 1918–	Trio	0110-perc	(p. London, Sept., 1966)
Bull	Concert	1110	(K)
Butterworth, A. 1923–	Trio (1962)	1110	Feldman
Butts, C. M.	Ode for low brass	0021/ 0011-bar	Pro Art, 1966
	Suite for brass	0210	Pro Art, 1966
Cabus, P. 1923–	Sonata a tre	1110	Maurer, 1962
Childs, B. 1926–	Trio	1110	CFE
	Divertimento (1959)	1110	CFE
Cowell, J.	Trio	1110	Camara, 1960
Cox, H.	Theme & Variations	1110	Maurer, 1967
Croley, R.	Sonata	0110-pf	Tritone, 1964
Dedrick, A.	Three to go	1110/0210	Kendor, 1966
Desprez, F.	Triptyque	1020	Maurer
Diercks, J. 1927–	Figures on China	1011	Tenuto, 1968
Donner, H. O. 1939–	Siamfoni	1110	(Ri)
Ducommun, S. 1914–	Petit Concert	1110	Horn Realm
Fink, R. 1914–	Modal Suite	1110	(K)
Flothuis, M. 1914–	Sonatine, Op 26 (1945)	1110	Donemus, 1946
Frackenpohl, A. 1924–	Trio	1110	Ensemble
Ginzburg, D.	Trittico	0210	IMP, 1963
Glasser, S. 1926–	Trio (1957)	0210	Musica Rara, 1959
Haan, S. de 1921–	Three Pieces	0111/0210	Hinrichsen, 1959
Haubiel, C. 1894–	Athanaeum Suite	1110	CP
Henry, O.	Variations	1110	Washington, Composer, 1961
Hogg, M.	Three Short Pieces	1110	(K)
Hughes, M.	Divertimento	1110	Tritone, 1964
Jong, C. de	Suite of Wisconsin Folk Music	1110	Templeton, 1964
Karjalainen, A. 1907–	Partita No. 1, Op 4	1110	MS? (Gor, Ri)
	Partita No. 2, Op 13	1110	(Ri)
Knab, A. 1881–1951	Sechzehn Choräle, 2 vols	0210	Br. & H.
Knight, M. 1933–	Cassation	1110	Tritone, 1962
Koepke, P.	Lonely River	0110-pf	Rubank, 1959
	Gaudy Dance	0110-pf	Rubank, 1959
Kohs, E. 1916–	Trio No. 1 (1957)	1110	CFE
Kox, H. 1930–	Kleine Suite (1958)	0210	Donemus, 1958
	Vier didactische Stukken	0210	Donemus, 1964

Kroeger, K. 1932–	Sonata breve	1110	Tritone, 1962
Kubizek, A. 1918–	Vier Stücke	0210	(K)
Leclercq, E.	Suite classique	1110	Brogneaux, 1959
Lessard, J. 1920–	Quodlibets	0210	GMPC, 1968
Lester	Three Pieces	0210	WIM
Lombardo, R.	Trio	1110	MBE
Louel, J. 1914–	Trio (1951)	1110	CeBeDeM, 1956
Lyon, D. 1938–	Little Suite, Op 11 (1966)	1110	Ascherberg, 1966
Macero, T. 1925–	Structure No. 2	0111	CFE
	Trio	0210	CFE
Maganini, Q. 1897–	Aria	0110-pf	(K)
Maniet, R.	Trio No. 1	1110	Maurer, 1958
Marek, R.	Trio	1110	King, 1959
Masso, G.	Trio	1110	Providence, 1966
Mayer, W. 1925–	†Country Fair (1962)	0210	Bo. & H., 1963
Meulemans, A. 1884–1966	Trio No. 1 (1930)	1110	Brogneaux, 1933
	Trio No. 2	1110	CeBeDeM, 1961
Moser, R. 1892–1960	Trio	1110	Horn Realm
Nagel, R. 1924–	Trio	1110	Mentor
Nelhybel, V. 1919–	†Trio	1110	GMPC, 1965
Orowan, T.	Trio, Op 1	0011-bar/ 0021	Musicus, 1965
Ostrander, A.	Suite	0210/1110	Musicus
Pelemans, W. 1901–	Sonata (1956)	1110	Maurer, 1956
Petersen, T.	Divertimento	1110	Kendor, 1964
Poser, H. 1917–	Kleine Suite	0210	Möseler, 1967
Poulenc, F. 1899–1963	†Sonata (1922)	1110	Chester, 1924
Presser, W. 1916–	Prelude, Fugue & Postlude	1110	Louisville, 1966
Quinet, M. 1915–	Sonata à trois	1110	CeBeDeM, 1961
Regner, H. 1928–	Spiel für drei Bläser	0210	Schott, 1960
	Three Pieces	0210	Grosch, n.d.; Schott
Reid, A.	November Nocturne	1110/ 0210-opt vib	Kendor, 1966
Roberts, W.	Walk in the Country	1110	Cor
Roussakis, N.	Composition	1110	Colombo, 1967
Ruelle, F.	Trio	1110	Maurer, 1965
Sanders, R. L. 1906–	Trio	1110	King, 1961

Scharrès, C.	Divertimento	1110	Brogneaux, 1958
Schmidt, W.	Sonatina	1011	WIM, 1968
Sear, W. E.	Demonstration Piece	0210	Cor
Šimai, P. 1930–	Introduzione ed Allegro (1958)	1110	SHF; Horn Realm
Spezzaferri, G. 1888–1963	Preludio e Fuga, Op 81 (1947)	0210	SZ
Srámek, V. 1923–	Trio (1956)	0210	SHV, 1962
Thielman, R.	Two Moods	1110/0210	Kendor, 1962
Thilman, J. P. 1906–	Trio-Musik	0210	Hofmeister; MV, 1953
Van der Moortel, A. 1918–	Divertimento, No. 2	1110	Maurer
Vellère	Two Essais	1110	Maurer
Werner, J. J.	Canzoni per sonar	1110	EMT, 1966
Westcott, F.	Prelude, Pavan & Galliard	1110/ 0111	Hinrichsen, 1962
White, J. 1938–	Trio	0011-pf	(MT, Sept., 1968
Wigglesworth, F. 1918–	Trio Sonata (1953)	0210	CFE
Wright, J. 1911–	Trio (1964)	1110	Horn Realm; BMIC
Wuorinen, C. 1938–	Trio Sonata	0210	CFE
Young, P. M. 1912–	Theme & Variations (1961)	1110	MS
Zbinden, J. F. 1917–	Trio de cuivres, Op 13	1110	Sidem, 1958

4.3 *Four Instruments*

Addison, J. 1920–	†Divertimento, Op 9	1210	Williams, 1954
Albert, K. 1901–	Quartet	4 br	(WWM)
Ameller, A. 1912–	Epigraphe pour un Morte heroïque	0031	
Andriessen, J. 1925–	Introduction & Allegro (1958)	1210	Donemus, 1958
Ashpole, A. 1892–	Three Quartets	4 br	(WWM)
Asriel, A. 1922–	Shakespeare-Suite	0220	MS (VDK)
Badings, H. 1907–	Drie Nederlandse Dansen (1950)	1210	Lispet
	Koperqwartet (1947)	1210	Jeanette
Baker, D. N.	Hymn & Deviations	1111	MBQ, n.d.
Barrell, B. 1919–	Suite, Op 21 (1959)	0220/2110	BMIC
Beckerath, A. von 1901–	Tanz, Magdlein, tanz	0220	Hieber, 1951

Beethoven, L. von 1770–1827	Three Equali (Arr. E. Kahn)	0130	Marks, 1947
Berger, J. 1909–	Intrada	0220/1210	King, 1961
Berghout, J. C. b. 1869	Suite	0031	Donemus
Bergsma, W. 1921–	Suite (1942)	0211	C. Fischer, 1946
Bernstein, L. 1918–	Fanfare for Bima	1111	G. Schirmer, 1950, 1962
Beversdorf, T. 1924–	Three Epitaphs (1955)	1210/0220	Interlochen, n.d.; Southern, 1966
Biersack, A. 1908–	Konzertante Musik	1210	Hofmeister, 1958
Boda, J. 1922–	Prelude, Scherzo, Postlude	1210	Louisville, 1965
Boedijn, G. 1893–	Quartet No. 2, Op 111	1210	Donemus, 1961
	Quartet No. 4	4 br	Donemus
Borowsky, F. 1872–1956	Morning Song	1210	Bo. & H.
Bozza, E. 1905–	Three Pieces	0031	Leduc, 1964
Bright, H. 1916–	Legende & Canon	0220/1210	AMP, 1953
Bruckner, A. 1824–96	Locus iste (Arr. M. Moore)	2110	Arco, 1967
Buchtel, F. L. 1899–	Choral & processional March	1210	Kjos, 1961
	Canzonetta	1210	Kjos, 1961
Burgon, G. 1941–	Divertimento (1964)	1210	Chappell, 1965
	Five Studies (1965)	0220	Chappell, 1967
	Fanfares & Variants	0220	Stainer, 1969
Butterworth, A. 1923–	Quartet (1962)	1210/0220	MS (CG)
	Scherzo (1958)	0220	Hinrichsen, 1965
Butterworth, N. 1934–	Four Motets	1210	Chappell, 1967
	Three XVI Century Motets	1210/0211	NWM, 1965
Cabus, P. 1923–	Lento	0220	Maurer, 1963
Catelinet, P. 1910–	Two Divertissements	1030	Hinrichsen
Cazden, N. 1914–	Three Directions, Op 39 (1941)	0220/ 0210-bar	AMP, 1949
Chailley, J. 1910–	Suite du XVe Siècle	1210	(K)
Chase, A.	Quartet No. 1	1210/0220	Camara, 1960
Cohen, S. B. 1891–	Quartet	1210	Belwin
	Four Travellers	1210	G. Schirmer, 1962

Cole, G.	Seven Impressions	0031	AMP, 1960
Conley, L.	Concert Polka	0220	Kendor, 1965
	Three early sacred Pieces	1210	Artransa, 1965
Coscia, S.	Concert Suite	3010	(K)
Cox, H.	Two Hymns	0220	Maurer
Cruft, A. 1921–	Four English Keyboard Pieces	1210	Williams, 1955
Cumberworth, S.	Overture	0220	(AMC)
Cundell, E. 1893–1961	Two Pieces	1210	Williams, 1957
Daems, H.	Grickse Suite	1210	Maurer
Dalby, M. 1942–	Divertimento (1966)	1210	BMIC
Dedrick, A.	Waltz for four	0220	Kendor, 1964
Dempster, S.	Quartet No. 1	0220	Ensemble, 1963
Desprez, F.	Jeunesse	0310-opt timp	Maurer, 1958
	Divertissement	0310-opt timp	Maurer, 1963
Diercks, J. 1927–	Quartet	1210	Tenuto, 1966
Dillon, H. 1912–	Marche & Chorale	0310	(K)
Donahue, R.	Five Pieces	0220	Tenuto, 1968
Donato, A. 1909–	Suite	1210	Interlochen, 1961
Drakeford, R. 1936–	Suite from Dr. Faustus (1962)	0220	BMIC
Dubensky, A. 1890–	Concerto grosso	0031	Ricordi, 1950
Fegers, K.	Frisch auf ins weite Feld	0220	Möseler, 1964
Felderhof, J. 1907–	Divertimento (1950)	1210	Donemus
Filippi, A. de 1900–	Suite	1210	Elkan, 1966
Fiorello, D. 1905–	Summer Music (1948)	1210	Educational Pubs.
Fitzgerald, B.	Lento	1210	Belwin
	Tarantella	1210	Belwin
Frackenpohl, A. 1924–	Quartet	0220	King, 1950
Gabaye, P. 1930–	Récréation	1110-pf	Leduc, 1958
Gardner, J. 1917–	Theme & Variations, Op 7	1210	OUP, 1953
Genzmer, H. 1909–	Musik für vier Bläser	0220	Peters
Geraedts, J. 1924–	Kleine Kopermuziek (1951)	1210	Donemus, 1953
Glatz, H.	Quartet (1964)	0130	BMIC

190

Glazunov, A. 1865–1936	In Modo religioso, Op 38 (Ed R. King)	1111 1111 1120	Belaieff, 1893 King Marks, 1948; IMC
		1210	Rubank
Grant, W. P. 1910–	Laconic Suite No. 1	1210	CFE
	Excursions: Suite No. 2	1210	CFE
	Brevities: Suite No. 3	1210	CFE
Guentzel, G.	Impromptu	1210	Barnhouse
	Festival Days	0220	Barnhouse
Haddad, E.	Quartet	1210	(MBE)
Haines, E. 1914–	†Toccata	0220/ 0210-bar	King, 1949, 1958
Hartley, W. S. 1927–	Solemn Music	0220	Presser, 1969
Heiss, H. 1897–	Trompetenmusik (1934)	0220	Br. & H., 1960
Heldenberg, A.	Quartet (1954)	1210	Brogneaux, 1954
Hemel, O. van 1892–	Four brass Quartets (1955)	1210	Donemus, 1955
Henry, O.	Quartet	1210	Composer, 1963
Holshauser, E. G.	First Theme & Chorale	0211	MS (MBE)
Hovhaness, A. 1911–	†Sharagan & Fugue	1210	King, 1950
Jacob, G. 1895–	Scherzo (1944)	1210	Williams, 1954
Jacques, M. 1944–	Divertimento No. 4 (1968)	1210	BMIC
Jones, E. L.	Soriano March	0220	CP, 1959; Elkan
Karkoff, M. 1927–	Quartet, Op 33 (1958)	1210	FST
Kay, U. 1917–	†Quartet (1952)	0220	Peer, 1958
Kayser, L. 1919–	Variazioni sopra In Dulci Jubilo	1111	Composer, 1964?
Keller, H. 1915–	Quartet	1210	King, 1954
Kerry, B.	Fanfare & March	1210	Chappell, 1967
Kesnar, M.	Intermezzo	1210	Presser, 1957
Ketting, O. 1935–	Sonata (1955)	1210	Donemus, 1957
King, R.	Prelude & Fugue	0210-bar	King, 1946
Klein, J. 1915–	Sonata	0220	AMP, 1950
Knight, M. 1933–	Three Quartets	0220	Tritone, 1962
	Six Quartets	0220	Tritone, 1966
Knox, C. 1929–	Solo for Trumpet	solo trp, 1110	Louisville, 1966
Koepke, P.	Canzona	0210-pf	Rubank, 1959
Koetsier, J. 1911–	†Kleine Suite, Op 33/1a (1947)	1210	Donemus, 1954
	Kleine Suite, Op 33/1b (1947)	0220	Donemus, 1957

	Quartettino, Op 33/2 (1950)	1210	Donemus
	Koraal en Fuga over Neem, Heer, mijn beide Handen, Op 33/3 (1947)	1210	Donemus
Kraft, K. J. 1903–	Augsburger Turamichele-Musik (1946)	0210-bells	MS (MGG)
Krapf, G.	Choral Intradas, 2 vols	0220	Concordia, 1963
Kreisler, A. von	Concert Piece	1210	Southern, 1965
	Music	1210	Southern, 1966
Kuusisto, I. T. 1933–	Music for Easter Sunday	4 br	(Ri)
Landré, G. 1905–68	Quartetto piccolo (1961)	1210	Donemus, 1962
Leontovich, H.	Two Ukranian Songs	1210	RS
Levy, F.	Concertpiece	1120	(K)
Lewallen, J.	Quartet (1952)	0110-ct, bar	MS (D)
Link, J. D. 1925–	Kleine Dresdner Spielmusik	0220	Hofmeister, 1963
Lo Presti, R. 1933–	Miniature	1210/0220	Shawnee, 1964
Lovelock, W. 1899–	Three Pieces	1210	Chappell, 1965
Lucký, S. 1919–	Quartet	1210	MS?
Lutyens, E. 1906–	The Tyme doth flete, Op 70; Prelude & Postlude	0220	Olivan
McCabe, J. 1939–	Fantasy, Op 35 (1965)	1210	Novello, 1966
McKay, F. H.	Adagio assai & Allegro vivace	0220	Presser; Gamble
	Four Pieces, Op 10	0220	Witmark
	Suite No. 2	0220/1120	Gamble
	Pageantry	0220/1210	Barnhouse, 1965
	Interlude	1210	Barnhouse
McKay, G. F. 1899–	Two Pieces in American Folk Style	0220/1210	Presser
Maganini, Q. 1897–	Medeovale	1210/0220	Musicus, 1940
	Lament	1210	Musicus
Melartin, E. 1875–1937	Quartet, Op 153	1210	(Gor)
Minkler, C.	Madrigal for brass	0220	Kendor, 1964
Mitchell, L. 1923–	Folk Suite	1210	Rochester, 1955
Mokrousoff, B. 1909–	Quartet	0220	MS? (G)
Müller-Zürich, P. 1898–	Choralfantasie: Christ ist erstanden	0210-org	MS? (MGG)
Muncaster, C. 1936–	Banbury Brass (1965)	0220	Chandos
Murphy, L.	Etude No. 1	1210/0220	Avant, 1964

Naginski, C. 1909–40	Divertimento (1939)	2110	MS (Fleisher)
Nelhybel, V. 1919–	†Piano-brass Quartet	1110-pf	GMPC, 1964
Nicholson, R. W. 1907–	March	4 br	(WWM)
Norden, H. 1909–	A solemn Musick, Op 15	0211	Bo. & H., 1950
Nuten, P.	Intermezzo	1210	(K)
Orrego-Salas, J. 1919–	Concertino, Op 54	1210	Peer, 1967
Osborne, W. 1906–	Canzone	1210	King
Ostrander, A.	Baroque Suite	1210	Musicus
Ostransky, L.	Suite	1210	Rubank
Otten, L. 1924–	Two Suites (1966)	1210	Donemus, 1967
Parfrey, R. J. 1928–	Little Suite (1967)	1210	BMIC
Parris, H. M.	Seven Moods	1210	EV, 1948
Parshall	Quartet in B♭	1210	Belwin
Peña, A.	Prelude & Fugue No. 3	4 br	Peer, 1968
Pfannenstiel, E. 1896–	Sechs Bläserstücke	0220	Möseler, 1967
Phillips, B. 1907–	Prelude	1120/0220	EV
Piket, F. 1903–	Dance & March	0220	AMP, 1952
Pisk, P. 1893–	Quartet, Op 72 (1951)	1210	CFE
Ploner, J. E. 1894–	Kleine Blechbläsermusik	1210	Grosch, n.d.
Polson, R.	Scherzo	0220	Interlochen, n.d.
Pozajić, M.	Skica	1210	UKBH, 1958
Praag, H. C. van 1894–	Sonata (1950)	1210	Donemus, 1950
Premru, R. E. 1934–	Quartet (1960)	1210	Premru Music
Presser, W. 1916–	Five Southern Songs	1120/0220	Elkan, 1967
Ramsoe, W. 1837–95	Quartet No. 1, Op 20	ct, ten hn, trb, tuba	Hansen, 1888
		0220	King, 1955; Ensemble
	Quartet No. 2, Op 29	ct, ten hn, trb, tuba	Hansen, 1888
		0220	King, 1955; Ensemble
	Quartet No. 4, Op 37	ct, ten hn, trb, tuba	Hansen, 1888
	(Ed R. King)	0211	King
	Quartet No. 5, Op 38	ct, ten hn, trb, tuba	Hansen, 1888
	(Ed R. King)	0211	King
Raphling, S. 1910–	Square Dance	0310	Musicus

Rasmussen, M.	Christmas Music	0211	King, 1959
Rathaus, K. 1895–1954	Invocation & Fanfare	1210	Bo. & H., 1955
Raymond, L.	Short Suite	1210	Avant, 1964
Regner, H. 1928–	Morgenruf	1210/0220	Möseler, 1961
Reinhold, O. 1899–1965	Musik (1953)	0210-org	MS (MGG, VDK)
Riegger, W. 1885–1961	Movement, Op 66	0210-pf	Peer, 1960
Rulst-Rema	Petite Fanfare	1210	Brogneaux, 1957
	Introduction & Finale	1210	Brogneaux, 1957
Rugolo, P. 1915–	Razing the 7th	0220	Alcove, 1965
Sabatini, G.	Puppet Waltz	1210	Camara, 1961
Salzberg, M.	Inventions Nos. 1 & 2	1210	CFE
Sanders, R. L. 1906–	Suite (1949)	0220	King, 1956
Scarmolin, 1890–	Improvviso	1210	C. Fischer
	Novelette	1210	Pro Art
	Pastel	1210	Bo. & H.
Schaeffer, D.	Hava nagila	0220	Pro Art, 1966
Schlag, E.	Joyful Divertissement	1210	C. Fischer
Schmitt, F. 1870–1958	Quartet, Op 109 (1946)	0031	MS
	Andante religioso from above	0031	Durand
Schmutz, A. D.	Air & Scherzo	1210	C. Fischer
	Choral Prelude	1210/0220	Ludwig, 1963
Schneider, W. 1907–	Tower Music	0220/1210	Noetzel, 1958
Schramm, H.	Chorale & Canon	4 br	(AMC)
Schuller, G. 1925–	Little Brass Music (1963)	1111	Mentor, 1967
Schulze, G.	Quartet (1908)	1210	Seeling
Schuster, G.	Intermezzo	1210	IMP, 1963
Sear, W. E.	Quartet	0211	Cor
Sehlbach, E. 1898–	Kleine Turmmusiken	0220	Möseler, 1957
Sertl, F.	Münchener Peterturmmusik	0220	Hieber, 1952
Shumway, S.	Intrada, Canzonet & Fugue	0220	Ensemble, 1963
Simon, A. 1850–1916	Sonatine, Op 23/1	1210	Jurgenson, 1889; Andraud
	Eight Quartets	4 br	Jurgenson, 1889
Smith, F.	Three Chorale Settings	0220/1111	King, 1962
Souris, A. 1899–	Choral, Marche & Galop	0220	CeBeDeM, 1956
	Petite Suite, Op 1	4 br	
Stabile	Suite	0220	Avant
Starer, R. 1924–	Dirge	0220	Presser, 1957

Stepanyan, A.	Nocturne	0031	
Stoker, R. 1938–	Five Movements (1964)	2110	BMIC
	Litany, Sequence & Hymn (1965)	0220	Hinrichsen, 1967
Stouffer, P.	Parade of the little green Spacemen	0310	Elkan, 1963
Straesser, J. 1934–	Music for brass	1210	Donemus, 1965
Strategeier, H. 1912–	Laat ons nu blij zijn	1210	Donemus
	Alleluia den blijden toon	1210	Donemus
Suter, R. 1919–	Fanfares et Pastorale	2110	(Schweiz)
Sydeman, W. 1928–	Fanfare & Variations	4 br	(AMC)
	Music for low brass	0031	(AMC)
Thilman, J. P. 1906–	Quartet	1210	Hofmeister, 1953
Thorpe, R. 1931–	Quartet	4 br	(WWM)
Trevarthen, R.	Sonata	1210	Louisville, 1966
Tuthill, B. C. 1888–	Fugue, Op 10/3	0220	C. Fischer, 1938
Uber, D.	Beachcomber's Dance	0220	Musicus
	Miniature Symphony	0220	G. Schirmer, 1955
	Two Compositions	1210/0211	Adler, 1960
	Two Pieces	0220/0211	Musicus
	Three Miniatures, Op 29	0031	Ensemble, 1967
Villa-Lobos, H. 1887–1959	†Chorôs No. 4 (1926)	3010	Eschig, 1928
Vinter, G. 1909–69	Fancy's Knell	4 br	Polyphonic, 1967
	Elegy & Rondo	4 br	Polyphonic, 1966
Walker, R.	Badinerie (1950)	1210	AMP, 1950
Walton, W. 1902–	Six Pieces, Set 1 (Arr. N. de Jongh)	0220	OUP, 1967
Werle, F. C. 1914–	March, Chorale & Fugue	0220	Musicus, 1956
Westcott, F.	Suite	1210/0211	Hinrichsen, 1962
Whear, P.	Prelude & Rondo	0211	Barnhouse, 1958
White, D. H. 1921–	Serenade No. 3	1210	(K)
White, F. H. 1884–1945	Fanfare for a Challenge to accepted ideas	1110-timp	G. & T., 1921
Whitney, M. C.	Quartet No. 1	0220/1210	C. Fischer,
Wickens, D. 1926–	Three Pieces (1961)	1210	BMIC
Wienandt, E. A.	Tu disois	1210	Pro Art, 1966
Wohlfahrt, F. 1894–	Festliche Fanfaren-Musik (1958)	0220	Sikorski, n.d.
Worthington, T.	Miniature Suite	4 br	Bo. & H., 1967
Wynne, D. 1900–	Suite (1959)	0220	MS (MGG)

	Quartet (Divertimento) (1962)	0220	BMIC
Zabel, F.	Four French Pieces (Arr. A. Ostrander)	1210	IMC, 1965
Zagwijn, H. 1878–1954	Prelude & Choral	1210	Lispet, n.d.
	Entrata giocosa (1952)	1210	Donemus, 1952

4.4 *Five Instruments*

Adler, S. 1925–	Five Movements	1211	King, 1965
Albert, K. 1901–	Quintet	5 br	(WWM)
Alexander, J.	Four for five	2210	(K)
Aliabev, A.	Quintet (Ed Usova)	2210	RS, 1960
Amram, D. 1930–	Fanfare & Processional	1211	Peters, 1968
Amy, G. 1936–	Relais	1220	(Times, 11 Oct., 1969)
Andriessen, H. 1892–	Suite (1951)	1220	Donemus
	Aubade (1952)	1220	Donemus
	Pezzo festoso	0220-org	Donemus, 1962
Andriessen, J. 1925–	Quattro Madrigale	1220	Donemus, 1962
Angelo, P.	Music for five brass instruments (1962)	1211	MS (MBE)
Archer, V. 1913–	Divertimento (1963)	1211	MBQ [1963]
Arnell, R. 1917–	Quintet	1211	Southern, 1968
Arnold, M. 1921–	†Quintet, Op 73	1211	Paterson, 1961
Ascher, R.	Quintet (1961)	1211	Mentor
Avarmaa, O. 1920–	Suite on Le Roi Renaud (1963)	1211	MBQ, 1964
	Theme & Variations	1211	MBQ [1967]
Bahret, A.	Quintet (1962)	1211	MS (MBE)
Baines, F. 1917–	Intrada & Fantasy	0230	Williams
Baker, D. N.	Passions	1211	MBQ [1966]
Balissat, J.	Sonata	1110-pf, perc	Horn Realm
Baron, S.	Impressions of a Parade; When Johhny comes Marching Home	1211	G. Schirmer, 1944, 1962
Bastien, G.	Exigence	1211	MBQ [1964]
Bazelon, I. 1922–	Quintet	1220	Bo. & H., 1965
Beaumont, A. 1937–	Sonata	0230	BMIC
Berman, M.	Quintet	1211	MBQ, n.d. [1967]
Beversdorf, T. 1924–	Cathedral Music	0220-org	King

Billingsley, W.	Suite (1955)	1211	MS (MBE)
Boreschansky, E.	Quintet	1211	MS (MBE)
Bornefeld, H. 1906–	Sonatine	0221	Hänssler
Bourgeois, D. 1941–	Quintet (1965)	1211	BMIC
Boutry, R. 1932–	Prélude, Choral et Fugue	1211	Leduc, 1967
Bowers-Broadbent, C. 1945–	Dialogue & Controversy	0220-org	(MT, Sept., 1966; WWM)
	Dogmas	4 br, timp	(WWM)
Bozza, E. 1905–	Sonatina	1211	Leduc, 1951
	Suite No. 2	1211	MBQ, 1967
	Suite	2210	
	Suite française	1211	Leduc, 1967
	Giration	1211	Leduc, 1967
Brant, H. 1913–	†Millenium IV	1211	(Schwann; MT, June, 1967)
Brehm, A. 1925–	Quintet	1211	(Gram, Nov., 1969)
Broiles, M.	Ensemble Profiles (1962)	1211	Mentor
Brott, A. 1915–	Mutual Salvation Orgy (1962)	1211	MBQ, n.d.
Brown, R. 1912–	Brass Quintet No. 2	1211	Avant, 1963
Bubalo, R. 1927–	†Three Pieces (1959)	1211	Galaxy, 1968
Cabus, P. 1923–	Elegie	1220	Maurer
Calvert, M. 1928–	Suite from the Monteregian Hills (1962)	1211	MBQ [1963]; Ensemble
	An Occasional Suite	1211	MBQ, 1967
Canning, T. 1911–	Four Christmas Pieces	1211	CFE
Cheetham, J.	†Scherzo	1211	Avant, 1965
Cherubini, L. 1760–1842	Eight Marches (Ed K. Haas)	3110	Mills, 1962
Childs, B. 1926–	†Variations sur une Chanson du Canotier (1963)	1211	MBQ, n.d.; Ensemble, 1965
	Quintet	1111-pf	CFE
	2nd Quintet	1211	CFE
Civil, A. 1929–	†Tarantango	1211	MS
Cobine, A.	Trilogy (1960)	1211	MBQ [1963]; Ensemble, 1966
Connolly, J. 1933–	Cinquepaces (1966)	1211	BMIC
Converse, F. S. 1871–1940	Two lyric Pieces, Op 106	0211-bar/ 1211	Rubank, 1939
Coscia, S.	Madrigal & Fugue	1211	(K)

Cowell, H. 1897–1965	Action in brass	1220	Musicus, 1943
	Supplication	0220-org	(K)
Croley, R.	Disquisition, Cyclic Chorale	1211	Tritone
Dahl, I. 1912–	†Music for brass instruments (1944)	1220-opt tuba	Witmark, 1949
Dela, M. 1919–	Divertissement (1963)	1211	MBQ [1963]
Dickinson, P. 1934–	Music for brass (1954)	0320	Novello
Dieterich, M.	Horizons	1211	Rubank, 1959
Dodgson, S. 1924–	Sonata (1963)	1211	MS (CG)
Drakeford, R. 1936–	Tower Music (1966)	1211	Novello, 1968
Dubois, T. 1837–1924	Alleluia (Arr. C. Kingsbury)	0310-org	Gray
Dunnigan, P.	Quintet	1211	MS (MBE)
Easdale, B. 1909–	†Cantilena (1962)	1211	MS (CG, MBE)
Elmore, R. 1913–	Meditation on Veni Emmanuel	0220-org	(K)
Etler, A. D. 1913–	†Quintet (1963)	1211	AMP, 1967
	Sonic Sequence (1967)	1220	Continuo, 1968
Ewald, V. 1860–1935	Quintet in b♭, Op 5 (1911) (Arr. R. King)	1211	King, 1957
Farberman, H. 1929–	†Five Images (1964)	1211	GMPC
Fleming, R. 1921–	Three Miniatures (3–4–5) (1962)	1211	MBQ, n.d.
	Quintet (1965)	1211	MBQ [1966]
Frackenpohl, A. 1924–	†Quintet (1961)	1211	EV, 1966
Goldstein, M.	Stillpoint (1962)	1211	MS (MBE)
Grant, W. P. 1910–	Lento & Allegro	1211	CFE, AMC
Gregson, E. 1945–	†Quintet (1967)	1211	Novello, 1968
Grey, G. 1934–	Divertimento pastorale (1968)	1211	BMIC
Gubby, R. 1911–	Entry of the Alumni	0230	(fp, 28 Nov. 1969)
Hamilton, I. 1922–	Quintet (1964)	1211	Schott, 1966
Hammond, D. 1917–	†Quintet	1211	Mentor
Hannenheim, N. von	Volksmusik	1211	
Harries, D. 1933–	Quintet, Op 30	5 br	(MT, Feb, 1969)
Harris, Arthur 1927–	†Four Moods (1957)	1211	Mentor, 1960

Hartley, W. S. 1927–	Quintet	1211	Tritone, 1963
	†Divertissement (1965)	1211	Ensemble, 1966
Haufrecht, H. 1909–	Introduction, Ceremonial & Passacaglia	1211	CFE
	Suite	1211	AMP, 1965
Heiden, B. 1910–	Four Dances (1967)	1211	Broude, 1968
Henkemans, H. 1913–	Aere festivo (1965)	0320	Donemus, 1966
Henry, O.	Four Bantu Songs	1211	Composer, n.d.
Hens, C. 1898–	Quintet	5 br	(La)
Hindemith, P. 1895–1963	†Plöner-Musiktag No. 1; Morgenmusik (1932)	0221	Schott, 1932
Hogg, M.	Invention	1211	(K)
Holmboe, V. 1909–	Quintet, Op 79 (1962)	1211	Hansen, 1967
Horovitz, J. 1926–	†Music Hall Suite (1964)	1211	Novello, 1969
Hoskins, W. B.	Allegro ostinato	1211	CFE
	Andante	1211	CFE
Howarth, E. 1935–	Variations	5 br	(MT, Sept., 1968)
Hübschmann, W. 1901–	Musik	0230	Hofmeister, 1952
Huggler, J. 1928–	Quintet	1211	CML, 1963
Ives, C. 1874–1954	Processional: Let there be light	0040-org	Peer, 1967
	†From the Steeples & the Mountains (1901)	0220-carillon	(Gram., Nov. 1969)
Jones, C. 1910–	Four Movements for brass	1211/1220	S. Fox, 1965
	Quintet (1957)	1211	Mentor, 1965
Jong, C. de	Essay	1211	(K)
Karlin, F.	Quintet	1211	MS (MBE)
Kiessig, G. 1885–	Intrada	1220	Parrhysius, 1938
King, R.	Prelude & Fugue	0220-org	King, 1953
Klerk, A. de 1917–	Intrada	5 br	Donemus
Koch, J. H. E. 1918–	Nach dem Winter da kommt der Sommer	0320	BVK, 1957
Korn, P. J. 1922–	Prelude & Scherzo	1211	Bo. & H., 1967
	Prelude & Scherzo	1220	Bo. & H., 1967
Korte, K.	Introductions	1211	EV, 1968
Kroeger, K. 1932–	Partita	1211	Presser, 1969
Kruyf, T. de 1937–	Aubade in due tempi	1211	Donemus, 1967
Kubik, G. 1914–	Celebrations (1958)	5 br	MS (MGG)

Kunz, A. 1929–	Three Fanfares (1964)	1211-opt timp, perc	CMC
Kvapil, J. 1892–1958	Quintet in e (1925)	1220	MS (Ga, MGG)
Lauber, J. 1864–1952	Dans le Montagne	1210-pf	Horn Realm
Lawner, M.	Chorale, Improvisation & Serenade (1963)	1211	(MS MBE)
Lebow, L.	Quintet	1211	Chicago Brass Ensemble
	Popular Suite	1211	(K)
Leclerc, M.	Par Monts et par Vaux	1211	Maurer, 1959
Legrady, T. 1920–	Suite (1963)	1211	MBQ [1963]
	Divertimento	1211	(K)
Lenel, L.	Introduction & Allegro (1962)	1211	Mentor
Levy, F.	Fantasy	1211	Cor
Lockwood, N. 1906–	Concerto for organ & brasses (1951)	0220-org	AMP
London	Quintet (1965)	5 br	(MT, Dec., 1965)
Lubin, E.	Partita	1211	MS (MBE)
McCabe, J. 1939–	†Rounds (1967)	1211	Novello, 1968
McGrath, J. J. 1889–1968	†Six Brevities, Op 31	1211	(Schwann)
McKay, G. F. 1899–	Sonatina expressiva	1210-bar	Southern, 1966
McKie, J. G.	Andante	1211	Ensemble, 1966
	Theme for a Carousel	1211	Ensemble, 1966
McLean, H.	Sonatina	1211	(AMC)
Maes, J. 1905–	Prelude & Allegro (1959)	1211	CeBeDeM, 1963
Maganini, Q. 1897–	A Flourish for a Hero	1220	(K)
Marshall, N. 1942–	Suite (1967)	1211	BMIC
Mašek, V. 1755–1831	Il Marcia per il giorna della Festa dei tre Re	0310–timp	MS? (MGG)
Masters, R. L.	Quintet	1220	Music Press
Maurer, L. W. 1789–1878	Scherzo & Lied (Ed R. Nagel)	2210/1211	Mentor, 1961
	†Three Pieces (Ed R. Nagel)	2210/1211	Mentor, 1960
	Four Songs (Ed R. Nagel)	2210	Mentor, 1967
Meester, L. de 1904–	Postludium	0220-org/ 0330-org	CeBeDeM, 1965
Micheelsen, H. F. 1902–	Ei du feiner Reiter: Variationen	0230	BVK, 1956
Mills, C. 1914–	Quintet	1220	CFE
Monnikendam, M. 1896–	Concerto in D	0220-org	Donemus, 1956

Morel, F. 1926–	Quintette pour cuivres (1962)	1211	MBQ, n.d.
Morgan, G.	Quintet (1959)	1211	MS (MBE)
Moss, L. 1927–	Music for five	1220/1211	Merion, 1965
Müller-Zürich, P. 1898–	Choraltoccata: Ein feste Burg, Op 54/1 (1953)	0220-org	BVK, 1956
	Choralfantasie: Wie schön leuchtet der Morgenstern, Op 54/2 (1953)	0220-org	BVK, 1956
Nagel, R. 1924–	March; This old Man	1211	Mentor, 1960
	Suite	1111-pf	Mentor
Nelhybel, V. 1919–	Quintet No. 1	1211	GMPC, 1968
Ostransky, L.	Character Variations on a modal theme	1211	Rubank, 1959
Papineau-Couture, J. 1916–	Canons (1964)	1211	CMC
Patterson, P. 1947–	Toccata for Ifor James	0211 solo hn	Mitchell
	Symphonia (1966)	1211	BMIC
Peeters, F. 1903–	Choral Fantasy on Christ the Lord is risen	0220-org	Gray, 1961
	†Intrada festiva, Op 93	0220-timp, ch ad lib	Peters, 1959
Persichetti, V. 1915–	Parable	1211	(K)
Petyrek, F. 1892–1952	Schlussmusik zum Eintedankfest	1211	Ullmann, 1940
Pfannenstiel, E. 1896–	Intrada No. 1 (Ed W. Schneider)	0320	Schott, 1962
Pfautsch, L.	Choral Prelude: If thou but suffer God to guide thee	0220-org	King, 1961
Phillips, P. 1930–	†Music for brass quintet	1220	(Gram, Nov. 1969)
Pinkham, D. 1923–	Sonata for organ & brasses	0220-org	CFE
	Gloria from Sinfonia sacra	0220-org	King, 1968
Pisk, P. 1893–	Introduction & Allegro (1962)	1211	MS (MBE)
Poot, M. 1901–	Impromptu	0011-saxhn, bar, pf	Eschig
Presser, W. 1916–	Folksong Fantasy	1211	Elkan, 1955
	Quintet (1965)	1211	Louisville, 1961
	Quintet No. 2	1211	(K)
Prévost, A. 1934–	Mouvement (1963)	1211	MBQ [1964]
Purdy, W. 1941–	Music for brass (1963)	1211	MBQ [1963]

Raph, A.	Call & Response	1211	Musicus, 1962
Rathaus, K. 1895–1954	Tower Music	0230/1220	AMP, 1960
Rebner, W. 1910–	Variations	1220	Modern, 1962
Reynolds, V.	Suite	1211	MS (D)
Riddle, N.	Three Quarter Suite	1211	MCA, 1966
Rieti, V. 1898–	Incisioni	5 br	GMPC
Roberts, W.	Three Headlines	1211	Cor, 1960
	Dixie	1211	Cor, 1961
Robinson, K.	Quintet (1963)	1211	MS (MBE)
Rolle	Quintet No. 1 (Ed H. Voxman)	1211	Rubank
	Quintet No. 2 (Ed. H. Voxman)	1211	Rubank
Sanders, R. L. 1906–	†Quintet in B♭ (1942)	1220	Music Press, 1948
Sauguet, H. 1901–	Golden Suite (1963)	1211	EMT, 1967
Schmidt, W. 1926–	†Variations on a negro song	1211	Avant, 1959
	Suite No. 1	1211	Avant, 1967
	Suite No. 2	1211	Avant
Schmutz, A. D.	Prelude & Gavotte	1211	SB
	Rondo in F	1211	SB
Schneider, W. 1907–	Kleine Feiermusik	0230/0221	Schott, 1967
Schule, B. 1909–	†Résonances, Op 58	1211	MS (MBE)
Schuller, G. 1925–	†Music for brass quintet (1961)	1211	AMP, 1962
Schwartz, E. 1936–	Three Movements	1211	MS (AMC)
Sear, W. E.	Quintet	1211	UBS
	Two Inventions	1211	Cor
Seeger, P. 1919–	Kleine Jagdgeschichte	1310	(K)
Siegner, E.	Invention in brass	1211	MBQ [1964]
Simon, A. 1850–1916	Four Quintets, Op 26	1211	Jurgenson, 1889
	No. 1 (Ed Wilson)	1211	Gamble
	No. 2 (Ed W. Sear)	1211	UBS
Snyder, R.	Variations on a Folk Theme	1211	S. Fox, 1968
Spears, J.	Four Miniatures	1211	Tenuto, 1968
Spirea, A.	Music for brass	1211	Israeli Composers League, 1962
Starer, R. 1924–	†Five Miniatures	2210	Southern, 1952
Steiner, G.	Quintet	5 br	(AMC)
Stevens, B. 1916–	Two Improvisations on Folksongs, Op 24 (1954)	0230	Galliard, 1964
Stoltz, W.	Symphony for brass	1211	UBS

Stratton, D.	Variations on an English Folk Tune	1211	Cor
	Chorale & Fugue	1211	MS (MBE)
Swain, F. 1902–	Solemn Salutation (1951)	2210	BMIC
Swanson, H. 1909–	Sound Piece (1952)	1211	Weintraub, 1953
Tanenbaum, 1924–	Structures	1211	CFE
Tice, D.	Four Pieces	0220-timp	Ann Arbor, 1956
Tisné, A.	Stances minoennes	1211	Leduc, 1967
Townsend, D. 1921–	Tower Music	1211	MS (MBE)
Trexler, G. 1903–	Quintet (1954)	0230	MS (VDK)
Tull, F.	Demonstration Piece	1211	Avant, 1964
Turner, R. 1920–	Four Fragments (1961)	1220	CMC
Uber, D.	Advanced Quintet	1211	Adler, 1960
	Chinese Legend	1211	(K)
	Greensleeves	1211	Musicus, 1960
	Adventures of a tin horn	1211	Musicus, 1962
	A Day at Camptown Races	1211	Musicus, 1957
	Lo, How a Rose e'er blooming	1211	Brodt, 1967
Valcourt, J.	Pentaphonie	1211	MBQ [1965]
Ward-Steinman, D. 1936–	Quintet	1211	MS (MBE)
Waxman, E. 1918–	†Capriccio (1962)	1211	MS (MBE)
Weille, B.	Quintet	1211	Cor
Werdin, E. 1911–	Kleine Suite	0320	Schott, 1958
	10 European Dances	0230	Möseler
Whear, P.	Invocation & Study	1211/1220	King, 1960
White, D. H. 1921–	Serenade in brass No. 3	1211	Shawnee, 1965
Whittenberg, C. 1927–	†Triptych (1962)	1211	(Schwann)
Wigglesworth, F. 1918–	Quintet (1956)	1211	CFE
Wilder, A. 1907–	†Suite (1959)	1211	Mentor, 1960
	Quintet No. 2	1211	(K)
	Effie joins the Carnival	1211	(K)
Würz, R. 1885–1965	Turmmusik Nr. 4: Abendmusik	0230	Br. & H., 1954
Young, P. 1912–	Music for brass	1211	MBQ, 1964
	Triptych (1962)	1211	MS (MBE)
Zaninelli, L. 1932–	Designs	0221/1220/0230	Templeton, 1963
Zindars, E.	Quintet	1211	King, 1958

Zipp, F. 1914–	Sonne der Gerechtigkeit	0220-org	BVK, 1968
Zverev, V.	Suite	1220	RS, 1959

4.5 *Six Instruments*

Applebaum, L. 1918–	†Three Stratford Fanfares (1953)	0330-opt tuba, timp, perc	Leeds (Can)
Atherton, P. 1910–	Diversions on a fourth	6 br	Polyphonic, 1965
Bales, G.	Fanfare for Easter Day	0220-org, timp	BMI (Can)
Bartsch, C.	Fanfare, Cantilène et Danse	1410	Maurer, 1965
Becker, A.	Paean	1211-bar	Remick
	Romance	1211-bar	Remick
Beckerath, A. von 1901–	Tower Music, Vol. 1	0330	Noetzel, 1957
Bender, J. 1909–	Come Holy Ghost, God & Lord	0230-org	(K)
Bezanson, P. 1916–	Prelude & Dance	1221	Interlochen, 1961
Böhme, O.	Sextet, Op 30 (1911)	1211-bar	Witmark, 1934
Borowsky, F. 1872–1956	Moods	1211-bar	Bo. & H., 1955
	Twilight Hymn	1211-bar	Bo. & H.
Bozza, E. 1905–	Bis	2211	Leduc, 1963
Brown, R. 1912–	†Concertino	1211-hp	Avant, 1965
Brugk, H. M. 1909–	Fanfare & Intrade	0330	Noetzel, 1959
Busch, C. 1862–1943	In festive Mood	1211-bar	Witmark
	Prelude & Choral	1211-bar	C. Fischer
Bush, G. 1920–	Homage to Matthew Locke (1962)	0330	Galliard, 1965
Cabus, P. N. 1923–	Intrada	1320	Maurer, 1964
Cadow, P. 1923–	Intrada	2220	Grosch, n.d. [1964]
Calabro, L. 1926–	Ceremonial March	0220-timp, perc	EV, 1963
Cazden, N. 1914–	Suite, Op 55 (1951)	1211-bar	AMP, 1958
Chandler, M. 1911–	Sinfonietta (1956)	0330	BMIC
Chase, A.	Fugue	1221	Camara, 1960
Clapp, P. G. 1888–1954	Suite in E♭ (1937)	1211-bar	Bo. & H., 1955

Conley, L.	Chaconne	1211-bar	Kendor, 1964
	Intrada	1011-2 ct, bar	Kendor, 1963
	Promenade	0011-3 ct, bar	Kendor, 1961
Constant, M. 1925–	Quatre Études de Concert (1957)	2110-pf, perc	Leduc, 1957
Converse, F. S. 1871–1940	Prelude & Intermezzo, Op 103	1211-bar	Bo. & H., 1938
Cooke, A.	Suite	2211	Cor
Cowell, H. 1897–1965	A tall Tale	1221	Mercury, 1948
Cruft, A. 1921–	Diversion: If all the world were paper (1959)	2220	Williams, 1960
Desprez, F.	Thème et Variations sur La Folia	0410-timp	Maurer
Dietz, N. C.	Modern Moods	1211-bar	AMP, 1951
Dunham, R. L.	Sextet	1211-bar	Bo. & H., 1955
Elmore, R. 1913–	Fanfare for Easter	0220-org, perc	Flammer, 1961
Fegers K.	Two Christmas Carols	0330	Möseler
Flagello, N. 1928–	†Lyra	1320	GMPC, 1964
Fox, F.	Concertpiece	1211-pf	MBQ
Friedlander, E. 1916–66	Suite (1965)	2211	CMC
Gibson, K.	Four Pieces	6 br	(MT, Feb., 1968)
Glass, P. 1937–	Sextet	2211	Novello, 1966
Glatz, H.	Hungarian Folksong Suite (1964)	0231	BMIC
Goeb, R. 1914–	Three Processionals	5 br-org	CFE
Goller, V. 1873–1953	Christ ist erstanden	2210-org	(K)
Grey, G. 1934–	Sonata (1965)	0330	BMIC
Haan, S. de 1921–	Six short Pieces	0330	Hinrichsen, 1956
Harding, J. & Sommer, J.	Two Dances	1211-timp	King
Hastetter, E.	Turmmusik: Volk auf dem Wege	0330	Schott, 1939
Haubiel, C. 1894–	Ballade	1011-2 ct, bar	CP
Haworth, F. 1905–	Gonfalon Suite (1961)	1211-bar	Horn Realm
Henry, O.	Dichotomy	2220	Composer, 1959
Herrmann, H. 1896–	Musica festiva	0330	Rahter, 1966
Hewitt-Jones, T. 1926–	Severn Bridge Fanfares (1966)	0330	MS (MT, Dec., 1966)
Hillert, R.	Three Christmas Carols	2220	Concordia, 1964
Hoddinott, A. 1929–	Fanfare for brass & drums	0320-drums	OUP, 1963

Jörns, H. 1911–	Turmmusiken	0420	(K)
Kabalevsky, D. 1904–	Sonatine I (Ed Barnes)	2220	Ludwig, 1961
Karg-Elert, S. 1877–1933	Wunderbarer König	0220-org, timp	Simon
Kaufman, W.	Passacaglia and Capriccio	1221	Shawnee, 1967
Kazdin, A.	Twelve Days of Christmas	1211-bar	King
Kelly, B. 1934–	Fanfares & Sonatina	2220	Novello, 1966
Ketting, O. 1935–	Drie Fanfares (1954)	0330	Donemus, 1957
Kiessig, G. 1885–	Five Pieces, Op 57	2211	Parrhysius, 1937
Koch, J. H. E. 1918–	Der Tag, der ist so freudenreich	032(1)-org	BVK, 1968
Koepke, P.	Scherzo	1211-bar	Rubank
Koerppen, A. 1926–	Zwei Sätzen uber dem Choral: Wir glauben all' an einer Gott (1959)	0330	Br. & H., 1960
Kraft, K. J. 1903–	Divertimento in B♭ (1934)	2220	MS (MGG)
Kroeger, K. 1932–	Canzona	2211	Tritone, 1962
	Canzona II	1211-bar	Tritone
	Canzona III	0330	Presser, 1967
Kummer, H.	Ein Sontagsmusik, Op 37	0330	Grosch, n.d.
Levy, F.	Fantasy	1211-timp	Cor
Lewis, M. 1925–	†Movement	1211-pf	
Löchel, A. 1920–	Weihnachtliche Turmmusik	1221	Schott
McKay, F. H.	Fantasy	1211-bar	Barnhouse, 1956
	Narrative Sketch	1011-2 ct, bar	Barnhouse, 1956
	Second Fantasy	1211-bar	Barnhouse, 1960
	Panel in oil colour	1211-bar	Barnhouse, 1966
	Concert Prelude	1211-bar	Barnhouse
	Prologue in E♭	1211-bar	Barnhouse
	Sextet in A	1211-bar	Barnhouse
	Romantic Mural	1211-bar	Barnhouse
McKay, G. F. 1899–	Prelude & Allegro	1211-bar	Barnhouse, 1956
	Legends	1011-2 ct, bar	Barnhouse, 1958
Malter, L. & Azarov, M.	Six Russian Folksongs	2211	Leeds
Marx, K. 1897–	Turmmusik, Op 37/1	0330	BVK, 1942
Meyers, C. D.	Rhapsody for brass	1211-bar	AMP, 1950
	Autumn Moods	1211-bar	CP
Miller, (E?)	Suite miniature	1211-bar	Belwin
Mills, C. 1914–	The brass Piano	0330	CFE

Mohler, P. 1908–	Fanfaren-Ruf. Op 38	0330	Schott, 1956
Morgan, D. 1933–	Divertimento	2220	BMIC; Horn Realm
Osborne, W. 1906–	Prelude	0320-bar	King, 1951
	Two Ricercari	2210-bar	King, 1948
Ostransky, L.	Passacaglia & Scherzo	1211-bar	Rubank, 1959
	Suite	1211-bar	Rubank, 1959
Otten, L. 1924–	Cassation (1950)	0330	Donemus, 1956
	Suite (1953; rev. 1966)	0330	Donemus, 1956, 1967
Parris, R. 1924–	Sonatina (1948)	0231	CFE
Patterson, P. 1947–	Fanfare & Rondo (1965)	2211	BMIC
Pelemans, W. 1901–	Sextuor	2220	Maurer
Pfannenstiel, E. 1896–	Feierliche Musik No. 3 (Ed W. Schneider)	0240	Schott, 1962
Phillips, I. C.	Three hunting Songs	2220	OUP, 1963
Pilss, K. 1902–	Vier Fanfaren	0330	Noetzel, 1962
Pinto, O. 1890–1950	Tom Thumb's March (Arr. H. S. Hannaford)	1211-bar	G. Schirmer, 1962
Pisk, P. 1893–	Five Variations on an old trumpet tune	1230	Peer
Raphling, S. 1910–	Little Suite	0330	Musicus, 1956
Reinhold, O. 1899–1965	Thema mit Variationen (1954)	2220	MS (VDK)
Salzedo, L. 1921–	Divertimento, Op 49 (1959)	0330	Lopés, 1959
Saucedo, V.	Toccata	2220	EV, 1963
Schilling, H. L. 1927–	†Fanfare, Ricercar, Hymnus (1963)	0330	Br. & H., 1964
	Intrada (1965)	0330/0321	Br. & H., 1967
Schmid, H. K. 1874–1953	Turmmusik, Op 105 b	0330	Br. & H., 1940
Schmutz, A. D.	Fantasy Sketch	1211-bar	C. Fischer
Siegmeister, E. 1909–	Sextet	1211-perc	MCA, 1968
Sommer, J.	Two Dances on the same theme	1211-bar	King
Sowerby, L. 1895–1968	Festival Musick	0220-org, timp	Gray, 1958
Sumerlin, M.	Andante & Fugue	1211-bar	Far West, 1965
Sust, J. 1919–	Suite: The Farm under the Elms	0041-bell	(Ga)
Uber, D.	Saint Louis Suite	1221	Adler
Verrall, J. 1908–	Suite	1211-bar	Merion, 1956
Viecenz, H. 1893–1959	Bläser-Suite (1953)	0330/2220	Hofmeister, 1956

Walters, D. L.	Air for brass	1211-bar	Pro Art, 1962
Walton, W. 1902–	Six Pieces, Set 2 (Arr N. de Jongh)	0330	OUP, 1967
Weinzweig, J. J. 1913–	Fanfare (1943)	0330-opt perc	CMC
Whettam, G. 1927–	Music for brass (1964)	0330	BMIC
White, D. H. 1921–	Diversions	1221	Colombo, 1967
Wishart, P. 1921–	Divertimento, Op 34 (1959)	0330	Hinrichsen
Würz, R. 1885–1965	Turmmusik No. 3 (Morgenmusik)	0330	Br. & H., 1954
Xenakis, I. 1922–	†Eonta (1964)	0230-pf	Bo. & H., 1967
Zipp, F. 1914–	Three Fanfares	0330-timp ad lib	

4.6 *Seven Instruments*

Alexander, J.	Festive Fanfare	2311	Wallan, 1965
Badings, H. 1907–	Pittsburgh Concerto: III Cymbals & Signals	6 br, perc, tape	Peters
Balkom, S. van 1922–	Septet	0330-carillon	Donemus, 1968
Berezowsky, N. 1900–53	†Suite, Op 24 (1938)	2221	Mills, 1942
Bliss, A. 1891–	†Three jubilant & three solemn Fanfares (1943)	0331	Novello
	†Two Royal Fanfares	0331	Novello, 1961
Borris, S. 1906–	Fanfare, Burletta, Canzone & March	2221	Peters
Brabec, E.	Bläsermusiken (1940)	3220	Ullmann, 1940
Castérède, J.	Prélude et Danse	0031-pf, 2 perc	Leduc, 1959
Cohn, A. 1910–	Music for brass instruments, Op 9 (1933)	0430/1330	Southern, 1950
Cowell, H. 1897–1965	Rondo	2320	Peters, 1959
Dickinson, P. 1934–	Fanfares & Elegies (1967)	0330-org	Novello
Diercks, J. 1927–	Mirror of brass (1960)	2221/0331	Tritone, 1962
Dodgson, S. 1924–	Suite (1957)	0331	BMIC
Dorward, D. 1933–	Divertimento for brass, Op 15 (1961)	2221	Galliard, 1966
Dubois, P. M. 1930–	Septuor	2221	Leduc, 1962
Elton, A. 1935–	Septet: Vietnam (1967)	0330-timp	BMIC
Etler, A. D. 1913–	Music (1938–9)	2221	MS (Ho 2)

Evans, R.	Festival Fanfare (1967)	1320-drum	BMI (Can)
Ferguson, H. 1908–	Two Fanfares	0430	(K)
Gebhard, L. 1907–	Burleske aus Op 6	2210-pf, timp	Schott, 1939
Gerschefski, E. 1909–	Septet (1938)	2221	(Fleisher)
Goeb, R. 1914–	Septet (1952)	2221	CFE
Greenberg, L. 1926–	Deptet (1965)	2111–2 pf	CMC
Griend, K. van der 1905–50	Blechbläsermusik (1931)	2221	Donemus, 1948
Hanna, J.	Song of the redwood Tree	2220-timp, speaker	King, 1964
Heisinger, B.	March for timpani & brass	0330-timp	C. Fischer, 1964
Heldenberg, A.	Septet, Op 6	0411-bar	Brogneaux, 1954
Herschmann, H. 1924–	†Meditation for brass	0430	Eulenburg, 1967
Huber, K. 1924–	Two Movements (1957–8)	2221	Schott, 1964
Inch, H. R. 1904–	Divertimento (1934)	2221	MS (Ho, R, T)
Jong, C. de	Three Studies	0331	Avant, 1966
Koch, J. H. E. 1918–	Sinfonietta	0330-timp	BVK, 1966
Komma, K. M. 1913–	Musik	7 br	Ullmann, 1940
Kopprasch, G. 19th Cent.	Septets	7 br	Peters
Kurz, S. 1930–	Sonatine, Op 8 (1952)	2221	Hofmeister, 1955
Langley, J. W. 1927–	Septet (1961)	0331	MS
Lecail, C. 1859–1932	Septet	trps, trbs	E. & S., 1921
Litaize, G. 1909–	Cortège	0330-org	EMT, 1951
Luening, O. 1900–	Entrance & Exit Music	0330-cym	Peters, 1966
Micheelsen, H. F. 1902–	Concerto	0330-org	BVK
Milhaud, D. 1892–	Fanfares from Le Trompeur de Seville, Op 152c (1937)	0331	(I)
Muczynski, R. 1909–	Allegro deciso, Op 4	2211-timp	Shawnee, 1962
Nelhybel, V. 1919–	†Numismata	2221	GMPC, 1965
Overton, H. 1920–	Fantasy (1957)	5 br, pf, perc	CFE
Patterson, P. 1947–	Panegyrikos (1967)	2320	Mitchell

o   209

Ruggles, C. 1876–	Angels (Rev. 1938)	0430	NME, 1943
Saint-Martin, L. de	In Memoriam	0330-org	Durand
Schmid, H. K. 1874–1953	Turmmusik, Op 105a	0510-org	Br. & H.
Seeboth, M. 1904–	Suite	0430	Heinrichshofen, 1940
Thilman, J. P. 1906–	Das Sieben-Bläser Stück	2221	Litolff, n.d. [1953]
Turner, R. 1920–	Fantasia (1962)	1220-org, timp	CMC
Velden, R. van der 1910–	Concertino	1211-2pf	CeBeDeM, 1968
Walker, D.	Hiroshima Epitaph	1211-pf, vib	MBQ [1964]
Weber, B. 1916–	Colloquy, Op 37	2221	CFE
Werle, F. 1914–	Variations & Fugue	0331	Rongwen, 1956
Whear, P.	Three Chorales	2230	
Widor, C. M. 1845–1937	Salvum fac populum tuum	0330-org	Heugel
Wills, A.	Fanfare	0330-org	Novello
Wright, D. 1895–1967	Sonatina	1011-2 ct, euph, bar	

4.7 *Eight Instruments*

Ahrens, J. 1904–	Konzert	2230-org	SM, 1961
Archer, V. 1913–	Introduction, Dance, Finale (1963)	1211-hp/pf, timp, drum	CMC
Benjamin	Six Ceremonial Fanfares	0530	(K)
Bingham, S. 1882–	Concerto for brass & organ	0330-org perc	Gray, 1954
Bliss, A. 1891–	†Royal Fanfares & Interludes (rev. version) (1960)	0331-perc	Novello, 1965
	Fanfare for Heroes	0330-timp, cym	Novello
Bowman, C. 1913–	Nocturne	8 br	(AMC)
Bozza, E. 1905–	†Sonatine	1311-2 ct	Leduc, 1951
Bresgen, C. 1913–	Bläsermusik	0430-perc	(K)
Brings, A.	Canzone	double brass quart	(AMC)
Brugk, H. M. 1909–	Suite	0331-timp	Noetzel, 1959
Burkhard, W. 1900–55	Zwei Choralpartiten, Op 75	2321	BVK

Cowell, H. 1897—1965	This is America	0431	CFE
Dale, G. 1935–	A Midland Concerto, Op 32	8 br	BMIC
Drakeford, R. 1936–	Suite	8 br	(WWM)
Dubois, P. M. 1930–	Trois Préludes en Fanfare	2221-timp	Leduc, 1965
Dupré, M. 1886–	Poème heroïque: À Verdun	0330-org, perc	
Franchetti, A. 1906–	†Three Italian Masques	1211-pf, perc, bass	Galaxy, 1969
Harris, R. 1898–	Chorale & Toccata	1330-org	Mills
Ives, C. 1874–1954	Chromatimelodtune	5 br, 3 perc	(Gram., Nov. 1969)
Jacob, G. 1895–	†Interludes from Music for a Festival	0430-timp	Bo. & H., 1955
King, R.	Prelude & Fugue	2021-2 ct, bar	King, 1953
Lebow, L.	Suite	1331	(K)
Leschetizky, T. 1830–1915	Zum Feierabend	3220-timp	Parrhysius
Lybbert, D.	Praeludium	0330-2 perc	Peters, 1964
Moerenhout	Fanfares I & II	0331-perc	(K)
Mueller, F.	Octet	1321-bar	Horn Realm
Otto, F.	Chorale Variations	0431	Colombo, 1967
Patterson, P. 1947–	Octet (1963)	2231	BMIC
Pfannenstiel, E. 1896–	Feierliche Musik No. 2 (Ed W. Schneider)	0350	Schott, 1962
Scheurer, R.	Scherzo	2221-timp	Presser, 1956
Schuller, G. 1925–	Fanfare	0440	MS (BMI)
Semini, C. F. 1914–	Armonie d'ottoni	4220	Horn Realm
Simpson, R. 1921–	Canzone	0431	Lengnick, 1958
Uber, D.	Double Round	0431/0440	Uber
	Gettysburg Suite	1331	Musicus
Vierne, L. 1870–1937	Marche triomphale pour le Centenaire de Napoléon	0330-org, timp	Salabert, 1921
Werle, F. 1914–	Four Sketches	0431	(K)
Winter, P. 1894–	Festfanfare (1960)	0331-timp	Peters, 1960
Würz, R. 1885–1965	Turmmusik No. 1: Intrada	0440	Br. & H., 1954
	Turmmusik No. 2: Weckruf und Choral	0440	Br. & H., 1954
Zillig, W. 1905–63	Serenade I (1927–8)	2221-ct	BVK, 1958

4.8 *Nine Instruments*

Adler, S. 1925–	Praeludium	2221-bar, timp	King, 1947
Bender, J. 1909–	Phantasy on the Chorale 'Come Holy Ghost, God & Lord'	0321-org, timp, cym	Concordia, 1961
Clérisse, R.	Symphonie pour les Soupirs du Roy	1231-bar, perc	(K)
De Lone, P.	Introduction & Capriccio	2221-timp, perc	Shawnee, 1966
Desprez, F.	Marche triomphale	0440-timp	Maurer, 1963
Dvorak, R.	Lament & Response	2231-bar	Colombo, 1966
Glickman, E.	Divertimento (1961)	1211-timp, 3 perc	MBQ, n.d.
Görner, H. G. 1908–	Intrada & Hymnus, Op 20	3330	Marbot, 1959
Hewitt-Jones, T. 1926–	Fanfare on a theme of John Blow	4310-timp	MS (CG)
Jaeggi, O. 1913–63	Fanfare	2330-tam-tam	Horn Realm
Ketelbey, A. 1875–1959	Fanfare for a ceremonial Occasion	0430-timp, drum	Bosworth [1962]
Klose, F. 1862–1942	Präludium und Doppelfuge	0440-org	Peters
Lachner, F. 1803–90	Nonet (Ed K. Janetzky)	4230	Hofmeister, 1955
	Andante in A♭ (1833)	4230	MS (MGG)
Loebner, R.	Musik für Blechbläser	2220-2 pf, perc	Gerig
Meyerowitz, J. 1913–	Short Suite	3321	Rongwen, 1956
Nelhybel, V. 1919–	†Three Intradas	2331	GMPC, 1964
Otten, L. 1924–	Cassation (1950)	2331	Donemus, 1956
Parris, R. 1924–	Lamentations & Praises (1962)	2331-timp ad lib	Peters, 1966
Pilati, M. 1903–38	Divertimento (1932)	4320	MS (MGG)
Riegger, W. 1885–1961	Nonet, Op 49	2331	AMP, 1951
Roger, K. G. 1895–1966	Suite, Op 62 (1950)	0440-timp	Moeck, 1960
Schäfer, D. 1873–1931	Musik für Bläser	2321-perc	(K)
Sheriff, N. 1935–	Destination 5 (1962)	0221-4 perc	IMI
Steiner, L.	Twelve Pieces	3141	Möseler, 1966
Weeks, J. R. 1934–	Jubilate	3320-org	Hinrichsen
Weinberger, J. 1906–67	Concerto for the Timpani	0440-timp	AMP, 1939

Zagwijn, H.	Cortège (1948)	0520-Bach	Donemus
1878–1954		trp, timp	

4.9 *Ten or more Instruments*

Adler, S.	Concert Piece	2331-2 bar,	King, 1947
1925–		timp	
	Divertimento	3331-2 bar	King, 1950
Alpaerts, F.	Fanfares d'Inauguration	4331-timp	Metropolis, 1953
1876–1954			
Alwyn, W.	Fanfare for a joyful	4331-timp,	OUP, 1964
1905–	Occasion	3 perc	
Anderson, L.	Suite of Christmas Carols	4441-bar	Mills
1908–			
Archer, V.	Fantasy in the form of a	4331-bar,	CMC
1913–	Passacaglia (1951)	timp	
Arnell, R.	Ceremonial & Flourish,	4330	AMP, 1948
1917–	Op 43		
	The Grenadiers	4331	Hinrichsen
Baervoets, R.	Fanfare héroïque &	4331-perc	Metropolis, n.d.
1930–	Fanfare joyeuse		
Barber, S.	Mutations from Bach	4331-timp	G. Schirmer, 1968
1910–			
Beadell, R.	Introduction & Allegro	3331-bar,	King, 1952
		timp	
Beckhelm, P.	Tragic March	4431-bar,	King, 1947
		timp, perc	
Beckler, S.	Three Pieces	4331-bar,	King
		org	
Bennett, R. R.	Humoresque No. 3	6661-perc	Peters
1894–			
Beversdorf, T.	Cathedral Music	4331-bar	Southern, 1966
1924–			
Beyer, H.	Suite	4330-timp	King
Bilik, J. H.	Sonata	4431-bar	S. French, 1962
Binkerd, G.	Three Canzonas	3331	Bo. & H., 1969
1916–			
Bliss, A. 1891–	Greetings to a City (1961)	4462-timp,	Peters
		perc	
Bonneau, P.	Fanfare	3321-timp,	Leduc
1918–		cym ad	
		lib	
Bottje, W. G.	Symphonic Allegro	4631-bar,	King, 1961
1925–		timp,	
		perc	
Bozza, E.	Fanfare héroïque, Op 46	4331-timp,	Leduc
1905–		perc	
	Ouverture pour une	4341-timp,	Leduc, 1963
	Cérémonie	perc	
Bradley, W.	Honeysuckle & Clover	4331	NME, 1948
Brant, H.	†Millenium No. 2 (1954)	8, 10, 10, 2-	CFE, 1954
1913–		4 perc, S	
		vocalise	

213

Bresgen, C. 1913–	Festliches Ruf, Op 71/1	0431-fanfare trp, timp	Vieweg
Brown, R. 1912–	Prelude & Fugue	4441-bar, timp, perc	Avant, 1966
Bumcke, G. b. 1876	Fünf feierliche Präludien, Op 72	0432-timp	Harth, 1954
Burnham, C.	Festival Chorale	4321-org	King, 1968
Castérède, J.	Trois Fanfares pour des Proclamations de Napoléon	4331-timp, perc, narrator	Leduc, 1954
Chou Wen-Chung 1923–	†Soliloquy of a Bhiksuni	4131-perc	Peters, 1961
Civil, A. 1929–	Symphony for brass & percussion (1950)	5341-2 ct, bass trp, 4 Wagner tubas, 6 perc	MS
Cobine, A.	Vermont Suite (1953)	3441-bar	King, 1957
Copland, A. 1900–	†Fanfare for the common Man (1943)	4231-timp, perc	Bo. & H., 1944, 1956
Cowell, H. 1897–1965	Fanfare for the Forces of Latin America	4330-perc	Bo. & H., 1943
Creston, P. 1906–	Fanfare for Paratroopers	4330-perc	Bo. & H., 1943
David, J. N. 1895–	Nun freut Euch, lieben Christen g'mein	br	Br. & H., 1937
	Introitus, Choral & Fuga über ein Thema Anton Bruckners, Op 25	4230-org	Br. & H., 1940
Debussy, C. 1862–1918	†Fanfares from The Martyrdom of St. Sebastian (1911)	6431-timp	Durand, 1911
De Young, L.	Divertissement	4431-bar, timp, perc	King
Diamond, D. 1915–	Ceremonial Fanfare	6431-2 timp, perc	Southern, 1962
Diemer, E. L. 1927–	Declamation	2421-bar, timp, perc	EV, 1967
Dukas, P. 1865–1935	†Fanfare pour précéder 'La Péri'	4331	Durand, 1912
Dury, M.	Three Fanfares	4330-perc	Maurer, 1956
Flagello, N. 1928–	†Chorale & Episode (1948)	4231	GMPC, 1964
	†Concertino for piano-forte, brass & timpani (1963)	2431-pf, timp	GMPC, 1964
Franken, W. 1922–	Torenmusik, 'De Geuzen'	4330–perc, carillon	Donemus, 1963
Frid, G. 1904–	Zeven Pauken en een Koperorkest, Op 69	4331-7 timp	Donemus, 1964

214

Fuleihan, A. 1900–	Fanfare for the Medical Corps	4331	Bo. & H., 1943
Ganz, R. b. 1877	Brassy Prelude, Op 33/1	4331	Mills, 1946
George	Suite de Chansons de Noël	4441	(K)
Geraedts, J. 1924–	Choral Fanfare	4331-timp, perc	Donemus, 1957
Giuffre, J.	Pharaoh (1956)	4631-2 bar, timp	MJQ, 1957
Glazunov, A. 1865–1936	†Fanfare for the Jubilee of Rimsky-Korsakov, 1890	4331-timp, perc	Belaieff, 1891
Globokar, V. 1934–	Fluide	9 br, 3 perc	Peters
Goldman, R. F. 1910–	March for brasses	2331-bar	(K)
	Hymn for brass choir (1939)	4432-bar, timp	NME, 1941; King, 1959
Goossens, E. 1893–1962	Fanfare for the Merchant Marine	4231-perc	Bo. & H., 1943
Gorecki, H. M. 1933–	Muzycka II	0440-2 pf, perc	PWM
Grant, W. P. 1910–	Prelude & Dance	4331	CFE
Grey, G. 1934–	Sonata for brass & percussion	0330-6 perc	Lopés, 1966
Gustafson, D.	When I can read my Title clear	3331-bar	Templeton, 1964
Hanna, J.	Suite	2421-bar	Tritone, 1961
Hanson, H. 1896–	Festival Fanfare (1938)	4431-timp	MS (Sibley Lib., Rochester, N.Y.)
	Fanfare for the Signal Corps	4431-timp, perc	Bo. & H., 1943
Hartley, W. S. 1927–	Sinfonia No. 3 (1963)	4531-bar	Tritone, 1966
Hartmeyer, J.	Negev: Tone Poem	3331-bar, timp	King, 1951
Haufrecht, H. 1909–	†Symphony (1955)	4330-timp	Bo. & H., 1967
Hindemith, P. 1895–1963	†Concert Music, Op 49 (1930)	4321-pf, 2 hp	Schott
Hogg, M.	Concerto for brass	3331-bar, timp	King, 1957
Holmes, P.	Suite	4331-timp	Shawnee, 1960
Jenni, D.	Allegro	4431-2 bar	CFE, 1958
Jesson, R. 1929–	Variations & Scherzo	3431-bar, timp, perc	King, 1954
Johnson, J. J. 1921–	Poem (1956)	4741-2 bar, db, perc	MJQ, 1961
Jolivet, A. 1905–	†Fanfares pour Britannicus (1946)	6441-2 perc	Bo. & H., 1962

215

Kaufmann, L. J. 1901–44	Music (1941) (Ed K. Janetzky)	4331	Hofmeister, 1957
Kay, U. 1917–	Suite for brass choir	4431	CFE, 1952
Kelterborn, R. 1931–	Invokatio	3331	BVK
Ketting, O. 1935–	Entrata to 'Fanfares 1956'	4831-timp, perc	Donemus, 1956
	Intrada festiva	4331-perc	Donemus, 1960
	Collage No. 9	6531-bar, perc	Donemus, 1963
King, R.	Seven conversation Pieces (1940)	0431-2 bar	King, n.d.
Kreisler, A. von	Two Chorales	4331	Southern, 1965
Langley, J. W. 1927–	Fanfare for Midland Youth	6441-timp, perc	MS
Lebow, L.	Suite for brass	3331-bar, timp, perc	King
Leopold, B. 1888–1956	Festive Music (Divertimento)	13 br, perc	(Ga)
Liadov, A. 1855–1914	†Fanfare for the Jubilee of Rimsky-Korsakov, 1890	4331-timp	Belaieff, 1891
Louel, J. 1914–	†Fanfares (1948)	4331-timp, cym	CeBeDeM
McKay, G. F. 1899–	Bravura Prelude (1939)	4441-2 bar	AMP, 1943
MacMillan, E. 1893–	Fanfare for a Festival (1959)	4331-timp, perc	CMC
Maganini, Q. 1897–	Shenandoah	2331-bar	Musicus, 1958
Maltby, R.	Ballad	4441-bass, gt, perc	(K)
Marks, J.	Introduction & Passacaglia	3331-bar, timp	King, 1951
	Music for brass & timpani	4331-bar, timp	King, 1954
Maxwell, C.	Music	6040	Horn Realm
	A mighty Fortress is our God	br	Horn Realm
Meriläinen, U. 1930–	Partita (1954)	4431	King, 1959
Merriman, T.	Theme & four Variations	2431-bar	AMP, 1951
Meulemans, A. 1884–1966	Eight Fanfares	4/8731-perc	MS (Gor)
	Suite	0551-perc	MS (Gor)
Miller (E.?)	Sinfonietta, Op 13	4331-bar	Belwin
Missal, J.	Fanfare, Chorale & Procession	4442-timp	S. Fox, 1962
	Jericho Suite	4441-bar, perc	(K)
Mohler, P. 1908–	Fanfaren-Intrada, Op 38	4331-timp	Schott, 1956

Nelhybel, V. 1919–	†Slavic March	3331-bar, 2 perc	GMPC, 1965
	Ancient Hungarian Dances	2331-bar, opt perc	Colombo, 1967
	Designs for brass	4331-bar	Bo. & H., 1966
	†Chorale	2331-bar	GMPC, 1965
	Concerto antiphonale	3452	Colombo, 1966
	Motet & Pavane	2321-2 bar, perc	Colombo, 1966
Niblock, J.	Triptych	4331-bar, timp	Interlochen, n.d.
Novy, D.	Sonatina	3330-timp	King,1960
Otterloo, W. van 1907–	Serenade (1944)	4431-hp/pf, cel, timp, perc	Donemus, 1948
Parris H. M.	Four Rhapsodies	4331	EV, 1948
Patterson, P. 1947–	Intrada	8431-timp	Mitchell
Petrassi, G. 1904–	Musica di ottone (1963)	4431-timp	SZ, 1964
Pisk, P. 1893–	Cortège	2331- 2 ct, bar	CFE
Piston, W. 1894–	Fanfare for the fighting French (1943)	4331- timp, 3 perc	Bo. & H., 1943, 1959
Presser, W. 1916–	Passacaglia & Fugue	4331-bar, timp, perc	Tritone, 1962
	Research	3331-bar	Tenut, 1967
Rautawaara, E. 1928–	†A Requiem in our Time, Op 3 (1954)	4431-bar, timp, perc	King, 1958
Read, G. 1913–	Sound Piece, Op 82 (1949)	4432-bar, timp, perc	King, 1950
	Choral & Fughetta	4432-2 bar	King, 1957
	Cherry Festival & Inter- lochen Bowl Fanfare	4331	MS (IL)
Reed, H. O. 1910–	Fanfares 4	4431-2 bar, perc	Mills, 1962
	Symphony	br, perc	(K)
Revueltas, S. 1899–1940	Canto de Guerra de los Frontes Leales (1938)	0332-pf, perc	(Slo)
Reynolds, V.	Theme & Variations	3331-bar, timp	King, 1952
	Prelude & Allegro (1947)	4331-2 bar, timp	King
Riegger, W. 1885–1961	†Music for brass choir, Op 45 (1948–9)	4/8, 10, 10, 2-timp, perc	Mercury, 1949
Roussel, A. 1869–1937	†Fanfare pour un Sacre païen (1921)	4430-timp	Durand
Roy, K. G. 1924–	Tripartita, Op 5	2331-2 bar	King, 1950

Samuel, H. 1927–	Praeludium (1950)	4231-org, perc	(CG, WWM)
Schmidt, F. 1874–1939	Fuga solemnis	3631-timp	UE [1940?]
Schmidt, W. 1926–	Chorale, March & Fugato	4331-bar	Avant, 1966
Schmitt, F. 1870–1958	†Fanfare from Antoine et Cléopatre, Op 69 (1920)	4331-perc	Durand, 1921
Schuller, G. 1925–	†Symphony for brass & percussion, Op 16 (1949–50)	4632-2 bar, timp, perc	Malcolm, 1959
Scott, W.	Rondo gioioso	4341-bar, timp, perc	King, 1956
Shahan, P. 1923–	Spectrums	4441-bar, timp, perc	King, 1955
	†Leipzig Towers	4441-bar, timp, perc	King, 1961
Shulman, A. 1915–	Top brass (Six minutes for twelve) (1958)	4431	Templeton, 1958
Smalley, R. 1943–	Pulses 5 × 4	5 groups: 3 trp, perc; 3 hn, perc; 3 hn, perc; 3 trb, perc; 3 trb, perc	Faber
Starer, R. 1924–	Serenade	4331	Southern, 1966
Stolte, S. 1925–	Fanfare	2331-perc	(VDK)
Strauss, R. 1864–1949	†Feierliche Einzug der Ritter des Johanniterodens (1909)	4, 15, 4, 2-timp	Schlesinger, 1909; Bo. & H., 1960
	†Wiener Philharmoniker Fanfare (1924)	8662-2 timp	Bo. & H., 1960
	†Fanfare zur Eröffnung der Musikwoche der Stadt Wien (1924)	8662-2 timp	Bo. & H., 1960
Sumerlin, M.	Fanfare, Andante & Fugue	3421-bar, perc	Far West, 1965
Taylor, C. H.	Inscriptions in brass	4331-bar, timp, perc	G. Schirmer, 1964
Tcherepnin, A. 1889–	Fanfare	4331-timp, perc	Bo. & H., 1964
Thomson, V. 1896–	Fanfare for France	4330-perc	Bo. & H., 1943, 1959
	Ode to the Wonders of Nature	2330-3 perc	G. Schirmer, 1968

Tippett, M. 1905–	Fanfare No. 1	4330	Schott
	Praeludium	6330-tub bells, perc	Schott, 1962
Tomasi, H. 1901–	Fanfares liturgiques	4331-timp, perc	Leduc, 1952
	Procession nocturne	4341-timp, perc, S; ch ad lib	Leduc, 1959
Tranchell, P. 1922–	Decalogue; Variations (1956)	0331-org, timp, perc	MS (CG)
Tull, F.	Soundings	6642-2 bar, timp, perc	Shawnee, 1967
Turner, G. 1913–	Fanfare, Chorale & Finale	4331	Arrow; G. Schirmer
Tyra, T.	Suite	4331-bar, timp	Southern, 1962
Uber, D.	Liturgy, Op 50	2431-bar, timp	Ensemble, 1967
Uldall, H. 1903–	Music for wind & percussion	4421-perc	
Viecenz, H. 1893–1959	Bläsermusik	4331	Hofmeister
Wagenaar, B. 1894–	Fanfare for Airmen (1942)	4331-timp, perc	Bo. & H., 1943
Wagner, L.	Fanfare, Scherzo & Allegro	4631-bar, perc	King, 1964
Walton, W. 1902–	Fanfare (Arr M. Sargent)	4331-timp, perc	OUP, 1965
Ward, R. 1917–	Fantasia (1953)	4331-timp	Highgate; Galaxy, 1957
Weiss, A. 1891–	Tone Poem (1957)	4431-2 bar, 2 timp, 4 perc	CFE, 1958
Woollen, R. 1923–	Triptych, Op 34	2431	Peters, 1960
Zador, E. 1894–	†Suite for brass	4331	Eulenburg, 1961
Zindars, E.	The brass Square	4431-timp, perc	King, 1955
Zuckert, L. 1904–	Prelude in modo antiguo (1964)	4331	CMC

4.10 *Unspecified Brass Ensembles*

Andriessen, J. 1925–	In Pompa magna	br, timp, perc	Donemus, 1966
	Entrada festiva	br, timp	Donemus, 1966
Bassett, L. 1923–	Designs in brass	br, perc	CFE

Binkerd, G. 1916–	Studenten-Schmauss	br, org	(Ho)
Bliss, A. 1891–	†Ceremonial Prelude (1965)	br, org, timp, perc	MS (MT, Aug., 1966)
Butterworth, A. 1923–	Three Impressions (1967)	br	(WWM)
Cabus, P. N. 1923–	Suite	br	(WWM)
Calabro, L. 1926–	Processional (1958)	br, perc	(Ho)
Campbell, S. S. 1909–	Fanfare	br	(WWM)
Canning, T. 1911–	Rondo	br, perc	CFE
Clapp, P. G. 1888–1954	Fanfare Prelude	20 br	(Blom)
Copley, I. A. 1926–	Suite	br	(WWM)
Cortes, R. 1933–	Introduction & Dirge	br, perc	CFE
Cowell, H. 1897–1965	Grinnell Fanfare	br, org	CFE
Cranmer, D. 1943–	Prelude & Fugue	br	(WWM)
Farquhar, D. A. 1928–	Divertimento	br	(WWM)
Franco, J. 1908–	Fanfare for brasses	br	CFE
Franken, W. 1922–	Musica di campanile	br, perc, carillon	Donemus, 1965
Freed, I. 1900–60	Symphony (1951)	br	(Ho)
Frid, G. 1904–	4 Schetsen, Op 72a	br	Donemus, 1966
Fuerstner, C. 1912–	Metamorphoses on a Chorale	br	(WWM)
Geddes, J. M. 1941–	Fanfare	br	(WWM)
Gow, D. 1924–	Sonata	br	(WWM)
Haan, S. de 1921–	Two Studies	br	(WWM)
Hasenoehrl, F. 1885–	Suite in four movements	br	(WWM)
Hawthorne-Baker, A. 1909–	Music	br	(WWM)
Hunt, O.	Music for brass & piano	br, pf	(MT, Feb., 1968)
Husa, K. 1921–	Divertimento	br, perc	(WWM)
Huybrechts, A. 1899–1938	Divertissement	br, perc	CeBeDeM, 1965
Kabelá⌣, M. 1908–	Symphony No. 3 in F, Op 33 (1948–57)	br, org, timp	(Ga, WWM)
Keldorfer, R. 1901–	Festliche Musik: Intrada, Chorale, Passacaglia & Fuge	br, org, timp	ÖBV, 1954

Kelly, R. 1916–	Chorale & Fugue	br, timp	CFE
Kilpatrick, J. F.	Concert Piece	br	(fp, May 1, 1951)
Kraft, K. J. 1903–	Concerto breve No. 2 in d	br, org	MS (MGG)
	Passacaglia (ca. 1942)	br	MS (MGG)
Kuusisto, I. T. 1933–	Three Introductions	br, org	(Ri)
Lindeman, O. 1929–	Counterpoint	br	(Ri)
Lovelock, W. 1899–	Fanfare: A Suite	br	Chappell, 1965
Macero, T. 1925–	In Retrospect	br, perc	CFE
Merikanto, A. 1893–1953	Drei Stücke & Zwei Fanfaren (1937–47)	br	(MGG)
Mojsisovics, R. von 1877–1953	Festmusik	br, org	(G)
Paynter, J.	Fanfaronade	br	Kjos, 1950
Redfern, P. E. 1908–	Suite in A	br	(WWM)
Rose, G.	Somerset Suite	br	(MT, Dec., 1968)
Salmenhaara, E. 1941–	Siam Phony	br	(Ri)
Scott- Maddocks, D. J. V. 1932–	Study	br, perc	(WWM)
Solomon, N.	Concerto	br	MS (CM Lib)
Spinks, C. 1915–	Concert Toccata	br, org	Lengnick
Stroe, A. 1932–	Concert Music	br, pf, perc	(MT, Dec., 1968)
Titcomb, E. 1884–	Prelude	br, org	(Ho)
Tschirch, R. 1825–72	Die St. Hubertus-Jagd	br	B. & B.
Van Hoof, J. 1886–1959	Sinfonietta	br	MS?
Weber, L. 1891–1947	Musik (1928)	br, org	Filser
White, J. 1938–	Symphony	br, org	(MT, Sept., 1965)
Wildgans, F. 1913–65	Concerto, Op 31b	br, org, perc	MS (MGG)
Wilson, T. B. 1927–	Sinfonietta	br	(WWM)
Winter, P. 1894–	Olympia-Fanfaren für XI Olymp. Spiele, 1936	br, timp	Voggenreiter
Woestijne, D. van de 1915–	Fanfares (1942)	br	(MGG)
Würz, A. 1903–	Drei Turmmusiken, Op 15	trps, trbs	(MGG)
Zbinden, J. F. 1917–	Concerto de Gibraltar	br pf	MS (MGG)

4.11 *Posaunenchor, Collections, etc.*

Bachmann, F.	Lass Dir unser Lob gefallen I	2–8 part	Rufer, 1950
	Posaunenchoralbuch zum Evangelischen Kirchengesangbuch	3–5 part	Rufer; Merseburger, 1953
	Zu Gottes Lob und Ehre: Supplements 1–60	3–6 part	Merseburger
	An hellen Tagen	4–5 part	(K)
Burghauser, J.	Old Czech Fanfares	various	SHV, 1961
Doflein, E.	Der Fuchstanz und andere Volkstänze	2 part	BVK, n.d.
Ehmann, W. 1905–	Bläser-Intraden zum Wochenlied	4–6 part	BVK, 1957
	Evangelisches Kantoreibuch	3–4 part 3rd ed.	Rufer, 1957
	Geistliches Zweierspiel für Bläser	2 part	BVK, 1956
	Alte Spielmusik für Bläser	4–6 part	BVK, 1964
	Jägerlieder	2–4 part	BVK, 1958
	Wanderlieder	2–4 part	BVK, 1958
	Blaser-Fibel II: Spielheft Weihnachtslieder	2–6 part	BVK, 1962 (K)
Ehmann, W. & Kuhlo, J.	Neues Posaunenbuch	4–5 part	
Ehmann, W. et al	Neue Spielmusik für Bläser	4–8 part	BVK, 1966
Franke, C.	Altdeutsche Volkslieder für Bläserchöre	4 part	Merseburger
Grad, T.	Europäische Spielmusik für Blechbläser	3–5 part	Möseler [1965?]
	Volksliedsätze	5–8 part	BVK, 1957
Häberling, A.	Frohes Zusammenspiel	2–5 part perc ad lib	Ruh, 1957
Hamm, W.	Dreissig Volkslieder	4 part	(K)
Hensel, W. 1887–1956	Wach auf	4 part	BVK
Hering, S.	Early Classics for brass ensembles	4 part	C. Fischer, 1964
Hoffmann, E.	Alte Bläsermusik aus der 16–18 Jh.	2–6 part	Merseburger,1956
	Bläsermusik: 53 Sätze Posaunenwerke d. Evang. Kirche		Berlin, Evang. Verlangsan- stalt, 1957
King, R.	Reformation Chorales	4 part	King, 1955
	24 Early German Chorales	4 part	King
Langstroth, I.	Five Dances (15th & 16th Centuries)	4 part	Presser, 1956
Kuhlo, J.	Neues Posaunenbuch I	4–5 part	(K)

Kuhlo & Bachmann, F.	Ruhmet den Herrn (Neues Posaunenbuch II)		Rufer, 1959
Lörcher, R. & Mühleisen, H.	Lobt Gott!	2–6 part	Aussaat-Verlag, 1956
Lubik	Madrigals & Pre-Classical Dances	4 part	EMB, 1959
Mönkemeyer, H.	Musik aus der Vorklassik	3 part	Schott, 1961
	Der Bläserchor: 5 vols	4 part	Moeck
Schilling, H. L. 1927–	Musica festiva: Bläsersätze des späten Mittelalters u. der Barockzeit (1470–1696)	3–7 part	Br. & H., 1966
Schlemm, H. M.	Lass Dir unser Lob gefallen II	2–8 part	Merseburger,1962
Schmitt, H.	Alte Bläsersätze	5–6 part	Schott
Schultz, H.	Deutsche Bläsermusik vom Barock bis zur Klassik		EdM, Vol. 2
Sertl, F.	Münchener Petersturm-musik, 2 vols	4 part	Hieber, 1951
	Unterhaltungsmusik aus dem 16 u. 17. Jahrhundert	5 part	Möseler
Ulf, O.	Augsburger Tafelmusik: Dances from the 16th & 17th Centuries	5–6 part	Möseler, 1963

5. Arrangements and Transcriptions for Brass Ensembles

5.1 *One Instrument*

	Ed Arr or transcribed by			
Gabrielli, D.	D. Shuman	†Ricercare No. 1	0010	Southern

5.2 *Two Instruments*

Bach, J. S. 1685–1750	A. Dedrick	Two-part Invention	0110	Kendor, 1964
	D. G. Miller	12 Two-part Inventions	0020	Ensemble
Fesch, W. de 1687–1761		Three Sonatas	0020	(K)
Gastoldi, G. G. ca. 1550–1622		Spielstücke	0020	BVK, 1950
Handel, G. F. 1685–1759	G. Pulis	Prelude	0020	Ensemble, n.d.
Jelich, V. b. 1596	W. Ehmann	†Parnassia militia: Ricercare	0110	BVK, 1966

5.3 *Three Instruments*

Anon. 13th Cent.	R. King	Two mediaeval Motets	1010-bar	King, 1956
		Two Pieces from The Glogauer Liederbuch	1110	Cor
Anon. ca. 1495	H. Heimler	†Trio	0030	(Day)
Bach, J. S. 1685–1750	D. G. Miller	24 Chorales	0030	Ensemble
	Kelleher	Sarabande	0030	Ensemble
	R. Myers	Fugue in G	0030	Ensemble
	G. Pulis	Polonaise	0030	Ensemble
Frescobaldi, G. 1583–1643	David	†Six Canzoni	0020-org	Schott
	Fetter	Canzoni Nos. 1 & 2	0030	Ensemble
Handel, G. F. 1685–1759	I. Rosenthal	Suite	1110	WIM, 1967
	G. Pulis	Sarabande: Arioso	0030	Ensemble
Hingston, J. d. 1683		†Fantasia	0110-org	(Day)
Josquin des Prés ca. 1445–1521	N. de Jong	Three Pieces	1110	Ensemble, 1966
Lassus, O. di 1522–94	G. Miller	†Adoramus te, Christe	0030	Ensemble
	M. Moore	Cantate Domino	0120	Arco, 1968
Lotti, A. ca. 1667–1740	A. Dedrick	Vere languores nostros	0030	Kendor, 1963
Lully, J. B. 1632–87	Muller	Airs de Table	0210/ 1110	Maurer, 1960
Palestrina, G. P. 1524–94	Schaeffer	Renaissance Ballade	0030	Pro Art, 1964
Purcell, H. 1659–95	D. G. Miller	Three Fantasias	0030	Ensemble
	W. Osborne	Trio Sonata	0030	Ensemble
	Elkan	Fanfare	0210	(K)
Scheidt, S. 1585–1672	Fetter	Gib uns heute unser taglich Brodt	0030	Ensemble
Schütz, H. 1585–1672	P. McCarty	Give ear, O Lord	0020-org	Ensemble, n.d.
Speer, D. b. ca 1625		†Sonata in e	0020-cont	
Spiegler, M.		Canzone I	0110-pf	IMC, 1966
Vivaldi, A. 1678–1741	Q. Maganini	Sonata da camera	0210	(K)
Willaert, A. ca. 1480–1562	L. Waldeck	Ricercar	1110	Cor

5.4 *Four Instruments*

Anon.		†Christ ist erstanden, from Liederbuch of Peter Schaeffer, Mainz, 1513	0130	
Antegnati, C. ca. 1550-ca. 1620	A. Lumsden	Canzona 9	0220	Musica Rara, 1969
Bach, J. S. 1685–1750	L. Waldeck	Contrapunctus I (Art of Fugue)	1111	Cor
	R. King	Contrapunctus I (Art of Fugue)	0210-bar	King
	R. King	22 Chorales	0210-bar	King, 1955
	Fetter	Chorales	0040	Ensemble
	R. King	16 Chorales	0040	King, 1958
		March, Chorale & Fugue	0210-bar	King, 1958
	R. King	Von Himmel hoch da komm' ich her	0210-bar	King
	J. Corley	Sarabande & Minuet	0210-bar	King
	Smith	Fugue XIV (Art of Fugue)	0220	Musicus, 1959
		Fugue XIV (Art of Fugue)	0220	Galliard, 1963
	S. Snieckowski	Five Fugues	1210	PWM, 1955
	Taylor	Fugue in D♭	1210	C. Fischer
	Taylor	Fugue in g	1210	C. Fischer
	Fetter	Three short Pieces	0040	Ensemble
	Fetter	Prelude & Fugue	0040	Ensemble
	Kelleher	Contrapunctus XIV	0040	Ensemble
	Smith	Contrapunctus I (Art of Fugue)	0040	(K)
	Mayes	Six 4-part Chorales	0220	Galliard
	R. Myers	Fugue in d	0040	Ensemble
	A. de Filippi	March, Chorale & Bourrée	1210	Elkan, 1966
	F. Zabel	Prelude & Fugue	1210	IMC, 1965
	Hanson	O sacred Head, sore wounded (2 settings)	0040	Ensemble
	G. Pulis	Polonaise	0040	Ensemble
	P. McCarty	Arioso	0040	Ensemble
	P. McCarty	Air	0040	Ensemble
	H. R. Ryker	Praeludium VII	0220	MBQ, 1967
	H. R. Ryker	Praeludium XXIV	0220	MBQ, 1967
Banchieri, A. 1567–1634	R. King	†Two Fantasias (Venice, 1603)	1120	King, 1964

P

	S. Beck	Two Fantasias	0220	Mercury, 1947
	Q. Maganini	Sinfonia	1210	C. Fischer
Barberis, M. de 16th Cent.	Fetter	Paduane: Chant d'Orlando	0040	Ensemble
Blitheman, W. d. 1591	R. Smalley	Gloria tibi trinitas No. 6	4 br	Faber
Byrd, W. ca. 1538–1623	E. E. Rogers	Pavane: The Earle of Salisbury	1110-org	Gray, 1966
Campra, A. 1660–1744	R. King	Rigaudon	0210-bar	King, 1960
Corelli, A. 1653–1713		Adagio & Pastorale	1210	IMC
Couperin, F. 1668–1733	R. King	Fugue (on the Kyrie)	0210-bar	King
	R. King	Two Pieces	0210-bar	King, 1959
		Rondo	1210	IMC
Couperin, L. 1626–61	R. King	Sarabande & Carillon	0210-bar	King, n.d.
Dandrieu, J. F. ca. 1681–1738		Rondo	1210	IMC
Daquin, L. C. 1694–1772	R. King	Noel suisse (from Nouveau livre de Noels)	0210-org	King, 1957
Dufay, G. d. 1474	Kelleher	Gloria	0040	Ensemble
Fischer, J. C. F. ca. 1665-ca. 1746	M. Moore	Two Marches	0220	Arco, 1966
	French	Der Tag, der ist so freudenreich	1210	Southern, 1969
Francisque, A. ca. 1570–1605	A. Raph	Suite from Le Trésor d'Orphee	0040	Ensemble
Franck, M. ca. 1579–1639	Fetter	Bergreigen	0040	Ensemble
Frescobaldi, G. 1583–1643	H. Aaron	Gagliarda	0020/ 1210	G. Schirmer, 1953
		Canzone 13	0220	Musica Rara
	M. Moore	Toccata	1210	Arco, 1966
Gabrieli, A. 1510–86	Smith	Ricercar	0310/ 0220	Musicus
	A. Lumsden	Ricercar del sesto tuono	0220/ 1120/	Musica Rara, 1957
	A. Lumsden	Ricercar del duodecimo tuono	0220/ 1120	Musica Rara, 1957
	Friedman	Ricercar	0040	(K)

Gabrieli, G. 1557–1612		Canzonas 1–4	0220	Musica Rara
	K. Brown	Sonata	0040	IMC
	R. King	†Canzona per sonare, No. 1, La Spiritata	1210	King, n.d.
	R. King	†Canzone per sonare, Nos. 2, 3 & 4	0210-bar	King, 1957
	A. Einstein	Canzoni per sonare (Venice, 1608)	4-pt	Mainz, 1933
Gasparini, Q. d. 1778	D. G. Miller	Adoramus te, Christe	0040	Ensemble
Gerle, H. 16th Cent.	L. Waldeck	Galliarde & Fugue	1111	Cor
Gervaise, C. 16th Cent.	Muller	Danses	0040	Maurer, 1959
Grétry, A. E. M. 1741–1813		Gigue	1210	IMC
Grillo, G. B. d. ca. 1622		Canzonas 11 & 12	0220	Musica Rara
Guami, G. ca. 1540– 1611	A. Lumsden	Canzonas 6 & 17	0220	Musica Rara, 1969
Handel, G. F. 1685–1759	R. King	March & Gavotte	0210-bar	King, 1956
	R. King	Bourrée & Minuet (Fireworks Music)	0210-bar	King, 1955
	H. Aaron	Chaconne (Almira)	0211	G. Schirmer, 1962
	D. G. Miller	Four Chorales	0040	Ensemble
	Williams	Largo from 'Xerxes'	0220	Southern, 1965
Ingegneri, M. A. ca. 1545–92	D. G. Miller	Tenebrae factae sunt	0040	Ensemble
Isaac, H. ca. 1450–1517	L. Waldeck	Canzona	0211	Cor
Jannequin, C. ca. 1475-ca. 1560		†Chantons, sonnons, trompettes	0220	(Day)
Josquin des Prés ca. 1445–1521	R. King	Motet & Royal Fanfare	0210-bar	King
	Q. Maganini	The King's Fanfare	1210	C. Fischer
Lappi, P. 16th Cent.	A. Lumsden	Canzoni Nos. 11 & 12	1210	Musica Rara, 1967
Lassus, O. di 1522–94	N. Butterworth	Four Tudor Canzonas	1210	Chappell

Law, A. 1748–1821 et al.	R. King	Three New England Hymns (from A Select Number of Plain Tunes, 1781)	0210-bar	King, n.d.
Locke, M. ca. 1630–1677	L. Waldeck	Suite No. 1	0211	Cor
	L. Waldeck	Suite No. 2	1111	Cor
Lully, J. B. 1632–87		Gavotte	1210	IMC
Luzzaschi, L. 1545–1607	A. Lumsden	Canzona, 10	0220	Musica Rara, 1969
Marini, B. d. ca. 1660		Canzona	0040	Ensemble, 1965
Maschera, F. ca. 1540–84	G. W. Lotzenhiser	Canzonc	2020/ 2110	C. Fischer, 1960
	L. Waldeck	Canzone	0211	Cor
	A. Lumsden	Canzonas 7 & 8	0220	Musica Rara, 1969
Merulo, C. 1533–1604	A. Lumsden	Canzona 5	0220	Musica Rara, 1969
Obrecht, J. 1450–1505	R. King	Tsat een Meskin (1501)	0130	King, 1958
	L. Waldeck	Tsat een Meskin	0211	Cor
Pachelbel, J. 1653–1706	R. King	Two Magnificats	1110-bar	King
Palestrina, G. P. 1524–94	R. King	Three Hymns	0210-bar	King, 1960
	R. King	Ricercar del primo tuono	1110-bar	King, n.d.
	L. Waldeck	Ricercar del primo tuono	0211	Cor
	H. Schultz	Lauda Sion	1210	Kendor, 1962
	H. Schultz	Mass; Iste Confessor	1210	Kendor, 1961
	L. Waldeck	Adoramus	1111	Cor
Pezel, J. C. 1639–94		Intraden für 1 cornet u. 3 Trombonen		Leipzig, Composer
Ponce	Kelleher	Ave, Color vini clari	0040	Ensemble
Praetorius, M. 1571–1621	R. Myers	Two ancient Carols	0040	Ensemble
	M. Moore	Bransle double	0220	Arco
Purcell, H. 1658–95	R. King	†Music for Queen Mary II	1110-bar	King, 1956
	T. Dart	March & Canzona for the Funeral of Queen Mary	0220-opt timp	OUP, 1958
		March & Canzona for the Funeral of Queen Mary	0040	Purcell GA, XXXI

	R. King	Allegro & Air from King Arthur	0210-bar	King, 1960
	J. Corley	†Two Trumpet Tunes & Ayre	0210-bar	King, n.d.
Reiche, E. 1667–1734		Vier und Zwanzig neue Quatricinia mit einem Cornet und drey Trombonen		Leipzig, J. Kolar, 1696
	A. Müller	24 neue Quatricinia	0130	Merseburger, 1927
	G. Müller	24 neue Quatricinia	1120	Merseburger, 1958
	D. G. Miller	24 neue Quatricinia	0220/ 0130	Ensemble, 1962
		Separate numbers from Neue Quatricinia		
		Five Quatricinia	0130	Gregorius, 1950
	R. King	Sonata No. 1	1110-bar	King, n.d.
	R. King	Sonata No. 7	1110-bar	King
	A. Fromme	Sonata No. 11	0130	S. Fox, 1961
	A. Fromme	Sonata No. 12 (Sonata chromatica)	0130	S. Fox, 1961
	R. King	†Sonata No. 15	0220	King, n.d.
		Sonata No. 15	1110-bar	Mercury
	R. King	†Sonata No. 18	1110-bar	King, 1960
	R. King	†Sonata No. 19	1111	King, n.d.
	W. Sear	Sonata No. 19	1111	Cor
	A. Ostrander	†Sonata No. 20	0220	IMC
	R. King	†Sonatas Nos. 21 & 22	1110-bar	King, 1957
	R. King	†Sonata No. 24	1110-bar	King, 1955
	A. Fromme	Baroque Suite (Sonatas Nos. 8, 12, 18, 19, 16)	1210	AMP, 1968
Scheidt, S. 1587–1654		†Canzon dolorosa	0130	(BBC, May, 1967)
	R. King	Three Christmas Chorales	1110-bar	King, 1958
	G. Ochs	Spielmusik: 5 Pieces	0220	Nagel, 1954
	G. Ochs	Suite in C	0220	Nagel, 1954
	R. King	Da Jesus an dem Kreuze stand	1011-bar/ 0040	King
Schein, J. H. 1586–1630	S. Beck	Banchetto Musicale: Intrada & Paduana	0220	Mercury
	W. Sear	†Padouana	1111	Cor
	N. Stone	†Padouana	0040	Bosworth

Schicht, J. 1753–1823	C. Surtees	Gross ist der Herr (1821)	0220	Chappell, 1967
Speer, D. b. ca. 1625		†Sonata	0040	Ensemble; IMC
	A. Baines	†Sonata No. 1 (1687)	0030-cont	Musica Rara, 1961
	A. Baines	†Sonata No. 2 (1687)	0030-cont	Musica Rara, 1961
		Two Sonatas	0130	IMC
	H. Schultz	†Sonata (1685)	cto, 2 trb, cont	EdM, 14, 1941, 1961
Spiegler, M.		Canzona II	0210-pf	IMC
Störl, J. G. C. 1675–1719	R. King	†Sonata No. 1	1110-bar	King, 1957
	D. G. Miller	Six Sonatas	0130/ 1120	Ensemble, 1962
	K. Brown	Six Sonatas, 2 vols	0130	IMC
	H. Schultz	†Six Sonatas	cto, 3 trb	EdM, 14, 1941
Susato, T. ca. 1500- ca. 1560	R. King	Three Dances (Antwerp, 1551)	1110-bar	King, 1955
Sweelinck, J. P. 1562–1621	R. Volkmann	Or sus, serviteurs du Seigneur	1120	Concordia, 1968
Taverner, J. ca. 1495– 1545	Fetter	Audivi	0040	Ensemble
Tomkins, T. 1572–1656	N. Butterworth	Mr. Church's Toye & other pieces	1210	Chappell, 1964
Tromboncino, B. ca. 1470-ca. 1535		†Frottola (1508)	0040	(Day)
Zingarelli, N. A. 1752–1837	R. Volkmann	Go not far from me, O God	0220	Concordia, 1966
	Carlsten	Adagio e presto	0220	Barnhouse, 1964

5.5 *Five Instruments*

Adson, J. d. ca. 1640	D. Greer	†Three Courtly Masquing Ayres, Nos. 19, 20, 21 (1621)	0230	Schott, 1963
	R. King	†Two Ayres for Cornets & Sagbuts	1210-bar	King, n.d.
Anon.	R. King	†Sonata (Bänkel- sängerlieder, ca. 1684)	1211	King, 1958

Anon.	G. Schünnemann	†Aufzug	0220-timp	EdM
Antegnati, C. ca. 1550-ca. 1620	A. Lumsden	Canzona 20	0230	Musica Rara
Asola, J. 16th Cent.	L. Waldeck	Dies Irae	1211	Cor
Bach, J. S. 1685–1750	R. King	Jesu, nun sei gepreist (Cantata 41)	0220-org	King
	R. King	Alleluia (Cantata 142)	0220-org	King, n.d.
	R. King	In dulci jubilo	0220-org	King
	J. H. Christensen	Three Chorales	0211-bar	Kendor, 1963
	Fote	Chorale & Fughetta	1210-bar	Kendor, 1963
	R. King	Contrapunctus I (Art of Fugue)	1210-bar	King, 1960
	R. King	Contrapunctus III (Art of Fugue)	1210-bar	King, 1955
	R. King	Contrapunctus V (Art of Fugue)	1210-bar	King, 1961
	J. Glasel	Contrapunctus IX (Art of Fugue)	1211	Mentor, 1959
	J. Menken & S. Baron	Three Chorales	1211	Bo. & H., 1959
	Gordon	Five Pieces	2210	(K)
	I. Rosenthal	Fantasie	1211	Artransa, 1965
	I. Rosenthal	Wir glauben all' an einem Gott	1211	Artransa, 1966
	Halverson	Jesu, meine Freude	0050	Ensemble
	Anderson	Prelude & Fugue in e	1211	WIM, 1968
	R. Nagel	Contrapunctus IV (Art of Fugue)	1211	Mentor
	H. R. Ryker	Praeludium VII: Praeludium XXII	1211	MBQ, n.d.
	I. Rosenthal	Air pour les trompettes	1211	Artransa, 1967
	W. Sear	Fugue XXII	1211	Cor
	W. Sear	Praeludium XXII	1211	Cor
Banchieri, A. 1567–1734	H. R. Ryker	Sinfonia	1211	MBQ, n.d.
Bonelli, A. fl. ca. 1600	R. King	†Toccata, Athalanta (from Il primo Libro Ricercari, 1602)	0210-bar, org	King, 1957

Brade, W. 1560–1630	R. King	†Two Pieces, from Neue ausserlesene Padouanen und Galliarden, 1609	1211/ 0220-bar	King, 1961
	H. R. Ryker	Four Dances Dances for five parts	1211 0230	MBQ, n.d.
Chilese, B.	A. Lumsden	Canzona 22	0230	Musica Rara
Coleman, C. fl. ca. 1650	A. Baines	Four Pieces for Sackbuts & Cornets	0230	OUP, 1962
Couperin, L. 1626–61	R. King	Chaconne	0210-bar, org	King, 1955
East, M. ca. 1580–1648	A. Fromme	Desperavi (1610)	1220	AMP, 1967
Ferrabosco II, A. ca. 1575–1628	V. Reynolds	†4 note Pavan	1211	(Gram)
Fischer, J. C. F. 1650–1746	L. Waldeck	Le Journal de Printemps	1211	Cor
	L. Waldeck	Bourrée & Minuet	1211	Cor
	L. Waldeck	Entrée & Rondo †Suite in a	1211 0310-timp	Cor
Franck, M. ca. 1579–1639	R. King	Two Pavans, from Neuer Pavanen, Galliarden u. Intraden, Coburgk, 1603	1210–bar	King, 1960
Frescobaldi, G. 1583–1643	A. Lumsden	Canzona 21	0230	Musica Rara
		Fugue & Capriccio	1211	(K)
Gabrieli, A. ca. 1520–86	L. Waldeck	Three Ricercari	1211	Cor
Gabrieli, G. 1557-1612		Canzona prima a 5	0230	King
	L. Waldeck	Canzona	1211	Cor
	R. King	†Sonata pian e forte, from Sacrae Symphoniae, 1597	0220-org	King
	R. King	†Canzoni primi toni	0220-org	King
	R. King	†Canzoni noni toni	0220-org	King
	J. Boeringer	Canzoni septimi toni a 8	0220-org	Concordia, 1967
	H. R. Ryker	Madrigale: Sacro tempio d'honor	1211	MBQ, n.d.

Composer	Arranger	Title	No.	Publisher
		Canzoni septimi toni Nos. 1 & 2	0220-org	King
Gesualdo, C. ca. 1560–1616	Upchurch	Three Madrigals	1220	Southern, 1965
	Freedman	Four Madrigals	0230	Leeds, 1964
Gibbons, O. 1583–1625	V. Reynolds	†In Nomine	1211	(Gram)
Grep, B. 16th Cent.	R. King	Paduana, from Ausserlesene Paduanen u. Galliarden, 1607	1210-bar	King
Guami, G. ca. 1540–1611	A. Lumsden	Canzona 19	0230	Musica Rara
Handel, G. F. 1685–1759	R. King	Overture to 'Berenice'	1210-bar	King
Haussmann, V. d. ca. 1614	F. Rein	Drei Tänze	0230	Br. & H., 1954
	H. R. Ryker	Paduane mit Galliarde	1211	MBQ, n.d.
Hessen, M. von 1572–1632	D. G. Miller	Pavana	0050	Ensemble
Holborne, A. d. 1602	S. Beck	Pavans, Galliards, Almaines... London, 1599	br	N.Y. Pub. Lib.
		Five Pieces	1210-bar	King, 1961
	J. Glasel	†Three Pieces	1211	Mentor, 1960
	R. King	†Two Pieces (Nos. 55 & 60)	1210-bar	King, n.d.
	T. Dart	†Suite	0230	OUP, 1959
	T. Dart	5-part Brass Music	0230	Musica Rara
	R. King	Six Pieces (Nos. 8, 25, 59, 53, 6)	1220	King
Isaac, H. ca. 1450–1517	H. R. Ryker	Canzona & Lied	1211	MBQ, n.d.
Josquin des Prés ca. 1445–1521	H. R. Ryker	Faulte d'argent, c'est douleur non pareille	1211	MBQ, n.d.
Kessel, J. 17th Cent		Sonata (1672)	1210-bar	King
Lanier, N. 1586–1666	W. Osborne	Almand & Saraband	1220	Campion, 1961
Lassus, O. di 1530–94	H. R. Ryker	Motet: Tristis est anima mea	1211	MBQ [1966]
le Jeune, C. 1528–1600	H. R. Ryker	Deba contre mes debateurs	1211	MBQ, n.d.

Locke, M. ca. 1630–77	A. Baines	†Music for His Majesty's Sackbuts & Cornets (1661)	0230	OUP, 1951
Lully, J. B. 1632–87	R. King	Overture to 'Cadmus & Hermione'	1210-bar	King
Marcello, B. 1686–1739	R. King	The Heavens are telling (Psalm XVIII)	0210-bar, org	King, 1957
	R. King	The Lord will hear (Psalm XIX)	0210-bar, org	King
Marenzio, L. 1553–99	H. R. Ryker	La Bella	1211	MBQ, n.d.
	H. R. Ryker	Solo e pensoso	1211	MBQ, n.d.
Maschera, F. ca. 1540–84	H. R. Ryker	Canzona	1211	MBQ [1966]
Merula, T. 17th Cent.	H. R. Ryker	Canzona: La Strada, Op 13 (Venice, 1637)	1211	MBQ [1966]
Merulo, C. 1533–1604	A. Lumsden	Canzonas 18, 23, 36	0230	Musica Rara
Monteverdi, C. 1567– 1643	S. Beck	Suite	0230/ 1211	Mercury
	D. Townsend	Sinfonia (1969)	1220	Colombo, 1968
O'Koever (16th Cent?)	V. Reynolds	†Fantasia	1211	(Gram)
Orologio, A. 16th Cent.	H. R. Ryker	Intrada No. 3	1211	MBQ [1966]
Pachelbel, J. 1653–1706	R. King	Allein Gott in der Höh sei Ehr	0210-bar, org	King
Palestrina, G. P. 1525–94	L. Waldeck	Agnus Dei	1211	Cor
Pezel, J. C. 1639–94		Hora decima musicorum Lipsiensium: 40 Sonaten f. 2 Cornette u. 3 Trombonen		Leipzig, G. H. Frommann 1670
	A. Schering	13 Sonatas: Nos. 1–6, 12–14, 27, 30, 39	0230	DDT, Vol. 63, 1928, 1959
	A. Lumsden	2 vols	0230/ 1220	Musica Rara, 1967
	D. G. Miller	12 Sonatas	0230	Ensemble, n.d.
	K. Brown	12 Sonatas Separate Sonatas from Hora Decima	0230	IMC

R. King	†Sonata No. 1	0221	King
R. King	†Sonata No. 2	0210-bar, org	King, 1957
F. Rein	†Sonata No. 2	0230	Br. & H., 1954
R. King	†Sonata No. 3	1220	King, 1958
	†Sonata No. 4		
J. Menken & S. Baron	†Sonata No. 5	1211	Bo. & H., 1959
	†Sonata No. 6		
N. C. Greenberg	†Sonata No. 12	1220	Mills, 1959
L. Waldeck	†Sonata No. 14	1211	Cor
R. King	†Sonata No. 22	1210-bar	King, 1956
R. King	Sonata No. 25	1210-bar	King, 1962
L. F. Brown	Sonata No. 27	1211	Rubank, 1958
F. Rein	Sonata No. 27	0230	Br. & H., 1954
N. C. Greenberg	Sonata No. 28	1211	Mills, 1958
	†Sonata No. 30		
	†Sonata No. 39		
	Fünffstimmigte blasende Musik, 1685. (76 Stücke f. 2 Cornette u. 3 Trombonen)		Frankfurt, B. Chr. West, 1685
A. Schering	Selections	0230	DDT, Vol. 63, 1928, 1959
K. Schlegel		1220/ 0230	Merseburger, 1960
A. Lumsden	3 vols	0230	Musica Rara, 1960, 1966
R. King	Six Pieces (Nos. 59, 25, 36, 29, 30, 64)	1210-bar	King, 1955
R. King	Three Pieces (Nos. 13, 63, 62)	1210-bar	King, 1960
D. G. Miller	Sixteen Dances	0230	Ensemble
K. Brown	Sixteen Pieces	0230	IMC
E. H. Meyer	Turmmusik: Auswahl von 18 Stücken (Hora decima u. Fünffstimmigte Blasmusik)	0230	Br. & H., 1930; New ed., 1954
A. Schering	†Zwei Suiten	0230	Br. & H., 1905; 1951
A. Schering	Turmmusik und Suiten (12 Sonatas from Hora decima, 16 Pieces from Fünffstimmigte Blasmusik)	0230	Br. & H., 1928; 1959

235

	W. Sear	†Intrada & Bal	1211	Cor
	W. Sear	†Bal & Sarabande	1211	Cor
	W. Sear	Allemande & Courante	1211	Cor
Praetorius, M. 1571–1621	R. King	In dulci jubilo (Musae Sioniae, 1607)	0210-bar, org	King
Purcell, H. 1659–95	J. Corley	Trumpet Voluntary	1210-bar	King, 1955
	J. Corley	Voluntary on the Old 100th	1210-bar	King, 1957
	R. King	Allegro & Air (King Arthur)	1211	King
	W. Sear	Fantasia on one note	1211	Cor
	W. Sear	Fantasia No. 5	1211	Cor
	W. Sear	Fantasia No. 8	1211	Cor
	G. Masso	Suite from 'Bonduca'	1211	Providence, 1968
	W. Sear	Trumpet Overture: Indian Queen, Act III	1211	Cor
Reiche, G. 1667–1734	R. King	Sonata No. 7 (Neue Quatricinia, 1696)	0210-bar, org	King
Rosenmüller, J. ca. 1619–84	L. Waldeck	Courante, Sarabande & Bal	1211	Cor
	L. Waldeck	Intrada	1211	Cor
	L. Waldeck	Sinfonia prima	1211	Cor
	K. Nef & H. J. Moser	Eleven Sonate da camera (1670)	2 cto, 2 trb, cont	DDT, 18, 1957
Scheidt, S. 1587–1654		Paduana, Galliarda, Alemande, Intrada, Canzonetta; 32 4–5 st. Instr. Sätze mit Bc		Hamburg, 1621; Ugrino, 1928
	V. Reynolds	†Canzon Gallicam	1211	(Gram)
	V. Reynolds	†Benedicamus Domino	1211	(Gram)
	V. Reynolds	†Galliard Battaglia	1211	(Gram)
	V. Reynolds	†Wendet euch um ihr Anderlein	1211	Gram)
	V. Reynolds	†Canzona Aechiopicam	1211	(Gram)

236

	V. Reynolds	†Canzona Bergamasca	1211	(Gram)
	C. de Jong	Canzona Bergamasca	1211	Ensemble, 1966
	D. M. Green	Suite	1211	Presser, 1964
Schein, J. H. 1586–1630	G. Hessler	Allemande & Tripla Nos. 1 & 2	0230/ 1211	Cor
	G. Hessler	Allemande & Tripla Nos. 6, 7 & 9	0230/ 1211	Cor
	G. Hessler	Allemande & Tripla No. 8	0230/ 1211	Cor
	G. Hessler	Allemande & Tripla Nos. 15 & 19	0230/ 1211	Cor
	Q. Maganini	Suite	0230	(K)
	R. King	Two Pieces (Banchetto Musicale, 1617)	1210-bar	King, n.d.
	W. Sear	Intrada	1211	Cor
Schütz, H. 1585–1672	H. R. Ryker	Sinfonia	1211	MBQ, n.d.
Simmes, W. 16th–17th Cent.	H. R. Ryker	Fantasia	1211	MBQ, n.d.
	V. Reynolds	†Fantasie	1211	(Gram)
Simpson, T. 17th Cent.	L. Waldeck	Theme & Variations	1211	Cor
Speer, D. b. ca. 1625	H. Schultz	†Sonata No. 1 (1685)	0040- cont	EdM 14, 1961
	H. Schultz	†Sonata No. 2 (1685)	0040- cont	EdM 14, 1961
	Brown	Two Sonatas	1030-org	(K)
		Two Sonatas	0230	Ensemble
		Two Sonatas	1220	IMC
Stoltzer, T. ca. 1475– 1526	R. King	Fantasia (Hypodorian)	0050/ 2030	King
Weelkes, T. ca. 1575– 1623	V. Reynolds	†Four Madrigals	1211	(Gram)

5.6 *Six Instruments*

Corelli, A. 1653–1713	R. King	Pastorale (from Christmas Concerto)	2210-bar	King, 1955
Couperin, F. 1668–1733		3 Movements from 'La Stein- querque'	1310-bar	Marks, 1967

Franck, M. ca. 1579– 1639	F. Rein	†Intrada (from Neue Musikalische Intraden . . . Nürnberg, 1608)	0330	Br. & H., 1955
	Long	Two Intradas	1211-bar	Rubank
Gabrieli, A. ca. 1520–86	A. Shuman	†Psalmus CXXLX: De profundis clamavi	0231	Southern
	A. Shuman	Agnus Dei	0231	Southern
	A. Shuman	†Ricercar del duodecimi toni	0231	Southern
Gabrieli, G. 1557–1612	A. Shuman	†Canzona a 6	0231	Southern
	R. King	†Canzon duodecimi toni (Sacrae Symphoniae, 1597)	1220-org	King, 1958
	A. Fromme	†Canzona Prima a 5	1221-opt, org	Mentor, 1961
Handel, G. F. 1685–1759	R. King	Three Pieces from The Water Music	2210-bar	King, 1955
Lassus, O. di 1522–94	R. Volkmann	Surrexit pastor bonus	1211-bar	Concordia, 1968
Locke, M. 1630–77	R. King	†Music for King Charles II	1310-bar	King, 1960
Pezel, J. C. 1639–94		Decas Sonatorum f. 2 Cornette u. 4 Trombonen (1669)		
Purcell, H. 1659–95	Barnes	March & Fanfare	1211-bar	Ludwig, 1963
	L. F. Brown	Trumpet Tune & Air	1211-bar	Rubank, 1950
	Q. Maganini	Fantasia on one note	1221	Musicus, 1960
Sweelinck, J. P. 1562–1621	R. Volkmann	Hodie Christus natus est	1211-bar	Concordia, 1966
	R. Volkmann	Angelus ad pastores act	1211-bar	Concordia

5.7 *Seven Instruments*

Bach, J. S. 1685–1750	R. King	Ricercar (from The Musical Offering)	1320-bar	King, 1956
Buonamente, G. B. d. 1643	R. King	†Sonata (from Sonate e Canzoni, 1636)	2211-bar	King, n.d.

Francisque, A. ca. 1570–1605	J. Berger	Suite: Le Trésor d'Orphée	2220-bar	King
Gabrieli, A. 1520–86	A. Shuman	†Ricercar del 12° tuono	0421	Southern
Josquin des Prés ca. 1440–1521		†Königsfanfaren	0330-timp	
Lassus, O. di 1522–94	R. King	†Providebam Dominum	1410-bar	King, n.d.
Monteverdi, C. 1567–1643	D. Greer	Three Sinfonias from 'Orfeo'	2230-opt org/ 0250-opt org	Faber, 1968
Schubert, F. 1797–1828	R. King	Eine kleine Trauermusik	2220-bar	King, 1959
Speer, D. b. ca. 1625	H. Schultz	Two Fanfares	0330-timp	EdM, XIV; BVK, 1961
Vitali, G. B. ca. 1644–92	B. Fitzgerald	Capriccio	1221-bar	Presser

5.8 Eight Instruments

Bach, J. S. 1685–1750	Hunsberger	Passacaglia in c	0080	Ensemble
	G. F. Ghedini	Ricercar	0330-2 pf	SZ
Bartolini, O.		Canzona 30	0440	Musica Rara
Bonelli, A. fl. ca. 1600	R. King	†Toccata: Athalanta (1602)	2220-2 bar	King, 1957
Bramieri, C.		Canzon: La Foccara	8 br	Peters
Buxtehude, D. ca. 1637–1707	R. King	Fanfare & Chorus (from Ihr lieben Christen)	2410-bar	King, n.d.
Chilese, B.		Canzonas 31, 32	0440	Musica Rara
Frescobaldi, 1583–1643		Canzona 29	0440	Musica Rara
Gabrieli, A. ca. 1520–86		†L'Aria della Battaglia	0440	
Gabrieli, G. 1557–1612		Sacrae Symphoniae		Venice, 1597
	R. King	†Canzon primi toni	0440	King, 1960
	P. Winter	†Canzon septimi toni No. 1	0620	Peters, 1960
	A. Shuman	†Canzon septimi toni No. 1	0431	Southern
		†Canzon septimi toni No. 1	2220-2 bar	Mercury, 1948

	R. King	†Canzon septimi toni No. 1	0440	King
	R. King	†Canzon septimi toni No. 2	0440	King, 1958
		Canzon septimi toni No. 3	0440	(BBC, May, 1967)
	R. King	†Canzon noni toni a 8	2420	King
	P. Winter	Sonata XIII (1615)	0620	Peters, 1960
	R. King	†Sonata pian e forte	1240-bar	King, 1958
	F. Stein	†Sonata pian e forte	0260	Peters, 1963
	Harvey	†Sonata pian e forte	2031-2 ct	EV
	R. Miller	†Sonata pian e forte	8 br	OUP, 1960
	G. Draper	O magnum Mysterium	3320	OUP, 1961
	Wolters	Jubilate Deo	0440	(K)
	G. W. Anthony	Antiphony No. 2	2240	Presser
	A. Lumsden	†Canzonas 27, 28	0440	Musica Rara, 1967
Gallus, J. 1550–91		Repleti sunt	0431	Cor
Guami, G. ca. 1540–1611	A. Lumsden	Canzonas 24, 25	0440	Musica Rara
Lappi, G.	A. Lumsden	Canzona 26	0440	Musica Rara, 1969
Massaino, T. ca. 1550–ca. 1609	C. Silliman	†Canzona a 8	0080	Ensemble, 1964
	R. King	†Canzona a 8	0080	King, 1964
Palestrina, G. P. 1525–94	L. Waldeck	Oratio Hieremiae	2231	Cor
Rognoni Taeggio, G. D. d. ca. 1626	P. Winter	†La Porta Canzone (1605)	0440	Peters, 1960
Schütz, H. 1585–1672	G. W. Anthony	Antiphony No. 1	0440	Presser, 1958

5.9 *Nine Instruments*

Bach, J. S. 1685–1750	F. Tull	Vom Himmel hoch	9 br	(K)
Campra, A. 1660–1744	R. Wetzler	Rigaudon	2331	Concordia, 1964
Gabrieli, G. 1557–1612		Sonata pian e forte	2241	Eulenburg

Massaino, T. ca. 1550– ca. 1609	R. Monteroso	†Canzona trigesimaterzo (1608)	0080-cont	Venice, 1608; DTÖ, CX, 1964
Monteverdi, C. 1567–1643	R. King	Sonata sopra Sancta Maria ora pro nobis (1610)	1420-2 bar	King
Schein, J. H. 1586–1630		Gagliarda	4221	Hinrichsen

5.10 *Ten or more Instruments*

Bach J. S. 1685–1750	Walker	Sarabande & Bourrée	4331-bar	Southern, 1966
	D. Gillis	Chorales	4231-2 ct, bar	Southern, 1963
	R. King	O Jesu Christ, meins' Lebens Licht (Cantata 118)	2430-bar	King
Berger, A.	D. Whitwell	Canzona	1422-bar	MF Co.
Bononcini, G. 1670–1747	M. Moore	Canon (1669)	0552	Arco, 1967
Cesti, P. A. 1618–69	B. Fitzgerald	Prelude to Il Pomo d'Oro	4332-bar	Presser, 1963
Clarke, J. d. 1707	F. Clark	†Trumpet Voluntary	4222-bar, org ad lib	Musicus, 1956
Gabrieli, G. 1557–1612	R. A. Boudreau	†Canzon noni toni a 12	0660	Peters, 1962
	F. Fennell	†Canzon noni toni a 12	3630	Ensemble
	R. King	†Canzon quarti toni	4263	King
	R. King	†Canzon duodecimi toni	2420-2 bar	King, 1958
	R. King	†Canzon octavi toni	2440-2 bar	King
		†Canzon septimi toni No. 1	2440	Baron
		Canzon No. 7	0640	Peters
	G. Benvenuti	Canzon duodecimi toni; †Canzon in echo duodecimi toni (1597)	8 cto, 2 trb	IMAMI 2, 1932
Massaino, T. ca. 1550– ca. 1609		Canzon	16 trb	Raverii, 1608; Musica Rara
Monteverdi, C. 1567–1643	D. Greer	Canzon quarti toni	15 br	Faber

Purcell, H. 1659–95	R. Smith	Symphony from The Fairy Queen, Act 4	2631-bar, timp King, 1957
	Brown	Trumpet Voluntary	2431-bar SB, 1958

6. Chamber music with parts for trombone(s)

6.1 *Two Instruments*

Braga, F. 1868–1945	Dialogo sonoro ao lunar sax, trb	IIM, 1946
Schwadron, A. A.	Short Suite cl, trb	Kendor, 1967

6.2 *Three Instruments*

Alsina, C. R. 1941–	Trio (1967) trb, vcl, perc	B. & B., 1969
Baeyens, H.	Introduction et Cantabile cl, trb/tuba, pf	Brogneaux, 1958
Banchieri, A. 1568–1634	Three Sonatas, Op 43: Suonarino trb, vln, cont	A. Vincenti, 1622
Behrend, F. 1889–	Kleine Kakteensammlung, Op 110 trb, vln, db	Composer, 1951
Bowman, C. 1913–	Trio trb, vla, vcl	Composer
Cima, G. P. fl. 1600	Concerti ecclesiastici: Sonata cto, trb, cont	Milan, 1610
Coperario, G. ca. 1575–1626	Fansies trb, vln, org	MS
Erb, D. 1927–	†In no strange Land trb, db, tape	(Gram, Nov. 1969)
Gaburo, K. 1926–	Poised IV (1966–7) trb, db, tape	(MT, Apr., 1968)
Ganassi, G.	Vespertina psalmodia: 3 Canzone trb, vln, cont	A. Vincenti, 1637
Harder, E. E.	Trio one 2 cl, trb	Composer, 1921
Horrod, N.	Trio hn, bn, trb	KaWe, 1967
Knight, M. 1933–	Selfish Giant Suite fl, cl, trb	Broude
Knipper, L. C. 1898–	Four Children's Miniatures, Op 24: No. 3, Song ca, trb, vln	Bo. & H.
Kroeger, K. 1932–	Toccata cl, trb, perc	(K)
Mariani, P. A.	La Guaralda trb, vln, cont	A. Vincenti, 1622
Masters, E. L.	Miniatures (1956) cl, trp, trb	MS

Milanuzzi, C. ca. 1590–ca. 1645	Canzon a 2 alla bastarda, from Op 6 trb, vln, cont	A. Vincenti, 1622
Nicolai, J. M. 1629–85	Two Sonatas a 2 trb, vln, cont	MS (MGG*)
Pepping, E. 1901–	Suite (1925) sax, trp, trb	MS (MGG, T)
Persichetti, V. 1915–	Serenade No. 6, Op 44 (1950) trb, vla, vcl	EV, 1964
Picchi, G. 16th–17th Cent.	Canzoni da sonar con ogni sorte d'istromenti: Canzon terza trb, vln, cont	A. Vincenti, 1625
	Sonata sesta a 2 trb, vln, cont	A. Vincenti, 1625
Riccio, G. B. 17th Cent.	Canzon la fineta trb, vln, cont	Magni, 1620
	Canzon la sauoldi trb, vln, cont	Magni, 1620
	Canzon la pichi in ecco con il tremolo trb, vln, cont	Magni, 1620
Scharwenka, X. 1850–1924	Sommertage auf Achensee, Op 89 trb, pf, timp	Kistner [ca. 1922]
Sedmidubský, M. 1924–	Concertino bn, trb, pf	SHV, 1965
Srámek, V. 1923–	Sonatina fl, ob, trb	SHV, 1964
Stewart, R.	Trio No. 5: Overture to Dr. Faustus cl, trb, vln	CFE
Tanenbaum, E. 1924–	Trio fl, trb, tenor vln	CFE
Thilman, J. P. 1906–	Concerti espressivi trb, pf, timp	Peters, 1966
Ucellini, M. ca. 1610–80	Sonata I trb, vln, cont	A. Vincenti, 1639
	Sonata seconda detta la bucefalasca trb, vln, cont	A. Vincenti, 1642
Weber, B. 1916–	Image in the Snow (1952) trb, vcl, cel	CFE
Wolf, J. J.	Transzendenz, Op 46 trb, db, tape	(Cz)

6.3 Four Instruments

Banchieri, A. 1568–1634	Sonata sopra l'aria del Gran Duca, Op 42 trb, 2 vln, cont	A. Vincenti, 1620
Bartali, A. 17th Cent.	Sonata a 3 trb, 2 vln, cont	MS (E*)
Bernardi, S. ca. 1576–1636	Sonata a tre, Op 12 trb, 2 vln, cont	A. Vincenti, 1621

Bertali, A. 1605–69 (same as Bartali above?)	Sonata a tre trb, 2 vln, cont	Musica Rara
Belli, G. 17th Cent.	Canzona trb, 2 vln, cont	Magni, 1613; Stein, 1621
Biber, H. I. F. 1644–1704	†Sonata a 3 (Ed K. Janetzky) trb, 2 vln, cont	Musica Rara, 1958
Bois, R. du 1934–	Musique d'atelier cl, trb, vcl, pf	Donemus, 1968
Capricornus, S. F. ca. 1629–65	Three Sonatas trb, 2 vln, cont	Nuremburg, 1660
Dias	Meu Bem sax, trp, trb, perc	(K)
Donner, H. O. 1939–	Ideogramme I fl, cl, trb, perc, 12 radios (or tape)	(Ri)
Ferro, M. A. 17th Cent.	Sonata quinta a 3 cto, trb, theorbo, cont	Venice, 1639
Gaburo, K. 1926–	†Line Studies (1957) fl, cl, trb, vla	Composer
	Musica da camera cl, trb, vla, pf	Composer
Hambraeus, B. 1928–	Transit No. 2 hn, trb, elec gt, pf	FST
Ives, C. 1874–1954	†Ann Street (1921) fl, trp, trb, pf	MS (Cowell)
	†From the Steeples (1901) trp, trb, 2 chimes/2 pf	Peer, 1965
Kempis, N. à 17th Cent.	Symphoniae, Op 2: Symphonia prima cto, trb, vln, cont	Phalese, 1647
	Symphonia secunda cto, trb, vln, cont	Phalese, 1649
	Symphoniae, Op 3: Symphonia prima trb, 2 vln, cont	Phalese, 1649
Kindermann, J. E. 1616–65	Sonate & Symphoniae (Ed F. Schreiber) 2 cto, trb, cont	Nuremburg, 1643; DTB, Filser, 1924
	Ballet G (Ed F. Schreiber) cto, trb, vln, cont	Nuremberg, 1643; DTB, Filser, 1924
	†Ritornello in G cto, trb, vln, cont	DTB, Filser, 1924
Klebe, G. 1925–	Seven Bagatelles, Op 35 basset hn, trb, hp, tubular bell	B. & B., 1961
Kubizek, A. 1918–	Vergnügliche Miniaturen, Op 28a cl, bn, trb, vln	Doblinger, 1966
Mellnäs, A. 1933–	Tombola (1963) hn, trb, elec gt, pf	Tonos
Mielczewski, M. d. 1651	Canzona No. 2 a 3 (Ed Z. M. Szweykowski & K. Sikorski) trb, 2 vln, bc	PWM, 1966

Mont' albano, B. 17th Cent.	Sinfonie: Castelletti trb, 2 vln, cont	Maringo, 1629
	Sinfonie: Fiumicello trb, 2 vln, cont	Maringo, 1629
Picchi, G. 16th–17th Cent.	Canzoni da sonar con ogni sorte d'istromenti: Canzon settima trb, 2 vln, cont	A. Vincenti, 1625
	Canzon ottava trb, 2 vln, cont	A. Vincenti, 1625
Rees, H.	The Cat's Paw among the Silence of midnight Goldfish trb, pf, elec org, perc, tape	(MT, May, 1969)
Rovetta, G. d. 1668	Salmi concertati, Op 1: Canzon seconda a 3 trb, 2 vln, cont	Magni, 1626, 1641
Salzberg, M.	Quartet (1953) ob, trb, vln, perc	MS (BQ, III, 3)
Sarason, L.	Quartet (ca. 1951) cl, trp, trb, hp	MS (BQ, III, 3)
Sheinkman, M. 1926–	Divertimento (1953) cl, trp, trb, hp	Litolff, 1957
Starer, R. 1924–	Cantamus: Concertino (1948) ob, trb, vln, pf	IMP, 1953
Stibilj, M. 1929–	Condensation trb, 2 pf, perc	BVK, 1968
Welin, K. E. 1934–	Manzit cl, trb, vcl, pf	FST
Vejvanowsky, P. J. ca. 1640–93	Sonata tribus quadrantibus (Ed J. Pohanka) trp, trb, vln, cont	SNKLHU, 1961 (MAB, Vol. 48)
Wyner, Y. 1929–	Passover Offering fl, cl, trb, vcl	CFE

6.4 *Five Instruments*

Antheil, G. 1900–59	Quintet (Sinfonietta) (1923) fl, bn, trp, trb, vla	MS (G)
Brown, E. 1926–	Times Five fl, trb, vln, vcl, hp, 4 channels of tape	AMP
Cardew, C. 1936–	Treatise trb, acc, elec gt, elec org, pf	
Cima, G. P. fl. 1600–	Concerti eccliastici: Sonata cto, trb, vln, violone, cont	Milan, 1610
Cuclin, D. 1885–	Quintet picc, ca, dbn, trb, pf	(L. & B.)
Duncan, J.	Divertimento (1947) trb, stg quart	MS (H*)
Ferro, M. A. 17th Cent.	Sonata ottava a 4 2 cto, trb, bn, cont	Venice, 1649
	Sonata undecimo a 4 2 cto, trb, bn, cont	Venice, 1649

Fitelberg, J. 1903–51	Capriccio fl, ob, cl, bcl, trb	Balan, 1931; Omega, 1948
Fux, J. J. 1660–1741	Sonata a 4 (Ed G. Adler) bn, trp, trb, viol, org	DTÖ, 19, 1902, 1959
Gauldin, R.	Movement (1952) fl, cl, bn, trp, trb	Young Composers Radio Awards, 1953
Goeb, R. 1914–	†Concertino trb, stg quart	CFE, 1952
Hartley, W. S. 1927–	Sonata da camera ob, 2 cl, bn, trb	Interlochen, 1958
	Suite (1951) fl, ob, cl, sax, trb	Interlochen, 1958
Holewa, H. 1905–	Quintet (1962) cl, trb, vcl, pf, perc	FST
Kohs, E. 1916–	Burlesca I (1945) fl, cl, bn, trb, timp (trb in No. 1 only)	MS (BQ, III, 3)
McCulloh, B. B.	Toccata (1949) trb, vla, pf, 2 perc	MS (BQ, III, 3)
Macero, T. 1925–	Allegro cl, trb, tuba, vln, vla	CFE
McKenzie, J. H. 1930–	Song (1952) trb, vib, timp, tam-tam, drums	Music for Percussion, 1956
Mills, C. 1914–	Paul Bunyan Jump sax, trp, trb, db, drums	CFE
Nelhybel, V. 1919–	Quintetto concertante trp, trb, vln, pf, xyl	GMPC, 1967
Picchi, G. 16th–17th Cent.	Canzoni da sonar con ogni sorte d'istromenti: Canzon decima 2 fl, 2 trb, cont	A. Vincenti, 1625
	Canzon duodecima 2 trb, 2 vln, cont	A. Vincenti, 1625
Pohle, D. 1620–ca. 1704	Sonata a 4 bn, 2 cto, trb, cont	MS (BQ, III, 4)
Porta, E. d. 1630	Canzon in risposta: La Luchina cto, 2 trb, vln, cont	Bologna, 1613
	Vaga Ghirlanda (1613) cto, 2 trb, vln, cont	
Premru, R. E. 1934–	Concertino fl, ob, cl, bn, trb	Musica Rara, 1961
Rabe, F. 1935–	Impromptu (1962) cl, trb, vcl, pf, perc	FST
Rathaus, K. 1895–1954	Little Serenade, Op 23 (1927) cl, bn, trp, trb, pf	MS (MGG, T)
Reisberg, H.	Quintet (1958) cl, bcl, trp, trb, pf	MS (BQ, III, 4)
Theile, J. 1646–1724	Sonata a 4 bn, trb, 2 vln, bc	MS (E*, MGG*)
Thomson, V. 1896–	†Sonata da chiesa (1925) cl, hn, trp, trb, vla	NME, 1944

Tuma, F. I. A. 1704–74	Sonata in e (Ed J. Racek & V. Belsky) 2 trb, 2 vln, bc	SHV, 1965 (MAB, Vol. 67)
Valentini, G. 17th Cent.	Sonata a 4 (ca. 1610) bn, cto, trb, vln, org	MS (Bibl. Kassel)
Vejvanowsky, P. J. ca. 1640–93	Sonata a 5 (1666) (Ed J. Pohanka) 2 trp, trb, 2 vln	SNKLHU, 1960 (MAB, Vol. 47)
Viadana, L. 1564–1645	Cento Concerti ecclesiastici, Op 12 Canzon francese cto, 2 trb, vln, cont	G. Vincenti, 1602
	Canzona a quattro a risposta cto, 2 trb, vln, cont	London, 1896
Vierdanck, J. b. ca. 1610	Sonata cto, 3 trb, bc	Rostock, 1641
Weckmann, M. 1619–74	Sonata a 4 (Ed A. Lumsden) ob, bn, trb, vln, cont	Musica Rara, 1957
	8 Sonate a 4 (Ed G. Ilgner) cto, bn, trb, vln, cont	EdM, 1942
	Nun freut euch (Ed G. Binkerd) ob, ca, bn, 2 trb	AMP, 1963

6.5 Six Instruments

Anderberg, C. O. 1914–	Hexaphoni cl, trp, trb, vln, db, pf	Suecia
Bean, C.	Sextet (1956) fl, ob, hn, trp, trb, tuba	MS (BQ, III, 4)
Cerha, F. 1926–	Enjambements (1959) fl, trp, trb, vln, db, perc	UE, 1963
Crosse, G. 1937–	Canto, Op 4 (1961, rev 1963) wind quint, trb	OUP
Finnissy, M. 1946–	Afar (1967) fl, cl, 3 trb, perc	BMIC
Galindo, B. 1910–	Sextet fl, cl, hn, bn, trp, trb	(Slon)
Grandi, O. M. 17th Cent.	Sonate per orgni sorte di stromente: Sonata decima nona a 5 4 trb, vln, org	Magni, 1628
Gwinner	Sechs Nederdeutsches Volkstänze 2 cl, 2 hn, trp, trb	Möseler
Hodier, A. 1921–	Osymetrios (1960) sax, trp, trb, db, pf, drums	MJQ, 1961
	Trope a Saint Trop sax, trp, trb, db, pf, drums	MJQ, 1961
Kindermann, J. E. 1616–65	†Intrada a cinque stromenti, in C 2 cto, 3 trb, cont	Nuremberg, 1643; Filser, 1924 (DTB, XXI, XXIV)
McCulloh, B. B.	Antigone Music ob, cl, bn, trb, vln, perc	MS (BQ, III, 3)
Mellnäs, A. 1933–	Per Caso (1963) sax, trb, vln, db, 2 perc	Tonos, 1964

Mohr, A.	Die Dorfmusikanten 2 picc, cl, bn, trb, vla	Andraud
Paz, J. C. 1897–	Tres Contrapuntos, Op 50 (1955) cl, trp, trb, vcl, cel, gt	MS (BQ, III, 4)
Ponc, M. 1902–	Hochzeitsleute auf dem Eiffels- turm: Szenenmusik cl, trb, vln, ¼ tone harm, ¼ tone pf, perc	MS (MGG)
Seiber, M. 1904–60	Two Jazzolettes (1929, 1932) 2 sax, trp, trb, pf, perc	Hansen, 1958
Valentini, G. ca. 1681–ca. 1740	Sonata a 5 2 cto, trb, 2 vln, cont	MS (BQ, III, 4)
Vejvanowsky, P. J. ca. 1640–93	†Sonata a 5 (Ed J. Pohanka) trp, alto trb, vln, 2 vla, cont	SNKLHU, 1960 (MAB, Vol. 49)
Villa-Lobos, H. 1887–1959	Chorôs No. 3: Pica Pao cl, sax, hn, bn, trb; mch ad lib	Eschig, 1928

6.6 Seven Instruments

Barbe, H. 1927–	Miniaturen zu einem Lustspiel von Shakespeare 0010–0110–0001–pf, 2 perc	BVK
Behrend, F. 1889–	Tanzsuite, Op 114 0111–0110–1010	Composer, 1955
Borris, S. 1906–	Intrada serena No. 1 1111–1110–0000	Sirius
Buonamente, G. B. d. 1643	Sonata a sei 0000–0040–2000–cont	A. Vincenti, 1636
	Canzona a sei 0000–0040–2000–cont	A. Vincenti, 1636
Castillo, R. 1894–	Fiesta 1111–0110–0000–perc	MS? (BQ, III, 4)
Cazzati, M. d. 1677	Sonata della la Vecchia 0000–0010–3100–violone, cont	A. Vincenti, 1648
Coscio, S.	Septet 1111–1110–0000	Baron, 1953
Doué, J. 1922–	Septet (1953) 1111–1110–0000	Heugel
Feldman, M. 1926–	False Relationships & the extended Ending 0000–0010–1010–3 pf, bells	
Frommel, G. 1906–	Concertino 1121–1010–0000	Schott
Gilbert, A. 1934–	Brighton Piece, Op 9 0010–1110–0010–2 perc	Schott
Grandi, O. M. 17th Cent.	Sonata vigesima a 6 0000–0030–3000–cont	Magni, 1628
Grandis, R. de 1927–	Canti sulle Pause 0000–sax–0010–1000–cel, vib, 2 perc	Tonos, 1961
Jolivet, A. 1905–	Rhapsodie 0011–0010–ct–1001–perc	Pathé-Marconi

Karjalainen, A. 1907–	Septet, Op 22 0111–1110–0000 (?)	MS? (Gor)
Kayn R. 1933–	Kammerkonzert 1111–1010–0000–perc	Sikorski, n.d.
Koechlin, C. 1867–1951	Le Jeu de la Nativité, Op 177 0101–ca–0110–0100–org, pf ad lib	MS (G, MGG)
Köper, K. H. 1927–	Musik für 6 Blasinstrumente u. Kontrabass 1010–sax–1110–0001	Modern
Layton, B. J. 1926–	Divertimento, Op 6 0011–0010–1010–hpcd, perc	G. Schirmer, 1963
Macero, T. 1925–	Four plus Four 0000–0210–1000–pf 4h	CFE
Maselli, G. F. 1929–	Divertimento 1100–0110–1001–pf	SZ, 1965
McCulloh, B. B.	Chamber Concerto (1947–8) 0000–0010–2200–pf, timp	MS (BQ, III, 3)
Motte, D. de la 1928–	Septet 0011–0110–1001–perc	BVK, 1966
Pablo, L. de 1930–	Coral, Op 2 1111–1110–0000	Modern, 1962
Picchi, G. 16th–17th Cent.	Canzoni da sonar con ogni sorte d'istromenti: Canzon decima quarta 0000–0040–2000–cont	A. Vincenti, 1625
	Canzon decima quinta 0000–0040–2000–cont	A. Vincenti, 1625
Satie, E. 1866–1925	Toute petite Danse pour la Piège de Méduse (1913) 0010–0110–1011–perc	Galerie Simon, 1921; G. Schirmer
Smalley, R. 1943–	Septet (1963) 1110–0110–0110– S & T solos in final section	(MT, Feb., 1968)
Stravinsky, I. 1882–	†L'Histoire du Soldat (1918) 0011–0010–ct–1001–perc, speaker	Chester, 1924
Sydeman, W. 1928–	Concerto da camera No. III solo vln–0000–bcl–0210–0000–2 perc	AMP, 1967
Sylvius, C. (=Coscio, S.)	Septet 1111–1110–0000	Baron, 1953
Vejvanowsky, P. J. ca. 1640–93	Sonata la posta (Ed J. Pohanka) 0000–0030–3000–cont	SNKLHU, 1961 (MAB, Vol. 48)
Wyner, Y. 1929–	†Serenade (1958) 1000–1110–0110–pf	CFE

6.7 *Eight Instruments*

Allen, P. H. 1883–1952	The Muses 1121–1110–0000	Whitney
Angerer, P. 1927–	Quinta Ton 1111–1210–0000	UE

Babbitt, M. 1916–	†All Set 0000–2 sax–0110–0001–pf, vib, perc	AMP [ca. 1957]
Chou Wen-Chung 1923–	Yu-Ko (1965) alto fl, ca, bcl–0020–1000–2 perc	Peters, 1968
Codivilla, F. b. 1841	Octet in E♭ 1111–2010–ct–0000	Pizzi, 1919
Dickinson, P. 1934–	Three Dances for a Ballet (1959) 1011–0110–0010–pf, perc	Novello
Engelmann, H. U. 1921–	Ezra Pound Music, Op 21 picc/fl 101–ca–0010–0011–perc	A. & S.
Fellegara, V. 1927–	Octet (1953) 1111–1210–0000	SZ, 1955
Gabrieli, G. 1557–1612	Sonata pian e forte (Ed G. Benvenuti) cto, 6 trb, vla	IMAMI, 2, 1932
Green, R. 1909–	Three Pieces for a Concert 1020–0210–0000–pf, perc	Marks, 1948
Henze, H. W. 1926–	†Concerto per il Marigny (1956) 0010–bcl–1110–0110–pf	Schott, 1956
Janáček, L. 1854–1928	†Capriccio picc/fl 000–0231–0000– pf lh	HM; SNKLHU, 1953
Krol, B. 1920–	Concerto da camera, Op 35 1001–bcl–1110–0001–pf	Simrock, 1961
Lang, M.	Schauspielmusik: Der Besuch der alten Dame 0111–0110–1000–pf, harm	MS (BQ, III, 4)
Lazarof, H. 1932–	Octet 1111–bcl–1110–0000	AMP, 1967
Lessard, J. 1920–	†Octet (1952) 1011–2210–0000	CFE
Matsushita, S.	Composizione da camera per 8 1010–0110–1010–pf, perc	Ongaku
Maxwell Davies, P. 1934–	Eram quasi Agnus 1011–dbn–0020–0000–hp, handbells	(Times, 20 June, 1969)
Newson, G. 1932–	Octet (1951) 1112–1110–0000	BMIC
Patterson, P. 1947–	Rebecca (1965) 0010–0010–1010–pf, prepared pf, perc, speaker	BMIC
Pentland, B. 1912–	Octet (1948) 1111–2110–0000	CMC
Pepping, E. 1901–	Concerto II (1926–7) cl, trb, 6 instruments	MS (MGG, S, T)
Picchi, G. 16th–17th Cent.	Sonata decima sesta 2001–0010–2000–cont	A. Vincenti, 1625
Rathbun, E. 1916–	Miniature (1949) picc-0111–1210–0000	CMC
	Parade (1949) 1111–1110–0000–perc	CMC
Riisager, K. 1897–	Sinfonietta (1924) 1012–0220–0000	Andraud

Schat, P. 1935–	Octet (1957) 1111–1210–0000	Donemus, 1959
Schibler, A. 1920–	Concerto pour le temps présent, Op 70 (1960) 1000–0010–1110–ondes M, pf, perc	UE
Smith, W. O. 1926–	Elegy for Eric 1010–0110–1001–vib, drums	MJQ
Stravinsky, I. 1882–	†Octet (1923; rev. 1952) 1012–0220–0000	RM, 1924; Bo. & H., 1952
Thilman, J. P. 1906–	News 1111–1110–0000–pf	n.p., Composer, 1956
Varèse, E. 1883–1965	†Octandre (1923) 1111–1110–0001	Curwen, 1924; Ricordi, 1956
Vejvanowsky, P. J. ca. 1640–93	Sonata vespertina a 8 (1665) (Ed J. Pohanka) 0000–0220–2000–alto vla, cont	SNKLHU, 1960 (MAB, Vol. 47)
Whittenberg, C. 1927–	Chamber Concerto 1010–0110–1011–perc	CFE
Wittinger, R. 1945–	Compensazioni, Op 9 1110–1110–1100	Br. & H.
Wuorinen, C. 1938–	Octet 0110–1010–1011–pf	M. & M., 1966
Zagwijn, H. 1878–1954	Cortège 5 melody instruments, 2 trb, timp	Donemus

6.8 *Nine Instruments*

Bertali, A. 1605–69	Suonata a nove 0001–0030–2 cto–2000–vla da gamba	MS? (F)
Bresgen, C. 1913–	Dorfmusikanten, Op 14 1101–0110–2001–perc	MS (MGG)
Brown, E. 1926–	Pentathis 1000–bcl–0110–1110–hp, pf	Composer, 1958; Schott
Cerha, F. 1926–	Exercises for 9 0000–bcl, sax, dbn–1111–0011	UE
Chavez, C. 1899–	Energia (1925) picc–1001–1110–0111	(K)
Feldman, M. 1926–	Numbers 1000–1011–1011–pf/cel, perc	Peters
Fisher, S. 1940–	Music for 9 instruments 0011–1111–1011	MJQ
Flowers, G.	A Miniature Suite 1121–0220–0000	Novello, 1965
Frankel, B. 1906–	Nonet 1111–1111–0000–acc	Mills, 1965
Froelich, T. 1803–36	Waltzer (Ed H. Scherchen) 1122–2010–0000	Ars Viva, 1954
Gerhard, R. 1896–1970	Nonet (1956) 1111–1111–0000–acc	KP, 1957; Mills, 1965

Guàccero, D. 1927–	'... Un Iter Segnato' 0111–0110–2110	Bruzzichelli, 1960
Hale, V. 1946–	Phantasmagoria No. 1 (1967) 0000–0120–2110–2 perc	BMIC
Hovhaness, A. 1911–	†Tower Music, Op 129 1111–2111–0000	Rongwen
Ives, C. 1874–1954	†Scherzo: Over the Pavements (1913) picc–0010–sax–0130–0000–pf, perc	Peer, 1954
Jelinek, H. 1901–	Three blue Sketches, Op 25 (1956) 1010–2 sax–0110–0001–vib, perc	Modern, 1956
Knipper, L. C. 1898–	Four Children's Miniatures, Op 24: No. 4, Finale 1010–ca–0111–1110	Bo. & H.
Krommer, F. V. 1759–1831	Harmonie à neuf parties 0222–2010–0000	Dufaut, n.d.
Laderman, E. 1924–	Nonette 1011–1110–1010–pf	OUP, 1969
Lekeu, J. 1870–94	Epithalame (1891) 0000–0030–2111–org	MS (MGG)
Lutyens, E. 1906–	Chamber Concerto, Op 8/1 (1939) 0111–1110–1110	Chester, 1947; Mills
Macero, T. 1925–	Structures No 4 0000–3 sax–0111–0001–pf, perc	CFE
McPhee, C. 1901–64	†Pianoforte Concerto (1928) 2111–1110–0000–pf	NME, 1931
Martín, E. 1915–	Concerto (1944) 1111–2210–0000	MS (BQ, III, 4)
Mayer, J. 1930–	Nonet (1963) 2000–0310–0001–2 bongoes	MS (CG)
Mayuzumi, T. 1929–	Olympics: Ballet 0000–2220–0001–pf, perc	Peters
Morgan, D. S. 1932–	Ricercar on Dunstable's 'O Rosa bella', Op 41 (1965) 1110–1010–1111	BMIC
Musgrave, T. 1928–	Chamber Concerto No. 1 (1962) 0111–1110–1110	Chester
Newson, G. 1932–	Concerto for Percussion & Wind (1967) 1111–1210–0000–perc	BMIC
Peixe, C. G. 1914–	Musik für 9 instrumente 1011–0110–1110–pf	Ars Viva [1954]
Rochberg, G. 1918–	Chamber Symphony (1953) 1011–1110–1110	Presser
Rychlík, J. 1916–64	†African Cycle (1961) 1111–2020–0000–pf	SHV, 1963
Schmeltzer, J. H. ca. 1623–80	Sonata XII a sette (1662) (Ed E. Schenk) 2 cto, 2 trp, 3 trb, bass, org	DTÖ, CXI, 1965
Schubert, F. 1796–1828	†Eine kleine Trauermusik in e♭ (1813) 0022–dbn–2020–0000	Br. & H., 1889; AMP; Ensemble

Smalley, R. 1943–	Missa Parodia II (1967) 1110–1110–1100–pf	Faber
Taneiev, S. I. 1856–1915	Marsch zum Mardi Gras bei Henri Duparc (1876) 0100–0030–0010–2 pf, harm, glock	MS (MGG)
Vejvanowsky, P. J. ca. 1640–93	Sonata a 8, Scti. Petri et Pauli (Ed J. Pohanka) 0000–0130–1200–basso viola, cont	SNKLHU, 1961 (MAB, Vol. 49)
Webern, A. 1883–1945	†Konzert, Op 24 (1934) 1110–1110–1100–pf	UE, 1948
Whittenberg, C. 1927–	Variations for 9 players in 2 parts 1111–1110–1001	CFE
Willman, A. A. 1909–	Concerto 1011–1110–1010–pf	MS
Wolff, C. 1934–	Nine (1954) 1010–1110–0020–pf, cel	Peters
Wolpe, S. 1902–	Concerto, Op 22 (1933–4) 1011–1110–1010-pf	MS (Ewen)
Zillig, W. 1905–63	Serenade II 0020–bcl–0110–ct–1110	BVK, 1960

6.9 *More than nine Instruments*

Amy, G. 1936–	Mouvements pour 17 instruments soloistes 1121–1110–2111–pf, 2 hp, perc	Heugel, 1959
Andriessen, H. 1892–	Suite (1954) 1212–1220–0000	Donemus
Andriessen, J. 1925–	Hommage à Milhaud (1945) 1111–sax–1110–1110	Donemus, 1948
	Rouw past Electra (1954) 1212–1220–0000–timp, perc	Donemus, 1955
Armstrong, D.	The Harsh World (1960) 1100–bcl, 4 sax–0220–0001–pf, gt, perc	Music Press
	The Protest (1960) 0010–2 sax–0110–0001–pf, perc	Music Press
Aubin, T. 1907–	Cressida Fanfare (1937) 0002–4331–0000–timp, perc	Leduc, 1961
	Vitrail: Fanfare 2000–4331–0000–timp, perc	Leduc, 1964
Beck, C. 1901–	Suite concertante 3332–2 sax–4331–0001–cel, timp, perc	Schott
Beckwith, J. 1927–	Montage (1953; rev. 1955) 2222–2220–0000–timp, perc	CMC
Belfiore, T. 1917–	Dimensioni (1959) 1122–2 sax–1110–0000–timp	SZ
	Paradigmi (1960) 2131–3220–0000–pf, xyl, 2 perc	SZ

Bennett, R. R. 1936–	†Calendar, (1960) 1011–0110–1110–pf, xyl, glock, perc	Mills
Benvenuti, A. 1925–	Three Studies (1960–1) 1101–1110–1110–pf, xyl	Bruzzichelli
Berg, A. 1885–1935	†Chamber Concerto 2 picc–2121–ca, bcl, dbn–2110–1000–pf	UE, 1953
Berio, L. 1925–	†Serenata I 1121–ca–1110–1111–pf, hp	SZ, 1957
Betts, L. M. 1918–	Suite da chiesa (1952) 2202–2220–0000–timp, perc	CMC
Birtwistle, H. 1934–	Verses for Ensembles 1111–1220–0000–3 perc	(fp, Feb. 12, 1969)
Blacher, B. 1903–	Virtuose Musik (1966) vln solo–2121–2110–0000–hp, timp, perc	B. & B., 1967
Boulez, P. 1925–	Éclat alto fl–0110–ca–0110–0110–cel, mand, vib, hp, pf	UE
	Polyphonies pour 18 instruments soloistes picc–1121–ca sax–1110–2221	Heugel
Bozza, E. 1905–	Overture for a Ceremony 0000–3 sax–4341–0000–timp, perc	Leduc
Brant, H. 1913–	†Galaxy II (1954) picc–0010–2110–0000–glock, 6 timp	CFE
Brün, H. 1918–	Gestures for Eleven 1111–1110–1101–perc	Apogee, 1967
Buczynski, W. J. 1933–	Chorale & five Variations (1960) 1112–2110–2111	CMC
Bush, G. 1920–	Fanfare & March: The Prince of Morocco 2121–4231–0000–timp, perc	Novello, 1965
Buxtehude, D. ca. 1637–1707	In dulci jubilo (Arr. G. Binkerd) picc–1222–3331–0000	AMP
Caturla, A. G. 1906–40	Bembé (1928) 1121–ca–021 0–0000–pf, perc	Senart
	Tres Danzas cubanas 1111–bcl–2111–0000–pf, perc	EV
Chandler, M. 1911–	French Suite (1962) 2232–2220–0000	MS (CG)
Chavez, C. 1899–	†Xochipilli Macuilxochiti (1940) picc–1010–0010–0000–6 perc	Mills, 1964
Christiansen, C.	The Toy Box 2122–2110–0000	Gehrmans
Clementi, A. 1925–	Ideogrammi Nr. 1 (1959) 2031–3210–0000–pf, xyl, 2 perc	SZ, 1960
	Sette Scene (1961) 2041–4 sax–3220–0001–pf, xyl, vib, 2 perc	SZ

254

Connolly, J. 1933–	Abraxas (1966)	BMIC
	1110–sax–0110–2111–hp, 2 perc	
Crosse, G. 1937–	†Concerto da camera, Op 6 (1962)	OUP, 1967
	1111–bcl–2210–1000–2 perc	
Dalby, M. 1942–	Sketches for young players (1966)	BMIC
	2200–0220–0001–bells, perc	
Devienne, F.	Overture	Hofmeister; M. &
1759–1803	2223–2210–serpent–0000–timp	M.
Donovan, R. 1891–	Design for Radio (1945)	CFE
	1010–3 sax–0320–0000–pf, timp, perc	
Fabian, W.	Musique de Concert	IPA, 1959
	2222–2221–0000–timp, tambura	
Edler, R.	Reflexions (1963)	Tonos
	0010–1010–1110–pf, xyl, vib, 3 perc	
Etler, A. D. 1913–	Concerto for clarinet	AMP, 1964
	0010–0330–0002–3 perc	
Felderhof, J. 1907–	Muziek (1930)	Donemus
	2222–sax–2211–0000–timp, perc	
Feldman, M. 1926–	Ixion	Peters
	3010–1110–0011–pf	
	Eleven Instruments	Peters
	alto fl–1000–1111–bass trp–1010–vib, pf	
	Atlantis	Peters
	1010–1110–0010–hp, xyl, vib, pf	
Ficher, J. 1896–	Ballet: Los Invitados, Op 26 (1933)	MS (Fleisher)
	1010–2 sax–0211–0000–pf, perc	
Finke, F. F. 1891–	IV Suite (1953)	Br. & H.
	2222–2231–0000–timp, perc	
Fortner, W. 1907–	Bläsermusik (1957)	Schott
	2222–ca, bcl, dbn–2110–0000	
Françaix, J. 1912–	†Sérénade (1934)	Schott, 1959
	1111–1110–2111	
Gabrieli, G.	Canzon quarti toni a 15 (1597)	IMAMI, 2, 1932
1557–1612	2 cto, 12 trb, vla	
Gerhard, R.	Sardana	MS
1896–1970	1121–ca–2111–0000–perc	
	Hymnody (1963)	OUP, 1964
	1110–1111–0000–2 pf, perc	
Goeb, R. 1914–	Concertant III	CFE
	3332–4331–0100 or 1111–2211–0100	
Grandis, R. de	Antruilles	BVK
1927–	1000–sax–2320–0001–hp, cel, gt, mouth-org, perc	
Griend, K. van der	Concertino (1932)	Donemus
1905–50	1121–1111–0000–pf, timp	
Grossi, P. 1917–	Composizione No. 4	Bruzzichelli
	1221–1210–2112	

Gudmundsen- Holmgren, P. 1932–	Two Improvisations, Op 9 (1961) 1100–1110–0001–pf, vib, 2 perc	Samfundet, 1962
Gwilt, D. 1932–	Suite (1965) 2121–2220–0000	Novello
Hale, V. 1946–	Phantasmagoria No. 2 (1967) 0000–0120–2110–3 perc	BMIC
Hamilton, I. 1922–	Sonatas & Variants 1111–2211–0000	Schott
Harrison, L. 1917–	Simfony in free style 17 fl, trb, 5 hps, cel, 8 viols, drum, bells	Peters
Hartley, W. S. 1927–	Concertino 0010–0010–4040–pf, perc	(IL)
Hartmann, K. A. 1905–63	Concerto for pianoforte (1953) 3033–0330–0000–pf, cel, timp, perc	Schott, 1953
	Concerto for viola (1965) 3033–0330–0100–pf, cel, timp, perc	Schott
Hemel, O. van 1892–	Concerto 3333–4331–0000	Donemus, 1960
	Three Contrasts 3333–sax–4331–0000–cel, xyl, timp, perc	Donemus, 1963
Henze, H. W. 1926–	Labyrinth (1951) 0100–bcl, sax–1110–0111–3 perc	Schott
	Concerto for pianoforte 2222–2221–0000–pf, timp, perc	Schott, 1957
	In Memoriam: Die weisse Rose (1965) 1001–ca, bcl–1110–2111	Schott
Hewson, R. 1938–	Concert Piece for wind (1963) 2222–4231–0000	MS (CG)
Hindemith, P. 1895–1963	Kammermusik No. 2, Op 36/1 (1924) 1111–bcl–1110–1111–pf solo	Schott, 1924
	Kammermusik No. 3, Op 36/2 (1925) 1111–1110–1011–timp	Schott, 1925
	Kammermusik No. 6, Op 46/1 (1929) 1121–1110–0032–vla d'am	Schott
	Kammermusik No. 7, Op 46/2 (1929) 2122–1110–0021–org	Schott
Hovhaness, A. 1911–	Symphony No. 17 for metal orchestra, Op 203 6000–0030–0000–5 perc	Peters, 1963
Hurník, I. 1922–	†Moments musicaux (1962) 1222–2110–0000	SHV, 1964
Ibert, J. 1890–1962	Concerto vcl solo–2222–1110–0000	Heugel, 1926

Jadin, L. E. 1768–1853	Symphony (Ed F. von Glasenapp) 2022–2210–0000	Hofmeister
Jolivet, A. 1905–	†Suite delphique (1942) 1110–2110–0000–ondes M, hp, timp, perc	Pathé-Marconi, 1957
Josephs, W. 1927–	Concerto a dodici, Op 21 (1960) picc–1111–ca, bcl, dbn–1111–0000	Weinberger
Ketting, O. 1935–	†Two Canzoni (1957) 1121–2110–0000–hp, cel, perc	Donemus
	Interieur: Balletmuziek (1963) 2221–2321–0000–cel, xyl, timp, perc	Donemus
Kilar, W. 1932–	Oda (Béla Bartók in Memoriam) vla solo–0000–4441–0000–6 perc	PWM, 1960
Kirchner, L. 1919–	†Concerto (1960) 1111–dbn–1220–1010–cel, 3 perc	AMP, 1962
Klebe, G. 1925–	Szene und Arie, Op 52 0000–0330–0080–2 pf	BVK, 1968
Klusák, J. 1934–	†Obrazy (Pictures) (1960) 2222–1210–0000	Composer, 1960; SHV, 1967
Kotonski, W. 1925–	Canto per complessa da camera 1121–1110–2111–hp, perc	Moeck, 1962; PWM
Křenek, E. 1900–	Capriccio (1955) solo vcl–1111–1110–0000–timp, perc	Schott; UE, 1959
Lampersberg, G. 1928–	Musik solo ob–0001–bcl–0110–1111–hp, cel, pf, perc	UE
Leleu, J. 1898–	Suite symphonique (1925) 2111–ca–1210–0000–pf, perc	Leduc, 1926
Lessard, J. 1920–	Concerto (1949) 2122–2210–0000	Merrymount [1951?]
Luening, O. 1900–	Synthesis 2222–4220–0000–perc, tape	Peters
Luening, O. & Ussachevsky, V. 1911–	Concerted Piece 2222–4220–0000–perc, tape	Peters
Macchi, E. 1928–	Composizione 3 1111–1110–1211	Bruzzichelli, 1960
Maxfield, R. V. 1927–	Structures, Op 23 (1953) picc–1111–ca–1120–0000	Composer, 1954
Maxwell Davies, P. 1934–	St. Michael (1957) 2222–3231–0000	Schott, 1963
	Shakespeare Music (1964) 2122–1010–2111–gt, perc	Bo. & H.
Mayer, W. 1925–	†Essay for brass & winds 1111–2211–0000–perc	Bo. & H., 1965
Mendelssohn, A. L. 1855–1933	Suite 2222–2230–0000–perc	Leuckart, 1916
Mercure, P. 1927–66	Pantomime (1948) 3322–4220–0000–timp, 2 perc	CMC; Ricordi

Messiaen, O. 1908–	†Couleurs de la Cité céleste (1963) 0030–2440–0000–gongs, bells, xyl, xylorimba, mar	Leduc, 1966
	†Et Exspecto Resurrectionem (1964) 5454–6442–0000–3 perc	Leduc, 1966
Meyerowitz, J. 1913–	Ecce Homo (1957) 2222–3221–0000–hp, perc	MS (BMI)
Mihalovici, M. 1898–	Étude en deux parties, Op 64 0021–0211–0000–cel, pf, 2 perc	Heugel, 1952
Milhaud, D. 1892–	†La Création du Monde (1923) 2122–sax–1110–2011–pf, perc	Salabert; Eschig, 1929
	Music for the film 'Gulf Stream', Op 208 1010–3 sax–0210–0001–pf, perc	(I)
Miroglio, F. 1924–	Espaces II (1962) 3333–4331–0000–2 hp, 8 perc	SZ
Nagel, R. 1924–	Divertimento (1951) 1111–2211–0000	CFE
Nicolescu, S. 1927–	Scenes (1962–5) 2111–ca, bcl–0110–0002–cel, xyl/vib, pf, perc	(RT, Mar. 5, 1969)
Nono, L. 1924–	Canti per 13 (1955) 1121–sax–1110–1111	Ars Viva
Otterloo, W. van 1907–	Intrada 0001–4441–0000–timp, perc	Donemus, 1958
Padovano, A. 1527–75	Aria della battaglia (1590) (Ed H. Schmitt) 2021–2231–0000–timp	Schott, 1967
Paz, J. C. 1897–	Theme & Variations (1928–9) 1122–bcl–2020–0000	MS (T)
	Overture 1111–1110–1111	MS (Fleisher)
Pepping, E. 1901–	Concerto I (1926) 0202–0220–0104	MS (MGG, S, T)
Persichetti, V. 1915–	Serenade No. 1 (1929) 1111–2211–0000	EV, 1963
Petrassi, G. 1904–	Estri (1967) 1010–bcl–1110–0111–cel/glock, vib, hpcd, 3 perc	SZ, 1967
Petyrek, F. 1892–1951	Arabian Suite (1924) 2122–2010–0001–hp, timp, perc	UE
Philipott, M. 1925–	Variations 1010–1110–2111	Heugel
Pittaluga, G. 1906–	Petite Suite 1011–0110–2110–hp	Leduc [ca. 1935]
Pluister, S. 1913– 1913–	Divertimento (1937) 2111–1110–0001–perc	Donemus, 1953
Poot, M. 1901–	Suite (1940) 2222–2220–0000–timp	UE
Poulenc, F. 1899–1962	Suite française d'après Claude Gervaise (1935) 0202–0230–0000–hpcd, perc	Durand, 1948

Pousseur, H. 1929–	Symphonies pour 15 soloistes (1954–5) 1111–1110–2111–2 hp, pf	UE, 1961
Prausnitz, F. 1920–	Episode 1111–1110–1100–pf	NME, 1949
Rajna, T. 1928–	Serenade (1959) 2111–2210–0000–pf, timp, perc, cymbalom	BMIC
Rathaus, K. 1895–1954	Intermezzo giocoso 3233–4331–0000–perc	BVK
Raxach, E. 1932–	Fluxion (1962–3) 1111–1110–2011–4 perc	Tonos
Rayki, G.	Burlesque 1122–3110–0000	UE
Reynolds, R. 1934–	Wedge (1961) 2000–0221–0001–pf, 2 perc	Peters
	†Quick are the Mouths of Earth (1965) 3100–0120–0030–pf, 2 perc	Peters, 1965
Riegger, W. 1885–1961	Introduction & Fugue, Op 74 3232–4331–0010–timp	AMP
Schäffer, B. 1929–	Permutazioni 1110–sax–0110–0100–pf, hp, perc	PWM
Schiske, K. 1916–	Divertimento, Op 49; Transformationen im goldenen Schnitt 0011–1110–2111	Doblinger, 1965
Schmeltzer, J. H. ca. 1623–80	Sonata II a otto (1662) (Ed E. Schenk) 0000–0030–cto–1300–bass, org	DTÖ, 111/112, 1965
Schmidt, W. A. 1925–	Concerto grosso for jazz combo & wind sextet 2 sax, trp, db, drums; 1000–ca–dbn–0111–0000	Modern, n.d.
Schuller, G. 1925–	Twelve by Eleven (1955) 1011–sax–1110–0001–hp, pf, vib, drums	(BMI)
	†Transformations (1956) 1011–sax–1010–0001–hp, vib, drums	Malcolm
	Atonal Jazz Study 1100–2 sax–2111–0001–pf, drums	MJQ
	When the Saints go marchin' in 0000–5 sax–2431–0001–drums	MS (BMI)
	Double quintet–wind quint & br quint	AMP
Schuyt, N. 1922–	Discorsi capricciosi (1965) 1222–1211–0000–perc	Donemus, 1965
Sear, W. E.	Antiphony 1111–2211–0000	M. & M.
Sheriff, N. 1935–	Music (1961) 3333–0010–0001–pf	IMI, 1961

Skalkottas, N. 1904–49	Andante sostenuto 1111–ca, dbn–1111–0000–hp/pf, timp, perc	UE, 1954
Smit, L. 1900–45	Concerto pour le piano (1937) 2222–3211–0011–pf, timp	Donemus, 1948
Steel, C. 1939–	Concerto for Organ, Op 28 (1966) 1111–1110–2000–org, perc	Novello
Stockhausen, K. 1928–	Kontrapunkte I (1953) 1011–bcl–0110–1010–hp, pf	UE, 1953
Stravinsky, I. 1882–	†Concertino (rev. 1952) 1112–ca–0220–1010	Hansen, 1953
	†Symphonies of wind instruments (1920; rev. 1947) 3232–ca, dbn–4331–0000	RM, 1926; Bo. & H., 1952
	†Ragtime (1918) 1010–1010–ct–2101–cymbalom, perc	Sirène, 1919; Chester, 1920
	†Ebony Concerto (1945) 0000–6 sax–1530–0001–hp, gt, pf, perc	Charling, 1946
	†Concerto (1924) 3322–4431–0001–pf, timp	RM, 1924; Bo. & H., 1954
	†Song of the Volga Boatmen picc–1111–2031–0000–perc	Chester
Surinach, C. 1915–	Apasionada 1111–1110–0001–pf, timp, perc	AMP
Sutermeister, H. 1911–	Pianoforte Concerto, No. 2 (1954) 2222–2220–0000–pf, timp, perc	Schott, 1955
Szabelski, B. 1896–	Aphorismen 9 (1962) 1110–0110–1110–2 perc	PWM
Tansman, A. 1900–	Sinfonietta (1924) 0010–0020–2111–pf, perc	UE, 1924
Toch, E. 1887–1964	Miniature Overture (1932) 2121–0210–0000–perc	Ars Viva
	Spiel für Blasorchester, Op 39 (1926) 2151–4431–0000–timp, perc	Schott
Tolar, J. K. 17th Cent.	Balletti e Sonate: Sonata a 10 0000–0130–2401–org	SNKLHU, 1959 (MAB, Vol. 40)
	†Sonata a 13 (Ed J. Pohanka) 0000–0240–2 cto–stgs cont	SNKLHU, 1959 (MAB, Vol. 40)
Tortani, L. 1921–	Musica No. 2 (1960) 3000–3 sax–0120–0000–hp, gong, timp	SZ
Valcárcel, E. 1932–	Dicotomia 0000–2220–2220	(K)
Varèse, E. 1883–1965	†Hyperprism (1923) 1010–3220–0000–16 perc	Ricordi
	†Integrales (1923) 2 picc–0120–0120–cb trb–0000–4 perc	Ricordi, 1956
	†Déserts (1954) 4 ww–10 br–pf, perc, tape	Ricordi, 1959

Vaughan Williams, R. 1872–1958	Scherzo alla Marcia (from Symphony No. 8) 2223–2230–0000	OUP
Vejvanowsky, P. J. ca. 1640–93	Sonata a 10 (Ed J. Pohanka) 0001–0220–2200–cont	SNKLHU, 1960 (MAB, Vol. 47)
	Sonata a 10 (Ed J. Pohanka) 0000–0230–2300–cont	SNKLHU, 1961 (MAB, Vol. 48)
Verhaar, A. 1900–	Kleine Dagmuziek: Aubade (1959) 2222–2221–0001–cel, timp, perc	Donemus, 1959
Vogt, H. 1911–	Sonata 2221–sax–0110–1011–hp, pf, perc	Alkor
Voss, F. 1930–	Variationen (1960) picc–2222–ca, bcl, dbn–4431– 0000–timp	Br. & H.
Warren, R. 1929–	Music for Harlequin 1122–2221–0000–timp, perc or 2222–4221–0000–timp, perc	Novello, 1966
Welin, K. E. 1934–	Nr. 3 (1961) 1110–bcl–1110–1001–pf	A. & S., 1962
Woestijne, D. van de 1915–	Sérénades (1946) 1033–2111–0001–pf, perc	CeBeDeM
Wood, R. W. 1902–	Concertino da camera (1955) solo vla–0001–bcl–0110–ct– 1011–timp	BMIC
	5 Soliloquies (1951) 1111–1110–2111	BMIC
Xenakis, I. 1922–	†Akrata (1964–5) 1121–bcl, 2 dbn–2321–0000	Bo. & H., 1968
	†Atrées (1962) 1010–bcl–1110–1010–2 perc	Ed Française
Zillig, W. 1905–63	Serenade IV 1111–1110–2111–cel, hpcd, perc	BVK
	Concerto for Cello & wind 2232–4221–0010	RVK
Zimmermann, B. A. 1918–	Cinque Capricci di Girolami Frescobaldi 3100–0330–2010–hp or 3 rec, ob d'am, 3 trp, 3 trb, 3 gamben, lute	BVK

7. Trombone(s) with voices

7.1 *Solo voice*

Armstrong, D.	The Younger Generation (1959) v; fl, cl, bn, trp, trb, vln, vcl, db, pf, perc	Music Press
Benhamou, M.	Mizmor 114 v; fl, hn, trp, trb, vln, vla, db, vib, mar	Jobert, 1967
Blacher, B. 1903–	Five Negro Spirituals v; 3 cl, trb, db, timp, perc	B. & B., 1963

Bliss, A. 1893–	Music for The Tempest (1921)	MS
	T, B; trp, trb, pf, timp, perc	
Brandl, J.	Sanctus	MS (E*)
1760–1837	4 v; trbs, bc	
Brott, A. 1915–	World sophisticate (1962)	CMC
	v; hn, 2 trp, trb, tuba, perc	
Castello, D.	3 Sonate	Magni, 1629
17th Cent.	S; trb, cont	
	2 Sonate	Magni, 1629
	S; trb, cont	
	2 Sonate	Magni, 1629
	2 S; trb, cont	
	2 Sonate	Magni, 1625
	2 S; 2 trb, cont	
Clarke, H. L. 1907–	Rondeau redoublé (1951)	MS (G)
	Bar; cl, trb, vcl	
Ernryd, B.	Introspection	(RT, Nov. 22,
	S, A, Bar; fl, trb, vla, db, hp	1968)
Feldman, M. 1926–	Intervals	Peters
	Bass-Bar; trb, vcl, vib, perc	
Forster, K. 1935–	Trois Chants d'après Apollinaire	Composer, 1957
	Bar; fl, trb, vln, xyl	
Franzoni, A.	Concerto a cinque (Sancta Maria)	Amadino, 1613
b. ca. 1585	S; 4 trb, cont	
Gay, H. W.	Proclamation & Judgement (1952)	MS (BQ, III, 3)
	Bar; 2 trb	
	Concerto grosso da chiesa (ca.	MS (BQ, III, 3)
	1954)	
	A; cl, trb, org	
Gielen, M. 1927–	Musica	UE, 1958
	Bar; trb, stgs, pf, timp	
Grandi, A. d. 1630	O beate benedi	A. Vincenti, 1629
	S, T; trb, 2 vln, cont	
Hammerschmidt, A.	Dialoghi oder Gespräche einer	Dresden, 1645;
1611–75	gläubigen Seele mit Gott	Artaria, 1901
	S, A, T, B; trb, cont	(DTÖ, VIII, 1)
	†Sonata super Gelobet seist Jesu	Zittau, 1662
	Christ	
	A; 2 trp, 4 trb, cont	
	†Sonata super Nun lob mein Seel	Zittau, 1662
	den Herrn	
	S; 2 trp, 4 trb, cont	
Harrison, L.	†Strict Songs I–IV (1956)	AMP
1917–	8 Bar; 2 trb, stgs, hp, pf, perc	
	Alma redemptoris mater	Peer, 1962
	Bar; trb, vln, tack pf	
Haubenstock-	Credentials, or Think, think,	UE, 1963
Ramati, R. 1919–	Lucky	
	sprechstimme; cl, trb, vln, pf,	
	vib, cel, 2 perc	
Ives, C. 1874–1954	†Song for the Harvest Season	NME, 1933
	(1894)	
	v; ct, trb, bass inst or org pedal	

Kuusisto, I. T. 1933–	Nunc Dimittis B; trb, org	(Ri)
Leonard, C. 1901–	The Grandsons (1943) Bar; 4 trb, pf	MS (R)
Lewkovich, B. 1927–	Cantata sacra T; fl, ca, cl, bn, trb, vcl	Hansen, 1960
Lockwood, N. 1906–	Mickey goes to School (1952) narrator; S, A, T; fl, cl, trb, perc	CFE
Lutyens, E. 1906–	And suddenly it's evening; Op 65 (1967) T; 2 trp, 2 trb, db, cel, hp, perc; hn, vln, vcl	Schott
Maxwell Davies, P. 1934–	†Revelation & Fall (1966) S; fl/picc, ob, cl/bcl, bn, hn, trp, trb, stg quint, hp, 3 perc	Bo. & H.
	†Leopardi Fragments (1962) S, A; fl, ob, cl, bn, trp, trb, hp	Schott, 1965
Milhaud, D. 1892–	Caramel mor (1920) v; cl, trp, trb, pf	Sirène, 1921
Monteverdi, C. 1567–1643	Sonata sopra Sancta Maria, ora pro nobis (Ed B. Molinari) S; 2 cto, 3 trb, 2 vln, vcl	Milan, 1919
Moore, D. 1893–1969	Ballade of William Sycamore (1926) Bar; fl, trb, pf	MS (G, MGG, R, T)
Nieman, A. 1913–	Genesis v; 4 trb, pf	(MT, Dec., 1968)
Petrassi, G. 1904–	Propos d'Alain (1960) Bar; ca, cl, trb, 2 vla, 2 vcl, mar, xyl, timp, 2 perc	SZ
Posch, I. d. ca. 1621	Dum complerentur dies Pentecostes 2 v; trb	Halbmeyer, 1623
	Haec est dies quam fecit Dominus 2 v; trb	Halbmeyer, 1623
Ravin, I.	Quartet (1943) S; ob, trb, elec gt	MS (AMC)
Roussel, A. 1869–1937	Jazz dans la Nuit, Op 38 (1928) T/S; 3 sax, 2 trp, trb, banjo, pf, perc	(G)
Schütz, H. 1585–1672	†Fili mi, Absalon (SWV 269) B; 4 trb, cont	Magni, 1629
	(Ed P. Spitta)	Br. & H., 1887
	(Ed K. Gerber)	BVK; King
	Attendite, popule meus, legam meam (SWV 270) B; 4 trb, cont	Magni, 1629
	(Ed P. Spitta)	Br. & H., 1887
	(Ed G. Kirchner)	BVK; Broekmans; G. Schirmer; Musica Rara

	†Meine Seele erhebt den Herren (SWV 344) S; 2 trb, cont (Ed Bittinger)	BVK
	†In te, Domine, speravi (SWV 259) A; trb, vln, cont (Ed P. Spitta) (Ed K. Gerber)	Magni, 1629 Br. & H., 1885 BVK
	Veni, dilecti mi, in hortum meum (SWV 274) 2 S, T; 3 trb, cont (Ed P. Spitta) (Ed G. Kirchner)	Magni, 1629 Br. & H., 1887 BVK
	Domiae, labia mea aperies (SWV 271) S, T; cto, bn, trb, cont (Ed P. Spitta) (Ed G. Kirchner)	Br. & H., 1887 BVK
	Du Schalksknecht (SWV 397) T; trb, 5 vcl (Ed Kamlah)	BVK
Schwaen, K. 1909–	Karl & Rosa, oder Lob der Partei MzS, Bar, speaker; fl, cl, bn, trp, trb, db, pf, perc	VNM
Smalley, R. 1943–	Two Poems of D. H. Lawrence (1965) Bar; cl, trb, pf	(MT, Nov., 1965)
	Three Poems of Friedrich Hölderlin (1965) S, T; fl, ob, bcl, hn, trp, trb, vcl, hpcd	(MT, Feb., 1968)
	Der Lattenzaum (1964) Bar; trb	(MT, Feb., 1968)
Štěpka, K. V. 1908–	Offering of Songs Bar; br, perc	(Ga, WWM)
Stravinsky, I. 1882–	†In Memoriam Dylan Thomas (1954) T; 4 trb, stg quart	Bo. & H., 1954
Viadana, L. G. da 1564–1641	Cento Concerti eccliastici, Op 12: O bone Jesu T; 2 trb, cont (Ed C. Gallico)	Vincenti, 1602 BVK, 1964
	Repleatur cor meum laude tua A, T; 2 trb	Emmeleus, 1626
	Benedicam Domino in omni tempore 2 T; 2 trb	Emmelaus, 1626
Whelen, C. 1927–	A Disturbance in Mirrors (1966) S; hn, 2 trp, trb, tuba	BMIC
Wolfurt, K. von 1880–1957	Der 90. Psalm, Op 44 (1948) B; 3 trb, 2 vln, org	MS (MGG)
Zuckert, L. 1904–	Song in brass (1964) v; 4 hn, 3 trp, 3 trb, vla, timp	CMC

7.2 *Mixed Chorus with Trombones*

Ahle, J. R. 1625–73	Be not afraid (Ed L. A. Lillehaug) S, 2 ch; 4 trb, cont	Concordia, 1964
Anderl, Q.	Deutsche Messe im Choralstyl für die Fastenzeit v, ch; 3 trb, org	UE
Bartmuss, R. 1859–1910	Der Tag der Pfingsten, Op 14 ch; trbs	Kahle, n.d.
Bassett, L. 1923–	For City, Nation, World T, ch; 4 trb, org	CFE
Brosig, M. 1815–87	Deutsche Choralmesse nach alten Choralmelodien ch; 4 trb	Leuckart, n.d.
Bruch, M. 1838–1920	An die deutsche Nation; Reformationslied, Op 73 ch; 3 trb, org	Simrock, n.d.
Bruckner, A. 1824–96	Psalm CXIV (1852–3) ch; 3 trb	MS
	Libera me, Domine (1854) (Ed V. Goller) ch; 3 trb, org	UE, 1911
	Christus factus est (1879) (Ed J. Döbber) ch; 3 trb	Schlesinger, n.d. [1886]
	Offertorium (1861) (Ed V. Goller) ch; 3 trb, org	UE, 1911; Peters
	†Ecce sacerdos (1885) ch; 3 trb, org	UE, 1911; Peters
	Christmas Motet ch; 3 trb, org	
	Let us celebrate God's name (Psalm 45) (Ed R. Peek) ch; 3 trb	Augsburg, 1968
Burroughs, B.	Praise God ch; 3 trb, timp	Broadman, 1968
Caldara, A. 1670–1736	Mass ch; 3 trb, org	MS? (AmZ 31, 1829)
Cohen, C. b. 1851	Missa pro Defunctis cum Responsoris Libera, Op 2 ch; 4 trb	Pustet, n.d.
	Te Deum, Op 3 ch; 6 trb	Pustet, n.d.
Degen, E.	Euch ist Heute der Heiland geboren! soli, ch, cong; trbs, org	Reiff, 1906
Dresden, S. 1881–1957	Psalm 99 (1950) ch; 4 trb, org	Donemus, 1959
Dufay, G. 1400–74	†Sine nomine ch; trb	

Eberlin, J. E. 1702–62	Litania in D ch; trbs	MS (E*)
Forster, J. 1838–1917	II Choralmesse ch; 3 trb, org	MS (MGG)
Gastoué, A. H. G. N. 1873–1943	Missa solemnis: Te Deum laudamus ch; trbs	MS (MGG)
Gebel, G. 1685–ca. 1750	Wir gingen alle in der Irre wie die Schäfe ch; 3 trb	MS (MGG)
Gleissner, F. b. 1760	Christus factus est ch; 3 trb	MS (E*, MGG)
Göroldt, J. H. 1773–1834	Cantata am 6 Sonntage post Trinitas ch; trbs, org	MS? (MGG)
Gregora, F. 1819–87	Mass ch; 3 trb	MS? (MGG)
Haller, M. 1840–1915	Te Deum laudamus, Op 1 ch; 5 trb	Pustet, n.d.
	Laudes Eucharisticae, Op 16 ch; trbs	Pustet, n.d.
	Missa: Assumpta est, Op 6 ch; trbs	Pustet, n.d.
	Requiem, Op 3 ch; 4 trb, org	Pustet, n.d.
Hanisch, J. 1812–92	Hymnus: Te Deum, Op 33 ch; 4 trb, org	Schwann, n.d.
	Auferstehungschor ch; 4 trb, org	Schwann; Seiling, n.d.
Harrison, L. 1917–	A joyous Procession & a solemn Procession ch; trbs, perc	Peters, 1963
Hauptmann, M. 1792–1868	Herr, Herr, wende dich zum Gebet, Op 38 v, ch; 4 trb, org	Siegel, n.d.
Hennig, K. 1819–73	Friedenspsalm (1854) soli, ch; trb, org, hp	MS (MGG)
Hennig, W. 1903–67	Herzlich tut mich erfreuen: Choralkantate ch, cong; trbs, org	Merseburger
Hovhaness, A. 1911–	Look toward the Sea, Op 158 Bar, ch; trb, org	Peters [ca. 1958]
Hüttenbrenner, A. 1794–1868	Libera ch; trbs	MS (MGG)
Kluge, K.	Welt-Totenfeier S, Bar, ch; trbs, org	Zeitgenöss, 1929
Leeuw, T. de 1926–	Psalm 118 ch; 3 trb, org ad lib	Donemus, 1966
Lewkovich, B. 1927–	Veni Creator Spiritus; Variations ch; 6 trb	Hansen
Marx, J. M. 1792–1836	Saint Jean-Baptiste ch; trbs, org	MS? (F)
Mašek, A. 1804–78	Salve regina ch; trbs	Berra, n.d. [ca. 1835]

Mayer, M.	Responsorium: Libera me, Domine ch; 3 trb	Pustet, n.d.
Mitterer, I. b. 1850	IV Cantiones, Op 32 ch; 4 trb	Pustet, n.d.
	Responsorium, Op 120 ch; 4 trb	Coppenrath, n.d.
Rehmann, T. B. 1895–	Goethe-Zyklus: Alles kündet dich an, Op 19a ch; 3 trb	Schwann
	Die Sonne tönt nach alter Weise, Op 19c ch; 3 trb	Schwann
Scheidt, S. 1587–1654	†Motet: Duo Seraphim clamabant (1618) ch; trbs, org	
Schmidt, A. b. 1772	Libera ch; 3 trb	Böhm, n.d.
Stein, A.	Tod und Auferstehung: Requiem ch; trbs, org	Reiff, 1913
Thiel, C. 1862–1939	Missa choralis in hon. S. Sebastiani, Op 18 ch; 3 trb, org	Schwann
Wanzura, C.	VII Brevissimae et solemnis Litaniae Laurentanae ch; trbs, org	Wessely, 1731

7.3 *Male Chorus with Trombones*

Anon. 15th Cent.	Breve Regnum mch; trbs	PWM
Beethoven, L. van 1770–1827	Trauergesang bey Beethovens Leichenbegängnis in Wien (Equali; Arr. I. X. Seyfried) mch; 4 trb	Haslinger, 1827
Böttcher, G. 1889–	O Herr, gib jedem deinen eignen Tod mch; 3 trb, timp, cym	Hug
Bruckner, A. 1824–96	Inveni David: Offertorium (1868) mch; 4 trb	Peters, 1961
	Vor Arneths Grab (1854) mch; 3 trb	Robitschek, 1954
Gessner, A.	Ad recipiendum Episcopum, Op 13 mch; 4 trb	Schwann, n.d.
Granzin, L.	Salvum fac Regem, Op 4 mch; trbs	Heinrichshofen
Hanisch, J. 1812–92	Missa pro defunctis, Op 15 mch; 2 trb, org	Pustet, n.d.
Herbeck, J. Ritter von 1825–80	Libera (1854) mch; 4 trb	Böhm, n.d.
Kammerlander, C. 1828–92	Libera, Op 58 mch; 3 trb, org	Böhm, n.d.

Kirchl, A. 1858–1936	Libera, Op 41 mch; trbs	Leuckart, n.d.
Kockelmans, G. 1925–65	Christus heri et hodie mch; 3 trb	Donemus, 1966
Kossmaly, K. 1812–93	Salvum fac Regem mch; 3 trb	Hoffarth, n.d.
Kretschmann, T. 1850–1919	Officium defunctorem mch; 3–4 trb	Procuré, n.d.
Kunz, K. M. 1812–75	Auferstehn mch; 4 trb	Aibl [ca. 1842]
	Paternoster mch; 4 trb	Aibl
Liszt, F. 1811–86	An den heiligen Franziskus von Paula mch; 3 trb, org, timp ad lib	T. & P., 1875
Moczynski, S.	Segne, Herr, unser Hirten! Op 71 Bar, mch; trbs	Schwann
Mühling, J.	Motette, Op 13 mch; 4 trb	Heinrichshofen, n.d.
Panny, J. 1794–1838	Festhymnus, Op 38 mch; 3 trb	Schott
Pfleger, C.	Libera me, Domine mch; trbs	Eberle, n.d.
Snel, J. F. 1793–1861	Rebecca; Serenade mch; 3 trb	Schott, n.d.
Wienhorst, R.	O Trinity, most blessed Light mch; trb, org	Concordia

7.4 *Chorus, Trombones and other Instruments*

Bernstein, L. 1918–	Chichester Psalms Solo, ch; 3 trp, 3 trb, stgs, 2 hp, perc	G. Schirmer
Bliss, A. 1891–	The World is charged with the Grandeur of God ch; 2 fl, 3 trp, 4 trb	Novello, 1970
Brahms, J. 1833–97	Begräbnisgesang (Ed D. Whitwell) ch; 2 ob, 2 cl, 2 hn, 2 bn, 3 trb, tuba, timp	MF Co.
Bruckner, A. 1824–96	Libera in f (1854) ch; trbs, vcl, db, org	(H. Redlich: Bruckner & Mahler)
Caldara, A. 1670–1736	Stabat Mater (Ed Meyerowitz) S, A, T, B, ch; trbs, stgs, org	
Fétis, F. J. 1784–1871	Messe de Requiem (1850) soli, ch; 6431–saxhn, bombardon, vcls, dbs, org, perc	MS
Gabrieli, G. 1557–1612	†In ecclesiis 2 ch; 3 cto, 2 trb, vla, org (Ed F. Hudson)	London, 1963
	Surreit Christus ch; 2 cto, 4 trb, 2 vla (Ed C. von Winterfeld)	Berlin, 1834

268

Geiser, W. 1897–	Symbolum 2 mch; 3 trb, vla, vcl, db, timp	BVK
Gerstenberger, K. T. 1892–1955	Festliche Musik mit Hymne, Op 23 ch; 7 fl, 3 ob, 4 cl, 3 bn, 8 trp, 7 trb, 3 tuba, 4 flghn, perc	MS (V)
Gluck, C. W. 1714–87	De profundis ch; trb, vla, vcl, db, org	Harmonia
Henze, H. W. 1926–	Choral Fantasy (1964) ch; trb, 2 vcl, db, org, timp, perc	Schott
	†The Muses of Sicily ch; 2 fl, 2 ob, 2 cl, 2 bn, 4 hn, 2 trp, 2 trb, 2 pf, timp	Schott, 1966
	Fünf Madrigale (1947) ch; fl, cl, bn, hn, trp, trb, stg quint	Schott
	Wiegenlied der Mutte Gottes (1948) boys' ch; fl, cl, hn, trp, trb, vla, vcl, db, hp	Schott
Heyl, M. 1908–	Requiem, Op 30 mch; ww, 4–12 trb, timp	Composer, 1950
Hovhaness, A. 1911–	The burning House, Op 185 soli, ch; 3 fl, 3 trb, 4 perc	Peters
Lilius, F. V. d. 1657	Jubilate Deo omnis terra ch; bn, 2 trb, 2 vln, vla, cont	PWM, 1959
Mältzel, G. 1624–93	Missa St. Godefridi (1666) ch; 4 trb, 3 violetti	MS (MGG)
	Missa diversi toni a 16 (1666) ch; 4 trb, stgs	MS (MGG)
	Missa variabilis a 15 (1668) ch; 5 trb, stgs	MS (MGG)
	Missa: Quid speramus ch; 3 trb, stgs	MS (MGG)
	Requiem (1678) ch; 4 trb, 4 vla, violone	MS (MGG)
	Te Deum (1671) ch; 2 clarini, 4 trb, org	MS (MGG)
	Missa (1671) ch; 2 clarini, 5 trb, org	MS (MGG)
Martinů, B. 1890–1959	†Field Mass (1939) Bar, mch; 2 picc, 2 cl, 3 trp, 2 trb, pf, perc	Melantrich, 1947; CHF
Maxwell Davies, P. 1934–	Te lucis ante terminum (1961) ch; 2 fl, ob, 2 cl, 2 trp, 2 trb, vcl, glock, gt	Schott, 1967
	Ecce Manus tradentis (1965) ch; fl, ob, bn, dbn, hn, 2 trb, hp, handbells	Bo. & H.
Mielczewski, M. d. 1651	Triumphalis dies ch; bn, 3 trb, 4 vln, org	MS (*MGG)

269

	Missa cerviensiana	MS (*MGG)
	ch; 4 trb, 2 vln, org	
	Missa triumphalis	MS (*MGG)
	ch; 4 trb, 2 vln, org	
	Missa Sancta Anna	MS (*MGG)
	ch; bn, 3 trb, 2 vln, org	
Moevs, R. 1920–	Cantata sacra (1952)	(Ho)
	Bar, mch; fl. 4 trb, timp	
Monteverdi, C.	Laetatus sum (1650)	
1567–1643	ch; bn, 2 trb, 2 vln	
	†Beatus vir (1640)	
	ch; 3 trb, 2 vln	
	Dixit Dominus (1640)	
	ch; 4 trb, 2 vln	
	Dixit Dominus, Domino meo	
	(1640)	
	ch; 4 trb, 2 vln	
	Et iterum venturus est	
	ch; 4 trb	
	Gloria in excelsis Deo (1631)	
	ch; 4 trb, 2 vln	
	†Laudate Dominum, omnes gentes	London, 1966
	(Ed D. Arnold)	
	ch; 4 trb, 2 vln	
	Magnificat	
	ch; 4 trb, 2 vln	
	Crucifixus	Sydney, n.d.
	(Ed E. Gross)	
	ch; 4 trb	
Mozart, W. A.	†Litaniae de B.M.V., K. 109 =74e	Diabelli [1835]
1756–91	(1771)	
	ch; 3 trb, stgs, org	
Perti, G. A.	Mass (1717)	MS (MGG)
1661–1756	ch; 2 trb, stgs, org	
	Mass in G	MS (MGG)
	ch; trb, stgs, 2 org	
Porena, B. 1927–	Cantata da camera	SZ
	Bar, mch; 3 trb, 6 vcl, timp	
Reichel, B. 1901–	Récit de la Crucifixion (1955)	MS (MGG)
	Bar, ch; 3 trb, stgs, org	
Rohwer, J. 1914–	Psalm-Motette (1959)	Br. & H.
	S, 2 A, mch; bn, trb, vcl, db,	
	org	
Schelle, J.	Ehre sei Gott in der Höhe	Hänssler
1648–1701	ch; bn, 2 trp, 2 trb, 2 vln, bc,	
	timp	
Schütz, H.	Magnificat (SWV 468)	BVK, 1962
1585–1672	(Ed W. Ehmann)	
	ch; 3 trb, 2 vln, bc	
	Kanzone: Nun lob, meine Seele	BVK
	(SWV 41) (Ed W. Ehmann)	
	2 ch; 3 trp, 2 trb, 3 vln, vla,	
	vcl, bc	

	Gesang der drei Männer im feurigen Ofen	
	3 ch; 2 trp, 2 trb, stgs, cont	
Stravinsky, I. 1882–	†Mass (1948)	Bo. & H., 1948
	ch; 2 ob, ca, 2 bn, 2 trp, 3 trb	
Tomeoni, P.	Magnificat	(MGG)
1729–1816	2 ch; 2 hn, 2 trb, 2 vln, org	
Vejvanovsky, P. J.	Missa brevis (1664)	(MGG)
1640–93	ch; 2 trp, 3 trb, 2 vln, db	
	Missa Visitationis B.M.V. (1665)	(MGG)
	ch; 2 trp, 3 trb, 2 vln, db	
	Missa Bonae spei (1679)	(MGG)
	ch; 2 trp, 3 trb, 2 vln, 2 vla, db, org	
	Missa Bonae valetudinis (1681)	(MGG)
	ch; 2 trp, 3 trb, 2 vln, 2 vla, db, org	
	Missa refugii (1682)	(MGG)
	ch; 2 trp, 3 trb, 2 vln, 2 vla, db, org	
	Missa martialis (1682)	(MGG)
	ch; 2 trp, 3 trb, 2 vln, 2 vla	
	Missa fidelitatis	(MGG)
	ch; 2 trp, 3 trb, 2 vln, 2 vla, db, org	
	Vidi Dominum (1677)	(MGG)
	ch; 3 trb, 2 vln, 3 vla, db, org	
	Medicamen contra pestem (1679)	(MGG)
	ch; 3 trb, 2 vln, 2 vla, db, org	
	Usquequo exultabuntur (1683)	(MGG)
	ch; 3 trb, 2 vln, 2 vla, db, org	
	Congregati sunt inimici nostri (1684)	(MGG)
	ch; 3 trb, 2 vln, 2 vla, db, org	
	Off. de Confessore	(MGG)
	ch; 3 trb, 2 vln, 2 vla, db, org	
	Motettum de tempore	(MGG)
	ch; 3 trb, 2 vln, 2 vla, db, org	
	Motettum de S. Caecilia	(MGG)
	ch; 2 trp, 3 trb, 2 vln, 3 vla, db, org	
	Confitebor tibi Domine (1660)	(MGG)
	ch; 3 trb, 2 vln	
	Vesperae de confessore	(MGG)
	ch; 3 trb, 2 vln, 3 vla, db, org	
Werndle, A. I.	Missa in D	MS (MGG*)
ca. 1700–54	ch; 2 trb, 2 vln, violone, org	
Ziani, M. A.	Requiem	(MGG)
1635–1715	ch; 2 trb, 2 vla, violone, org	

7.5 *Mixed chorus with brass ensemble*

Ahrens, J. 1904–	Ecce sacerdos (1949) ch; 0220–org	SM, 1953

	Drei Festmotetten: No. 2 (1949) ch, cch; 0221	SM, 1952
	Vier Hymnen ch; 0241	SM, 1953
Amory, A. H.	Orangelied ch; 4231–timp	Arnheim
Andriessen, H. 1892–	Cantata Bar, ch; 0311–org	Donemus
Angell, W. M. 1907–	Children of America ch; br	(WWM)
Archer, V. 1913–	Apocalypse S, ch; 6 br, timp	MS?
Arnatt, R.	Communion Service for the people ch, cong; 0220–org	Gray
Auer, J.	Fünf Hymnen zur Fronleichnams-Prozession, Op 10 ch; br	Coppenrath
Bach, J. S. 1685–1750	O Jesus, Lord, my Light & Life (Cantata 118) ch; 0420	
Balazs, F. 1919–	Casualty & Christmas ch; 4231–timp, perc	CFE
	Two Poems ch; br, perc	CFE
Bales, G.	Jubilate Deo ch; 0330–perc	Waterloo, 1966
Bartmuss, R. 1859–1910	Fünf liturgische Feiern (Vespern), Op 37 ch; 0210–org	Hug
Bauer, J.	Fünf Fronleichnams-Hymnen, Op 2 ch; br, org	Böhm
Beach, P. W.	Rejoice in the Lord ch; 0321–timp	SB
Beck, C. 1901–	Der Tod des Oedipus (1928) S, T, B, ch; 0220–org, timp	Schott, 1929
Beethoven, L. van 1770–1827	Gottes Macht und Vorsehung (Arr F. Burkhart) ch; 0220/2320/4331–timp ad lib	Doblinger
Bemmann, O.	Reformations Kantate ch; br/org	Siegel
Bender, J. 1909–	Nun bitten wir den heiligen Geist ch; 0420–org	BVK, 1957
	Awake thou Spirit, who didst fire ch; 0220–org	Concordia
	Christ is arisen ch; 0220	Concordia
	God the Father, be our Stay ch; 0220–org	Concordia

	Psalm 130 ch; 2210/0320	Concordia
	Psalm 150 ch; 2210/0320	Concordia, 1957
Bergt, C. G. 1772–1837	Herr Gott, dich loben wir, Op 13 ch; trps, trbs, org, timp	Hofmeister [ca. 1815]
Bieger, F.	Zwölf Begräbnisgesänge, Op 12 ch; flghn, althn, bass trp, trb	Böhm
Bieger, F. et al.	Vier Veni Sancti Spiritus ch; 0210–bass trp/org	Böhm
Bieske, W. 1913–	Vater unser im Himmelreich ch; 0220	BVK, 1962
Binkerd, G. 1916–	Festival Procession ch; br	CFE
Bissell, K. W. 1912–	People look East soli, ch; br, org, timp	Waterloo, 1966
	Newfoundland (1964) narrator, ch; 0221–2 bar, euph	CMC
Blanchard, W. G.	An Anthem of Praise ch; 0310–org	Boston, 1958
Blumner, M. T. W. 1827–1901	Hymne (1890) ch; br	MS?
Boelee, H.	Looft God met zingen en met spelen ch; br, org	Harmonia
Bornefeld, H. 1906–	Du meine Seele, singe ch; 0420–org, timp	BVK, 1954
	Herr Jesu Christ, dich zu uns wend ch; 0220–org	BVK, 1955
	Lobt Gott, ihr frommen Christen (1952) S, T, ch; br, org, perc	BVK
Boulanger, L. 1893–1918	Psalm XXIV ch; 4341–hp, org, timp	Durand, 1924
Bowman, C. 1913–	Festival Te Deum ch; 5 br	Composer
	Magnificat MzS, ch; 5 br	Composer
Braal, A. de 1909–	Profetie: Jesaja 25, 26 (1951) Bar, ch; 2220–pf	Donemus
Braun, C.	Heilig ist der Herr, Op 31 ch; 7 br, org	Zumsteeg
Bruckner, A. 1824–96	Cantate in D: Auf, Bruder, auf zur hohen Festen (1852) 4 soli, ch; 3210	MS
	Litanei (1843–5) ch; br	(H. Redlich: Bruckner & Mahler)
Brugk, H. M. 1909–	An die Musik ch; 2221–timp	Böhm
	Festmesse, Op 20 S, A, T, B, ch; 0330–org, timp	MS

	Bläser-Messe, Op 30 ch; 0220-tenhn	Schott, 1965
Brunner, E.	Zweites Requiem, Op 8 ch; 4 br/org	Coppenrath
Bunge, S. 1924–	Hymne ch; br, carillon, perc	Donemus, 1965
Burkhard, W. 1900–55	Te Deum, Op 33 (1931) ch; 0110–org, timp	Schott, 1932
Busarov, D.	We praise Thee, O God ch; 0220–org, opt timp	Concordia, 1964
Busser, H. 1872–	Messe de St. Etienne ch; 0110–org, hp, perc	Lemoine
Buxtehude, D. 1637–1707	Fanfare & Chorus from 'Ihr lieben Christen' (Arr. R. King) ch; 2420–org	King
Canning, T. 1911–	An Offering of Carols & Rounds ch; 0220–perc	CFE
	Rogation Hymn ch; 0220	CFE
	Festal Procession ch; br, perc	CFE
Cassels-Brown, A. K. 1927–	Magnificat & Nunc dimittis ch; br, org	(WWM)
Christou, J. 1926–	Mass (1953) ch; br, perc	(La)
Cochereau, P. 1924–	†Paraphrase de la Dédicace ch; br, org, timp	
Cohen, K. H. 1851–1938	Fünf Fronleichnamshymnen, Op, 11 ch; 2231	Schwann
Converse, F. S. 1871–1940	Psalm: 'I will praise Thee, O Lord' ch; br, org, pf	Birchard, 1929
Cousins, M. T.	Hymn to the Sublime ch; 4331–timp, perc	MS (ASCAP)
Cowell, H. 1897–1965	Supplication ch; 0220–org, timp ad lib	Peters, 1962
Croce, G. 1557–1609	Benedictus es, Domine 2 ch; 0440	Möseler [1969]
Cruft, A. 1921–	Benedictus ch; 4310	Bo. & H.
Dello Joio, N. 1913–	†To St. Cecilia ch; 3331	C. Fischer, 1958
	Proud Music of the Storm ch; 3331-org	Marks, 1967
	Years of the Modern ch; br, perc	Marks, 1968
Demattia, A.	10 Gesänge zur Feier der Fronleichnamsprozession ch; 4 br	Coppenrath
Deschermeier, J.	Gesänge zur Fronleichnams- prozession, Op 18 ch; br	Feuchtinger

	Leichtes Requiem mit Libera, Op 26 ch; flghn, trp, bass trp, trb	Feuchtinger
	Psalm 50, Op 48 ch; br	Pietsch
Dirksen, R.	Christ, our Passover ch; 0220–org, timp	Gray, 1965
	Hilariter ch; 0220–org, timp	Gray, 1960
	Communion Service for Easter ch; 4 br, org, timp	Gray
Doppelbauer, J. F. 1918–	Festliche Kantate: Lobe den Herrn ch; 0220	Coppenrath
	Tantum ergo, Op 15 (1949) ch; 2221–org	MS (V)
Doret, G. 1866–1943	Cantate du Centenaire ch; br	MS? (MGG)
Drakeford, R. 1936–	Festival Jubilate ch; 0220–org	MS (CG, WWM)
Driessler, J. 1921–	Darum seid getrost, Op 28 T, ch; 0330–org, timp	BVK
Ebner, L.	Missa Jubilate Deo, Op 8 ch; 0210–cornu alto	Pustet
Edenhofer, A.	Vier Marienlieder ch; 9 br	Coppenrath
Elmore, R. 1913–	Psalm of Redemption A, Bar, ch; 0330–org, perc	J. Fischer, 1961
Erhard, K. 1928–	Gesänge zur Fronleichnams- prozession ch; 0220	Böhm
Ett, C. 1788–1847	Missa pro Defunctis ch; br	Böhm
	Pange lingua ch; 8 br	Böhm
Fiebig, K. 1908–	Halleluja, Lob, Preis und Ehr ch; 1210–org	Merseburger, 1949
Filke, M. 1855–1911	Ecce sacerdos magnus, Op 97 ch; 0220–org	Böhm
	Ostermotett, Op 60/2 ch; 2220–org, timp	Böhm
	Vaterlandslied, Op 56 ch; 0031–tenhn, timp	Siegel
Fissinger, E.	When Johnny comes marching home ch; 0330–timp, drum	SB, 1958
Forster, H.	Hymnen zu Prozession und Andachten mit ausgesetzen Allenheiligsten ch; br	Böhm
	Zwei Pange lingua, Op 11b ch; 4 br	Böhm
Franco, J. 1908–	As the Prophets foretold T, B, ch; 1210–carillon	CFE

Fromm, H. et al 1905–	And Death shall have no dominion (1954): Six Pieces in memory of Dylan Thomas ch; br	(BQ, VI, 3)
Führer, R. 1807–61	Ecce sacerdos magnus ch; 2010–org, timp	Hoffmann
Gabrieli, G. 1557–1612	†In Ecclesiis (1615) (Arr W. Damrosch) 2 ch; 0330–org	G. Schirmer
	†Jubilate Deo (Arr G. W. Woodworth) ch; 0440–org	G. Schirmer
Garden, C.	Come, ye servant people ch; 0220–org, timp ad lib	Gray
Gaugler, T.	Latein-Messe, Op 14 ch; 0220–althn, org	Böhm
	Missa, Op 18 ch; br, org	Beyer
Gelbke, J.	Der 100 Psalm, Op 17 ch; br, timp	Kistner
Ghisi, F. 1901–	Sequenza e Giubilo (1945) ch; br, pf, perc	MS? (MGG)
Gleich, F. 1816–98	Hymnus nach Worten der Offenbarung St. Johannis, Op 23 soli, ch; 0230–org, timp	Hoffarth
Goldsworthy, W. A.	O be joyful ch; 0110–org	J. Fischer, 1960
Goller, V. 1873–1953	Der Heiland ist erstanden, Op 28 ch; 0220–org	Coppenrath
	Hymnus: Te Deum laudamus, Op 50 ch; br, org	Coppenrath
	Loreto-Messe, Op 25 ch; br, org	Coppenrath
	Prozessionsgesänge für d. hoch-heil. Fronleichnamsfest, Op 32 ch; br	Coppenrath
Gottschick, F. 1928–	Komm trost der Nacht, O Nachtigall ch, cch; 0220	BVK
Gounod, C. 1818–93	Messe dite de Clovis ch; 0440–org	Choudens
Grabner, H. 1886–	Ein feste Burg: Kantate ch; br	MS? (MGG)
Grainger, P. 1882–1961	I'm seventeen come Sunday (1905) ch; br	Schott
	Marching Tune (1905) ch; br	Schott
Greith, J.	Ecce sacerdos magnus, Op 47 ch; 2231	Schwann
Grell, A. E. 1800–86	Te Deum ch; br	MS? (AmZ 42/1840)

Groh, J. jun.	Vokalmesse ch; 0220	Hoffmann
Gruber, J. 1855–1933	Vier Gesänge, Op 123 ch; 0220	Coppenrath
Grunenwald, J. J. 1911–	Messe heroïque (1945) soli, ch; 0330–2 org	MS (MGG)
Güttler, J.	Requiem No. 2, Op 12 ch; br, org	Pietsch
Häser, A. F. 1779–1844	Te Deum laudamus ch; br, org	MS? (AmZ, 32/1840)
Hafner, J. 1901–	Domine Deus ch; br	Schwann
Haller, M. 1840–1915	Jubiläums-Festlied, Op 56 ch; 9 br, pf	Coppenrath
	Missa sexta, Op 13 ch; 9 br, org	Coppenrath
Hammerschmidt, A. ca. 1611–75	Jauchzet, ihr Himmel ch; 0230–bc	BVK
	Triumph, triumph, Victoria ch; 0230–bc	BVK
Hanisch, J.	Fünf Hymnen zur Fronleichnams-Prozession ch; 4 br	Coppenrath
Harmat, A. 1885–	150. Psalm ch; 0221–org, timp	MS? (G, MGG)
Harris, R. 1898–	Alleluia (1945) ch; br, org	MS (Ewen)
Hemel, O. van 1892–	Herdenkings-Hymne (1955) ch, cch; 4332–2 ct, tenhn, timp, perc	Donemus, 1956
Herrmann, H. 1896–	Chorwerk der Gemeinschaft, Op 81 (1932) ch; br, perc	B. & B.
Hess, E. 1912–	Schweitzergebet (1940) ch; br	Hug
Hessenberg, K. 1908–	Kantate von dankbaren Samariter, Op 57 (1952) ch; br, org	Merseburger
Hilber, J. B. 1891–	Missa pro patria (1941) ch; br, org	Willi
Hillert, R.	May God bestow on us His grace ch; 0320	Concordia
Hiltscher, W. 1913–41	Mit Fried und Freut ich fahr dahin (1937) ch; 0220	Br. & H.
Hindemith, P. 1895–1963	†Apparebit repentina Dies (1947) ch; 4231	Schott, 1947
Höllwarth, J.	Prozessions-Gesänge ch; 4 br	Gross
	Te Deum ch; 4 br	Gross
Hoft, N.	Vaterlandische Hymne: O Bayerland, Op 60 ch; br	MS (P)

Hohlfeld, C. 1922–	Kleine Spruchmotette zum Ernte- dankfest ch; 0220–org	Br. & H.
Hoof, J. van 1886–1959	Missa: De Deo (1937) ch; br	MS (MGG)
	Te Deum (1949) ch; br	MS (MGG)
Horn, A. 1825–93	Deutsches Kaiserlied, Op 65 ch; br	Kistner
Horst, A. van der 1899–1965	Choros IV 2 ch, cong; br	Donemus
	Rembrandt-Cantata: Choros V (1956) ch; br	Donemus
Hoskins, W. B.	Jerusalem from the Mountain ch; 0110–pf	CFE
Hotter, J. B.	Trauerlieder ch; br	Böhm
Hovhaness, A. 1911–	Glory to God, Op 124 S, A, ch; 4440–sax, org, timp, perc	Peters, 1958
	Ave Maria ch; 0220–hp	AMP, 1958
Huber-Andernach, T. 1885–	Graduale und Offertorium, Op 28 ch; 0220	Hug
Huston, J.	A Canticle of Thanksgiving ch; 0220–org	Gray, 1959
Ireland, J. 1879–1962	Vexilla Regis soli, ch; br, org	Galliard
Ives, C. 1874–1954	†Three Chorales for a Harvest Festival (Ed H. Cowell) ch; trps, trbs, db, org	Mercury, 1950
Jaeggi, O. 1913–63	Pange lingua (1951) ch; 0320–org, timp	Paulus
	Kleine Marien-Kantate (1950) ch; 0320–org, timp	MS (MGG)
James, D. 1901–	Nativity Hymn ch; 0220–pf/org	J. Fischer, 1959
James, P. 1890–	Psalm 149 S, ch; 0320–org	Gray, 1960
Janáček, L. 1854–1928	Hospodine pomiluj (1896) soli, 2 ch; br, org, hp	MS? (G)
Jerger, W. 1902–	Kantate: Es schaut der weite Kreis der Erde (1926) S, ch, cch; br, org	Böhm, 1936
Jochum, O. 1898–	Karfreitagskantate, Op 35a ch; br	Böhm, 1932
	Ostergesänge, Op 35b ch; br	Böhm, 1932
Johnston, D. O.	Missa brevis (1957) ch; 0321–bar, timp, cym	Interlochen, n.d.
Jolley, F.	Gloria in excelsis S, ch; 0331–org, perc	Shawnee, 1954

	Holy Lord God of Hosts ch; 0331–org, pf	Shawnee, 1955
Jones, R. W.	Magnificat & Nunc dimittis ch; 0330–org, timp	Gray, 1968
Jongen, J. 1873–1953	Mass soli, ch; br, org	MS?
Josquin des Prés ca. 1440–1521	Absalom, fili mi (Arr T. Marier) ch; 0220	King, 1958
Kammerlander, C. 1828–92	Tantum ergo & Genitori, Op 66 ch; 8 br, timp	Böhm
Karjalainen, A. 1907–	Kuin laula raikuva, Op 51 cch; 0330	(Ri)
Keller, J. M.	Sanctus & Benedictus ch; 4240–timp	Böhm
	Pange lingua & Tantum ergo ch; 8 br	Böhm
Kempff, W. 1895–	Te Deum ch; trps, trbs, org, timp	MS? (ZfM 92/1925)
Kempter, K. 1819–71	Grablied, Op 93 ch; 2010	Böhm
	Pange lingua, Op 56/1 ch; br	Böhm
Kirk, T.	O come, let us sing ch; 0221–timp, cym	SB, 1959
Klerk, A. de 1917–	Missa ad modum tubae ch; 4 br	Donemus
Koch, J. H. E. 1918–	Komm, heilige Geist, Herre Gott ch, cong; 0320	BVK, 1962
	Darum wachet S, A, ch; 0220–org	BVK, 1959
	Steht auf, ihr liebe Kinderlein ch, cong; 0320– fanfare trb ad lib, timp ad lib	BVK, 1954
	†Christ lag in Todesbanden ch; 0221	BVK, 1957
Koerppen, A. 1926–	Zwei Hymnen (1952) ch; 2331	MS (V)
Krapf, G.	Easter Antiphon ch; 0220	Concordia, 1964
Krieger, F. 1902–	Festliches Tantum ergo ch; 1220	Schwann
Kromolicki, J. 1882–	Alleluja, Op 16 ch; 0220–org	Böhm, 1929
	Fünf eucharistische Hymnen, Op 24a ch; 2221–timp	Böhm
	Te Deum, Op 43 ch; 0220–org	Böhm
Kronsteiner, H. 1914–	Kleine Festmesse (1948) ch; 0220–org	Doblinger, 1949
Krug, A. 1849–1904	Hymne an Germania, Op 79 ch; br	Kistner, 1898
Kühne, B.	Lauda Sion ch; br	Coppenrath

	Veni Creator spiritus ch; br	Coppenrath
	Weinachtsgesang ch; br	Coppenrath
Kurpinski, K. 1785–1857	Messe ch; trps, trbs, org, timp	MS? (F)
Kuusisto, I. T. 1933–	Rejoice, O young man ch; br	(Ri)
Lang, H. 1897–	Die Gedanken sind frei ch, mch, cong; 0331–timp	Leuckart, 1961
	Die Sonnengesang des heiligen Franziskus, Op 52 ch, cch; 3331–timp, perc	Schott, 1957
Langlais, J. 1907–	†Missa: Salve Regina (1954) 2 ch; 0350–2 org	MS? (MGG)
Lassus, O. di 1530–94	Providebam Dominum (Arr R. King) 2 S, A, ch; 1410–bar	King
Laube, A. 1718–84	Te Deum ch; 2 clarini, trb, org, timp	MS? (MGG)
Lauer, E.	Hymne an Deutschland, Op 14 ch; 0331–org, timp	Hochstein
Layton, B. J. 1926–	Three Dylan Thomas Poems, Op 3 (1954–6) ch; 2220	G. Schirmer, 1964
Lechthaler, J. 1891–1948	30th Psalm, Op 10 ch, cch; 8 br, org	Böhm, 1928, 1952
Leitner, C. A.	Fronleichnams Hymne ch; 4 br, org	Böhm
	Drei Fronleichnamslieder cch; 4 br	Böhm
	Sechs sehr leicht ausführbare Messen ch; 4–9 br	Böhm
Leonard, C. 1901–	Song of the Universal (1941) S, ch; br, org, perc	(R)
Levy, E. 1895–	De Profundis (1919) ch; br, org, timp	MS? (MGG)
	Hymnus symphonicus (1936) ch; br, org	MS? (Ewen, MGG)
Lipp, A.	Feierliches Auferstehungslied, Op 57 ch; br	Feuchtinger
	Fronleichnamsgesänge, Op 73 ch; br	Böhm
	Vier latein Gesänge, Op 14 ch; 5 br	Böhm
	Schützengel-Messe, Op 46 ch; 0310–opt org	Böhm
	Vier Veni Sancti Spiritus ch; 4 br	Böhm
Lissman, K. 1902–	Leuchte, scheine, goldne Sonne ch; 0330	Tonger

Liszt, F. 1811–86	In domum Domini ibimus ch; 0220-org, timp	Br. & H., 1936
	Nun danket alle Gott (1883) ch/mch; 0231-org, timp	Br. & H., 1884
	Te Deum laudamus I ch; 2220-org, timp	Br. & H., 1936
Lourié, A. V. 1892–	Motet: De ordinatione angelorum (1942) ch; 5 br	The Thomist, 5, 1943
Lubrich, F. 1862–1952	Dir . . . Kaiser Heil, Op 59 ch; br	Hoffman
Lutyens, E. 1906–	Encomion, Op 54 (1963) ch; br, perc	Schott
McCabe, J. 1939–	Great Lord of Lords (1966) ch; br, org, timp	Novello
McGuire, F.	Blessed art Thou, O Lord God ch; 0220-timp	Gray, 1965
McKay, G. F. 1899–	Choral Rhapsody, Op. 39 ch; 4330-timp	(ASCAP)
Macpherson, S. 1865–1941	Communion Service in E♭ ch; br	Novello
Marchant, S. 1883–1949	Te Deum (1931) ch; br, org	OUP
Marshall, J.	Lord most high ch; 0320/1310-org	Abingdon, 1965
Martin, A. 1825–56	Marche funèbre ch; 0330	MS? (F)
Martin, R. P. 1914–	†Libera me ch; 2020– org, perc	Ouvrières, 1957
Marx, K. 1897–	Mein schönste Zier und Kleinod bist ch, cong; 0220	BVK, 1956
	Nun freut euch, lieben Christen gmein ch, cong; 0320	BVK
Masséus, J. 1913–	Camphuysen-hederen ch; 0331	Donemus, 1968
Meinardus, L. S. 1827–96	Wanderlied, Op 17 ch; br	Br. & H.
Mellers, W. 1914–	Two Motets (1946) ch; 4230	OUP
Meredith, M.	Recessional ch; br, org	MS? (MGG)
Meuerer, J.	Auferstehungschor, Op 16 ch; 0220-org	Schwann
	Missa, Op 25 ch; 0130/1030	Pustet
	Missa in hon. St. Joannis Bapt., Op 19 ch; br, org	Böhm
	Requiem, Op 4 ch; trps, trbs, org	Pustet
Meyerowitz, J. 1913–	How Godly is the House of God (1955) ch; 2220-org, timp	Rongwen, 1959

Micheelsen, H. 1902–	Christ ist erstanden ch; 0330	BVK, 1960
	Allein zu dir, Herr Jesu Christ ch; 0330	BVK, 1953
	O Christenheit, sei hoch erfreut ch; 1550	BVK, 1950
Missal, J.	Gloria in excelsis Deo ch; 4342-bar, timp	SB, 1962
Mitterer, I. 1850–1924	Ave Maria, Op 108 ch; br	Coppenrath
	Chor zum Empfange eines Bischofs ch; br	Coppenrath
	Festchor: Wie schön die Füsse dessen sind ch; 9 br	Coppenrath
	Die Jubel-Kaiser-Festhymne, Op 154 ch; br	Pressverein
Mittmann, P.	Papst-Hymne, Op 109 ch; 9 br	Böhm
Mohler, P. 1908–	Festliche Liedkantate (1956) ch; br, timp	MS? (Rie)
	Wandspruchkantate (1956) ch; br, timp	MS? (Rie)
Monnikendam, M. 1896–	Veni Creator (1959) ch; 0110-org	Donemus
	Christ-Mass ch; 0110-org	Donemus
	Missa solemnissima in honorem Sancti Willibrordi ch; 0330-org	Donemus, 1959
	Missa festiva ch; 0220-org	Rossum, 1955
	Hymne A, ch; br	Donemus, 1957
Monteverdi, C. 1567–1643	Sonata sopra Sancti Maria ora nobis (Arr R. King) S, ch; 0420-2 bar	King
Moser, R. 1892–1960	Ode an die Allmacht, Op 96 (1957) ch; br, timp	MS (MGG)
Muckenthaler, L.	Hymne: Dich, Maria, hoch erhoben, Op 1 ch; 6 br	Böhm
Müller, O. b. 1870?	Hymnus: Pange lingua gloriosi, Op 3 ch; 2210-db, org, timp	Böhm
Müller-Zürich, P. 1898–	Herr, nun selbst den Wagen halt ch; 0320-org	MS (V)
Mussa, V. E.	Hohenzollernlied, Op 34 ch/mch; br	Zumsteeg
Nekes, F. 1844–1914	O Crux ave, Op 33 ch; br	Schweitzer

Nelson, R. 1929–	Dedication & Praise ch; 2 br choirs	(Ho)
	Fanfare for a Festival ch; 0331-org, timp	Bo. & H., 1960
Neukomm, S. 1778–1858	Missa pro defunctis 2 ch; br, org	Peters, 1815
Niblock, J.	Vanity of Vanities ch; 2220-org, timp	Interlochen, n.d.
Nowak, L. 1911–	Concertante MzS, ch; 0240	CFE
Nuffel, J. van 1883–1953	Te Deum (1944) ch; br	MS? (MGG)
Odorich, P.	Two Ave Maria ch; 2010-org	Böhm, n.d.
	Offertorium ch; 2010-org	Böhm, n.d.
Pachelbel, J. 1653–1706	Nun danket alle Gott (Arr R. King) ch; 0220-org	King, 1959
	All praise and thanks to God (Arr A. Lovelace) ch; 0220	Brodt, 1959
Peeters, F. 1903–	†Intrada festiva, Op 93 ch; 0220-org, perc	Peters, 1959
Peregrinus, J.	Drei Gesänge für das heilige Fronleichnamsfest, Nos. 1 & 2 ch; br, org	Böhm
Pfautsch, L.	Christ, Foundation, Head & Cornerstone ch; 0320/org	Lawson, 1960
	Hymn Anthem on Christian, dost thou see them ch; 0320	Abingdon, 1962
	I want a Principle within ch; 0220	Abingdon, 1965
Philipp, F. 1890–	Ecce sacerdos, Op 55 ch; 2231-org	Schwann
	Ernste und frohe Kanons, Op 76 (1952) ch; 6 br, timp	Böhm
	Feierliches Einzugspräludium und Choral, Op 62 ch; br, timp	Böhm
	Festliche Andacht zur heiligen Eucharistie, Op 45 (1932–45) ch, cch, cong; 7 br, org, timp	Schwann
	Hymne für eine Priesterfeier, Op 54 (1943) ch; 4 br, org, timp	Schwann
	St. Franziskus-Feier, Op 64 ch, cch, cong; 7 br, org, timp	Schwann
Pinkham, D. 1923–	Festival Magnificat & Nunc dimittis ch; 1210-org	Peters, 1963

	Christmas Cantata (Sinfonia sacra) ch; 0451	King, 1958
	Angelus ad Pastoris ait fch; 043(1)	King, 1959
	Psalm 81 (1959) ch; 0220-org	CFE
	Easter Cantata ch; 2431-cel, timp, perc	Peters, 1962
	Requiem A, T, ch; 2220-db/org/pf	Peters, 1963
	This is the Day ch; 0431-timp	CFE
	Lamentations of Jeremiah ch; 2220-db, timp, 2 perc	Peters
	Canticle of Praise S, ch; br, perc	E. C. Schirmer, 1968
Pisk, P. A. 1893–	Prayer for the twentieth century (1932) ch; br	CFE
Pizzaro, D.	An Easter Laud ch; 5 br, org, timp	Gray, 1958
Polzer, O.	Missa festiva ch; 2220	Weinberger
Praetorius, M. 1571–1621	In dulci jubilo (1607) (Arr R. King) ch; 0220	King, 1959
Purcell, H. 1659–95	Music for Queen Mary II (Arr R. King) ch; 1110-bar	King, 1959
Raubuch, E. 1909–	Tu es Petrus: Hymnus ch; 1110-org	Schwann
Reda, S. 1916–	Te Deum laudamus (1950) 2 ch; 0331	BVK, 1951
Reichel, B. 1901–	Cantique de confiance ch; 0220-org	MS (BQ, VII, 1)
	Musique liturgique de Pâques ch; 0330-org, timp	MS (BQ, VII, 1)
Reimann, F.	Christus ist erstanden ch; br, org	Hoffmann
Reimann, I. 1820–85	Libera ch; 0110-ten hn	Pietsch
	IV Stationen mit Pange lingua ch; br	Pietsch
	Vexilla regis & Ecce quomodo ch; br	Pietsch
Rein, W. 1893–1955	Komm, trost der Nacht, O Nachtigall ch, cch; 023(1)	Schott
	Du meine Seele, singe ch, cong; 0220	BVK, 1956
	Macht hoch die Tür ch, cong; 0220	BVK, 1956
	Zu Bethlehem geboren ch; 0220/0330	BVK, 1962

Renner, J.	Auferstehungslieder, Op 35	Pustet
1832–95	ch; br	
	Missa quarta, Op 32	Pustet
	ch; br	
	Te Deum, Op 37	Pustet
	ch; br, opt org	
Rettich, W. 1892–	Ballade vom Werewolf, Op 62	MS (V)
	(1928)	
	ch; br, timp	
Reuland, J.	Laus Deo	Harmonia
	ch; br	
Reynolds, R. 1934–	Blind Men	Peters, 1967
	ch; 0331-pf, perc	
Ropek, J. 1922–	Mass in C	(WWM; fp 25
	ch; 0220-org	Oct., 1968)
Rowlands, D.	Degrees	(RT, 4 Sept, 1969)
	ch; br quint	
Rubbra, E. 1901–	Veni, Creator spiritus, Op 130	Lengnick, 1966
	ch; 4231	
Rungenhagen, C. F.	Festkantate (1840)	MS? (AmZ 42,
1778–1851	ch; br	1840)
Sapp, A. D. jun.	How like the month of May	CFE
1922–	ch; 0330	
Schaefers, A. 1908–	Gott ist gewaltig	B. & B.
	ch, cch; 0230	
	Zwei Hymnen nach Texten der	B. & B.
	Apokalypse (1954)	
	ch; 3231	
Scherr, J.	Deutsches Requiem	Aibl
	ch; 2010-org	
Schgraffer, J.	Kurzes und leichtes Stabat Mater,	Böhm
	Op 22	
	ch; br, org	
Schmid, A.	Dies Irae	Böhm
b. 1772	ch; 2210	
Schmid, F. X.	Deutscher Trauergesang	Böhm
	ch; 4040	
Schnabel, J. I.	Zwei Lieder zu Ehren des heiligen	Leuckart
1767–1831	Johann von Nepomuk	
	ch; br, org	
	Deutsches Litanei	Leuckart
	ch; br, org	
Schönsee, G.	Deutsche Hymne	Challier
	ch; br	
Schroeder, H.	Fünf Hymne zur Fronleichnams-	Schwann
1904–	prozession	
	ch; 2231–2 tenhn	
	Magnificat	Schwann, n.d.
	ch; 0331	
	Te Deum	Schott, 1933
	ch; 023(1)	
Schulhoff, E.	Manifesto (1930)	(Ga)
1894–1942	5 soli, 2 ch, cch; br	

285

Schumann, G. A.	Drei Choral-Motetten, Op 75/3	Lienau
1866–1952	S, ch; 3031-org, timp	
Schütz, H.	Psalm 8: Herr unser Herrscher	BVK
1585–1672	(SWV 27) (Ed. Huber)	
	2 ch; 0320-org	
	Psalm 150 (1619) (Arr T. Marier)	King, 1958
	2 ch; 0530-org	
Schwarz-	Signum magnum (1958)	MS (MGG)
Schilling, R.	ch, cong; 4440	
1904–		
Schwenke, J. F.	Lob- und Dank-Kantate, Op 40	MS (AmZ 47,
1792–1852	ch; 0140-org, timp	1845)
Scull, H. T. 1898–	Cantate Domino (Psalm 98)	Williams, 1958
	ch; 0330-cym	
Snel, J. F.	Deux Chants de Fête	Terry
1793–1861	ch; hns, trbs	
Spengel, J. H.	Der 39 Psalm, Op 7	Leuckart
1853–1936	ch; br, timp	
Staempfli, E.	Liberté (1944)	MS (MGG)
1908–	soli, ch; br, pf, timp	
Stanford, C. V.	St. Patrick's Breastplate	MS (Stainer)
1852–1924	ch; 0230-org, perc	
	Te Deum in C (1909)	
	ch; br, drums	
Stehle, J. G. E.	Huldigungslied, Op, 71	Schwann
b. 1839	ch; trps, trbs	
Štépka, K. V.	In the Footsteps of the Hussites	(Ga)
1908–	(Canto bellicoso) (1953)	
	ch; br, timp	
Stern, H. 1901–	Lobt Gott, ihr Christen alle	BVK, 1956
	gleich	
	ch, cong; 0320	
	Das alte Jahr vergangen ist	Hänssler
	ch, cong; br	
Stier, A. 1880–	Ich habe nun den Grund gefunden	BVK
	ch; 1210-vln, timp ad lib	
Stockhausen, K. H.	Momente II (1965)	
1928–	S, 2 ch; 0440-2 elec org, 3 perc	
Storch, A. M.	Ermanne dich, Deutschland!	Cranz
1815–87	soli, ch; br	
	Fest-Motto ch; br	Cranz
Stuntz, J. H.	Heldengesang in Walhalla	Falter
1793–1859	ch; 5210	
	Grabgesang	Aibl
	ch; 4030	
Täglichsbeck, T.	Fünf Chorgesänge, Op. 29	Falter
1799–1867	ch; 2230-oph	
Tagg, L. E.	Hodie Christus natus est	SB, 1962
	ch; 2220/0420	
Thaller, J. B.	Auferstehungslieder, Op 3	Coppenrath
	ch; br, timp	
	Missa tertia (Requiem)	Böhm
	ch; br, org	

Thiel, C. 1862–1939	Jauchzet dem Herr alle Lande, Op 21 ch; 0230	Schwann
Thompson, R. 1899–	A Feast of Praise ch; br, hp/pf	E. C. Schirmer [1963]
Titcomb, E.	Hymn-Anthem on Adeste Fideles S/T, ch; 0220-org	Peters, 1962
	Rejoice we all, and praise the Lord S, ch; 0220	Gray, 1959
Titone, A. 1934–	Quattro Haikai di Bashô ch; 0310	Composer, 1959
Tittel, E. 1910–	Missa magnus et potens, Op 15 ch; 2220-org	Schwann
	Requiem mit Libera, Op 34 ch; br, org	Styria
	Sonnenhymnus, Op 47 (1950) ch; 0431-bass trp	Öst. Sängerbund
Toepler, A. 1888–	Hymnen zur Fronleichnams- prozession und für feierliche Sakramentsandachten ch; br, org	Schwann
Tomasi, H. 1901–	Procession nocturne S, ch; 4341-timp, perc	Leduc, 1959
Tremmel, M. 1902–	Der 150 Psalm, Op 20 ch; 2220-org, timp	Coppenrath
Vaughan Williams, R. 1872–1958	†O clap your hands 2 ch; 7 br, org, perc	Stainer, 1920
Vecchi, O. 1540-ca. 1604	O dulcis Ilsu 2 ch; 0440	Möseler [1969]
Vinter, G. 1909–69	†The Trumpets B, ch; br, perc	
Waldbroel, W. 1896–1952	Ecce sacerdos (1951) ch, cong; 4 br	SM, 1952
Walter, K. 1862–1929	Festmesse ch; 2220-org	Doblinger, 1953
	Weihnachtsmesse ch, cch, cong; 0330-org	Styria
Walton, K.	Fanfare for Easter ch; 0220	Kjos, 1958
Ward, W. R.	Father, we praise Thee ch; 2331-bar	Marks, 1957
Warner, R.	Come thou long-expected Jesus S, ch; 0310-org	Gray, 1958
Weber, L. 1891–1947	Lass die Wurzeln unseres Handels Liebe sein ch; 10 br	Schott
Wedig, H. J. 1898–	Das ewige Allelujah (1953) ch; 1220	Wildt
	Komm; trost der Nacht, O Nachtigall ch, cch; 0330-timp	MS (V)
Weinberger, K. F. 1853–1908	Recht und Treu, Op. 24 ch; br	Böhm

Weismann, W. 1900–	Weihnachtshymnus: Vom Turm die Glocken brummen ch; 0220-org	Br. & H., 1938
	Wessobrunner Gebet ch; 0220-org	Br. & H.
Wenzel, E. 1896–	Choralkantate: Wach auf, wach auf, 's hohe Zeit (1953) ch; 0210	MS (V)
	Gott des Himmels und der Erden ch, cong; 0231	BVK
	Nun freut euch, lieben Christen g'mein ch, cong; 0210-org	Hänssler
Werner, F. 1898–	Jesus Christus herrscht als König, Op 33b (1952) ch; 0330-timp	Schultheiss
Whettam, G. 1927–	Thus spake Solomon ch; 0330-org, timp	Ascherberg
Wildgans, F. 1913–65	Eucharistische Hymnen (1954) S, B, ch; 12 br, 3 pf, perc	Doblinger, 1958
Willan, H. 1880–	Sing to the Lord of harvest (Arr M. E. Hogg) ch; 1211-bar	Concordia, 1960
Witt, F. X. 1834–88	Missa in honorem St. Luciae Op 11a ch; br, org	Coppenrath
Wittmer, E. L. 1905–	Deutsche Erde, Kantate ch; br	Hochstein, n.d.
Wöss, J. V. von 1863–1943	Te Deum, Op 3a (1888) ch; 2230-org, timp	Böhm
Wood, J. H. (b. 1915?)	Only-begotten Word of God eternal ch; 1220-org	Concordia
Wyton, A. 1921–	Easter Canticle ch; 0220-timp	Gray
	This joyful Eastertide ch; 0220	Gray
Zaininger, B.	Berühmtes Libera, Op 16 ch; br	Böhm
Zipp, F. 1914–	Such, wer da will, ein ander Ziel, Op 50 ch, cong; 0420-timp ad lib	BVK, 1956
	Choral-Kantate: Wachet auf ruft uns die Stimme (1955) ch; 0220-org	BVK
	Choralfeier: Ist Gott für mich, Op 45 S/T, 2 ch; br, org, opt timp	Merseburger
	Choralkantate: Lobt Gott getrost mit Singen, Op 37 ch; br	Merseburger
Zoll, P. 1907–	O Lied ch; 2331	MS (V)

Zulehner, C. ca. 1770–ca. 1830	Freimaurer-Kantate ch; br	Schott

7.6 *Male chorus with brass ensemble*

Abt, F. 1819–85	All Deutschland: Festgesang, Op 201 mch; br	Siegel
Ahle, J. N.	Du starker Fels im Meer! Festgesang T, Bar, mch; 9 br	Coppenrath
Ames, W.	O Read mch; br	CFE
Anschütz, C. 1815–70?	Festlied: Hohenzollern hoch T, mch; br	MS? (AmZ 42, 1840)
Appel, K. b. 1812	Zwei Lieder, Op 70 mch; br	Forberg
Argento, D.	The Revelation of St. John the Divine T, mch; 3220-pf, hp, perc	Bo. & H., 1968
Attenhofer, C. 1837–1914	Waldfahrt, Op 54 mch; 4210	Hug
Aysslinger, R.	Begrüssungs-Chor, Op 41 mch; br	André, 1903
Barber, S. 1910–	†A Stopwatch & an ordnance Map, Op 15 (1940) mch; 4031-timp	G. Schirmer, 1954
Baumann, F. C.	Zur Fahnen-Feier-Festgesang, Op 12 mch; br	UE
Baussnern, W. 1866–1931	Wer weiss wo Bar, mch; 0220-timp	Rhein
Becker, A. E. A. 1834–99	Psalm 84, Op 79 mch; 0130-timp	Br. & H., 1895
Becker, V. E. 1814–90	Gesänge, Op 25 mch; br, timp	Glaser
	Zwei Gesänge, Op 108 mch; hns, ct, trb, pf	Glaser
	Die Rose Deutschlands, Op 68 mch; br, timp	Kahnt
	Sedania; Festkantate, Op 91 mch; br, timp	Kahnt
Bergmann, E.	Jesurum, Op 61 Bar, mch; br, perc	Fazer, 1967
Bieger, F.	Missa in hon. S. Francisci Seraphici, Op 11 mch; 2 bass trp, althn, trb	Böhm
Blum, C. L. 1786–1844	Siegeslied der Kreuzfahrer bei Eroberung des heiliges Grabes, Op 67 mch; br	Schott
Börner, A.	Hohenzollernlied, Op 38 mch; 3010	Heinrichshofen

Brah-Müller, K. F. 1839–78	Friede den Entschlafenen mch; 0230-2 ct, timp	Zechlin
Brambach, K. J. 1833–1902	Gott der Herr, Op 62 mch; br	Kistner
	Nänie, Op 67 mch; 4031-timp	Kistner
Breu, S.	Bundesfeier, Op 50 mch; 4231-2 E♭ trp, bar, timp	Kistner, 1897
Bruch, M. 1838–1920	Männerchöre, Op 19 mch; 2230-timp	Siegel
Bruckner, A. 1824–96	Das Deutsche Lied (1892) mch; 4331	UE
	Germanenzug (1863) mch; 4431–2 ct, ten hn	Kränzl [1865]; Robitschek [1892]
	Lasst Jubelklänge laut erklingen (1854) mch; br	(H. Redlich: Bruckner & Mahler)
	Helgoland (1893) mch; br	(G)
Bülow, H. von 1830–94	Bayrische Volkhymne mch; 9 br	Aibl
Burkhard, W. 1900–55	Sechs Chor-Duette, Op 22 (1928) mch; 0110	Hug
Burkhart, F. 1902–	Das grosse Licht (1952) mch; 4431-timp	Doblinger
Canning, T. 1911–	The Temptation of Jesus narrator, mch; 2231-perc	CFE
Cassels-Brown, A. K. 1927–	Jubilate mch; br	(WWM)
Converse, F. S. 1871–1940	Laudate Dominum, Op 22 mch; 0230	Boston
Daxsperger, L. 1900–	Vaterland (1923) mch; 2220	MS (V)
de Filippi, A. 1900–	Three Poems mch; br	MS (R)
Deigendesch, K.	Der Geworbene, Op 32 mch; flghn, althn, trb, bar, pf	Böhm
Enckhausen, H. 1799–1885	Der 100 Psalm, Op 50 mch; br	Nagel [ca. 1840]
Eyken, J. A. van 1822–68	Turmlied soli, mch; br, timp	Brauer
Faisst, I. G. F. 1823–94	Hymne: Dem Herrn mch; br, timp	Kränzl [ca. 1866]
	Vier Kriegs- und Siegeslieder, Op 28 mch; br	Forberg [ca. 1871]
	Des Sängers Wiederkehr, Op 30 mch; br, db, drums	Ebner
	Schillerkantate, Op 31 mch; br	Ebner
	Siegespsalm, Op 29 mch; br	Forberg [ca. 1871?]

Filke, M. 1855–1911	Lobgesang zum Herrn, Op 65 mch; br, timp	Forberg
	Soldling und Bauer, Op 86 mch; br, timp	Siegel
Fink, C. 1822–1911	Der 95 Psalm, Op 28 mch; br, timp	Br. & H., [ca. 1865]
Frackenpohl, A. 1924–	Shepherds, rejoice T/Bar, mch; 3031-bar	King, 1958
Frid, G. 1904–	Das Sklavenschiff, Op 51 T, Bar, mch; 4331-pf, xyl, timp, perc	Donemus, 1956
	Ballade, Op 71 mch; br	Donemus, 1965
Fromm, E. b. 1835	Das Helden Auferstehung, Op 2 soli, mch; br	Glaser
Girschner, C. F. J. 1794–1860	Psalm: Gross ist der Herr, Op 12 mch; br	Wagenführ [1835]
Goller, V. 1873–1953	Hymnus: Te Deum laudamus, Op 45a mch; 4 br	Coppenrath
Grabner, H. 1886–	Sonnengesang (1949) mch; 2211-timp	Schwann
Graener, P. 1872–1944	Der Retter ist nicht weit mch; 4330-dbn, timp, pf/org	Eulenburg
Graf, H. 1926–	Nancy-Lied 1477 (1949) mch; 0330-timp, perc	MS (V)
Häser, A. F. 1779–1844	Hymne mch; br, org	MS? (AmZ 42, 1840)
Haller, M. 1840–1915	Motette: Tu es Petrus, Op 49 mch; br	Pustet
Hartmann, J. P. E. 1805–1900	Orla Lehmann mch; br, 2 pf	Samfundet, 1917
Haszlinger, J. von	Die Fünf des ersten Freiheitkampfes mch; hns, trbs, timp	MS? (AmZ 47, 1845)
Hauptmann, M. 1792–1868	Motette: Ehre sei Gott in der Höhe, Op 36/3 mch; 2030	Siegel
Heller, J. G.	Jagdchor, Op 34 mch; br	André
Hermann, W.	Ans Vaterland, Op 27 mch; br	Siegel
Herzogenberg, H. 1843–1900	Begräbnis-Gesang, Op 88 mch; 403(1)	RB [1896]
Heyblom, A. W. A.	Vrijheidslied, Op 42 mch; br	Br. & H.
Hofer, J.	Trostspruch an Deutsch- Oesterreich, Op 8 mch; br	Bosworth
Hol, R. 1825–1904	Hollands Glorie, Op 24 mch; br	Lichtenauer
Holst, G. 1874–1934	†A Dirge for two Veterans mch; br, drums	Curwen, 1914

Horn, A. 1825–93	Marschlied, Op 25 mch; 221(1)	R. & E.
	Des Sängers Welt, Op 44 mch; 3011	Br. & H.
Huber, W. S. 1898–	Kantate nach Gedichten von C. F. Meyer mch; 2220-org, timp	Hug
Isenmann, C. 1839–89	Lobgesang, Op 107 mch; 3311-timp	Forberg
	Der Sänger Festgruss, Op 31 mch; br	Kistner
Jadassohn, S. 1831–1902	Hymnus: Gott ist gross und allmächtig, Op 45 mch; 2020	Siegel
James, P. 1890–	General Booth enters into heaven (1932) mch; 0110–2 pf, perc	Witmark, 1933
Jochum, O. 1898–	Zuversicht: Hymne, Op 42 mch; br	Böhm, 1932
Kabeláč, M. 1908–	Cantata: Weichet nicht zurück, Op 7 (1939) mch; br, perc	MS (G, MGG)
Kammerlander, C. 1828–92	Hohe Sängerkunst, Op 74 mch; 9 br, timp	Böhm
	Sänger-Reichtum, Op 78 mch; 9 br, timp	Böhm
Keller, H. 1915–	The Raider (1943) mch; br	MS (R)
Kelly, R. 1916–	The Torment of Job mch; 0330-pf, perc	CFE
Kirchner, H. 1861–1928	Festgesang, Op 25 mch; br, pf	Rohlfing
Koch, J. H. E. 1918–	Lob der Musik mch; 0320	Nagel, 1967
Köllner, E.	Hohenzollernlied, Op 124 mch, cch; 2221–2 ten hn, timp	Kahnt
	Hohenzollernlied, Op 149 mch; br	Forberg
	Die Königserl im Spreewald, Op 128 mch; 0231-timp	Kistner
	Zwei Waldlieder, Op 75 mch; 2210	Pabst
Křenek, E. 1900–	Jagd Im Winter, Op 74 (1933) mch; br, timp	MS (V)
Kreutzer, C. 1780–1849	Siegesbotschaft mch; 2210-timp	Eulenburg
Krizkovsky, K. P. 1820–85	SS. Cyril & Methodius: Cantata (1861) mch; br, pf	Stary
Kubik, G. 1914–	Litany & Prayer (1943) mch; 4331-perc	Southern, 1953

Lang, H. 1897–	Bundeslied mch; 4331	Schott
La Tombelle, F. de 1854–1928	Le Chant du Travail mch; br, sax	Fougeray, n.d.
Leitner, C. A.	Vier Hymnen zu Prozession und Andachten mch; br	Böhm
	Requiem & Libera mch; 4 br	Böhm
Lichner, H. 1829–98	Der deutsche Baum, Op 67 mch; br	Siegel
	Deutsches Bundeslied, Op 68 mch; br	Siegel
	Seid uns! Op 65 mch; br	Siegel
	Wanderlied, Op 69 mch; br	Siegel
Liebe, L. 1819–1900	Das Göttliche: Kantate, Op 60 soli, mch; br	Coppenrath
Lindpaintner, P. J. 1791–1856	Chant funèbre mch; 5030	Zumsteeg
Lissmann, K. 1902–	Beherzigung mch; 1110	Tonger
	Zum Sehen geboren mch; 0330-timp	Tonger
Liszt, F. 1811–86	Licht, mehr Licht (1849, rev. 1856) mch; 0230	Schuberth [ca. 1860]
	Festgesang: Carl August weilt mit uns mch; br, org, perc	Kistner, 1887
	Nun danket alle Gott mch; 0230-org, timp	Br. & H., 1884
	Psalm XVIII (1860) mch; 4231-timp	Schuberth, 1871
	Requiem (1868) 2 T, 2 B, mch; 0220-org, timp	Repos, 1868; Kahnt, 1870
Mangold, J. W. 1796–1875	Festkantate mch; br	MS? (AmZ 46, 1844)
Marx, J. 1882–1964	Morgengesang (1910) mch; 4340-org, timp	UE
Matthes, R. 1897–	Kantate: Gezeiten des Lebens S, sprechstimme, mch; br, org, timp	MS (V)
May, H. von 1913–	Vermahnungsgesang mch; 0320	Hug
Mayer, J. A. 1855–1936	Finnisches Reiterlied mch; br	Zumsteeg
Mendelssohn, F. 1809–47	Festgesang an die Künstler, Op 68 (1845–6) 2 T, 2 B, mch; 2221 (Ed. T. Sokol) 2 T, 2 B, mch; 4431-bar	Simrock King, 1960

	Festgesang: Begeht mit heil'gen Lobgesang mch; Choir I 4430-oph; Choir II 2230 (Ed. T. Sokol)	Br. & H. King
	Festlied zur Enthüllung der Statue Friedrich August von Sachsen (1843) 2 mch; br	MS (MGG)
Metzger, J. C.	In heiligen deutschen Osten, Op 173 mch; br	Robitschek
Meyer-Obersleben, M. 1850–1927	Gruss und Willkomm, Op 37 mch; br	Siegel
Meyerbeer, G. 1791–1864	Bayerischer Schützenmarsch (1829) soli, mch; br	MS (G)
Meyerowitz, J. 1913–	Ave Maria Stella (1954) mch; 3331	Rongwen
Mittmann, P.	Unter Kolpings Eiche, Op 124 mch; 9–12 br	Böhm
Mohler, P. 1908–	Das Leben: Präludium, Op 5 (1932) mch; 0331-timp	Hochstein, 1936
Monnikendam, M. 1896–	Ballade des Pendus (1949) mch; 2220-pf, timp, perc	Donemus, 1952
	Veni Creator S, mch; 1010-org	Donemus, 1960
Moser, R. 1892–1960	Friedensgebet, Op 64/4 mch; 0130	Hug
Mussa, V. E.	Hohenzollernlied mch; br	(P)
Neithardt, H. A. 1793–1861	Sechs Kriegslieder, Op 82 mch; hns, trbs	Wagenführ [ca. 1834]
Nekes, F. 1844–1914	O Crux ave, Op 33b mch; br	Schweitzer
Neumann, H.	Rhein-Preussens Kriegerlied, Op 47 mch; 0440-timp	Fürstner
Ortner, A.	Bayerisches Lied, Op 38 mch; br	Aibl
Othegraven, A. von 1864–1946	Advent Kantate über zwei Volkslieder, Op 70 S, mch; 0230-org, timp	Leuckart, 1927
	Drei Gesänge, Op 10 mch; 4231-timp, perc	Siegel
Otto, E. J. 1804–77	Sängergruss, Op 124 mch; br	Leuckart
Petrassi, G. 1904–	†Coro di morti (1940–1) mch; 4431-db, 3 pf, timp, 4 perc	SZ, 1953

Philipp, F. 1890–	Eichendorff-Zyklus, Op 16 (1924)	Müller
	No. 1	
	mch; 1031-timp	
	No. 2	Schultheiss
	mch; 1031-2 pf, timp	
	Ernste und frohe Kanons, Op 31 (1952)	Böhm
	mch; 6 br, timp	
	Festgruss, Op 73	Böhm
	mch; br, perc	
Piston, W. 1894–	Carnival Song (1938)	Arrow, 1941
	mch; 4331	
Ploner, E. 1894–	Deutsches Weihelied, Op 11 (1924)	MS (V)
	mch; 2221-timp	
Podbertsky, T. b. 1846	Altgermanischer Siegesgesand, Op 100	Siegel
	mch; 0511	
	An das Feuer, Op 51	Siegel
	mch; br	
	An der Nordstrom, Op 103	Lyra
	mch; 0331	
	Germanischer Schlachtgesang, Op 140	Forberg
	mch; 0231	
	Leyer und Schwert, Op 123/3	Siegel
	mch; br, pf	
Quenzel, H.	Der Deutsche Sang, Op 2	Forberg
	soli, mch; br	
Radermacher, F. 1924–	Von den Wolken (Wolkenlieder)	Volk
	mch; 1110	
Rebling, G. 1821–1902	Festgesang, Op 38	Heinrichshofen
	mch; br	
	Die Jungfrau von Magdeburg, Op 40 mch; br	Heinrichshofen
Rein, W. 1893–1955	Türmerlied	Schott
	mch; 0331	
	Freiheit, die ich meine (1955)	Schott
	mch; br	
Reinecke, C. 1824–1910	Der Jäger Heimkehr, Op 90	Siegel
	mch; 4010	
	Festgesang, Op 192	RB
	mch; br	
Renner, J. 1832–95	Missa tertia, Op 31	Pustet
	mch; br	
Reutter, H. 1900–	Hymne an Deutschland	Schott
	mch; 2331-timp	
Rheinberger, J. 1839–1901	Ballade: Die Rosen von Hildesheim, Op 143	Kistner
	mch; br	
Richli, J.	Ein Ständchen beim Herrn Burgermeister: Humoreske	Hug
	mch; br	

Richstätter, M.	Begrüssungschor, Op 17 mch; br	Ulrich
Riegel, F.	Volkshymne zum 700 jährigen Jubiläum des Hauses Wittelsbach mch; br	W. Schmid
Röder, E.	Des deutschen Sängers Bannerlied, Op 36 mch; br	Bratfisch
	Hymnus, Op 14 mch; 4030	Fritzsche
Roussel, A. 1869–1937	Le Bardit des Francs (1926) mch; 2231–timp, 2 perc	Durand
Rudnick, W.	Heil Hohenzollern, Op 75 mch; br	Preiser
	Rheinsage, Op 55 mch; 4231–timp	Siegel
Rudolph, O.	Deutsche Treue, Op 27 mch; br	Siegel
Samuel, A. A.	Léopold Ier, Op 40 (1880) mch; br	MS? (MGG)
	L'Union fait la force, Op 27 (1855) mch; br	MS? (MGG)
Schauseil, W.	Festgruss mch; br	Kistner [ca. 1867]
Schiwy, J.	Die Fahnenweihe, Op 13 mch; br	Siegel
Schletterer, H. M. 1823–93	Der Landsknecht, Op 56 mch; br	Kistner
Schneider, J. C. F. 1786–1853	Hymne: Jehova, Dir frohlockt der König, Op 94 mch; 4230–db, timp	Trautwein [1834]
Schnyder, C.	Gebet für das Vaterland mch; 2 flghn, 2 trp, 4 althn, trb, bombardon	Hug
Schoeck, O. 1886–1957	Eichendorff-Kantate, Op 49 (1933) Bar, mch; 0031–pf, perc	Hug, 1934
Schroeder, H. 1904–	Hymnen zur Fronleichnams- prozession mch; 2241	Schott
Schubert, F. 1797–1828	Geisterchor aus Rosamunde, Op 26/4 mch; 0330	Br. & H.
Seeger, P. 1919–	Pfälzische Liedkantate mch; br	Schott
Seidel, O.	Ein Gruss an den Kaiser mch; br	Vieweg
Siefhardt, W.	Bundeslied, Op 2 mch; 2231	Kahnt
Siegl, O. 1896–	Bauernhymne mch; 2221	Hochstein

	Liederehung mch; 2220	Hochstein
Soltans, N.	Mailied, Op 16	André
	mch; br	
Speidel, W.	Deutsche Völker allesamt, Op 42	Zumsteeg
1826–99	mch; br	
	Kaiserlied, Op 57	Schweers
	mch; 4431–oph	
Stade, F. W.	Worte des Glaubens	Kahnt
1817–1902	mch; br	
Stein, B. b. 1873	Ein Bild aus fernen Tagen, Op 24	Vieweg
	mch; br	
	Dem Kaiser Heil! Op 26	Kothe
	mch; br	
	Rotbarts Testament, Op 32	Vieweg
	mch; br	
Steinhäuser, C.	Schlacht von Sedan	Oertel
	mch; br	
Steinhauer, C.	Zwei Rheinlieder, Op 33	Leuckart
1852–1934	No. 1: Der Rhein	
	mch; br, timp	
Storch, A. M.	Jagdlied, Op 102	Cranz
1815–87	mch; br	
	Liedertafel, Op 100	Cranz
	mch; br	
	Soldatenmut	Cranz
	mch; br	
Strohbach, S. 1929–	Lob der Musik (1953)	Br. & H.
	mch, cch; 2330	
	Das Wort und das Musik (1960)	Br. & H.
	mch, cch; 2330–timp	
	Proprium Missae in Festo. Scti.	Br. & H.
	Bartholomaei Apostoli	
	mch; 2221–timp ad lib	
Stürmer, B.	Choralkantate: Nun danket alle	Merseburger
1892–1958	Gott	
	mch; 3330–timp	
	Herrlich der Tag	Tonger
	mch; 2330–perc	
	Das Ludwigsburger Te Deum	Tonger
	mch; 3330–timp	
	O Tag, O Sonne	Tonger
	mch; 2330–perc	
Stuntz, J. H.	Bankett-Lied zu dem Maskenzug	Falter [1840]
1793–1859	der Künstler	
	mch; 4510–oph, timp	
	Bardengesang	Aibl
	mch; 4511–oph	
	Den Bayerischen Schützenmarsch	Aibl
	mch; 4310	
	Die Burgfrau	Aibl
	mch; 5010–oph	
	Schützenruf	Aibl
	mch; 2511–oph	

Tardos, B. 1910–	German Mercenaries Song (1942) mch; br	MS? (G)
Tauwitz, E. 1812–94	Fahnenschwur, Op 127 mch; br	Robitschek
	Festchor, Op 113 mch; br	Wetzler
	Festgruss der deutsch-böhmischen Verein, Op 73 mch; br	Wetzler
	Hoch Österreich, Op 100 mch; br	Robitschek
Tietz, P.	Festlicher Lobegesang, Op 53 mch; br	Kahnt
Tresch, J. B.	Zwei Miserere und Benedictus zu feierlichen Begräbnissen, Op 7 mch; br	Germann
Tschirch, R. 1825–72	Des Löwen Erwachen mch; br	Schlesinger
Unger, H. 1886–1958	Heimatsgefühl mch; 4230	Tonger
	Sonnenaufgang (1952) mch; 4230	Tonger
Verhulst, J. J. H. 1816–91	Vlaggelied, Op 35 mch; br	Weygand, 1850
	Bij het Graf, Op 34 mch; br	Weygand, 1855
	Missa pro defunctis, Op 51 mch; 2231–org, perc	Theune; Van Eyck, 1854
Wassermann, K. d. 1902	Dem Vaterlande! Op 38 mch; br	Kahnt
Weber, B. 1912–	Kling auf, mein Lied mch; 2331	Schott
Weegenhuise, J. 1910–	Domine salvum fac (1950–9) mch; 4331	Bank, 1959
Wehrli, W. 1892–1944	Festlied, Op 31 (1933) mch; 8 br, timp	Hug
	Kantate über das Beresinalied mch; 0210	Hug
Weinzierl, M. von 1841–98	Fahnenlied, Op 78 mch; br	Robitschek
	Fahnenlied, Op 89 mch; br	(P)
Willemsen, H.	Es gilt dem Lied mch; br	Oertel
Wiltberger, A. b. 1850	Kaisergruss, Op 51 mch; 9 br	Schwann
Wittmer, E. L. 1905–	Bekenntnis mch; 0330–timp	Braun-Peretti
	Psalm 146 (1950) mch; 0330–timp	Hochstein
Wolf, L. C.	Persergebet, Op 26 T, mch; br	Reinecke
Wood, T. 1892–1950	The Rainbow (1950) T, Bar, mch; br	Stainer

Wynne, D. 1900–	Cantata: Owain ab Urien mch; br	(MT, July, 1968)
Zedtler, A.	Gott schirme dich, mein Vaterland, Op 35 mch; br	(P)
Zöllner, H. 1854–1941	Hohenzollernlied, Op 34a mch; br	Klinner
	Dem jungen Kaiser: Festhymne Op 88d mch; br	Siegel
	Nachtlied mch; 2030–harm/pf	Hug; Kistner
	Dem neunzigjährigen Kaiser: Festhymnus, Op 38 mch; br	Siegel
	Preis der deutschen Musik, Op 52 mch; br	Siegel
	Der Tod des Herrn, Op 84 mch; br	Wernthal
	Trauerode auf dem Tod des Kaisers Wilhelm, Op 38b mch; br	Siegel
	Zur Schillerfeier, Op 86 mch; br	Leuckart
Zoll, P. 1907–	Freude mch; 2220	Braun-Peretti
	Gelöbnis mch; 3330–timp	Schwann
	Spruch mch; 2220	Braun-Peretti
Zopff, H. 1826–83	Deutscher Triumphgesang, Op 23 mch; br	Kahnt
Zuschneid, K. 1856–1926	Lenzfahrt, Op 22 mch; br	Br. & H.

Publishers

Agent in U.K.

Abingdon	Abingdon Press, 201 Eighth Ave. So., Nashville, Tenn. 37303.	
Adler	Henry Adler, Inc., 136 W. 46th St., New York, 36, N.Y.	
Aibl	*Josef Aibl-Verlag, Munich. (Now UE).	
Alcove	Alcove Music, N. Hollywood, Calif.	
Alkor	Alkor Edition GmbH, Kassel. (See BVK.)	
Amadino	*R. Amadino, Venice.	
AMP	Associated Music Publishers, Inc., 609 Fifth Ave., New York 10017.	Schott
Amphion	Éditions Musicales Amphion, 26–28 Rue de la Pépinière, Paris 8.	UMP

Agent in U.K.

Andraud	Albert Andraud, Cincinnati. (Now Southern.)	
André	Musikverlag Johann André, Frankfurterstr. 28, Offenbach a.M.	
Ann Arbor	University Music Press, 340 Maynard St., Ann Arbor, Mich.	
Apogee	Apogee Press, Cincinnati, Ohio.	
Arco	Arco Music Publishers, N. Hollywood, Calif.	
Arnheim	Arnheim, Mastrigt.	
Arrow	Arrow Music Press Inc., 17 E. 42nd St., New York, N.Y.	
Ars-Viva	Ars-Viva-Verlag GmbH, Mainz. (Now Schott.)	
Artaria	*Artaria & Co., Vienna.	
Artia	Artia Verlag, Ve Smeckach 30, Prague 2.	Bo. & H.
Artransa	Artransa Music, Los Angeles, Calif.	
A. & S.	Ahn & Simrock Musikverlag, Meinekestr. 10, Berlin 15; Schutzenhofstr. 4, Wiesbaden.	
Ascherberg	Ascherberg, Hopwood & Crew, Ltd., 16 Mortimer St., London, W.1.	
Augsburg	Augsburg Publishing House, 426 S. 5th St., Minneapolis, Minn.	
Avant	Avant Music, 2859 Holt Ave., Los Angeles 34, Calif.	
Balan	Verlag Benno Balan, Berlin.	
Barnhouse	C. L. Barnhouse Pub. Co., 110 B. Ave. East, Oskaloosa, Iowa.	
B. & B.	Bote & Bock KG., Hardenbergstr. 9a, Berlin-Charlottenburg 2; Sonnenbergerstr. 14, D-62, Wiesbaden.	Schott
B. & C.	British and Continental Music Agencies, Ltd., 8 Horse & Dolphin Yard, London, WIV 7LG.	
Bank	Annie Bank, Anna Vondelstr., Amsterdam.	Chester
Baron	M. Baron, Box 149, Oyster Bay, Long Island, N.Y.	
Belaieff	Ed. Belaieff, 10 Sq. Desnouettes, Paris 15; Kronprinzstr. 26, Bonn.	Bo. & H.
Belwin	Belwin Inc., 250 Maple Ave., Rockville Centre, Long Island, N.Y.	Leeds
Benjamin	Anton J. Benjamin, 239/241 Shaftesbury Ave., London, W.C.2; Werderstr. 44, Hamburg 13.	
Berra	*Marco Berra, Prague.	
Beyer	*H. Beyer, Langensalza.	
Billaudot	Éditions Billaudot, 14 Rue de l'Echiquier, Paris 10.	UMP

Agent in U.K.

Birchard	C. C. Birchard & Co., 221 Columbus Ave., Boston, Mass. (See SB.)	
BMI (Can)	BMI Canada Ltd., 41 Valleybrook Drive, Don Mills, Ont.	A. A. Kalmus
Böhm	Musikverlag Anton Böhm, Ludwigstr. 3, Augsburg, D.	Hinrichsen
Bo. & H.	Boosey & Hawkes, Ltd., 295 Regent St., London, W.1; 30 W. 57th St., New York 19; 4 Rue Drouet, Paris 1; 26 Kronprinzstr. Bonn; Sydney; Toronto; Johannesburg.	
Bosse	G. Bosse-Verlag, Regensburg. (See BVK.)	
Boston	Boston Music Co., 116 Boylston St., Boston 16, Mass.	
Bosworth	Bosworth & Co., 14–18 Heddon St., London, W. 1; Hohestr. 133, Cologne; Vienna.	
Bratfisch	Musikverlag Georg Bratfisch, 865 Kulmbach.	
Braun-Peretti	Braun-Peretti, Bonn.	
Br. & H.	Breitkopf & Härtel, Walkmühlstr. 52, Wiesbaden; Breitkopf & Härtel VEB, Karlstr. 10, Leipzig, DDR–701.	British & Continental, London
Brauer	*Brauer, Dresden.	
Broadman	Broadman Press, Nashville, Tenn.	
Brodt	Brodt Music Co., Charlotte, N. Carolina.	
Broekmans	Broekmans & van Poppel, Van Baerlstr. 92, Amsterdam.	A. A. Kalmus
Brogneaux	Éditions Brogneaux, 73 Paul Jansonlaan, Brussels.	
Broude	Broude Brothers Music Publishers, 56 W. 45th St., New York 36.	Schott
Brown	M. Brown, New York. (See Colin.)	
Bruzzichelli	Edizioni Aldo Bruzzichelli, Borgo Sanfrediano 8, Florence.	Hinrichsen
BVK	Bàrenreiter-Verlag KG, Heinrich Schütz Allee 29, Kassel-Wilhelmshöhe; 32–4 Great Titchfield St., London, W.1; P.O. Box 115, New York 34; Basle; Paris.	
Camara	Camara Music Publishers, 229 W. 52nd St., New York 19.	
Campion	Campion Press, Philadelphia, Pa.	
CB	Cundy-Bettoney Co., Inc., 96 Bradley St., Hyde Park, Boston 36, Mass.	
CeBeDeM	Centre Belge de Documentation Musicale, 3 Rue de Commerce, Brussels.	Lengnick
CFE	Composers Facsimile Edition, American Composers Alliance, 2121 Broadway, New York 23.	

Agent in U.K.

Challier	*C. A. Challier & Co., Berlin. (Now Birnbach.)	
Chappell	Chappell & Co., Ltd., 50 New Bond St., London, W.1; 609 5th Ave., New York 10017; Schwanthalerstr. 51, Munich; 4 Rue d'Argenson, Paris 8; Stockholm.	
Charling	Charling Music Corporation, New York.	
Chester	J. & W. Chester Ltd., 7 Eagle Court, London, E.C.1.	
Choudens	Éditions Choudens, 138 Rue Jean-Mermoz, Paris 8.	UMP
CMC	Canadian Music Centre, 33 Edward St., Toronto 2, Ont.	
CML	Chamber Music Library, New York. (See S. Fox.)	
Colin	C. Colin, 1225 6th Ave., New York 19.	
Colombo	Franco Colombo Inc., 16 W. 61st St., New York 10023.	
Concordia	Concordia Publishing House, 3558 South Jefferson Ave., St. Louis 18, Miss. 63118.	
Continuo	Continuo Music Press, Inc. (See Broude.)	
Coppenrath	Musikverlag Alfred Coppenrath, 8262 Altötting.	
Cor	Cor Publishing Co., 67 Bell Place, Massapequa, N.Y.	
CP	Composers Press. (See Elkan, Southern.)	
Cranz	Musikverlag August Cranz KG, Elise-Kirchner-Str. 15, Wiesbaden.	
Curwen	Faber/Curwen, 38 Russell Sq., London, W.C.1.	
DDT	Denkmäler Deutscher Tonkunst. (See Br. & H.)	A. A. Kalmus
Diabelli	*A. Diabelli, Vienna.	
Doblinger	Ludwig Doblinger KG, Dorotheen-gasse 10, Vienna 1.	A. A. Kalmus
Donemus	Donemus-Stichting voor Documentatie van Nederlandse Muziek, Jacob Obechtstr, 51, Amsterdam.	Lengnick
Drago	A. Drago, Magenta.	
DTÖ	Denkmaler der Tonkunst in Österreich. (Agent: Akademische Druck- und Verlags-anstalt, Graz.)	A. A. Kalmus
Dufaut	*Dufaut & Dubois, Paris.	
Durand	Éditeurs Durand et Cie., 4 Place de la Madeleine, Paris 8.	UMP

Agent in U.K.

DVM	Deutsche Verlag für Musik, Karlstr. 10, Leipzig, DDR–701.	British & Continental, London
Eberle	*Eberle, Vienna.	
Ebner	*Ebner, Stuttgart.	
Ed. Française	Éditions Françaises de Musique, ORTF, Paris.	
EdM	Das Erbe deutscher Musik. (See BVK.)	
Educational Publications		
Elkan	H. Elkan, 1316 Walnut St., Philadelphia, Pa.	
EMB	Editio Musica, 5 PF 322, Budapest.	Bo. & H.
Emmeleus	*E. Emmeleus, Frankfurt.	
EMS	Edition Music Service.	
EMT	Éditions Musicales Transatlantiques, 14 Ave. Hoche, Paris 8.	UMP
Ensemble	Ensemble Publications, Box 98, Bidwell Station, Buffalo, N.Y. (See C. Fischer.)	
E. & S.	*Evette & Schaefer, Paris. (Now Leduc.)	
Eschig	Éditions Max Eschig, 48 Rue de Rome, Paris 8.	Schott
Eulenburg	Eulenburg & Co., Cobbs Wood Estate, Brunswick Rd., Ashford, Kent.	
EV	Elkan-Vogel Co. Inc., 1712–1716 Sansom St., Philadelphia, Pa. 19103.	UMP
Faber	Faber Music Ltd., 38 Russell Sq., London, W.C.1.	
Falter	*M. Falter & Sohn, Munich.	
Far West	Far West Music, Los Angeles, Calif.	
Fazer	Oy Musukki Fazer Musik AB, Aleksanterinkatu 11, Helsinki.	
Feuchtinger	Franz Feuchtinger, Regensburg.	
Filser	Dr. Benno Filser Verlag GmbH, Augsburg.	
C. Fischer	Carl Fischer Inc., 62 Cooper Sq., New York 10003.	
J. Fischer	J. Fischer & Bros., Harristown Road, Glen Rock 17, N.J. 01452.	
Flammer	H. Flammer Inc., New York.	
Forberg	Robert Forberg Musikverlag, Sedanstr. 18, 532 Bad Godesberg.	
Fougeray		
S. Fox	Sam Fox Publishing Co., 11 W. 60th St., New York 20; 21 Denmark St., London, W.C.2.	
S. French	S. French, New York.	
Fritzsche	Fritzsche, Hanover.	

FST	Föreningen Svenska Tonsättare, Tegnérlunden 3, Stockholm. (See Suecia).	
Fürstner	Adolph Fürstner Ltd., 55 Iverna Court, London, W.8.	
Galaxy	Galaxy Music Corp., 2121 Broadway, New York 10019.	Galliard
Galerie Simon	Galerie Simon, Paris.	
Galliard	Galliard Ltd., Queen Anne's Road, Great Yarmouth, Norfolk.	
Gamble	Gamble Hinged Music Corp., 312 S. Wabash, Chicago 5, Ill.	
Gaudet	Éditions E. Gaudet, Paris. (Now Salabert.)	
Gehrmans	A. B. Carl Gehrmans Musikvorlag, Vasagatan 46, Stockholm 1.	Bo. & H.
Gerig	Musikverlag Hans Gerig, Drususgasse 7–11, Cologne 1.	
Germann	*E. Germann, Regensburg.	
Gervan	Gervan, Brussels.	
Girod	*E. Girod, Paris.	
Glaser	*K. Glaser, Leipzig.	
GMPC	General Music Publishing Co., New York.	Novello
Gray	H. W. Gray Co., Inc., 159 E. 48th St., New York 17.	Novello
Grosch	P. Grosch, Lisztstr. 18, Munich 8.	
Gross	*Gross, Innsbruck.	
G. & T.	Goodwin & Tabb, Ltd., Borough Green, Sevenoaks, Kent	
Halbmeyer	*Halbmeyer, Nuremberg.	
Hansen	Wilhelm Hansen Musik-Vorlag, Gothersgade 9–11, Copenhagen.	Chester
Hänssler	Hänssler-Verlag KG, 7 Stuttgart-Hohenheim.	Novello
Harmonia	Harmonia-Uitgave, Roeltjesweg 23, Hilversum.	A. A. Kalmus
Harth	Harth Musikverlag, Leipzig.	
Haslinger	*T. Haslinger, Vienna. (Now Lienau.)	
Heinrichshofen	Heinrichshofen's Verlag, Bremenstr. 52–58, Wilhelmshaven; Amsterdam; Locarno.	Hinrichsen
Henmar	Henmar Press, Inc., 373 Park Ave. South, New York 10016.	Hinrichsen
Henn	Edition Henn, 8 Rue de Hesse, Geneva.	UMP
Heugel	Heugel & Cie., 2 bis Rue Vivienne, Paris 2.	UMP
Hieber	Max Hieber, Kaufingerstr. 23, Munich 2.	
Highgate	Highgate Press, 2121 Broadway, New New York 23.	

Hinrichsen	Hinrichsen Edition, Ltd., 10–12 Baches St., London, N.1.; 119–125 Wardour St., London, W.1.	
Hiob	H. Hiob, Berlin.	
HM	*Hudební Matice, Prague. (Now SHV.)	
Hochstein	Musikverlag Hochstein & Co., Heidelberg.	
Hoffarth	*L. Hoffarth, Dresden.	
A. Hoffmann	*A. Hoffmann, Striegau.	
W. Hoffmann	*W. Hoffmann, Weimar.	
Hofmeister	Musikverlag F. Hofmeister, Eppsteinerstr. 43, Frankfurt a.M. 6; VEB Friedrich Hofmeister Musikverlag, Karlstr. 10, Leipzig DDR–701; Hofheim.	British & Continental, London
Holly-Pix	Holly-Pix Music Publishing Co., N. Hollywood, Calif.	
Horn Realm	The Horn Realm, Box 542, Far Hills, N.J. 07931.	
Hug	Hug & Co., Limmatquai 26–28, Zürich.	Hinrichsen
IIM	Instituto Interamericano de Musicologia, Montevideo.	
IMAMI	Instituzioni e monumenti dell arte musicale italiana	
IMC	International Music Co., 509 5th Ave., New York 17.	A. A. Kalmus
IMI	Israeli Music Institute, P. O. Box 11253, Tel-Aviv.	A. A. Kalmus
IMP	Israeli Music Publications, Ltd., P.O. Box 6011, Tel-Aviv.	Chester
IPA	Israeli Publishers Agency, P. O. Box 11180, Tel-Aviv.	
Interlochen	Interlochen Press, National Music Camp, Interlochen, Mich.	
Jeanette	Edition Jeanette, Bilthoven.	
Jurgenson	*P. Jurgenson, Moscow. (Now RS.)	
Kahle	*Kahle, Dessau.	
Kahnt	C. F. Kahnt, An der Hofstatt 8, Lindau, Bodensee.	
KaWe	Edition KaWe, Brederode Str. 90, Amsterdam 13.	
Kendor	Kendor Music Inc., Delevan, N.Y. 14042.	
King	Robert King Music Co., 7 Canton St., N. Easton, Mass. 02356.	
Kistner	*F. Kistner, Leipzig. (Now K. & S.)	
Kjos	Neil A. Kjos Music Co., 525 Busse Ave., Park Ridge, Ill.	
Klinner	*Klinner, Leipzig.	
Kothe	*Kothe, Leobschütz.	

Agent in U.K.

KP	Keith Prowse Music Publishing Co., Ltd., 21 Denmark St., London, W.C.2.	
Kränzl	*J. Kränzl, Ried.	
K. & S.	Kistner & Siegel, Luisenstr. 8, Lippstadt.	
Lawson	Lawson-Gould Music Publishers Inc., 609 5th Ave., New York, 17.	Curwen
Leduc	Alphonse Leduc & Cie., 175 Rue St. Honoré, Paris 1.	UMP
Leeds	Leeds Music Corp., 322 W. 48th St., New York 36; Leeds Music Ltd., 139 Piccadilly, London, W.1.	
Leeds (Can)	Leeds Music (Canada) Ltd., 215 Victoria St., Toronto 2, Ont.	
Lemoine	Éditeurs Henri Lemoine & Cie., 17 Rue Pigalle, Paris 9; 37 Bd. du Jardin-Botanique, Brussels.	UMP
Lengnick	Alfred Lengnick & Co. Ltd., Purley Oaks Studios, 421a Brighton Road, S. Croydon, Surrey.	
Leuckart	Musikverlag, F. E. C. Leuckart KG, Prinzenstr. 7, Munich 19.	Novello
Lichtenauer	*Lichtenauer, Rotterdam.	
Lienau	Robert Lienau, Lankwitzerstr. 9, Berlin-Lichterfelde-Ost.	Hinrichsen
Lispet	J. J. Lispet, Hilversum.	
Litolff	Henry Litolff's Verlag, Forsthausstr. 101, Frankfurt a.M. (See Peters.)	Hinrichsen
Lopés	Lopés Edition, 430 Strand, London, W.C.2.	
Louisville	Louisville House, Louisville, Ky.	
Ludwig	Ludwig Music Publishing Co., 557 E. 140th St., Cleveland 10, Ohio.	
Lyra	Lyra-Verlag, Vienna.	
MAB	Musica Antiqua Bohemia. (See SNKLHU.)	
Magni	*Magni, Venice.	
Malcolm	Malcolm Music Ltd., 157 W. 57th St., New York 19.	
Marbot	Marbot, Bornstr. 12, Hamburg.	
Maringo	*G. B. Maringo, Palermo.	
Marks	Edward B. Marks Music Corp., 136 W. 52nd St., New York 19.	
Maurer	Éditions Maurer, 7 Ave. du Verseau, Brussels.	
MBE	Modern Brass Ensemble, 42–25 80th St., Elmhurst 73, N.Y.	
MBQ	Montreal Brass Quintet Series, 145 Graham Boulevard, Montreal 304, Quebec.	
MCA	MCA Music, 543 W. 43rd St., New York 10036.	Leeds Music

Mentor	Mentor Music Inc., 123 Dietz St., Hempstead, N.Y.	
Mercury	Mercury Music Corp., 47 W. 63rd St., New York 23.	Schott
Merion	Merion Music Inc., Presser Place, Bryn Mawr, Pa.	
Merrymount	Merrymount Music, 47 W. 63rd St., New York 23.	
Merseburger	Merseburger Verlag GmbH, Alemannstr. 20, Berlin-Nikolassee.	Hinrichsen
Metropolis	Metropolis S.P.R.L., 24 Ave. de France, Antwerp.	
MF	MF Co., Box 351, Evanston, Ill. 60204.	
Mills	Mills Music. Inc., 1619 Broadway, New York 10019; 20 Denmark St., London, W.C.2; Brussels.	
Mitchell	Mitchell & Martin Publishing Ltd., c/o Pollard & Co., 24–25 Princes St., Hanover Sq., London, W.1.	
MJQ	MJQ Music Inc., New York. (c/o AMP.)	
M. & M.	McGinnis & Marks, 408 2nd Ave., New York 10.	Hinrichsen
Modern	Edition Modern, Walhallastr. 7, Munich. (Now Hans Wewerka.)	
Moeck	Hermann Moeck Verlag, Hannoverschestr. 43a, Celle.	Schott
Möseler	Karl Heinrich Möseler Verlag, Gr. Zimmerhof 20, Wolfenbüttel.	Novello
Morris	E. H. Morris & Co., 35 W. 54th St., New York 19.	
Müller	*F. Müller, Karlsrühe.	
Musica Rara	Musica Rara, 2 Great Marlborough St., London, W.1.	
Music for Percussion	Music for Percussion, 1841 Broadway, New York 23.	
Music Press	Music Press Inc., New York. (See Mercury.)	
Musicus	Edition Musicus, 333 W. 52nd St., New York, 10019.	
MV	Mitteldeutscher Verlag GmbH, Robert Blumstr. 37, Saale, Halle.	
Nagel	Nagel's Verlag, Kassel. (See BVK.)	
NME	New Music Editions, Presser Place, Bryn Mawr, Pa.	A. A. Kalmus
Noetzel	Otto Heinrich Noetzel Verlag, Wilhelmshaven.	Hinrichsen
Nordiska	A/B Nordiska Musikförlaget, Pipersgatan 29, Stockholm 10.	Chester
Novello	Novello & Co., Ltd., Borough Green, Sevenoaks, Kent.	

Agent in U.K.

NWM	New Wind Music Co., 23 Ivor Place, London, N.W.1.	
ÖBV	Österreichischer Bundesverlag, Schwarzenbergstr. 5, Vienna 1.	
Oertel	Musikverlag Johannes Oertel, Karntnerplatz 2, Hannover-Waldhausen.	
Olivan	The Olivan Press, 49 Selvage Lane, London, N.W.7.	
Omega	Omega Music Edition, 353 E. 52nd St., New York 10022.	
Ongaku	Ongaku-no-Tomo Sha, Inc., Tokyo.	
ÖS	Österreiche Sängerbund.	
OUP	Oxford University Press, 44 Conduit St., London, W.1; 200 Madison Ave., New York 10016.	
Pabst	*Verlag P. Pabst, Leipzig. (Successor, Musikverlag W. Gebauer, Wiesbaden).	
Panton	Panton, Besední 3, Prague 1; Sládkovičova 11, Bratislava.	Faber Music
Parrhysius	Arthur Parrhysius, Berlin.	
Paterson	Paterson's Publications Ltd., 36–40 Wigmore St., London, W.1.	
Pathé-Marconi	Pathé-Marconi, Paris.	
Paulus	Paulus-Verlag, Lucerne.	
Peer	Peer International Corp., 1619 Broadway, New York 19; Klärchenstr. 11, Hamburg 39.	
Peters	C. F. Peters Musikverlag, Forsthausstr. 101, Frankfurt a.M.; 373 Park Ave. South, New York 10016.	Hinrichsen
Philippo	Éditions Philippo, 24 Blvd. Poissonière, Paris 9.	
Piedmont	Piedmont Music Co., New York.	
Pietsch	*Pietsch, Ziegenhals.	
Pizzi	*Umberto Pizzi e Co., Bologna. (Now Bongiovanni.)	
Polyphonic	Polyphonic Reproductions, Pipers Wood, Peaslake, Surrey.	
Preiser	Preiser, Liegnitz.	
Premru	Premru Music, 33 Springfield Gardens, London, N.W. 19.	
Presser	Theodore Presser Co., Presser Place, Bryn Mawr, Pa.	A. A. Kalmus
Pressverein	Pressverein, Brixen.	
Pro Art	Pro Art Publications, 469 Union Ave., Westbury, N.Y.	A. A. Kalmus
Procuré	Procuré du Clergé, Arras.	
Pustet	F. Pustet, Gutenbergstr. 8, Regensburg	Hinrichsen
PWM	Polskie Wydawnictwo Muzycne, Foksal 18, Warsaw.	A. A. Kalmus

Agent in U.K.

Rahter	D. Rahter Musikverlag, Werderstr. 44, Hamburg 13. (See Benjamin.)	
Raverii	*Raverii, Venice.	
RB	*Verlag J. Rieter-Biedermann, Leipzig. (Now Peters.)	
R. & E.	Musikverlag Ries & Erler, Charlottenbrunnerstr. 42, Berlin-Grünewald.	Hinrichsen
Reiff	J. J. Reiff, Karlsruhe.	
Reinecke	*Reinecke, Leipzig.	
Remick	Remick Music Corp., 488 Madison Ave., New York 22.	
Repos		
Rhein	*Rheinischer Musikverlag, Bonn.	
Ricordi	Edizioni G. Ricordi & C. S. P. A., Via Berchet 2, Milan; The Bury, Church St., Chesham, Bucks; 16 W. 61st St., New York 23; 3 Rue Requepine, Paris; Buenos Aires.	
RM	Edition Russe de Musique, 22 Rue d'Anjou, Paris.	Bo. & H.
Robitschek	Musikverlag Adolf Robitschek, Vienna; Wiesbaden.	
Rochester	Rochester Music Publications, Fairport, N.Y.	
Rohlfing	Rohlfing Sons Music Co., Milwaukee, Wis.	
Rongwen	Rongwen Music Inc., 56 W. 45th St., New York 36. (See Broude.)	
Rossum	Wed. J. R. van Rossum, Minnebroedstr. 1–3, Utrecht K.	A. A. Kalmus
RS	Russian State Publication Co. (Music), Moscow 200; Leningrad.	Anglo-Russian Music, 16 Manette St., London, W.1.
Rubank	Rubank Inc., 5544 West Armstrong Ave., Chicago 30, Ill.	Novello
Rufer	Rufer, Gütersloh.	
Ruh	Verlag von Ruh & Walser, Adliswil; Zürich. (Successor, E. Ruh.)	
Salabert	Éditions Salabert, 22 Rue Cauchet, Paris 9.	UMP
Samfundet	Samfundet til Udgivelse af Dansk Musik, Kronprinsessgade 26, Copenhagen.	
SB	Summy-Birchard Publishing Co., 1834 Ridge Ave., Evanston, Ill. 60204.	A. A. Kalmus
Schauer		
E. C. Schirmer	E. C. Schirmer Music Co., 600 Washington St., Boston 11, Mass.	
G. Schirmer	G. Schirmer Inc., 3 East 43rd St., New York 17.	Chappell

Agent in U.K.

Schlesinger	*Schlesingersche Buch- und Musik-Handlung, Berlin. (Successor, Lienau.)	
C. Schmidt	C. F. Schmidt, Cäcilienstr. 62, Heilbronn.	Hinrichsen
W. Schmidt	W. Schmidt, Leipzig; Nuremberg.	
Schott	B. Schott's Söhne, Weihegarten 5, 6500 Mainz; 48 Great Marlborough St., London, W.1; 30 Rue St. Jean, Brussels.	
Schuberth	J. Schuberth & Co., Moritzstr. 39, Wiesbaden.	
Schultheiss	Musikverlag Carl L. Schultheiss KG, Denzenbergstr. 35, 74 Tübingen.	Hinrichsen
Schwann	Verlag L. Schwann, Charlottenstr. 80–86, Düsseldorf.	Hinrichsen
Schweers	Schweers & Haake, Mittelstr. 3, Bremen 1.	
Schweitzer	Schweitzer, Aachen.	
Seeling	J. G. Seeling, Dresden.	
Senart	Éditions Maurice Senart & Cie., 20 Rue du Dragon, Paris 6. (Now Salabert.)	
Shawnee	Shawnee Press Inc., Delaware Water Gap, Pa. 18327.	
SHF	Slovenský Hudobný Fond, Gorkého, 19, Bratislava.	
SHV	Statní Hudební Vydavatelství, Palackého 1, Prague 1.	
Sidem	Éditions Sidem, Geneva.	
Sidemton	Sidemton Verlag, Cologne.	
Siegel	*C. F. W. Siegel, Leipzig. (See K. & S.)	
Sikorski	Musikverlag Hans Sikorski, Johnsallee 23, Hamburg 13.	KP
Simon	*Karl Simon, Steglitz 35, Berlin. (Now Br. & H.)	
Simrock	Musikverlag N. Simrock, Dorotheenstr. 176, Hamburg 39; 239–241 Shaftesbury Ave., London, W.C.2.	
Sirène	*La Sirène Musicale, Paris. (Successor, Eschig.)	
Sirius	Sirius-Verlag, Wiclefstr. 67, Berlin, N.W. 21.	
SM	Süddeutscher Musikverlag (Willy Müller), Märzgasse 5, Heidelberg.	Novello
SNKLHU	Statní Nakladatelství Krásné Literatury, Hubdy a Umeňí, Prague. (Now SHV.)	
Southern	Southern Music Publishing Co. Inc., 1619 Broadway, New York 19; P.O. Box 329, San Antonio, Texas 78206.	Bo. & H.

Agent in U.K.

Stainer	Stainer & Bell, Ltd., Lesbourne Rd., Reigate, Surrey.	
Stary	*Stary, Prague.	
Stein	*N. Stein, Frankfurt a.M.	
Steinbacher	E. Steinbacher, Karlsrühe.	
Styria	Styria Musikverlag, Graz; Vienna; Cologne.	
Suecia	Edition Suecia, Stockholm. (See Gehrmans.)	
SZ	Edizioni Suvini Zerboni, Galleria del Corso 4, Milan.	Hinrichsen
Templeton	Templeton Publishing Co., 10 E. 43rd St., New York 17.	
Tenuto	Tenuto. (See Presser.)	
Terry	*Terry, Brussels.	
Tetra	Tetra Music Corp. (See Broude.)	
Theune	*Theune, Amsterdam.	
T. & J.	Musikverlag Tischer & Jagenberg, Prinzenweg 3, 813 Starnberg.	Novello
Tonger	P. J. Tonger Musikverlag, Bergstr. 10. Rodenkirchen/Rhein.	
Tonos	Tonos-Musikverlag, Ahastr. 7, Darmstadt 6100.	British & Continental
T. & P.	*Taborsky & Parsch, Budapest.	
Trautwein	Trautwein, Berlin.	
Tritone	Tritone Press, Hattiesburg, Miss.	
Uber	David Uber Music Publishing Co. (See Musicus.)	
UBS	University Brass Series. (See Cor.)	
UE	Universal Edition AG, Karlsplatz 6, Vienna; 2–3 Fareham St., London, W.1.	
Ugrino	Ugrino Verlag, Elbchaussee 499a, Hamburg-Blankensee.	
UKBH	Udruzenje Kompozitora Bi. H., Sarajevo.	
Ullmann	E. Ullmann, Reichenberg.	
Ulrich		
UMP	United Music Publishers Ltd., 1 Montague St., London, W.C.1.	
Van Eyck	G. H. Van Eyck, The Hague.	
Vieweg	Musikverlag Chr. Friedrich Vieweg, Ringstr. 47a, Berlin-Lichterfelde-West.	Musica Rara
A. Vincenti	*A. Vincenti, Venice.	
G. Vincenti	*G. Vincenti, Venice.	
VNM	Verlag Neue Musik, Leipzigerstr. 26, 108 Berlin.	British & Continental
Voggenreiter	Voggenreiter-Verlag, 532 Bad-Godesberg.	
Volk	Arno-Volk Verlag, Cologne.	
Wagenführ	H. Wagenführ, Berlin.	

311

Agent in U.K.

Wallan	Wallan Music, New York.	
Waterloo	Waterloo Music Co. Ltd., 3 Regina St. North, Waterloo, Ont.	
Weinberger	Musikverlag Josef Weinberger GmbH, Steinweg 7, Frankfurt a.M.; 10–16 Rathbone St., London, W.1.	
Weintraub	Weintraub Music Co., 240 W. 55th St., New York 19.	
Wessely	*A. W. Wessely, Prague.	
Westend	Westend-Verlag, Wilhelmshaven. (Now Noetzel.)	
Wetzler		
Weygand	*Weygand & Beuster, The Hague.	
Whitney	Whitney Blake, 243 W. 72nd St., New York 23.	
Wildt	Wildt, Stuttgart.	
Willi	Willi, Cham.	
Williams	Joseph Williams Ltd., London. (See Galliard.)	
WIM	Western International Music Co., 2859 Holt Ave., Los Angeles, Calif. 90034.	
Witmark	M. Witmark & Sons. 488 Madison Ave., New York 22.	
Zanibon	Edizioni Gugliemo Zanibon, Piazza del signori 24, Padua.	Hinrichsen
Zechlin		
Zeitgenöss	Edition Zeitgenöss, Berlin.	
Zimmermann	Musikverlag Wilhelm Zimmermann, Wohlerstr. 10, Frankfurt a.M.; Querstr. 28, Leipzig C.1.	Novello
Zumsteeg	Musikverlag G. A. Zumsteeg, Hamburg.	

Appendix

TWENTIETH-CENTURY TROMBONE MAKERS

Alexander	Gebr. Alexander, Bahnhofstrasse 9, Mainz 65.
Bach	Vincent Bach (See H. & A. Selmer, Inc.)
Baldwin	(See Gretsch.)
Beltone	Sorkin Music Co., Inc., 559 Sixth Ave., New York N.Y. 10011.
Besson	Besson & Co., Ltd., 15 West St., London, W.C.2.
Blessing	E. K. Blessing Co. Inc., 1301 W. Beardsley Ave., Elkhart, Ind. 46514
Böhm & Meinl	Böhm & Meinl, Isardamm 667, 8192 Gartenberg/Obb.
Boosey & Hawkes	Boosey & Hawkes, Ltd., 295 Regent St., London, W.1.
Buescher	Buescher Band Instrument Co. (See H. & A. Selmer, Inc.)
Bundy	(See H. & A. Selmer, Inc.)
Concerto	Worldwide Musical Inst. Co., Inc., 404 Fourth Ave. New York, N.Y. 10016.
Conn	C. G. Conn Corporation, 1101 E. Beardsley Ave., Elkhart, Ind. 46515.
Couesnon	Couesnon et Cie., 105 Rue Lafayette, Paris.
Courtois	A. Courtois, 8 Rue de Nancy, Paris 10.
Couturier	E. A. Couturier Band Inst. Co., La Porte, Ind.
Doina	State Brass Inst. Factory, Maria Hagi Moscu 5, Bucharest.
Dolnet	Établ. Dolnet, 31 Rue de Rome, Paris 8.
Enders	M. Enders, Mainz.
Finke	Helmut Finke, 4901 Exter uber Herford Nr. 327, Westfalien.
Frank	William Frank Co., 2033 Clybourn Ave., Chicago, Ill.

Getzen	The Getzen Co. Inc., Elkhorn, Wisc. 53121.
Glier	A. C. Glier, Markneukirchen.
Gretsch	Fred. Gretsch Mfg. Co., 60 Broadway, Brooklyn, N.Y. 11211; 218 S. Wabash Ave., Chicago, Ill. 60604.
Heckel	F. A. Heckel, Dresden.
Hess	Hess, Klingenthal
Hirsbrunner	Fritz Hirsbrunner & Sohn, Sumiswald, Canton Berne
Holton	Frank Holton & Co. (See Leblanc.)
Hüller	F. X. Hüller & Co., Diespeck bei Neustadt/Aisch.
Hüttl	A. R. Hüttl, Hauptstrasse 36, Baiersdorf/ Mittelfranken.
Keilwerth	J. Keilwerth, Königstadterstrasse 165, 6085 Nauheim Kr. Grosz-Gerau.
King	The H. N. White Co., 5225 Superior Ave., Cleveland, Ohio 44103.
Kruspe	Ed. Kruspe, Schillerstrasse 22, Erfurt.
Kühnl & Hoyer	Kühnl & Hoyer, Markt Erlbach, Bayern.
Lätzsch	H. Lätzsch, Ostertorstrasse 2, Bremen.
Lafayette	(See Couesnon).
Lafleur	J. R. Lafleur & Son, 147 Wardour St., London, W.1.
Langhammer	H. Langhammer & Sohn, Ringstrasse 19, 3559 Frankenberg/Eder.
Lavelle	Grossmann Music Corp., 1278 West 9th St., Cleveland, Ohio 44113.
Leblanc	G. Leblanc Corp., 7019 Thirtieth Ave., Kenosha, Wisc. 53141.
Leistner	W. Leistner, Poolstrasse 12, Hamburg.
Lidl	J. Lidl, Brno. (Export, Ligna, 41 Vodickova, Prague 2).
Lorenz	A. Lorenz, Markneukirchen.
Martin	Martin Band Inst. Co. (See Wurlitzer Co.)
Meinl & Lauber	Meinl & Lauber, 8192 Gartenberg /Obb., Schwalbenweg 2.
Meyer	Karl Meyer, Germany.
Miller	M. von Miller, Dehmstrasse 5, Lauf (Pegnitz).
Miraphone	Produktivgenossenschaft der Graslitzer Musik-instrumentenzeuger, 8264 Waldkraiburg/Obb., Postfach 23; Miraphone Corp., P.O. Box 909, 8484 San Fernando Rd., Sun Valley, Calif. 91352.

Monke	W. Monke, Gutenbergstrasse 59–61, D 5 Köln-Ehrenfeld.
Mücke	P. Mücke, Magdeburg.
Muck	Rudy Muck Co. Inc., 233 Nenins St., Brooklyn, N.Y.
Olds	F. E. Olds & Son, Inc. (Now Chicago Musical Inst. Co., 7373 N. Cicero Ave., Chicago, Ill.60646.)
Orsi	Prof. R. Orsi, Via Zuretti 46, Milan.
Piering	R. Piering, Adorf.
Piquemal	Gaëtan Piquemal, Paris.
Reisser	Chr. Reisser, Ulm/Donau.
Revere	Revere, Paris
Reynolds	(Now Chicago Musical Inst. Co., 7373 N. Cicero Ave., Chicago, Ill. 60646.)
Schenkelaars	H. Schenkelaars, Ruysdaelbaan 33, Eindhoven.
Scherzer	Scherzer, Augsburg.
Schilke	The Schilke Co., 223 W. Lake St., Chicago, Ill. 60606.
Schmidt	C. F. Schmidt, Berlin.
Schwarz	R. Schwarz, Königstrasse 6a, Hannover.
Selmer (1)	H. Selmer & Cie., 4 Place Dullin, Paris 18.
Selmer (2)	H. & A. Selmer, Inc., Box 337, Elkhart, Ind. 46515.
Spring	August Spring, Berlin.
Thibouville-Lamy	Thibouville-Lamy, Paris; J. Thibouville-Lamy & Co., 34 Aldersgate Street, London, E.C.1.
VEB	VEB Blechblas- und Signalinstrumentenfabrik, Postschliessfach 3, Markneukirchen, Sa.
Vega	Vega Co., 155 Columbus Ave., Boston 16, Mass.
Wetzel	H. Wetzel, Lindenallee 21, Hamburg.
Williams & Wallace	Williams & Wallace, Los Angeles, Calif.
Wurlitzer	Wurlitzer Co., P.O. Box 807, Elkhart, Ind. 46515.
Yamaha	Yamaha Europa GmbH, 2 Hamburg 50, Stresemannstrasse 313a.
York	York Band Inst. Co. Inc., 1600 Division Ave. South, Grand Rapids, Mich. 49502.
Zimmermann	Julius Heinrich Zimmermann, Leipzig.

SELECT BIBLIOGRAPHY

Arnold, D., *Con ogni Sorte di Stromenti: some practical Suggestions*, Brass Quarterly, II, 3, 1959.

Bach, V., *Embouchure and Mouthpiece Manual*, V. Bach Corporation, 1954.

Bahnert, H., Herzberg, T. and Schramm, H., *Metallblasinstrumente*, Leipzig, Fachbuchverlag, 1958.

Baines, A., *The Trombone*, Grove: Dictionary of Music and Musicians, 5th Ed., Macmillan, 1954.
  European & American Musical Instruments, B. T. Batsford, 1966.

Bate, P., *The Trumpet & Trombone*, Ernest Benn, 1966. New York: Norton, 1966.

Benade, A. H., *Horns, Strings & Harmony*, Doubleday & Co., 1960.

Benade, A. H. and Gans, D. J., *Sound Production in Wind Instruments*, Annals of the New York Academy of Sciences, 155, 1968.

Berlioz, H., *Instrumentationslehre*, ergänzt u. revidiert von Richard Strauss, Leipzig, 1905.

Besseler, H., *Die Entstehung der Posaune*, Acta Musicologica XXII, 1950.

Blandford, W. H. F., *Handel's Horn & Trombone Parts*, Musical Times 1160–2, Oct., Nov., Dec., 1939.

Bouasse, H., *Instruments à Vent*, Librairie Delagrave, 1929.

Brass Mouthpieces: A Symposium, The Instrumentalist, I, 7, 1952.

Bridet, A., *Histoire des Instruments à Vent*, Lyon, Beal. 1945

Buck, P., *Acoustics for Musicians*, Oxford University Press, 1918.

Campbell, R. A., *A Study of the Effects of selected interior Contours of the Trombone Mouthpiece*, M. Mus. Thesis, University of Texas, 1954.

Carse, A., *Musical Wind Instruments*, Macmillan, 1939; New York: Da Capo, 1965.
  The History of Orchestration, Kegan Paul, 1925; New York: Dover Books, 1964.
  The Orchestra from Beethoven to Berlioz, Heffer, 1948.

Culver, C. A., *Musical Acoustics*, McGraw Hill, 1956.

Dankworth, A., *Jazz: An Introduction to its Musical Basis*, Oxford University Press, 1968.

Dart, T., *The Repertory of the Royal Wind Music*, Galpin Society Journal, XI, 1958.

Daubeny, U., *Orchestral Wind Instruments*, Reeves, 1929.

Donington, R., *The Instruments of Music*, Methuen, 1949; 3rd rev. Ed., 1962. New York: Barnes & Noble, 1962.

Dunstan, R. D., *Some Acoustical Properties of Wind Instruments*, Proceedings of the Musical Association, 44, 1917–18.

Ehmann, W., *Neue Blechblasinstrumenten nach alten Modellen*, Hausmusik, 22, 1958.

trans. M. Rasmussen, *New Brass Instruments based on Old Models*, Brass Quarterly, I, 4, 1958.

Was guett auf Posaunen ist, Zeitschrift fur Musikwissenschaft, 17, 1935.

Elsenaar, E., *De Trombone, haar Onstaan, Ontwikkeling, Bouw, Techniek, Gebruiz enz.*, Lispet, 1947.

Farkas, P., *The Art of Brass Playing*, Brass Publications, 1962.

Flandrin, G. P. A. L., *Le Trombone*, Encyclopédie de la Musique et Dictionnaire du Conservatoire, 2e. Partie, Vol. 3, Delagrave, 1927.

Forsyth, C., *Orchestration*, Macmillan, 1914; reprinted 1922, 1926, 1929, 1944.

Galpin, F. W., *The Sackbut, its Evolution & History*, Proceedings of the Musical Association, 33, 1906.

Old English Instruments of Music, Methuen, 1910; 4th Ed. rev. T. Dart, 1965. New York: Barnes & Noble, 1965.

A Textbook of European Musical Instruments, Williams & Norgate, 1937, 1956.

Geiringer, K., *Musical Instruments: their History from the Stone Age to the present Day*, trans. Bernard Miall, Allen & Unwin, 1943; 2nd Ed., 1959. New York: Oxford University Press, 1945.

Gevaert, F. A., *Nouveau Traité d'Instrumentation*, Lemoine, 1885.

Gorgerat, G., *Encyclopédie de la Musique pour Instruments à Vent*, Éditions Rencontre, 1955.

Gray, R., *The Treatment of the Trombone in contemporary Chamber Literature*, A.M.D. Thesis, Eastman School of Music, Rochester, 1956.

The Trombone in Contemporary Chamber Music, Brass Quarterly, I, 1, 1957.

Hague, B., *The Tonal Spectra of Wind Instruments*, Proceedings of the Royal Musical Association, LXXIII, 1947.

Harrison, F. and Rimmer, J., *European Musical Instruments*, Studio Vista, 1964.

Hofmann, H., *Über den Ansatz der Blechbläser*, Barenreiter, 1956.

Husted, B. F., *The Brass Ensemble: Its History and Literature*, University of Rochester Press, 1961.

Jahn, F., *Die Nürnberger Trompeten-und Posaunenmacher im* 16. *Jahrhundert*, Archiv für Musikwissenschaft, 7, 1926.

Jeans, Sir J., *Science and Music*, Cambridge University Press, 1937. New York: Dover Books, 1937.

Karstädt, G., *Posaune*, Die Musik in Geschichte und Gegenwart, Vol. 10, Bärenreiter, 1949–1968.

Kent, E. L., *The inside Story of Brass Instruments*, C. G. Conn, 1956.

Kenton, E. F., *The 'Brass' Parts in Giovanni Gabrieli's Instrumental Ensemble Compositions*, Brass Quarterly, I, 2, 1957.

Kingdon-Ward, M., *In Defence of the Trombone*, Monthly Musical Record, 80, 1950.

Kleinhammer, E., *The Art of Trombone Playing*, Summy-Birchard Company, 1963.

Koechlin, C., *Traité de l'Orchestration*, Eschig, 1949.
    Les Instruments à Vent, Presses Universitaires de France, 1948.

Kunitz, H., *Die Instrumentation: Teil* 8, *Posaune*, VEB Breitkopf and Härtel, 1963.

Kurka, M. J., *A Study of the Acoustical Effects of Mutes on Wind Instruments*, F. E. Olds and Sons, 1961.

Lafosse, A., *Méthode complète de Trombone*, 2 vols, Leduc, 1921.

Langwill, L. G., *An Index of Musical Wind-Instrument Makers*, 2nd Ed., Edinburgh, The Author, 1962.

Lloyd, Ll. S., *Music and Sound*, Oxford University Press, 1951.
    The Musical Ear, Oxford University Press, 1940.

Mahillon, V., *Les Instruments à Vent; I, Le Trombone*, Mahillon, 1907.

Mahrenholz, C., *Über Posaunenmusik*, Musik und Kirche, I, 1929.

Martin, D. W., *A Physical Investigation of the Performance of Brass Musical Instruments*, New York: D. van Nostrand Co., 1957.

Miller, D. C., *The Science of Musical Sounds*, Macmillan, 1922.
    Sound Waves, their Shape and Speed, Macmillan, 1937.

Miller, G., *The Military Band*, Boosey and Co., 1912.

Monk, C. W., *The Older Brass Instruments: Cornet, Trombone and Trumpet*, Musical Instruments through the Ages, (Ed. A. Baines), Penguin, 1961.

Olsen, H. F., *Musical Engineering*, McGraw Hill, 1952.

Piston, W., *Orchestration*, Gollancz, 1955. New York: Norton, 1955.

Porter, M. M., *The Embouchure*, Boosey and Hawkes, 1967.
    Problems of the Embouchure, Brass Today, Besson, 1957.

Rasmussen, M., *Two early 19th Century Trombone Virtuosi: Carl Traugott Queisser and Friedrich August Belcke*, Brass Quarterly, V, 1, 1961.

Read, G., *Thesaurus of Orchestral Devices*, Pitman, 1954.

Richardson, E. G., *The Acoustics of Orchestral Instruments*, Arnold, 1929.

Sachs, C., *Real-Lexicon der Musikinstrumente*, Berlin, 1913; Hildesheim, 1964.
Handbuch der Musikinstrumentenkunde, Breitkopf and Härtel, 1920, 1930.
The History of Musical Instruments, W. W. Norton, 1940; Dent, 1942.
Die Modernen Musikinstrumente, Max Hesse, 1923.

Schlesinger, K., *Trombone*, Encyclopaedia Britannica, 11th Ed., Vol. XXVII, New York, 1911.
Modern Orchestral Instruments, Reeves, 1910.

Seashore, C., *The Psychology of Music*, McGraw Hill, 1938.

Taylor, C. A., *The Physics of Musical Sounds*, English Universities Press, Ltd., 1965.

Terry, C. S., *Bach's Orchestra*, Oxford University Press, 1932; 2nd Ed., 1961.

Vogel, M., *Die Intonation der Blechbläser: Neue Wege im Metallblasinstrumentenbau*, Dusseldorf, 1961.

Weingartner, F., *Die Posaunen in Mozarts Requiem*, Die Musik, 5, 1905–6.

Wellesz, E., *Die neue Instrumentation*, Max Hesse, 1928.

Widor, C. M., *The Technique of the Modern Orchestra*, trans. E. Suddard, Joseph Williams, 1906.

Wörthmüller, W., *Die Nürnberger Trompeten-und Posaunenmacher des 17. und 18. Jahrhunderts*, Mitteilungen des Vereins für Geschichte der Stadt Nürnberg, 45, 1954.
Die Instrumente der Nürnberger Trompeten-und Posaunenmacher, Mitteilungen des Vereins für Geschichte der Stadt Nürnberg, 46, 1955.

Wood, A., *The Physics of Music*, Methuen, 1944; 6th Ed., 1962. New York: Barnes and Noble, 1968.

Young, F. J., *Posaune: Akustik*, Die Musik in Geschichte und Gegenwart, Vol. 10, Bärenreiter, 1949–1968.
The Natural Frequencies of Musical Horns, Acustica, X, 1960.

Index

Erlangen, Rück Collection, 36

Farkas, P., 82*n*
Fink, G. W., 85
Finke, Helmut (maker, Herford), 153
Flute, 59, 112
Forsyth, C., 59, 125
France,
    abandonment of alto trombone, 108
    brass ensembles, 154
    players' use of duplex instrument, 90
    seventeenth-century bass attachment, 84
    use of narrow-bore trombone, 59
    use of three tenor trombones, 71, 108
Fux, 106–7

Gabrieli, Giovanni, 106
Galpin, Canon F. W., 29, 94
Gautier, M., 147*n*
Geiringer, K., 94*n*, 117
Germany,
    brass ensembles, 152–4
    composers' use of four trombones, 102
    later use of alto trombone, 108–9
    makers' description of attachment, 90
    ousting of E♭ and F bass trombones, 86
    pedalton, 62
    popularity of contrabass trombone, 97
    Posaunenchöre, 153
    Stadtpfeifer, see Stadtpfeifer
Giovanna, Matteo di, 30
Glissando, 66–76, 79, 112, 121, 144, 152
    alto trombone, 115
    'half-valve', 121
    harmonic, 144
    lip-, 67, 72–5, 144
    notation, 70–4
    tenor-bass trombone, 70, 92
    vocal, 144
Globokar, Vinko, 146
Gluck, 106–7, 117–18, 125, 134
Gontershausen, H. W. von, 121*n*
Grace notes, 74–6
Gray, Robert, 155

Grock, 145
'Growl', 144–5
'Gutbucket', *see* Jazz

Haas, W. W., 34
Hainlein, Hanns, 34
Halfpenny, Eric, 31*n*
Hall, Harry H., 117*n*
Handle, *see* Bass trombone; Contrabass trombone
Harp, 83, 112
Haydn, Franz Josef, 152
Haydn, Michael, 125
Hérold, 60
Heyde, Dr. H., 36*n*
Hindemith, 130, 138
Holborne, Anthony, 154
Holst, 65
Horn, 55, 85, 96, 110, 112–13, 120, 124–5, 127, 141, 152–3
    crooks, 86
    double horn, 86, 101
    factitious notes, 61
    hand horn, 42
    lip glissando, 74

Intonation, 54, 78, 97
    adjustment by player, 43, 101
    in alternative positions, 64
    defects caused by valves, 121, 123
    effect of mutes, 52
    effect of temperature, 43
    fifth position, 56
    first position, 21, 55–7, 96
    fourth position, 56
    just intonation, *see* Acoustics: just temperament
    'lipping down', 42, 56
    playing sharp, 42
    second position, 56–7
    seventh position, 55–6
    sharp leading-notes, 57
    sharp low C on F attachment, 88
    sixth position, 56
Italy,
    abandonment of alto trombone, 108
    use of valve trombone, 121

Janáček, 86
Jazz, 152, 154*n*
    'blue notes', 144